Daughter OF PROPHECY

MILES OWENS

REALMS
A STRANG COMPANY

Most STRANG COMMUNICATIONS/CHARISMA HOUSE/SILOAM/REALMS products are available at special quantity discounts for bulk purchase for sales promotions, premiums, fund-raising, and educational needs. For details, write Strang Communications/Charisma House/Siloam/Realms, 600 Rinehart Road, Lake Mary, Florida 32746, or telephone (407) 333-0600.

DAUGHTER OF PROPHECY by Miles Owens
Published by Realms
A Strang Company
600 Rinehart Road
Lake Mary, Florida 32746
www.realmsfiction.com

This is a work of fiction. Names, characters, places, and incidents are products of the author's imagination or are used fictitiously. Any similarity to actual people, organizations, and/or events is purely coincidental.

Cover design by studiogearbox.com
Cover illustration by Cliff Nielsen
Map design by studiogearbox.com

Published in association with the literary agency of Janet Kobobel Grant, Books & Such, 4788 Carissa Ave., Santa Rosa, CA 95405.

Library of Congress Cataloging-in-Publication Data

Owens, Miles.
 Daughter of prophecy / Miles Owens.
     p. cm.
 ISBN 1-59185-799-6 (pbk.)
 I. Title.

PS3615.W475D38 2005
813'.6--dc22

2005014488

First Edition

05 06 07 08 09 — 987654321
Printed in the United States of America

To Dr. Gwen Faulkner, 1947–1999. Glorious Christian lady, English teacher, drama director, and my first reader. Red-penciled margin notes and writing school were in session. Our last time together that poignant night less than a week before she succumbed to breast cancer, she rose in her bed and gripped my hands. "My greatest regret," she whispered as we both cried, "is that I never wrote my novel. Finish yours."

Here 'tis, dear lady. I believe you would have liked it.

Acknowledgments

Grateful thanks to:

Crystal Miller, Wendy Lawton, and Audrey Dorsch, who took over the critiquing and editing chores afterwards. Thank you so much.

Len Goss, cherished friend and writing mentor. Bless you, dear brother. I owe you more than I can repay.

All my hometown encouragers for their unflagging support and prayers, especially: David and Debra Adams, Gary and Joan Brett, Rev. Eddie and Beth Blalock, Chet and Terry Thompson, Scott Barton, Lee McKinney.

Janet Grant, my agent. May our "marriage" continue to be a blessing.

Jeff Gerke, senior editor at Realms, who would not let *Daughter of Prophecy* be anything less that what it is now.

I saved the most important for last: Patti, my wife and love of my life. Her belief never wavered. I drew strength from that. Always will.

CAST OF CHARACTERS

THE ROGOTHS OF CLAN DINARI

Lord Tellan: kinsmen lord of the Rogoth family in the Dinari clan

Rhiannon: Tellan's daughter

Lady Mererid: Tellan's wife

Creag: Tellan's elder son

Phelan: Tellan's younger son

Girard: Tellan's loreteller and advisor

Llyr: Tellan's rhyfelwr (champion) and advisor

Serous: head herdsman

Lakenna: Rhiannon's tutor; member of the Albane sect

Branor: High Lord Keeper and advisor to Lord Tellan

OTHER IMPORTANT CHARACTERS

Maolmin: High Lord of the Dinari clan; excellent swordsman

Abel: Maolmin's loreteller

Breanna: Abel's daughter

Gillaon: kinsmen lord of the Tarenester family in the Arshessa clan

Harred: Gillaon's rhyfelwr (champion); master swordsman

Elmar: Harred's brother-in-law

Ryce Pleoh: wool merchant from the Sabinis clan

King Balder: the current king

Queen Cullia: the current queen

Prince Larien: Balder and Cullia's son; the only heir

Lady Ouveau: advisor to Queen Cullia

Lady Zoe: beautiful pagan woman from the Isle of Costos

Larbow: raider from the Rosada tribes; leader of his family group

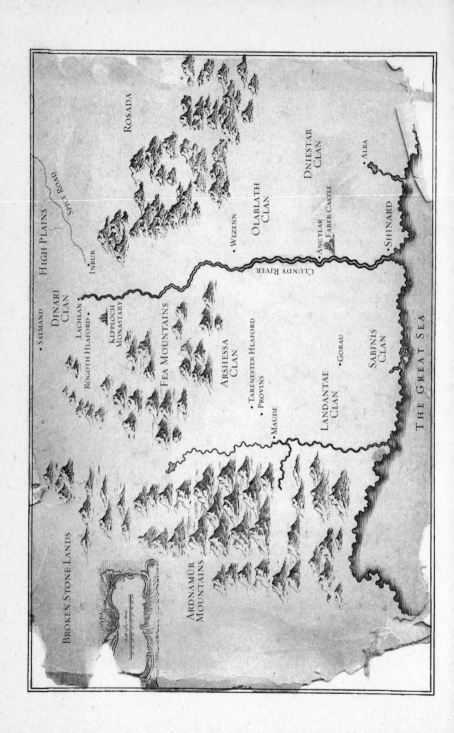

PROLOGUE

"NOW YOU CAN push, m'lady," Drysi the midwife announced in weary triumph. "The babe was coming sideways, but I've turned it. Push, and soon this one will be at your breast for its first meal."

Sweat plastered Lady Eyslk Rogoth's hair to her scalp, turning the red tresses a muddy brown. Her gown was drenched and clung to her bulging belly. She took several quick breaths around a rope of fabric clenched between her teeth, then bore down. The lines around her mouth deepened; her neck muscles bulged. A low groan accompanied the effort for several heartbeats. Then with a gasp the young woman fell back against the pillows.

The bedroom was sparsely furnished. Flanking Lady Eyslk's canopied bed were two red oak wardrobes, sturdy and well made. Opposite the bed stood a washstand and a dresser with a hand mirror hanging from a peg. Several chests lined the far wall. Above them hung a tapestry with the Rogoth banner: a white ram with triple spiral horns.

Upon arriving, Drysi had ordered the bedroom's two wooden shutters opened in hope of a breeze to cut the heat of the lanterns placed around the bed. The damp night air remained still. The only movement through the windows was moths. Their weaving about the lights threw darting shadows across the tapestries on the far wall. Two women, an elderly servant and the wife of the Rogoth loreteller, attended their lady, one standing on either side of the bed.

1

Drysi wiped the sweat from her brow. "Again. Push."

Lady Eyslk's throaty groan lasted several heartbeats before it too ended in a gasp.

The midwife frowned as a flow of dark blood began leaking out between the white legs. She glanced up at the noble lady's face. It was pale—much too pale. "Bring me my bag," Drysi snapped. "Hurry!"

The servant scurried over with the worn leather bag. Drysi quickly wiped the blood and fetal fluids from her hands, then rummaged in the bag's depths for a small pouch tied with a rawhide string.

"Put a pinch of this powder in a mug of hot water and make the lady drink it—all of it!" She brought out her forceps. They were constructed of iron strips with the spoon-like ends fitted with leather covers. After coating the outside of the leather with an herbal salve, she deftly slipped them into the birth canal and maneuvered the ends on either side of the baby's head.

Lady Eyslk lifted her lips from the mug and moaned. It was early for such a measure, but the amount of blood told Drysi to get this babe out now.

Lady Eyslk had been in labor many turns of the glass before Lord Tellan and his warriors had tracked Drysi down on the road as she returned from attending another birth. Lord Tellan himself had lifted her from the seat of her small two-wheeled cart and placed her in his open carriage. It had been a wild, careening ride back, with Tellan's face a stone mask as he kept the horses at a killing pace.

Drysi had been surprised to see a group of monks kneeling in the main room of the Rogoth hlaford when Tellan hurried her straight to Lady Eyslk's room. One looked up as they hurried by and said, "May the Eternal guide your efforts."

She hoped the monks were still praying. Lady Eyslk and the babe were going to need all the help they could get.

"Has she drunk all of the mug?"

"Only half—"

"That's enough. Give her something to bite on."

The servant placed the cloth rope back into Lady Eyslk's mouth.

"Hold her arms and shoulders. Keep her steady."

Drysi waited as the servant took one arm. The wife of the Rogoth loreteller gripped the other. She was heavy-chested with wide hips and could drop babies as easily as making water. So unlike Lady Eyslk's long, slender build. Drysi and the loreteller's wife glanced at each other. The worry in the other's eyes mirrored Drysi's own.

The forceps were in place. Blood continued to pour out, creating a growing red pool on the sheets. It had to be now.

Drysi gripped the handles and braced herself. "Hear me, m'lady! You push with everything you have. For the little one's life, push!"

Lady Eyslk's grunt turned into a full-throated wail as her effort and Drysi's brought the crown of the head into view.

"Again! For both of your lives, *push!*"

Eyslk's scream filled the room as the entire head emerged. Drysi threw the forceps down, reached in, and helped rotate the tiny shoulders. The head was covered with a thick mat of hair; skin color was the normal whitish blue. The babe twisted its head and blinked. Good enough.

"Now, one last time. Give me one more long, hard push."

The babe—a girl—came into the world. Drysi placed her on Eyslk's stomach, then raced to stop the hemorrhaging. "Give Lady Eyslk the rest of that mug, then another. If she throws it up, give her more until she keeps it down!"

Reaching into her bag again, she took out several hand-sized pieces of brown moss. They had been steeped in broth concocted from a type of bread mold, then air-dried. She placed two inside the gaping birth canal. That helped. She placed another and watched the bleeding slow to a trickle.

Glancing up at Lady Eyslk's pale, slack face, the midwife added her prayers to those of the monks. The young woman had been in intense labor for many hourglasses. That and the amount of blood she'd lost had killed many a new mother. Was she strong enough to come back, or would she continue on a downward spiral?

"Tell the monks to pray harder. I am doing all I can, but she needs more."

Drysi inserted another piece of moss, then stood and stretched her back. Numb with fatigue, she walked to a stand, poured water into a basin, and washed her hands and arms. Then she went back to check the little one.

The newest Rogoth lay comfortably on her mother's belly, cord still attached. The loreteller's wife began sponging off the mucus and blood while cooing softly at the babe. "She is strong and hungry. Do we let her nurse? With all the bleeding, you want to pull the afterbirth now, or wait a bit?"

The midwife pondered. Nursing helped the mother expel the afterbirth. But in Lady Eyslk's case, more bleeding would be sure to follow. Drysi checked her bag. Only three moss pads were left. From Lord Tellan's face on the road, she had not dared ask to go home and replenish her supplies.

She eyed the mother. Lady Eyslk's color was some better. Her breathing was rapid and shallow but already slowing down. The young mother was doing better than expected at this point. The monks' prayers must have been helping.

The servant lifted the lady's head and brought the mug to her lips. Eyslk swallowed, then opened her eyes. "Is it all right? Is my baby healthy?"

"Yes." Drysi breathed easier. "You have a fine, healthy girl." She made her decision. "Let it nurse now."

The loreteller's wife placed the babe at Eyslk's breast, then showed the new mother how to place a finger to keep the little one's nose free to breathe.

"Rhiannon. If it was a girl, it was to be Rhiannon," Eyslk whispered, watching her daughter nurse with vigor. "I am sure your lord father and the others are anxious to see you," she finished weakly before closing her eyes and resting back against the pillow.

"Be not in a hurry, m'lady," the loreteller's wife said. She placed both hands on broad hips and sniffed. "It does them good to wait until we allow entrance. As soon as you pass the afterbirth, we will sponge both you and Mistress Rhiannon clean and change the sheets. I will help you into a fresh gown and brush your hair. You dab on some perfume. Only then will it be proper for Lord Tellan to behold his lady wife and daughter. The monks can come after him."

The afterbirth came out easily and in one piece. Drysi tied and cut the cord. Only two moss pads were needed to stop Eyslk's new bleeding.

Drysi begin packing her supplies while the servant and the loreteller's wife made ready. This was Drysi's third time attending a noble birth. Labor brought women mercilessly to level ground. It was the same for all: a womb and a babe demanding to be born. And in the struggle to bring new life into the world, Death hovered over every bed, noble-born or commoner.

Tonight Death had almost won. But her skill and the monks' prayers had beaten him back one more time.

The women finished their ministrations to mother and babe. Drysi waited patiently. She had learned it was best to wait until after the father saw the new one—especially a first-timer like Lord Tellan—before mentioning her fee. Although they were of noble status, the Rogoths were not wealthy. Even so, Drysi felt certain Tellan would give her beyond the normal amount.

Besides, she always found it interesting to watch fathers and their firstborn. With a girl some were openly disappointed; others were smart enough to try and mask it. Most were awestruck, girl or boy.

Tellan Rogoth came into the room walking on air. He stopped at the bed and gazed at Eyslk. As the two regarded each other, Drysi doubled the amount she had planned to ask.

Lady Eyslk's eyes shone as she presented her babe. "A fine, healthy girl, my lord husband. Rhiannon de Murdeen en Rogoth, Clan Dinari." Tellan received his daughter awkwardly, then held her out in midair as if examining a new tunic.

Drysi smothered a snort. Typical.

"Tsk, m'lord." The loreteller's wife stepped up. "Hold her thusly. Babes need warmth and closeness." She soon had him cradling his daughter to his chest.

Then it was the loreteller's turn. He had entered with Tellan but remained by the door until now. The Rogoth loreteller was a short stump of a man; his wife easily made two of him. He wore the multicolored vest of his office, a well-recognized garment that allowed loretellers to move unchallenged throughout the Land, inviolate even in the midst of battle, to chronicle the history of the six clans.

In a deep, rich voice Loreteller Girard intoned: "On this date, thirty days before the summer solstice, in the year twelve hundred and one after the Cutting of the Covenant, was Rhiannon de Murdeen en Rogoth born into the Rogoth kinsmen of Clan Dinari. Be it known to all that, I, Loreteller Girard, am a witness to that fact and find her a well-formed babe with no blemishes or defects."

Girard held out his hand. Tellan removed his clan dagger from the sheath at his waist, placed it the loreteller's hand, and then held out his daughter's right foot. Girard made a small nick in the babe's heel; she promptly wrinkled her face and vented her disgust at the whole affair. Girard took a sheet of parchment and pressed it to the bloody heel.

"I will finish this by the noon meal, m'lord, and have it in the Annals for your inspection."

Rhiannon's wail stilled abruptly upon her return to Eyslk's breast. Drysi was about to step forward when the monks came traipsing in, four of them. She bit back an exasperated sigh. What were Keepers of the Covenant doing here anyway? In all her years, this had never happened. It had been a long, demanding night: two babes delivered safely and a good hourglass's travel to home yet ahead. She ground her teeth. If these monks started one of their interminable ceremonies, they could keep Tellan tied up well past dawn.

But no, the black-robed Keepers simply crowded respectfully around the bed. Three of the four looked in their late teens or early twenties. The fourth was older, late thirties perhaps. Tall and broad of shoulder, he had huge hands with the longest fingers Drysi had ever seen. The younger three took turns praising the babe and Lady Eyslk with a familiarity that bordered on family. The older monk remained quiet with a patient smile on his lips. He kept eying the bedroom door, giving Drysi the impression he was as eager to leave as she was.

Suddenly, the older monk's placid demeanor changed. He stepped back from the others, frowning fiercely. His eyes darted between the other three monks and then rested on the one closest to Lady Eyslk at the head of the bed. The younger monk's mouth hung open, and he had an unfocused gaze.

Drysi waited, but when nothing happened, she shouldered her bag and moved toward Lord Tellan. He stood away from the bed next to the loreteller, beaming with—

"Thus saith the Eternal!"

She froze in astonishment, as did everyone else in the room.

The young monk reached down and gripped Lady Eyslk's hand. Face aglow in religious fever, he spoke again:

"'Have I not given my word,' says the Eternal, 'that my covenant of peace will remain? Did I not say through my prophet these words: For the mountains shall depart and the hills be removed, but my kindness shall not depart from thee, neither shall this covenant of my peace be removed?'"

The monk raised his other hand to the ceiling. The long sleeves of his black robe slid back to revel a well-muscled arm. "Thus saith the Eternal! 'This babe at the breast will be a Protectoress of the Covenant. She will be a tool in my hands to strengthen it and return its fullness to the Land while bringing the Mighty Ones and their creatures to heel again.'"

The moment passed, and the expression on the young monk's face returned to normal. Wavering slowly, he lowered his hand and looked around sheepishly.

Several voices started together, excited.

But then another voice rose. "No! No!" overrode all else. "This will not be!" The older monk's voice was deep, liquid. It sent a bone chill through Drysi.

The monk surged at Lady Eyslk and seized the babe from her breast. "She must die!"

He swung the little one high above his head, but before he could do more, the other three monks swarmed him. They grappled around the bed with the crying babe still held high. Then the struggling mass fell back onto the bed on top of Lady Eyslk. The side railing broke with a loud crack, tipping everyone to the floor.

The young monk who had given the prophecy wrenched the babe free and came scrambling out of the pile, only to be jerked back by the outstretched hand of the older monk, who kept babbling: "No! No! Must die!"

Tellan flew into the melee. With obvious effort he pried away the crazed monk's hand, then lifted both his newborn and the young monk holding her and carried them to the far side of the room. He set them down and then whirled with dagger in hand.

The demented monk shook off the other two and rose menacingly to his feet. Eyes pulsing red, he glared past Tellan to the babe and spoke with a calm certainty that sent fresh chills down Drysi's spine.

"The Mighty One of the North rules here. Give her to him, and you will live and prosper. Refuse, and all in your house will perish with her." Then the monk came single-mindedly for the babe. To Drysi's startled eyes, it seemed he grew in size with every step.

Bravely, the small loreteller dove and wrapped his arms around the monk's leg, only to be dragged across the wooden floor effortlessly before being battered aside with a sharp blow.

Then Tellan launched himself at the advancing monk. As the two came to grips, it seemed to Drysi that the floor trembled. The lord's dagger plunged into the other's body twice, but the monk, now looming a full head taller than Tellan, only shuddered at each blow while attempting desperately to dodge around to the babe, babbling over and over, "Must die. Must die."

The loreteller's wife took the crying babe from the young monk. "Do something!"

The man gaped at the fight in the middle of the room. "This can't be happening. The Covenant prevents..."

"You've read all those parchments! Help Lord Tellan!"

The man swallowed hard. Coming to his full height, he flung out an arm with a long finger pointing at the crazed monk and bellowed, "In the name of the Eternal, I bind you!"

Still grappling with Tellan, the monk spat, "You lack the power!" He jerked a hand free and dealt Tellan a blow that dropped the new father to his knees. The monk kicked him aside and, leaving a trail of blood on the hardwood floor, came again for the babe.

The young monk stepped in front. "I bind you and any power you draw from the Mighty Ones!"

The other's tread faltered as he spat, "Weakling! You understand nothing."

The other two monks joined the fray. "We bind you! In the Eternal's name and the Covenant, you are bound!"

The wounded monk shuddered—and slowed.

The three continued the verbal fight. "We bind you! In the Eternal's name and the Covenant, you are bound!"

Tellan struggled to his feet. Dagger in hand, he reengaged, striking repeatedly. The monk seemed weaker, his intensity gone. After more blows, he sank to his knees. A low keening issued from his mouth, and a foul odor permeated the room. Then he crumbled prostate and lay still.

Tellan wavered, breathing hard. Then he sheathed his dagger and ran to the broken bed. "Midwife!" he bellowed in an agonized voice.

Drysi hurried over with a sinking feeling in her heart. Lady

Eyslk lay crumpled half on the bed, half on the floor, the lower part of her gown soaked in blood.

"He was so strong," one of the other monks said, "we couldn't help falling on her."

Tellan cradled his wife's limp body in his arms. "Eyslk? Eyslk!" He stroked her face. "Don't leave me!"

Drysi took her one remaining moss pad—but it was too late. She looked at Eyslk's stilled face and glazed eyes and suddenly felt old beyond her years.

"I'm sorry, m'lord. She is gone."

Chapter One

RHIANNON

H ER HOME WAS a ruin.
Rainwater collected in cracks where the stone floor
had buckled from intense heat. Faint tentacles of
smoke rose from fallen roof beams, charred and blackened, the
flames quenched by the heavy drizzle.

Rising above the acrid smell of wet soot was the odor of death.
It wafted up through the early morning mist, clinging inside Rhiannon's nostrils and making her filly skittish. The horse gave
a low snort and pranced sideways, reluctant to approach any
closer. Rhiannon urged the filly forward, applying pressure with
her left calf while pulling on the right rein. Her two younger half-
brothers were having similar difficulty with their mounts.

Her father and his escort of three clan warriors reined in
their horses at the waist-high stone fence that surrounded the
structure. They sat silently, contemplating the destruction with
grim faces.

Rhiannon eased up by the men and looked, stunned and
uncomprehending, at what was left of the Rogoth hlaford, the
dwelling of the kinsmen lord. She had been born here and lived
all of her almost sixteen years here. Even with the sight and smell
right before her, the fact of it was hard to grasp. The hlaford
would be rebuilt, of course, but that did not dim the numbness
of the loss. Losing irreplaceable keepsakes collected throughout
her childhood hurt more than she would have thought.

For nobility the structure was modest, even for a clan as poor as the Dinari. Nestled on a knoll rising from the valley floor, it was a simple two-story structure sixty cubits in length and thirty wide. The ground floor was constructed of stone; timber beams and rough hand-hewn planks comprised the second story. And, to her stepmother's great pride, both levels boasted glass windows.

Now the panes were shattered, the wooden frames scorched. Soot-streaked chimneys rose forlornly on either end of the building, the larger north one for the kitchen hearth, the south one for the room where Tellan had received petitioners and conducted matters as lord of the Rogoth kinsmen.

The Rogoth loreteller had galloped ahead of the party and was now examining the field full of dead and ravaged sheep. Rhiannon watched as he walked with the herdsmen. They pointed to the ground in several places. Then the loreteller climbed back on his horse and trotted to the smoldering ruin. His face was grim.

Her father stepped off his roan stallion as the loreteller rejoined them. Tellan Rogoth was tall, with pale white skin and black hair just beginning to show traces of gray. His oft-laundered breeches and tunic were frayed, the leather of his boots cracked and the soles well worn. After this year's wool was finally sold, all of the family would be fitted for new clothes and boots.

He handed his reins to one of the men, then strode through the open gate with the grace of a deadly fighter. Stopping at the burned structure, he stood with both fists on his hips. "Man or beast?" he growled darkly, glaring at the debris as if his gaze would make it relate the happenings of the night. "Girard!" he called out, sweeping an arm from the smoldering rubble to the blood-spattered corpses in the field. "What say you, loreteller? Two legs or four?"

Rhiannon's disquiet increased. This was no idle question. Her father asked if this was an attack or warning toward him because of the Rogoth kinsmen's stand against the hard-eyed wool merchants from Clan Sabinis.

"Beasts, m'lord," Girard said flatly. "We can find prints of neither man nor horse. Claws and fangs are responsible for the bloodletting among the sheep."

"And my hlaford, loreteller? This honored dwelling where my wife and children sleep secure under its peace? Claws and fangs did this as well?"

Girard pressed his lips together, frowning as he contemplated his answer. The Rogoth loreteller was round of face with heavy jowls. His short, bandy legs barely reached below his horse's belly. "Lore dating from before the Cutting of the Covenant recounts similar incidents," he began hesitantly. "Torn throats, dismembered bodies, unexplained fires as this one here."

Tellan glanced back with eyebrows raised. "You seek to spin a tale of winged horrors of the night?" His voice carried a trace of derision, but even so, his knuckles whitened around the hilt of his sword. "Has the Eternal suddenly blessed you as he did the Founders? You declare with certainty that siyyim and similar creatures stalk the Land again?"

"As you know, m'lord, it has been years since anyone has been gifted at that level." Girard rubbed his hand nervously across the stubble on his chin. "But for some reason I feel strongly about this. Come and see the heavy claw marks in the ground. And the deep gouging of the grass. Whatever attacked must be several times the weight of a horse. The prints are abundant in the middle of field where the sheep lay, there and nowhere else. Serous and his herdsmen have searched. No tracks lead into the field or away."

Tellan turned to face his loreteller. "And the ground here around the hlaford? I see no prints or claw marks."

"Our lore recounts how such creatures flew to the roofs, breathed fire on the thatch, then circled above before swooping down to catch those forced out by the smoke and flames."

Rhiannon exchanged startled looks with her half-brothers. Creag was thirteen and ever desirous to appear fearless. Nonetheless, he cut his eyes to the sky, head swiveling back and forth as he anxiously searched the rolling mass of gray clouds.

Phelan's gaze flicked from Girard to Tellan, then to Rhiannon.

13

The boy was ten, small for his age and frail. He had his father's pale skin and black hair. Catching her eye, Phelan grinned with excitement, teeth biting down on his lower lip, clearly relishing the prospect of seeing such mythical beasts.

Rhiannon did not share his enthusiasm. She brushed a hand across the hilt of her sword, taking comfort in its weight resting in the scabbard hanging from a broad belt buckled around her waist. On her fourteenth birthday, her father had given in to her pleading and presented her this scaled-down version of his broadsword. Since then she had joined her brothers in daily lessons with their arms instructor, infuriating Creag by continually besting him in bouts with their wooden practice swords.

Returning to the big roan, Tellan took the reins and swung easily into the saddle. He led them toward the sheep in the nearby field. The grassy hillsides around the hlaford were rock-strewn. Further on, a series of ridges undulated upward to the higher peaks towering in the distance. Below, a wide stream snaked through the middle of the valley floor, bubbling and frothing its way to the join the Clundy River several leagues away.

On warm summer days, Rhiannon and her brothers wove fish traps from rushes gathered in the quiet eddies of the stream. Then they waded into the snowmelt with bare toes clinging to the slippery stones along the bottom, placing the traps between rocks that narrowed the current, emerging with chattering teeth and blue lips. Later, they returned to lift the baskets out and carry the trout home to be cleaned and cooked for dinner.

The clouds hid the sky completely, a solid gray sheet seemingly close enough to touch, as was often the case in the Dinari highlands. Its rugged hills produced two things superbly: sheep with prize wool that could be woven into waterproof garments, and hard-muscled warriors, each equal to any three men from the other five clans. Or so the Dinari boasted.

But Rhiannon's beloved highlands had not produced anything in living memory that could wreak such havoc as she saw now. The sight chilled her more than the long predawn ride in the cold drizzle. Less than a hundred paces away from her home the bloody carcasses of several score of sheep dotted the surrounding field. Recently shorn, their white bodies lay in stark contrast against the green grass. The animals' throats were ripped open. But even more ominous to Rhiannon was the number of limbs torn from their bodies and flung paces away.

She struggled with the filly again as they came to where the majority of the sheep had been slain. The horse pranced about with light feet, head swinging side to side, blowing low snorts at the mangled corpses. Rhiannon collected her mount with gentle but steady pressure on the bit. "Easy, easy."

Phelan nudged his horse up alongside. "You think winged horrors did this?" he whispered in awe.

"I don't know," Rhiannon shook her head. "A pack of wolves could kill this many, but..." She swallowed as a cold twist rippled through her stomach. "But their feeding would not tear bodies apart in such a manner."

Every carcass in sight had its throat torn away by what must have been sharp teeth and the power of massive jaws. Plus, Rhiannon noted, most of the severed limbs lying scattered about had the bones sliced—or bitten—completely through.

Her father's head herdsmen, Serous, came forward to hold the stallion's bit while Tellan dismounted. Serous was of average height and painfully thin. Both his hands were gnarled, the joints red and swollen. "Not a pleasant sight, m'lord. As a boy, then a man, I've been herding sheep nigh on fifty years, and I never seen the like."

A murmur of agreement came from the other herders. They shifted back and forth on nervous feet, eyes flicking between their lord and the dead sheep.

The loreteller dismounted and walked with his short-legged, rolling gait to an area of torn grass. He turned back and pointed down. "Here, m'lord. This is what I am talking about."

Rhiannon slid off, handed the reins to Phelan, then followed her father to where the loreteller stood. The marks were easily distinguished in the soft, wet soil. Long clumps of grass had been gouged up where one or more creatures had pivoted and twisted. The deep parallel lines sliced through the dirt had to have come from sharp claws or talons. Looking at the width of the footprints, Rhiannon realized that the loreteller was correct—the creatures that did this were large.

"From what our men have told me, m'lord," Girard said quietly, "and from the evidence of my eyes, I can come to but one conclusion: winged horrors of the night."

Rhiannon looked up and caught her father's gaze. Worry was evident behind his eyes as he looked from her to her brothers, to the three warriors, then back to her again. His hand dropped to his sword hilt.

Two days past Tellan had taken his family and lone household servant to the town of Lachlann, a ride of more than two turns of the glass. They were staying in four of the upper rooms of the largest inn. This unusual move had been necessitated by his involvement in the tense negotiations concerning the wool trade. Tellan had not wanted to leave his wife and children alone during what promised to be a time of unrest.

When a messenger woke them at the inn an hourglass before dawn, Rhiannon had asked to come home along with her father, with Creag and Phelan echoing her plea. Their mother, Lady Mererid, was gone to interview a prospective tutor for the three of them, taking five of the Rogoth warriors with her as an escort. She was not expected back in Lachlann until late in the day. Considering the tension in the town between the Sabinis merchants and other small Dinari lords allied with the Rogoth kinsmen, her father had agreed to bring Rhiannon and the boys along.

From the lines creasing his brow, she could read his thoughts: he had brought them from one danger into a greater one.

Stone-faced, Tellan surveyed the ravaged sheep. "Tell me what you saw, Serous."

"The fire at the hlaford woke me, m'lord. The roof was aflame."

Serous had only two upper teeth, both slanting sideways. He kept running his tongue around them in a nervous tic. "At first I was concerned for your lordship's safety, but then I remembered how everyone was in Lachlann. As I came running up, the hlaford looked like a huge torch. The flames was being fanned by..." He looked at those around him, then down at his feet.

The nervous movement among the other herdsmen ceased. They waited with pensive faces.

Tellan reached out and gripped the old man's shoulder. "Serous de Rogoth en Caillen, you strapped on your sword and rode by my father's side every time the kinsmen were called out. And you have served me with honor these last years. Tell it straight and know I will believe you."

Serous took a deep breath. "It was like Girard says, m'lord. Him being a great loreteller and such, he has seen it true. Winged horrors of the night. That's what they had to be, just like in the old stories. At least four of them. As you said, m'lord, I was a warrior until my joints started to swell, and no man can say he seen my backside when cold steel was drawn." He stood up straight. "Fearsome I was. Ask them that knew me when I could grip a sword."

"No need to ask. I know your mettle."

The old herdsman's Adam's apple bobbed as he regarded Tellan with watery eyes. "I ran from them things, m'lord," he confessed softly, his weathered face twisting in misery. "I left the sheep unattended and ran for my life. The other herders were just following my lead when they ran, too. Then the winged horrors was free to do this." He paused, then lifted his chin. "I have a few coins put by. So do the rest of us. It won't be near enough to repay your loss, but it is all we have. If you want me to end my service, I will."

Tellan smiled grimly. "Serous, if any of you had stayed, we would be burying fools this morning. I have no need of fools. Cowards try to excuse their absence. Rogoth warriors do not hide behind words. In Serous Caillen and his herdsmen I have such men. Keep your coins. You are more valuable than any metal jingling in a bag."

Rhiannon watched self-respect return to the old man's countenance. The other herdsmen squared their shoulders, their chins held higher. She glanced at the three men-at-arms. To a man, they sat straighter in their saddles, grim pride breaking through their stoic demeanor.

Serous's lips trembled for a moment. He blinked rapidly, then turned his head. Clearing his throat, he hawked and spat before looking back.

"Tell me more about the attack on the hlaford," Tellan said.

"When the winged horrors realized no one was coming out, one of them dropped through the roof—the flames didn't seem to bother it none. Then it flew back out and screeched at the others. That's when they took to the sheep. It was a killing rage, m'lord. Pure and simple. They didn't kill to feed; it was anger and frustration."

The herdsman paused, then gave Tellan a level look. "M'lord, I swear I could hear the winged horrors talking as they flew around the hlaford. It was strange and awful sounding, but I could understand them right enough. They kept chanting: 'Red hair. Red hair. Kill red-haired girl.'"

Everyone looked at Rhiannon. The blood chilled in her veins as her curly mane of dark red tresses suddenly felt heavy on her scalp.

Chapter Two

RHIANNON

THE DRIZZLE STOPPED as they rode back to Lachlann. The sun began to burn through the clouds, sending rays of light to contrast the grayness. A layer of fog clung to the hollows while the upper ridges poked in and out of the misty blanket like undulations of a sea monster.

On the left side of the trail, the ground rose away up the hillside, ablaze with yellow, gold, and red flowers blooming in broad swathes across the steep hillsides. Scattered trees dotted the landscape. Periodically, patches of blue-gray granite thrust up from the underlying bedrock like giant teeth chewing through the thin soil. A ring of flowers mimicking multicolored necklaces encircled many of the boulders. Only a few paces to Rhiannon's right, the hillside sloped away steeply over broken terrain until it gave way to open air beneath.

When they left the hlaford everyone had been on alert, although the legends said winged horrors flew only under the cover of darkness. The three warriors had strung their bows and now rode with arrows notched. After an uneventful length of travel, Tellan told them to sheathe their bows but remain watchful. Everyone drew deep breaths and sat easier on their mounts.

It was spring in the highlands. In the sky, birds roamed the air currents with deft dips and weaves, their calls seeming to urge greater efforts from each other as they celebrated winter's retreat. Even so, the wind still carried a hint of a chill with the sun only halfway above the horizon.

Rhiannon and her brothers rode behind their father and Girard. Kinsmen lord and loreteller were in heated discussion about the attack. Two warriors rode a stone's throw ahead as forward scouts; the third brought up the rear several paces behind the party. The rocky trail was barely wide enough for three horses to walk abreast.

Rhiannon listened to Creag and Phelan discuss the winged horrors and the sheepherders' actions.

"The herdsmen should have been dismissed," Creag pronounced with iron conviction. "I would have done so first thing."

"Why?" Phelan asked, puzzled.

"Now they will think they can get away with not doing their duty."

"How can they be expected to fight winged horrors with just their staffs? You heard Father say they would have been foolish to do that."

Creag's lip curled. "Next time they see danger, they will run away again."

"They will stay and fight next time," Rhiannon said. "They will walk barefoot over hot coals if Father asks it of them."

Creag shook his head, snorting in disagreement. They passed a mound of grass-choked ruins. Loreteller Girard claimed it was a former temple dedicated to the old gods pulled down centuries ago during the Cleansing when Destin Faber led the effort to rid the Land of pagan worship.

A fresh wind gust molded Rhiannon's dark green cloak to her back. The front edge tangled around the hilt of her sword and flapped maddeningly. When she tugged it loose, the wind snatched it out of her grip, blowing the cloak before her, held on only by the clasp at her neck.

Her filly, Nineve, broke into a fast trot, startled at the sudden appearance of the material waving above her head. Rhiannon grappled with the cloak with one hand while reining back her mount with the other. Nineve was still green and needed at least another year of hard training. Rhiannon was growing weary of the constant struggle.

Creag snickered. "If you put your arms through the straps inside your cloak the wind couldn't blow it loose."

"The straps hinder drawing my sword," she snapped, fighting to rearrange the cloak.

"You make just one swing, and it will be all you can do to keep Nineve from running off. Then the cloak will be in your face and your sword will be—"

"At least I hit what I swing at instead of missing the gourd by two handsbreadth and breaking a good sword on the post."

"Not on Nineve. Last time you tried that on her, she threw you. While you were trying to catch her, I knocked off every gourd—"

"At a trot. I knocked them off at a canter—"

"Only the last two. You were so busy trying to control her that you missed the first three!"

"I will hear no more of this mindless chatter," their father growled. He looked back over his shoulder. "Rhiannon, join me and Girard. There are things you need to know. Creag, we will discuss the same with you next."

She gave her brother a sour look, then urged the filly up to squeeze between the two men. Her being called first would put Creag in a pout the rest of the day.

"Lord Tellan has asked me to be sure you understand our lore about winged horrors," Girard said.

"I listen to learn, loreteller."

"Before Destin Faber and the Cutting of the Covenant, winged horrors of the night and other such creatures could be loosed by the Mighty Ones."

Rhiannon nodded. This was common knowledge—and the subject of many nighttime stories told by Ove, their household servant.

"The Covenant," the loreteller continued, "severely limited the Mighty Ones' power, and the appearances of those creatures virtually ceased."

"That is what the Keepers of the Covenant assure us each

year when we bring our tithe."

A flock of birds flew across the path, then wheeled abruptly away from the ridge to the right and the drop-off beyond. Nineve turned her head that way; her ears flicked forward. Rhiannon pulled her around, but the filly pulled against the bit to look right again. The birds' calls faded into the distance.

"Less commonly known," Girard said, "are the reports of appearances through the centuries. Keepers respond to them and keep their own records. But no one among the six clans has produced a carcass verified by a Loreteller Assembly. Most such incidents are considered flights of fantasy."

Tellan spoke. "But you believe last night's attack to have been winged horrors?"

"Yes, m'lord. Strongly."

"So advise us, loreteller. If winged horrors were sent to 'kill red-haired girl,' who loosed them? And why?"

Nineve stumbled, her gaze fixed at the low ridge to their right. Rhiannon pulled the filly's head around, but the horse tossed her head and looked back. Her father's roan kept turning its head to the right as well. Girard's old gelding, however, plodded along unconcerned, with relaxed ears and droopy eyes. Rhiannon had never seen the animal excited over anything. She glanced again at the ridge, chewing the inside of her lip thoughtfully. It was daylight, many turns of the glass before nightfall. Still . . .

"Only Serous claims to have heard that," Girard was saying. "Our lore makes no mention of the Mighty Ones' beasts talking. None of the other herders heard anything. I asked them out of Serous's hearing. They were as surprised with that as the rest of us." Girard shook his head. "If you are thinking of the incident by that deranged monk after Rhiannon's birth—"

"It has been almost sixteen years without any further attempts on Rhiannon," Tellan said. "Like you, I think we can discount what Serous said." He leaned forward, his dark eyes glittering. "But my questions remain: Why were winged horrors sent to destroy the Rogoth hlaford? And who sent them?"

Chapter Three

LAKENNA

"MY LORD HUSBAND indulges Rhiannon shamefully," Lady Mererid said as they jostled about in the carriage. "It is my hope that your presence will help me lead her to put aside this warrior obsession."

Lakenna retied the scarf that secured her hair against the stiff breeze. "This time can be difficult for young ladies."

They were half a day's journey from Lachlann. The road was muddy and rocky. More than once Lakenna had determinedly kept her eyes focused inside the carriage, trying not to speculate on how much room the wheels had before the road gave way to air and the breathtaking scenery beyond. Foothills, Lady Mererid had called them. To Lakenna, they were small mountains. A long valley stretched below the winding road, blue with morning mist. She could see tops of trees, some type of evergreens judging by the foliage and the crisp scent.

Lakenna brought her gaze back inside the carriage where she sat across from her new employer. The seats were bare wood. Every bump in the road pounded through the tutor's hips, coursed up her spine, and rattled the top of her skull, which made talking risky. Several times her teeth had clacked together, once catching the side of her tongue painfully. A faint metallic taste of blood still lingered.

The wind blew wisps of hair across Lady Mererid's face. Lakenna envied the noble lady's long elegant fingers as Mererid tucked the wayward strands back under the hood of her cloak.

A deep wine-red, the cloak was made of the highest quality wool embroidered in a flower and leaf pattern. Mererid's dress was a lighter shade of red with the bodice and hem outlined by delicate lace. Around her neck she wore a necklace of gold links with a small cameo pendant nestled in the hollow of her throat.

"I never met my lord husband's first wife, but I am told that Rhiannon favors her strongly. Lady Eyslk died during Rhiannon's birth." Mererid fussed with another windblown strand of hair. "This is my second marriage as well. I lost my first husband and year-old son to lung fever only weeks after Lady Eyslk's death."

Lakenna's insides roiled. She had lost her father to this dread disease years ago. And just six months ago her betrothed had succumbed to it. He had just finished building their cottage when the constant clearing of his throat started. The next day, his flushed face and chills confirmed… Lakenna firmly put those thoughts aside.

Another strong jolt bounced her on the hard seat. The carriage was well made but unadorned. It had no sides or top, and the wind had a bite that made Lakenna glad for the wool blanket she had wrapped around her legs and feet. Two bench seats faced each other. She sat behind the driver, directly across from Mererid. A grizzled warrior handled the reins of the pair of horses that pulled the carriage along at a fast clip. Two warriors rode ahead and two behind, all mounted on shaggy-haired, sturdy horses. Each rider had a broadsword strapped behind his back and a strung bow and quiver of arrows in leather sheaths hanging from the saddle. A pack mule tied to the rear of the carriage carried Lakenna's bags and her precious hoard of hand-copied sections of Holy Writ carefully wrapped in waxed parchment.

Lakenna Wen was twenty-five, slender, with an angular face dominated by a bold nose between eyes recessed in their sockets. Her dark hair was in a bun and covered by a scarf that the gusts kept trying to rip off. Her skirt was farmer brown wool, her blouse a crisp white linen with a double row of pleats. A gray cloak that was too thin for the chilly highland spring barely kept her teeth from chattering.

Squinting at the rocky hillsides through wind that made her eyes water, Lakenna tried not to question her reason for being here. Lord Tellan's letter inquiring into her services had been well written, his offer of payment in coin adequate, and the proposed duties he outlined reasonable.

But there was the difference in faith. The conservative Dinari clan was well known to be a stronghold of the most orthodox of Keeper monks. The Kepploch Monastery was the most famous in the Land and was close to Rogoth lands. The Keepers of the Covenant were enemies with her own breakaway sect of believers, called Albanes, their differences longstanding and irreconcilable.

And she was single, only months removed from burying the man she had been days away from marrying. Another pang rippled through her stomach. Mercifully, the lung fever outbreak had been a mild one, with Loane only one of a double handful succumbing to the disease before the outbreak ended as mysteriously as it begun.

Lakenna shifted on the hard seat and glanced out at the countryside without seeing it, hands clenched tightly in her lap. Most Albane maidens were married by fifteen or sixteen. Being single at twenty-five was beyond the point of embarrassment. It bordered on hopeless.

Loane had been three years her junior, and many had considered him no prize: under average height and beanpole thin, with a face that was all misplaced parts—a mouth too small for his teeth, potato nose, and long, pointed chin. But he loved her, and she had grown to love him.

When Lord Tellan's letter came, she tried to dismiss it—and found that she could not. She had been unable to commune with the Eternal since Loane's death. Even more so since…the other. So when the letter arrived, she had not been able to pray and seek guidance about such a major change. Albane teachers of doctrine proclaimed that the Eternal's forgiveness was available to all, and Lakenna knew they spoke truth. Still...her guilt kept her from accepting this truth for herself.

Even so, something kept prodding her to accept Lord Tellan's offer. She had met with Lady Mererid yesterday in the large trading center of Inbur on the border of Dinari lands. The interview had gone well, and Lakenna had agreed to one year of service tutoring the three Rogoth children plus no more than five others from Lord Rogoth's retainers.

"Tell me more about my charges," she said. Noble children could be difficult.

Mererid smiled a mother's smile. "Of the three, Phelan is the best student. He is the youngest and has been a sickly child. On two different occasions the Healer feared the poor boy would not survive the latest bout of fever and advised us to call a monk to prepare for the funeral. However, Phelan always rallied. He has not been seriously ill for more than a year." She paused. "Then there is Creag. He is thirteen. He is so serious, so determined to be found worthy. He counts the days until he turns sixteen and can take his place in the adult world." Lakenna could tell Mererid chose her next words carefully. "He is the slowest at learning and...feels it keenly."

"What do you mean, m'lady?"

"Our previous tutor, an older monk, was determined that the heir should excel. He was hard on the boy. Creag does not learn at the same pace as Phelan or Rhiannon—when she tries. But once Creag finally grasps it, he does not forget. Loreteller Girard is impressed with Creag's memory for dates and names. But the boy has trouble reading even the simplest passages from Holy Writ, and his writing is atrocious. It drove Keeper Astwin to despair."

"But Creag learns well mouth-to-ear?"

"Pardon?"

"If you read to him or explain it to him with words, he does better?"

"Well, that is how Master Girard teaches clan lore. He keeps saying how pleased he is with Creag. Without the loreteller's praise, I don't know what the boy would do." Mererid regarded Lakenna frankly. "Girard joined with me to convince Tellan to search for a tutor who was not a monk. It was his loreteller contacts that led us to you."

Lakenna was surprised. "I wondered why a Dinari lord living so close to the Kepploch Monastery was interested in engaging my services. As I understand it, clan loretellers and the Keepers work closely together. And yet your loreteller recommended me to take the place of one of their monks?"

"We are familiar with the Albanes' reputation for producing gifted teachers. And everyone Girard talked to had nothing but the highest praise for you in particular. I am so pleased you decided to accept our offer."

Lakenna smiled politely. "Tell me more about Rhiannon."

"She is growing into an extraordinarily beautiful young woman, and yet all she thinks about is becoming a clan warrior. She wears her sword continually. Yes," Mererid sighed in response to Lakenna's perplexed look, "and practices every spare moment. I begged Tellan not to give it to her, but . . ." Mererid turned her head and gazed at the countryside. "As I said, Rhiannon is the image of her mother. I have come to realize that Lady Eyslk holds a place in my husband's heart I cannot touch." Her voice was flat, her face emotionless. "When he looks at Rhiannon—well, he indulges her. He teaches her as he would a son and heir."

"Which Creag sees as disapproval of him," Lakenna said, warming to the challenge, wondering what the Eternal had in store for the boy.

"It is not that bad. Truly. Tellan is good to all of them. He prepares both Creag and Phelan as his duty requires; he just includes Rhiannon as well. Which makes my role of teaching her a noblewoman's responsibilities difficult."

"I look forward to meeting her," Lakenna murmured neutrally.

"You should know that there is another reason Tellan teaches her as he does." Again, it was apparent that Mererid composed her words carefully. "At Rhiannon's birth...well, first let me explain about certain monks at Kepploch during that time. A number of the younger ones were searching the writings in both theirs and other monasteries' archives, attempting to separate myth from fact around Destin Faber and the Cutting of the Covenant. They sought to recover an understanding of the warfare in the heavenlies that occurred during the Founding."

Lakenna's jaw dropped. Keepers had attempted to do what the Eternal had called Albanes to do? She listened intently.

"Rhiannon's mother, Lady Eyslk, became interested in the monks' efforts and helped them as she could. She wrote to other nobles among the six clans asking them to search for old letters and other writings that mentioned their ancestors' role during those days. Many responded, and what they sent was of great benefit to the monks' study. When Lady Eyslk's time came in her pregnancy, that group of Keepers came to the hlaford and were in attendance, praying for both mother and the coming babe. The moment Rhiannon was born, one Keeper seemed to have a special...insight." Mererid paused. "I was not present, of course. What I know is from what Loreteller Girard has told me."

"What kind of insight?"

Mererid related the happenings of that dark night. "I am sure Tellan's indulgence of Rhiannon's warrior desires comes from that time."

"I see," Lakenna said, thoughts whirling. "What became of the monk who made the prophecy?"

"He left the monastery soon thereafter and has risen high in the Keeper hierarchy."

"Thank you for telling me this," Lakenna said. "I do look forward to working with Rhiannon. She must be a special child."

Mererid reached under her feet, brought out a bag, and removed three articles wrapped in soft leather. "Last fall, unbeknownst to Tellan, I commissioned these from the silversmith in Inbur. I picked them up this morning before we left."

DAUGHTER OF PROPHECY

Lakenna reached out to take the hand mirror, comb, and brush, all crafted of silver. The mirror was half a cubit in length with a fluted handle and a ring through the end for hanging. Its circle of reflecting glass measured a handsbreadth in diameter, the silver edges decorated in a twisted rope design. The same twisted rope design outlined the edges of the brush and comb in detail so exquisitely wrought it had to be the work of a master craftsman. Lakenna sighed inwardly. She would never own anything like this. "They are beautiful."

"These are for Rhiannon," Mererid said. "It is my hope they will bring some femininity into her life to help counteract the harshness of her training. One of my aunts died this past winter. I will tell Tellan she left these to me. I had to bargain a diamond bracelet and two gold rings with the silversmith. If Tellan knew, he would erupt into a towering rage."

Reluctantly, Lakenna handed the three pieces back, regarding Mererid with growing respect. The other woman carefully wrapped them in the leather and placed them inside the bag.

They bounced along in silence for a while, Lakenna lost in thought as she attempted to come to terms with Lady Mererid's revelation.

Suddenly she felt a familiar urge build inside, as if the Eternal was calling her to pray. She dismissed it quickly. *How could he be speaking to me after my failure?*

Her mother and friends had questioned her decision to come here to the Dinari highlands and accept service virtually within sight of the legendary Kepploch Monastery. She had responded to their concerns with, "The Eternal is telling me to go. How can I refuse?"

But the truth had been something other than what she had said. She had mouthed reasons no Albane could argue with. But her real reason was too painful...

She pushed that aside. Here she was less than a day after accepting the position, and the possibilities before her were mind-boggling. A young heir to restore, a girl to prepare for

29

something to do with the Covenant.

The urge to pray built inside her. Again.

How can I?

But the feeling grew stronger, insistent, more demanding until she could no longer discount it. The Eternal was indeed prodding her to pray. Pray for... protection? Pray against... evil?

Puzzled, she glanced at the escorts. They rode alertly alongside the carriage but seemed unconcerned. Swinging her head back, she caught Mererid's eyes.

"Teacher? Is something the matter?"

Lakenna opened her mouth, then closed it. Was this some aftermath of the story the noble lady had just told her? But that thought was pushed aside as the feeling surged again with extreme urgency, and Lakenna knew she had to respond.

"Lady Mererid, will you join with me in prayer? I feel... I feel that... evil... stalks someone. It must be Lord Rogoth or the children! We need to pray the covering of the Covenant over them," she said with a fierceness that surprised her and widened Mererid's eyes in alarm. "We need to pray *now*."

Chapter Four

RHIANNON

THE BAY GELDING Phelan rode was named Munin. Until Rhiannon had talked her father into letting her start training Nineve, the gelding had been her mount. Munin was calm and unflappable, responding immediately to knee and voice commands. He was almost as well taught as her father's stallion.

Training a young horse was more of a challenge than Rhiannon had anticipated. She tried not to begrudge Phelan his easy ride as hers pranced along requiring constant attention and a firm hand. Phelan rode along beside her, chattering away while Tellan and Master Girard informed Creag about the winged horrors.

"Before Mother left yesterday," Phelan said, "she said our new tutor may be a woman. I didn't know women could be monks."

"She is not a monk."

"Why?"

"Why what? Why can't women be monks or why a woman tutor? You do not have to be a monk to be a tutor."

The breeze picked up just then, causing a clump of bitter-grass growing by the trail to wave about. Nineve decided that was excuse enough to startle in alarm. She shied to the side, bumping into Munin. Rhiannon collected the filly and reined her back to the bush. The only way to train a mount not to balk at unusual objects was to make them approach it. When they got close to the grass again, Nineve snorted, then pranced sideways, still convinced the waving clump held terrors untold.

The rear guard reined his horse up and watched Rhiannon's struggle with a bemused expression. Tellan, Girard, Creag, and the two forward guards continued, unaware of the delay behind them.

"I'll ride Munin up to show her it's safe," Phelan offered.

"No," Rhiannon said through clenched teeth as Nineve whirled away yet again. After several more tries she finally got the filly within a sword's length of the bittergrass and declared victory.

"What happened to Keeper Astwin?" Phelan asked when she joined him back on the trail.

"He couldn't teach Creag to read." She worked her fingers up the reins to shorten her grip.

"He taught me to read. He never gets angry with me. If you tried harder, he wouldn't shout at you, either."

Rhiannon made a noncommittal sound.

"He only gets red in the face and shouts when he has to ask you the same question two or three times because you weren't paying attention or when you forget and wear your sword into the room."

Unbidden, her hand dropped to the hilt of her sword. It was a simple straight blade, sharp on both edges. When she had first held it, it had seemed small compared with her father's. She had learned its weight after practicing only a few of the drills the arms instructor showed her. Her muscles had strengthened, and now she could wield the blade with greater swiftness and for a longer length of time before having to rest.

"Father can wear his sword into the room," she said.

"Only that one time, and Keeper Astwin glared and wouldn't say another word until Father unbuckled the scabbard and hung it on the wall next to yours. Every time since, he takes it off before he..." His words trailed off when she raised her hand in a gesture for quiet.

She listened to the silence. The creak of saddle leather seemed loud, so too the crunch of hoofs in the dirt. Overhead, the sky was empty, the chatter of birds gone. Nineve walked straight, but her head was turned to the right, her ears upright and alert. Rhiannon checked Munin. The gelding was looking at the ridge, too. Her concern became more urgent.

Glancing over her shoulder, she saw that both the warrior and his horse were interested in whatever was happening below sight of the rocky ledge. He reached down, slid his bow out of its sheath, and nocked an arrow.

"Mistress Rhiannon," he warned, "we need to gallop ahead and join the rest of them."

She opened her mouth to urge Phelan on when she heard her father shouting, "Rhiannon! You and Phelan get up here!" His voice cracked with authority while conveying his concern. He had turned around and was cantering back to them. The stallion's muscles rippled and nostrils flared as he bore Tellan down the trail.

She pressed her heels into Nineve's side, but instead of leaping ahead, the horse slowed abruptly, pivoted directly to the right, and snorted. Dirt swirled among the rocks bordering the ledge. The filly gave a louder, longer snort. Rhiannon's skin pricked; the hair on her arms stirred. The air thickened. Her heart hammered.

Two winged horrors soared up over the ridge.

They were more fearsome than Rhiannon had imagined from the stories. Many times the size of a horse, they were heavy chested with long leathery wings shaped like an eagle's and a long, whiplike tail. In the air, they kept their four feet pulled tightly against their bodies. Wedge-shaped heads attached to serpentine necks swung back and forth surveying the humans before them.

The nearest creature's eyes glowed when its gaze came to Rhiannon. Opening its mouth to reveal a double row of sharp teeth, it let out an ear-piercing screech and beat straight for her.

Nineve neighed in stark terror and bolted down the trail, nearly unseating Rhiannon. She had barely managed to right herself in the saddle when a third winged horror appeared over the ridge ahead and swooped for them. Unbidden, Nineve swerved smartly to the left and raced up the boulder-strewn hillside.

Dimly, Rhiannon realized that the creatures were neatly separating her from the rest of the party. Swallowing her fear, she leaned forward over the filly's shoulders and urged more speed. The long mane brushed her face; her cloak clasp tugged strongly against her neck as it blew behind, flapping in the wind generated by the all-out gallop.

But within a few bounds a large shadow passed overhead, and a horror landed before them, long rear legs unfolding to absorb the shock. The creature's skin was a mottled lizard-green, hairless and grainy. Shorter front legs attached to the body just forward of the wings possessed three wickedly curved claws with a smaller opposing thumb for grasping. The beast crouched with its huge wings spread, hissing, ready to spring.

Nineve came to a jolting, stiff-legged stop that propelled Rhiannon face forward onto the horse's neck. Desperately grabbing a fistful of mane, she managed to stay on as the filly pivoted back in the direction of Phelan and the warrior. But two winged horrors dropped to the ground to block that avenue of escape. Again Nineve whirled—and right before them was the open mouth of a fourth beast! Its hot, fetid breath filled Rhiannon's nostrils as sharp fangs descended—

Her father galloped into the creature's side. The impact knocked the horror sideways and buckled the legs of the stallion. Tellan leaped adroitly out of his saddle onto Nineve, cradling Rhiannon in his arms as they rolled to the ground.

The stallion regained its balance first and kicked out at the horror. Shrieking in rage, the beast struggled back to its feet and with a swing of its heavy head batted the horse away several paces.

Nineve seized that opportunity to bolt past the other horrors closing in. The beasts paid the filly no mind as she raced by with bridle reins dragging the ground; they had eyes only for Rhiannon, regarding her with the cold-eyed menace of a pack of wolves cornering their prey.

"Red hair," they hissed, the sound coming out of the hooked beaks guttural and grotesque. "Kill red-haired girl."

The intensity of their malevolence toward her froze Rhiannon's breath in her throat as the words rippled up and down her skin.

Then she remembered her sword. She started to reach for it but realized she already held it before her! Both hands gripped the hilt correctly, the point up in the ready position, wavering slightly.

"This way!" Tellan shouted. His sword was drawn as well. Reaching out with his free hand, he pulled her toward a formation of boulders several paces away.

As they ran, a horror raced ahead at an angle to cut them off, moving with astonishing speed on those long rear legs while holding out its wings for balance. Skidding to a stop in front of the rocks, it wheeled about with a viperous grace to face them. Clearly the beasts were treating the humans and their weapons with contempt. Such assuredness was even more frightening to Rhiannon than the size of the creatures themselves.

The horror's abdomen heaved repeatedly. Its long neck rippled in a series of waves, and the skin behind the jaws expanded into a round ball. The mouth opened, and Rhiannon stared in disbelief at the red-orange glow like that of a blacksmith's forge behind the tongue. It shot forth—

The fletching of an arrow appeared in the creature's left eye.

The horror roared, part scream of pain, part death throe. It flung its head skyward, a long plume of flame billowing from its mouth before collapsing into a heap.

The rear warrior galloped by, the Dinari battle cry on his lips. In one smooth motion, he nocked and loosed another shaft while guiding his horse by knee pressure alone into the midst of the three pursuing creatures. This time the arrow's point hit just below the eye of the closest one but dropped to the ground without penetrating. As the man nocked another, the horrors leaped into the air with mighty flaps of their wings. The warrior loosed twice more as they flew overhead, aiming for the underbelly. Both arrowheads bounced harmlessly off the green skin.

Tellan and Rhiannon ran on and swung sharply around one end of the uprising of rocks. Many times the height of a man, the formation measured twenty strides in length and six wide. Bare boulders marked each end with a mixture of large stones, gravel, and grass comprising the middle. It offered scant protection, but anything was better than the open ground.

Rhiannon gasped for breath while her father hurriedly surveyed the jumble of rocks in the middle. He pointed to an open space between a group of man-high stones two-thirds of the way up. "We'll crawl up there and let them be our shields."

The words were barely out his mouth when two horrors plopped down on either end of the boulders; the third stayed in the air and circled directly above. The two on the ground regarded the humans with unblinking yellow eyes, then began the particular stomach heaving that Rhiannon now recognized as preparation to belch fire.

The two forward guards joined the rear one and skidded up from the opposite end. Leaping from their mounts, they knelt and drew back their bows. But the horror they aimed at disdainfully pivoted its rear to them.

"Up these rocks, men!" Tellan bellowed, his grip an iron band around Rhiannon's arm as he pulled her up the steep slope. "Then you can shoot down at their faces."

Halfway up, however, the loose soil gave way under her feet, and she fell heavily in a cascade of dirt and pebbles, almost losing her grip on her sword. Yanked to her feet by Tellan's strength, she stepped on the hem of her dress and stumbled back to her knees. When he pulled at her this time, his footing gave way and he slid, hitting the slope on his side. Digging into the dirt with his fingers and feet, he somehow managed to keep them both from rolling back down. They scrambled up to the narrow spaces between the stones just as a shadow passed overhead.

The horror still in the air glided down at them, wings extended, round ball bulging behind its jaws. "Red hair," the beast snarled, the words guttural and grating. "Kill red-haired girl."

"Down!" Tellan panted as the horror opened its mouth.

Rhiannon dove to the ground face-first just as the blast of flames broke over them. Sobbing out loud, she threw her hands over her head and tried to press herself into the soil as unseen fingers of heat touched the back of her legs. Her mouth was full of dirt, and her muscles twitched as she fought the urge to curl into a ball and cry. Growing heat came from her lower legs. Looking back, she saw that the bottom of her skirt was on fire. She stared wide-eyed as the flames spread, her muscles frozen. Her courage drained away. She was opening her mouth to scream in black despair when her father rolled over her legs, using his body to smother the fire.

"Pick up your sword, Rhiannon. We Dinari face foes with cold steel in our hands!" One side of his face was blistered from the blast, his hair singed, his tunic charred. He came to crouch, resting his blade across his knees, fingers clasping and unclasping the hilt. "Use these rocks as a shield and thrust for their eyes. These beasts think to have an easy time of it. You and I will show them different."

His confident manner restored her. She picked up her sword and came to her knees. Her whole body trembled. Her mouth was dry, and she had no moisture to spit out the dirt still coating her tongue and lips. But she peered up at the threat from the sky, ready to join her father in the fight.

The horror was almost on them again when an arrow arched up from the other side of the slope, impacting the creature right below the eye. It jerked up, screeching in surprise. Two other shafts followed close behind with the same accuracy, one hitting the head and the second narrowly missing. The horror swerved away, flapping its wings to circle around.

Tellan called out, "Good shooting!"

A scrambling sound came from below. Rhiannon whipped around.

The other two horrors pounded up the slope, half running,

half flying, rear legs churning, wings flapping. They projected a driven purpose fueled by raw hatred as they chanted, "Red hair, red hair. Kill red-haired girl!"

They sprinted straight at her, heads low to the ground, eyes glowing, front claws extended. Rhiannon brought her sword up, but her father jerked her behind a rock, covering her with his body. With an ear-shattering roar, the horrors crashed over them with the elemental fury of storm-driven waves.

Tellan pulled her sharply aside as front claws scored the granite only inches above her head. They crawled toward the next boulder.

Then a heavy rear foot slammed down, the ground shuddering under the impact that knocked them both flat.

Wickedly sharp talons curled into the dirt right before her face. A rank, oily musk filled her nostrils. She looked up at the lighter-colored underbelly and realized a horror straddled them. The wedge-shaped head swung down, mouth opening to reveal huge yellow teeth.

Her father rolled off her, sword ready, an angry growl coming from his throat. The creature's head came straight at her. Tellan surged, grunting as he stabbed for the eye—then he was gone!

The horrors bellowed in triumph.

Rhiannon scrambled to her knees, numb with disbelief. Her father's broadsword was in the mouth of one of the beasts! It spat the twisted metal out, then gazed back down at her, eyes pulsing in demonic fury.

Frantically, Rhiannon searched for her sword. Her hands finally bumped across the hilt, and she brought it up. Both beasts hissed and stepped toward her—

When suddenly she felt something *shift*.

The two horrors felt it as well. They halted, looked at each other in seeming bewilderment, their ferocity draining away like water from a cracked bucket. Out of the corner of her eye, Rhiannon noticed the third beast cartwheeling through the air, wings flapping in a desperate effort to maintain flight. It slammed into the ground with a heavy, dust-raising thud and remained motionless.

Looking back at the two before her, Rhiannon thought they seemed smaller, and the round ball behind their jaws had disappeared.

The three warriors pounded over the top of the outcropping, screaming the Dinari battle cry, bows drawn and arrows nocked. They knelt as one, took careful aim at the confused beasts, then loosed the arrows. This time the arm-long shafts penetrated deeply into flesh.

One horror collapsed at her feet with an arrow protruding from its eye. The other screeched in surprised pain as two arrowheads dug into the bones of its face, one just forward of an eye, the second a finger's length away. Whimpering, it whirled and fled back down the slope. It did not get far. With the speed of long practice, the warriors sent two more volleys into the now vulnerable horror.

It died at the foot of the rock formation, six feathered shafts embedded in its chest.

Rhiannon watched what happened next in stunned disbelief. Within the space of a few heartbeats, the bodies of the two horrors crumbled inward and blew away like dust, leaving only the bloodstained arrows to mark where they had fallen. The other two beasts that had died away from the outcropping crumbled away as well, disappearing in the spring breeze as if they had never been.

Tellan came limping back up the slope. "Daughter, are you all right?" He squatted beside her, his eyes full of love and concern as he checked her from head to toe.

She nodded, dazed. "What happened to you?"

"The horror grabbed my sword in its mouth, and before I could let go, it flung me down the slope." He rolled his shoulders and grimaced. "I am bruised, but nothing seems broken."

Relief washed over Rhiannon like warm oil. Leaning her head against the rough surface of the stone, she took a deep breath. Never had life been so sweet! The breeze was a gentle caress across her skin; the damp, earthy smell of the rock was as fragrant as her stepmother's finest perfume. She could feel every ridge and contour of the sword hilt in her hands.

The sword she'd drawn without realizing it!

She had risen with it in her hands after her father had rolled her off Nineve. She had come to her feet, sword held correctly, ready to face the winged horrors like a true Dinari warrior!

She basked in that fact for a moment. Then, incredibly, she started to shiver.

Girard came scrambling up the slope. "I gathered up Creag and Phelan, m'lord, and kept them a safe distance away. They are unharmed." The loreteller walked to where the closest beast had died; he picked up the arrow. "Lore come to life. And then gone." He shook his head. "No wonder many accounts are disputed."

"But we can kill them," declared Nerth, who had killed the first one. "Aim for the eyes."

Tellan rose stiffly to his feet. "Can you explain what happened just now, loreteller? What allowed the beast at the bottom to be penetrated when just moments before arrows bounced off?"

"Aye, m'lord. And the horror not being able to stay in the air." Girard rolled the shaft back and forth in his fingers. "Then there is their appearance during the day when every account of accepted lore only mentions them during the night."

"Night!" the youngest warrior exclaimed. "We can't hit their eyes at night!" He licked his lips. "I thought winged horrors were just stories. They can come from anywhere. We won't be safe anywhere..."

Tellan touched his arm. "Easy, son. You acquitted yourself well today. And will do so again."

The lad visibly gathered himself. He glanced at the other two warriors, embarrassed.

"And we have Covenant," Girard said. "Some stories say Destin Faber discovered how to cut these creatures off from the power they drew from the Mighty Ones. That rendered them vulnerable to swords and arrows. Many loretellers consider those accounts untrustworthy." He regarded Tellan soberly. "But that must be what happened here."

"How were these horrors cut off from their power?"

"Perhaps someone, some group, or the monks at Kepploch learned to pray as did Destin Faber and the Founders."

"How did they know that we needed this kind of prayer at this moment?"

"How indeed, m'lord? How indeed?" Girard tapped the arrow-head on his palm. "We have conflicting accounts about the battles before the Cutting of the Covenant. But if our lore is correct, then a siyyim had to be watching just now, controlling the horrors' actions."

Rhiannon frowned. "A siyyim?"

"Spirit beings second in power only to the Mighty Ones." Girard paused, clearly struggling to come to grips with all this. "Some say that under the right circumstances a siyyim could take control of a human body and use it to carry out the Mighty Ones' desires. Dinari clan lore does not recognize those tales."

Tellan growled. "Where is this siyyim? If it was controlling this attack, we must expect it to continue."

Rhiannon's breath caught. She checked the hillsides and up and down the trail. Nothing.

"I agree, m'lord," Girard said. "Mistress Rhiannon will not be safe until it has been dealt with."

Tellan looked at her closely. "Rhiannon? You sure you're all right?"

She nodded numbly, although the trembling was increasing and she did not think she could stand. A siyyim was after her! And after her still! Her breathing became ragged; her teeth chattered, grinding against the dirt that coated the inside of her mouth. She ran her tongue around, trying to build up enough moisture to spit the dirt out.

More winged horrors could appear at any moment!

Tellan squatted beside her again. Cupping her chin, he gazed straight into her eyes. "I am so very proud of you. You faced those beasts eye to eye and did not waver."

She opened her mouth to tell about drawing her sword—but to her surprise, she found both her arms wrapped tightly around his neck.

Tellan enclosed her in his arms and rested his cheek on her head. "Sweet girl, my brave sweet girl." He stroked her hair. "From the moment you were born, you have been special, very special indeed. Never fear, we shall hunt this siyyim and kill it or bind it or whatever we need to do."

She knew what he referred to. All of her life she had taken secret pride in her birthing prophecy that she would be "Protectoress of the Covenant." The prophecy was seldom mentioned, and no one—not even the monks at Kepploch—had any idea what it meant. She had envisioned grand and heroic deeds accomplished to the acclaim of all. The account of the struggle with the deranged monk and her mother's death only added to the mystique. But never, never, had Rhiannon thought it would be like this!

Although part of her mind protested that a warrior would not do so, she buried her face in the security of her father's chest and allowed deep shuddering sobs to overtake her.

Chapter Five

HARRED

LACHLANN LAY NESTLED on a flat shelf of land in the Clundy River valley. The river was still young here, barely beginning its journey to the Great Sea. It cascaded through the middle of town with violent energy, frothing and whirling down the boulder-cluttered bed. An arched stone bridge wide enough for two wagons to squeeze by each other linked both sides of town.

The east bank was considered the most prestigious, and it was there that Lachlann's prize inn, the Bridge Across, was located. Like most buildings in the region, the ground floor was constructed of river stone. A second and third story of whitewashed boards jutted out two arm lengths around the structure, topped by a sharply pitched thatched roof. Several paces behind the main building a stable provided lodging for the patrons' horses.

Inside the inn's double doors, tightly woven rush mats protected the floor from muddy feet. Immediately to the left, an arched entranceway opened into the dining room with a score of red oak tables and a roaring fireplace. At the end of the main hall, a winding staircase graced by a polished, hand-carved railing led up to the second and third floors. Each level had eight well-appointed rooms facing each other across a wide hallway. Every room had a window.

The sun had slid below the horizon an hourglass ago, and the dining room was bursting at the seams with Dinari merchants who traveled the circuit of wool sales. Eager to provide their newly wealthy clan members opportunities to lighten their coin purses, the merchants brought a variety of expensive wares— linens for gowns and cloaks, swords and daggers, dyes, furs, brightly colored tapestries, saddles, beveled glass for windows, and gems and rare spices from the fabled lands in the Southern Sea. Most of the merchants knew each other and gave nods of recognition as they settled into their chairs and waited for the young waitress to bring tonight's dish.

One table along the far wall drew more than its share of attention. Lord Gillaon Tarenester, an Arshessa lord from the foothills of the Ardnamur Mountains, and a young warrior sat waiting to be served. The Dinari merchants caught one another's eye, then glanced at the two Arshessa clansmen, then back to each other. Some lifted eyebrows, some pursed lips, others remained blank-faced.

The room stilled when three Sabinis wool merchants strode into the dining room with a flutter of rich garments. The first two greeted the innkeeper by name, then went straight to their reserved table in the far corner. The third merchant slid by with only a slight nod of his head. He was a weasel of a man, almost completely bald except for a thin fringe around his lower scalp. His eyes moved among the diners until they found Lord Gillaon, then the merchant's face closed into a neutral mask. He scurried on to the table.

Behind the merchants strutted their three hired bodyguards. All eyes in the room darted warily to the two Arshessa several paces away. The guards paused, their gazes resting on Lord Gillaon. The atmosphere in the room changed.

Gillaon remained calm and assured, ignoring the stares of the guards. The nobleman was short, barrel-chested, with iron-gray hair, and projected immense energy and purpose. Tonight he was fashionably dressed in a white linen shirt and dark trousers. The knee-length cloak fastened at his shoulders was trimmed in ermine. He wore a pair of knee-high leather boots shining with polish.

All Dinari were aware of Gillaon's discussions with Lord Tellan to acquire the wool from the Rogoths and other smaller Dinari kinsmen. The Arshessa clan was proposing to bypass the Sabinis' stranglehold on shipping by hauling the goods across the Ardnamur Mountains into the pagan Broken Stone Land. It was a move bold enough to crack the Sabinis' monopoly and benefit every Dinari clansman.

But no deal had been struck. Everyone anxiously awaited tomorrow's meeting.

The warrior sitting next to Lord Gillaon might have been twenty. He had dark hair and even darker eyes to go along with chiseled features. The warrior wore leather breeches, a soft gray woolen shirt, and similar boots as his lord's. His mouth firmed and his eyes narrowed as, unlike Lord Gillaon, he glared back at the three mercenaries.

The biggest of the three guards stepped toward the Arshessa table.

The noise level dropped. Everyone held his breath. Several sat frozen with spoons of food halfway to their mouths.

After looking contemptuously at Lord Gillaon the guard turned back to his companions. "Best we eat down there," he sneered, lifting his chin toward the direction of the wool merchants' table. "The air on this end of the room seems . . . tainted." The other two snickered loudly in agreement before they sauntered off to join their employers.

The warrior was halfway to his feet, eyes flashing and right hand reaching for a sword hilt that was not there. Lord Gillaon gripped the man's arm and whispered curtly. The warrior hesitated for a heartbeat, then settled stiffly back into his chair.

All present let out a pent-up breath and returned to their meals.

Harred swallowed his anger. From the look in his lord's eyes, he knew he had erred.

"They did that under orders from their Sabinis masters," Lord Gillaon lectured coldly, his face expressionless. "Why?"

"My pardon, m'lord."

"I do not want your apology! I want you thinking!"

Harred watched as his lord's gaze swept the dining room. Normally, when Gillaon Tarenester was angry, his face would wither a tree. Not so tonight. The man's expression was bland with a hint of a smile on his lips.

The innkeeper came up to inform them that the meal was coming soon. Gillaon nodded pleasantly and continued. "Harred de Tarenester en Wright, your skills are formidable. You are the best swordsmen we Tarenesters have produced in my memory—and your prime is yet to come. Beyond that, I believe you have the potential to become more than a gifted warrior. But if you are to remain by my side as rhyfelwr, you must learn to control both your emotions and facial expressions and to use your mind as a weapon."

Harred took a deep breath. He unclenched his fists, relaxed his shoulders, and tried to appear as calm as his lord. He grappled with the swirling subtleties involved in what he had naïvely assumed would be a straightforward process of buying wagonloads of wool. You offered more than anyone else did, and it was yours. That seemed simple, as had everything else in his life to this point—which had been man to man, sword against sword, with the strongest and quickest walking away the acknowledged winner.

But he was learning that if his clan bought Dinari wool, it could have an effect on the balance of power among the six high lords. That level of maneuvering was beyond Harred. But for the moment, it meant he must ignore sneering comments made by ill-mannered, pot-bellied ruffians whose loyalty was to a coin purse.

"Think upon this as a different type of battle, fought with different weapons," Lord Gillaon went on, continuing his closed-face inspection of the dining room. "While I have no doubt that you could have killed all three, what would you have gained me? The Sabinis would be almost blameless. One of their hired guards said something indiscriminate. They render an apology while commenting on how difficult it is to hire good men. And my rhyfelwr would have proved himself a quick-tempered lout while calling my judgment into question."

Gillaon swung his gaze back to fix Harred with an anvil-hard stare. "And my judgment, my trustworthiness, is what I am attempting to prove here more than anything else. All that would have gone to the Sabinis side of the ledger at the bargain price of three hired blades!"

Harred had no reply. Thankfully, further conversation was halted when the young waitress wove smoothly among the tables toward them. Perched on her shoulder was a round tray of dishes. From brief conversations during previous meals, Harred knew her to be the innkeeper's daughter. Fifteen or sixteen years of age, she was pretty, with a long neck and slender figure. Her dark blond hair was pulled back and tied with a leather string.

She lowered the tray with practiced skill and placed a loaf of dark brown bread, several yellow clay dishes, and two pewter mugs on the table. "The white sauce on the mutton may be a little hot if you are not used to it," she warned. Then she looked straight at Harred. "If you want anything else, let me know." She held his gaze just long enough. As she left, she managed to brush a hip lightly against his shoulder.

The promise in her eyes and her warmth as she moved by caused Harred to turn his head—until he crossed Lord Gillaon's icy blue eyes.

"Not to worry, m'lord," Harred said. "There will be no problem. I have told the other warriors that if I catch any of them being distracted by a woman while we are here, the next time they carry a ladylove to the blankets they will be seriously impaired. The same applies to me."

Gillaon kept him fixed with the stare a moment longer before nodding curtly. "Have you heard anything more about Lord Tellan's hlaford burning?" he asked while tearing a chunk from the dark loaf.

Harred breathed an inward sigh of relief. The issue of his responding to the taunt from the guards was over. That was one reason he held his kinsmen lord in such high regard: Gillaon Tarenester was a hard man, but fair. Err or displease him, and he would point it out and explain why in no uncertain terms, and then it was over.

But do not make the same mistake again.

"Only what we have all heard, m'lord. After Lord Tellan and the others returned this afternoon, everyone was saying it must have been a kitchen fire."

"Hmmm." One of the plates contained slices of a crumbly white cheese. Gillaon placed one on the bread and bit into it. "I stayed at the Rogoth hlaford in the fall when I first approached Lord Tellan about his wool. It was the smallest hlaford I have ever seen. At that time, the only household servant was that toothless old crone upstairs. Everyone there then is here at the inn now." Gillaon took another bite and chewed thoughtfully. "The messenger galloped up bringing news of the fire a glass before dawn?" Harred nodded. Gillaon gave him a level look. "I wonder who had been cooking," he asked in a tone not expecting an answer.

Conversations like this with his kinsmen lord were still a novelty to Harred. Though he had seen the man almost daily since entering his service three years previous, Gillaon had been a distant, revered figure. Harred had been stunned when Gillaon had asked him to function as rhyfelwr when they left the Tarenester hlaford. In the three warrior clans—Arshessa, Landantae, and Dinari—a lord's rhyfelwr served as commander of the men-at-arms and was considered an advisor equal to the loreteller. It was unheard of for a youth of nineteen to hold such an exalted position. Harred understood this trip to be a test, and, until the incident with the guards, he thought he had done well. The counselor function had not been an issue. But Harred could not imagine Gillaon Tarenester needing advice from anyone—rhyfelwr or loreteller.

The more he learned about Gillaon's dealings, the more Harred realized how much he had to learn. But whatever it took, he would please his kinsmen lord. Tasting the challenges and benefits of that elevated position only a few days, Harred knew he would never again be satisfied with the life of a common warrior.

He picked up a slice of cheese and sniffed. It was strong and sharp. He took a small bite and found that it tasted as it smelled: too strong to be eaten alone. He pulled off a chunk of the bread. It had a rich, nutty favor, blending well with the sharp cheese. Another yellow clay dish contained dried apples. Harred ate one and took another bite of bread and cheese. The meals he had eaten at The Bridge since arriving yesterday had been excellent, much better than the plain fare served at the inns they had stayed in on the journey here.

Looking at the plate of browned meat drizzled in white sauce, he remembered the waitress's warning and sliced off only a small section. The mutton was spicy—and full of fire! Quickly, he reached for the mug. The cool well water helped, but for only a moment. As soon as he swallowed, the flames returned with even greater vengeance. Sweat popped out on his forehead as he emptied the mug in a vain effort to seek relief.

"Eat some cheese," Gillaon advised, blue eyes dancing in humor. "It will cut the heat somewhat."

Harred took his lord's advice. The cheese did help, but a distinct glow still lingered. Another mouthful of cheese and more bread dulled the sensation to a tolerable level.

"I was served this dish by the Rogoths during my visit in the fall," Gillaon said. "After everyone quit laughing at my plight, they told me the cheese would help. Springing this on unsuspecting guests seems to be a Dinari form of welcome. They must figure that anyone who survives it good-naturedly is worthy of further hospitality." He smiled wryly. "It did seem that our discussions went better afterwards."

Harred wiped his forehead with a linen cloth, then shoved the meat aside and reached for the dried apples. "Speaking of fire, m'lord, is the incident at the Rogoth hlaford going to change the meeting tomorrow?"

As was often his wont during the trip, Gillaon responded to a question of Harred's with one of his own. "You were with me when Lord Tellan's party returned this afternoon. What did you make of their condition?"

Harred fingered a chunk of bread as he took his time answering. He had assumed that the combat and counselor responsibilities of rhyfelwr were two distinct functions. But tonight a whole new perspective was dawning on him, and he found the possibilities exciting.

"At that time, m'lord, I thought nothing unusual, but now I wonder. Lord Tellan's skin was blistered, his hair and clothes singed. The bottom of the daughter's dress was burned, and her blouse looked as if she had been rolling in the dirt. I assumed they both had been fighting the fire." Harred tapped the chunk of bread on the table in emphasis. "But the two boys were clean, as was the loreteller. I can't see them standing idly by watching the father and sister. And you have said the hlaford is at least two hourglasses away. With the time necessary for the messenger to come and for them to return, any fire should have been over by the time they arrived."

"Exactly." Gillaon's tone was pleased. "Further, Lord Tellan was leading his horse when they arrived back. Its shoulder was swollen. When I asked about it, Tellan said the animal had pulled up lame outside of town. A shoulder lameness of that severity while on the road? Not likely." Gillaon pursed his lips. "When I inquired about the fire, he politely informed me that it was nothing. Typical closed-mouthed Dinari. But I noticed a glint in his eyes that I am certain did not come from the destruction of the hlaford. He said no lives were lost." Gillaon gave Harred a level look. "I tell you, something else kindled a fire inside Tellan Rogoth today—flames that only spilled blood will douse."

Harred was silent for a moment. People were finishing their meals, and the noise level was increasing with the after-dinner talk. A minstrel strolled in and began tuning his lyre. A murmur of anticipation swept the room.

"Whatever it was happened to both him and the daughter," Harred said.

"Yes."

"She was as unruffled as he was when they went upstairs."

"She's Dinari. She sat by Tellan's side during our talks this fall. She listened and asked several questions. I was impressed." Gillaon's eyes swept the room again as he took another bite of cheese and chewed slowly. After he swallowed, he cocked an eyebrow at Harred. "She will soon be of age to be called Lady Rhiannon and accept suitors. Though her family is not wealthy, her combination of intelligence and beauty is a rare find. If you were noble-born kinsman, she would be worth a lot of effort."

Some instinct warned Harred to be careful. It was not seemly for a commoner to discuss a noble maiden in such a manner. Nobles *had* married commoners. Bards sang of Lady Elegan and Ober, for instance. But that tragic union of widowed High Lady and sailing master echoed the sentiment of most.

"I am sure many young nobles will be asking their fathers to approach Lord Tellan once she is eligible for courtship," Harred said, surprising himself. That sounded like something Gillaon would have said.

His lord regarded him with quiet approval. "Good. You're learning. That is how to answer all such comments and questions while we are here. State a truth without it meaning anything." He took a swallow from the pewter mug, then patted his lips with a cloth. "Do your best to remain by my side tomorrow. But be prepared for an effort to be made to separate us. If that happens, one or more of those guards will be in your face. Their little comedy just now was only plowing the ground."

Gillaon's eyes flashed, and his small frame loomed large across the table. "It is not by happenstance that the Sabinis have controlled the wool and other trade all these years. Have no doubt that we will be in battle tomorrow, kinsman. But there will be neither drawn weapons nor lives taken. Later perhaps, but not tomorrow and not here."

Harred nodded slowly. He found himself looking forward to this new challenge. "I'll be ready." Carefully he continued, "M'lord, why the importance of a simple wool sale?"

Gillaon tore off a chunk of bread. "Clan Sabinis is the wealthiest of the six clans. They control the Land's banking, which allows them to dominate the most profitable trade. Additionally, Queen Cullia is a Sabinis. It is universally acknowledged her family's wealth saved the Faber throne from bankruptcy. With King Balder's long-standing bad health, Cullia has become the true power. She profanes her oath to leave clan ties behind by using her influence to extend Sabinis power. Their fingers are into everything. Most importantly for us, they have gained control of all the harbors and shipping interests. Without their cooperation, no one can ship goods to the lucrative markets across the Great Sea."

Gillaon paused while the young waitress refilled their mugs. Harred kept his eyes on his plate until she moved away.

"But cracks are appearing," Gillaon continued. "Cullia over-reached when she announced Prince Larien's betrothal to a Sabinis maiden, which would give them three queens in a row. The other clans voiced such displeasure that the betrothal was broken. The prince is twenty-two and well past the age to be married and producing an heir. With King Balder's health failing, the Ruling Keeper has declared a Rite of Presentation." Gillaon snorted. "Every seamstress in the Land will be sewing her fingers to the bone. But I digress. The Sabinis realize this business with Tellan Rogoth is just our opening move. Next year at the Radael all six High Lords will ink trade agreements for the coming three years. If we Arshessa have shown we can break the Sabinis monopoly in this area, the other clans will be more amenable to believing we can do so in others."

"So the Dinari are already with us?" Harred asked as he glanced around the room.

"Lord Tellan certainty is. This fall when I offered four silvers per standard weight bale, his jaw almost hit the floor. He's been getting less than two from the Sabinis." Gillaon grimaced. "Unfortunately Maolmin Erian, the Dinari High Lord, is against us. He arrived this afternoon. He has close ties to the Sabinis, and my sources say he is most upset with Tellan."

"He and his rhyfelwr arrived soon after Lord Tellan's party returned. Surely, the High Lord was not involved in the fire—"

"If he was, either Tellan or Maolmin would be dead now."

"M'lord, most consider High Lord Maolmin to be the best swordsman in the Land—maybe the best ever. His quickness and strength are said to be unbelievable."

"That would not have stopped Tellan. Would it have you?"

"No," Harred admitted.

"Maolmin knows our plans will weaken his bargaining at the Radael. He and his rhyfelwr came on ahead to plan with the Sabinis. The rest of his party should arrive anytime. We need to be prepared to shield the Rogoths from any…conflict."

"How so?"

Gillaon's look betrayed nothing. "Which of our warriors do you trust the most?"

"Elmar," Harred said without hesitation.

"Where is he?"

"He was going to the stable to tend the stone bruise on your horse."

"As soon as you escort me back upstairs, find him. I want the two of you to strike up a conversation with any Rogoth warriors you can find. We need to find out what really happened to Tellan and the girl today."

The Mighty One of the North's displeasure washed over the siyyim like a winter storm battering a rocky beach and sent waves of cold fear rippling through the body he inhabited. His dominion of the appropriated body faltered. The bowels loosened and threatened to let go. With iron will, he reestablished control.

Is the girl dead?

"No, Mighty One." The North knew, of course. But this was how it was done. The siyyim steeled himself even as he seethed in rage. "The attack on the hlaford should have succeeded! How was I to know Tellan would take the girl to Lachlann two days early?"

You allowed all four to be destroyed! You know how difficult it is to get one, much less four, past the Covenant's barrier.

Two more pulses of raw displeasure slammed through the mist, the second on the heels of the first. The demon reeled, almost losing control of the bowels again. He was startled at the level of rage displayed. After all, he was not a minor underling.

"I was too far away to maintain total control. I must protect my position. We cannot have any hint of . . ."

And on the road?

"The power necessary to whip them into a daylight attack took all my concentration. And then . . ." the siyyim had been dreading this part of the tale . . . "two different sources entered into the spirit realm and hit me with the authority of the Eternal. I was prepared for one. The second caught me off guard. I lost my link with the horrors, and the Rogoth warriors did the rest."

Two different sources? Silence reigned in the mist as the North digested that unwelcome news. *You should have killed the girl years ago. With the new development, the other Mighty Ones are even more insistent she be removed from the playing board.*

The lesser demon seethed again. He had reasons for taking this long. His revenge had been slow and sweet. "She shows no sign of walking in her prophecy. I have kept her family growing poorer each year. They lack the prestige and resources to even hope to . . ."

The Mighty One of the West in particular fears the girl's potential. The West boasts she is ready to position one of her lilitu and threatens that if I do not see this matter resolved, she will.

The siyyim began to see the reason behind the North's rage. Lilitu were very powerful, just one rank below a siyyim like himself.

I am the one who has labored for generations to bring the Faber dynasty to this low ebb. Only one healthy male remains. Never before have we been this close! I WILL BE THE ONE TO REAP THE REWARDS OF ENDING THE COVENANT, NOT THE WEST! DO NOT FAIL ME!

Another pulse of rage slammed through the mist, and the siyyim was left quivering on the floor, struggling to maintain control of the body.

Chapter Six

RHIANNON

RHIANNON STEPPED OUT the rear door of the inn and headed for the stable. It was past time to feed Nineve. When her father had agreed she could begin training a mount for herself, she vowed to be the only one to feed, groom, and saddle the horse.

Besides, Rhiannon desperately needed time alone to think through the events of the morning without Phelan's endless questions. Even her room was not suitable for contemplation. The new tutor—Rhiannon had been surprised at how young the woman was—had taken her meal into Rhiannon's room to eat. The two of them would share the room until other arrangements were made.

So when the family servant took Creag and Phelan downstairs to the washroom, Rhiannon slipped out with them. She had already bathed, having spent a long time soaking in the tub soon after arriving back at the inn.

Now, as she moved away from the inn and into the night, her scalp prickled as the star-studded sky seemed to loom above her with unseen menace. In her mind she heard the guttural hiss: *Kill red-haired girl.*

Her breath caught and her steps faltered. Again she saw unblinking yellow eyes. Her mouth felt the grit of dirt; her legs tingled with the remembered heat of flames. Her heart thudded; cold sweat beaded on her skin.

Stop this! she commanded herself firmly. *I will not give in to fear!*

I am Dinari. Lifting her chin, she grasped the hilt of her sword. *Thrust for their eyes.* She strode on.

The yellow glow of lanterns shone through the open stable doors. As she entered, the familiar odors of horses, oiled leather, hay, and manure mingled in her nostrils. A walkway divided the building in half with a row of stalls facing each other. Two stalls in the middle were enclosed, one for feed storage and the other serving as living quarters for the old man who ran the stable. His door was shut with no light showing through the cracks.

Already at some tavern, Rhiannon thought as she lifted the heavy latch on the feed room door. Every morning the man's sour breath and shaking hands gave ample evidence of how he spent his nights.

She filled a bucket with oats from a wooden bin and carried the feed to Nineve's stall. Rhiannon was pleased to hear the filly whicker at the smell of the oats. The poor thing had been wide-eyed and trembling when the party had found her several measures from where the winged horrors had attacked. Rhiannon did her best to calm her mount during the ride back to Lachlann, but knew more smooth words and hand rubbing were needed.

After emptying the bucket into the trough, Rhiannon scattered the oats around several fist-sized stones. Nineve was a greedy eater, taking such hasty mouthfuls of grain that she risked having half-chewed boluses lodge in her throat. Rhiannon followed her father's advice and put the stones in the feed trough to force the horse to nibble around them and eat slower.

Nineve moved up eagerly and stuck her head in the trough. Relieved, Rhiannon stroked the horse's neck fondly, murmuring, "I should have known it would take more than a few winged horrors to keep you from eating."

The filly lifted her head and shifted irritably before taking another mouthful of grain. Knowing that Nineve preferred to be left alone during this time, Rhiannon eased back out and went into the next stall to check on her father's stallion.

The big roan stood in the middle of the enclosure, the

shadows concealing the injured right shoulder. That leg was cocked, all weight supported on the other three legs. His ears were flat, eyes half-closed in pain. Rhiannon put a rope around the horse's neck and led him out of the stall into the walkway. The stallion shuffled along awkwardly, extremely reluctant to put any weight on the right foreleg.

In the better light, Rhiannon's heart twisted. The swelling from the impact with the winged horror was impressive, much larger than when they had arrived back in Lachlann. Now easily a cubit in circumference and rising a double handsbreadth above the body, it stretched the skin taut and caused the hair to ruffle.

Tears came to her eyes. "Thank you," she whispered as she rubbed the velvet soft muzzle. "You are a true Dinari warrior just like your rider."

"That be one bad bruise," came a voice from behind her.

She whirled, hand tight on the sword hilt. One of Lord Gillaon's men stood just inside a stall on the other side of the walkway.

"Yes, it is," she said, trying to calm her racing heart. "He was . . . kicked on the road this morning."

The man glanced again at the shoulder, a slight frown creasing his brow. "It be twice as big as when Lord Tellan brought him in." He spoke with the thick brogue characteristic of one from the higher regions of the Ardnamur Mountains. She had seen him here last night tending to one of the Arshessa horses. "Unless something be done soon," he continued, "it be even worse by morning."

"Our medicines and herbs are back at our stable at the hlaford. We applied a liniment the stableman said was good for this type of injury." She bit her lower lip. "It has not stopped the swelling nor eased his pain. I was about to inform my father about this." She squared her shoulders. "He would have checked already, but he has pressing matters at the moment."

"Aye. I'm sure that be true."

She searched his face for any hidden meaning but found none. The man was below average height and heavily built. He had a settled, unflappable manner. And although he was young, early twenties at the most, his hair was thinning noticeably and his belly bulged over his belt.

"If it be agreeable," he offered, "I'll make a stinkweed and brown moss poultice for his shoulder. It be perfect for this type hurt. Come morning, the swelling be down or winged horrors can carry me away."

Rhiannon's blood chilled. "What do you mean?" she asked with admirable control, her hand dropping again to the sword hilt. The stallion's ears flicked upright, and she felt his neck brush against her right arm as he pressed forward.

The Arshessa regarded her with puzzlement even as a stillness descended upon him. "I meant no offense, Mistress Rogoth. Simply offering help. You be saying you have no medicines. I carry a good supply in my bags. You can let one of your father's men apply them."

"What did you mean about winged horrors?"

His eyes never left hers. "That be a common expression of my mother's. Growing up, she always be warning me and my sisters how if we don't be acting proper, winged horrors come to carry us away."

Rhiannon sensed truth and breathed easier. "Your poultice will be much appreciated...?"

"Elmar. Elmar de Tarenester en Stuegin, Clan Arshessa."

"Mistress Rhiannon de Murdeen en Rogoth, Clan Dinari. Please, prepare and apply the poultice. I will help."

"This be a foul-smelling one, and the brown moss part might stain your hands. Best to let me."

"I have applied this poultice before. Two sets of hands makes it easier."

He gave her a quick look of reassessment. "My bags be at our camp a few lengths behind the stable." He made to leave, hesitated, then turned back. "Mistress Rhiannon, next time you prepare to draw your sword, make sure there be room to pull it clear. Your sword arm be blocked by the horse." He gave a soft smile. "I could have had my hands around your throat while you be struggling to step aside."

Chagrined, she realized he was correct. Her ears warmed. "Yes, I see. Thank you."

Elmar nodded. "I'll get what we need for the poultice."

While Rhiannon waited, she pondered the winged horrors for the twentieth time. Her father and Girard thought the attack on the hlaford was tied in with the Sabinis or High Lord Maolmin, or both. But if that was true, why the single-minded focus the horrors had to kill the red-haired girl?

No, Rhiannon decided, the attack had to be involved with her birthing prophecy, the same reason the monk had tried to kill her at her mother's breast. But why no other attempts until almost sixteen years later? What had changed?

Hopefully the monks at Kepploch would know.

Upon arriving back at the Bridge Across, Tellan had sent a sealed letter to the monastery, hand carried by two warriors with instructions to ride as fast as their weary horses would allow. The letter detailed both attacks and asked for monks to be sent to the inn.

Rhiannon rubbed the stallion's muzzle and hoped the Keepers would arrive soon. She wanted to learn how they knew to pray as they did to cut the horrors off from their power. And how long did that cutting off last? A day? A week? Just the one incident? If the siyyim sent more winged horrors of the night, surely the monks would know to pray again.

Wouldn't they?

As a child, she had considered the monks at Kepploch all wise and all knowing. When Keeper Astwin came as her first tutor, she peppered him with questions about her prophecy. And her future. That led to long talks about the Eternal, the Covenant, and the Founding. With childlike faith, she went with Tellan and Mererid to Kepploch, and in a ceremony there, pledged to serve the Eternal all her days. She left aglow in religious fervor, sure the quest was about to begin.

But long years went by—and nothing happened. She began to grow confused, then frustrated. Creag grew old enough to join the schooling, and then Phelan. Discussions with Keeper Astwin about her prophecy gradually ceased. Life went on. She quit reading Holy Writ. And quit praying. Lately, now that she was almost of age, she had begun thinking the Eternal had forgotten about her. And that neither he nor the Mighty Ones were involved in daily life, after all.

She gnawed her lower lip. That was before today, of course.

She heard footsteps approaching the stable. The camp must be closer than she had thought for Elmar to return so soon.

But it was not the Arshessa soldier who strode into the stable. It was the Dinari High Lord, Maolmin, the best swordsman in the land.

His dark eyes seemed to glow when they rested upon her.

Chapter Seven

HARRED

H ARRED WALKED TO the stable to get Elmar. Together they would go to the taverns to find some Rogoth warriors to pump for information about what had happened at Lord Tellan's home.

He entered the stable—and his warrior instincts screamed danger. Down the way among the shadows cast by the lanterns he noticed a girl, the Rogoth daughter, standing by a horse. A man approached her. The man was too big to be Lord Tellan, and the girl did not have a welcoming expression on her face. Her hand dropped to her sword hilt, and she stepped away from the horse when the man halted before her. The man wore a sword as well, and although both hands remained clasped behind his back, Harred could tell by the tensed shoulders the man was poised to draw.

Harred gritted his teeth. He was without his sword; he had only his clan dagger. But the sense of unease surged so strongly he *knew* the girl was in danger. Feeling naked, he strode quickly down the walkway.

"Begging your pardons," he called into the stable. "Have any of you seen a fat, ugly Arshessa tending Lord Gillaon's horse?" As he closed, Harred gathered his muscles, preparing to dive into a ball, bowl the man's feet out from under him, then roll up while throwing a handful of dirt in the face. Then get the girl's sword—

The man whirled in a blur, sword appearing in his hands as if by magic.

Harred blinked. How could anyone move so fast! He slowed a step as he realized who this must be.

"Leave us!" High Lord Maolmin snarled, his mouth an ugly slash.

"And if I don't?" Harred said softly, dangerously. He stopped within an arm's length of the gleaming steel point. He was an Arshessa clansman, and no one—this High Lord or King Balder himself—had the right to address him in such a manner. Only his kinsmen lord could, and that solely because Harred was in his service.

Maolmin Erian was a lithe, strong man with a proud face that feared no foe. Eyes black as cabochons regarded Harred while movement rippled in their depths like pebbles dropped into a dark pool. The tip of the sword lowered a fraction. Harred tensed—

"Yes," the girl said with a clear, strong voice, "Elmar will be returning any moment now. He is bringing a poultice for my father's horse."

Harred watched Maolmin struggle within himself. Finally, the stiffness drained out of the high lord's muscles; the look in his eyes eased. He shook himself like a dog, then sheathed his sword before flicking Harred a dismissive glance.

"My pardon, you startled me." He looked around the stable as if seeing it for the first time. "I came to arrange stalls for two more horses. My loreteller and his daughter have arrived. They were told the stable is full." He placed both fists on his hips and jutted his chin forward. "Bring the stableman."

"He is not here, High Lord," the girl said. "Can these two horses be stalled together? Our horses can be rearranged to free a stall."

"Of course they can be kept together! See to it." He turned and stomped away.

The girl's eyes flashed with anger at the imperious tone. Seeing her this close, Harred agreed with his lord's assessment. Dark red hair, green eyes, pale skin, tall, high-breasted figure—she was indeed stunning. But why the sword? Gillaon believed she would be worth a lot of effort. Harred wasn't so sure. The young nobleman who won her hand might discover he had more than he bargained for.

She flicked a strand of hair from her face and raised her chin. "Will you hold the stallion while I arrange the horses?" she said. Harred nodded, and she handed him the rope. "I am Mistress Rhiannon de Murdeen en Rogoth, Clan Dinari. Thank you for...." Her words tailed off.

"I am Harred de Tarenester en Wright, Clan Arshessa. You are welcome for..." He let his voice tail off in like manner.

She bit back an amused snort. Then Harred felt the impact of those green eyes as she gave him a glance before heading to the stalls.

Oh yes, he thought, watching her long-legged stride. *Worth a lot of effort indeed.* But even if he was in a position to pursue her, he preferred a woman without any attached steel.

Movement at the front of the stable caught his eye. Elmar came ambling in with a pot and two sticks.

"I knew it be too good to last," his brother-in-law grumbled as he set the pot down. "When I leave, this horse be attached to pure beauty. When I return, it just be you. Why you scare her off? She be wanting to help me, side by side, shoulder to shoulder." He sighed. "I guess it be for the best. After your lecture about women here, your sister be glad I be coming back whole and able to function at my normal high standard."

"I would hate to have to answer any awkward questions. She has always been able to tell when I lie."

"What's this about you having to lie?" Rhiannon asked as she came down the hallway after moving the horses.

Harred and Elmar looked at each other.

"Ah...uh..." Elmar's voice tailed off.

"Go ahead," Harred urged, smothering a grin. "Tell her."

Elmar reddened. "Well, mistress, er..." He shot a glance at Harred.

"This handsome fellow is married to my oldest sister," Harred said. "He's begging me not to tell her about all the young girls he's been trying to..."

Elmar snorted in disgust.

Rhiannon laughed. She had a good one, deep and rich. It warmed the stable. "I will tell my father about the stallion's shoulder. He'll want to come to see it and to thank you, Elmar. Please wait while I go get him." She made to leave, then hesitated. She cocked an eyebrow at Harred. "If I see any girls, should I tell them where to find Elmar?"

"Best not, mistress," Harred replied solemnly. "He'd risk losing more than you know."

Those vivid green eyes studied him again. Then she flashed him a quick smile, turned and left, her right hand gripping her sword hilt, her red mane bouncing.

Harred watched her stride away and swallowed. *Worth whatever it may take.* Then he shook himself. It wasn't going to happen. Elmar took one of the thin, flat sticks and handed the other to Harred. With gentle strokes, they began applying the thick, strong-smelling paste to the stallion's shoulder and leg.

"Was High Lord Maolmin here when you went to make the poultice?" Harred asked.

"No. That be him I saw leaving?"

Harred nodded. "I felt strongly he was about to harm the girl."

"Things be that bad?"

"Lord Gillaon believes Tellan is ready to wet his sword." In low tones Harred related Gillaon's speculation that the Rogoth fire was not as straightforward as it seemed.

Elmar grunted. "Could be. When I step out from the stall and offer to make this poultice, she jump straight up. Half that Dinari chastity belt was out of the scabbard before she hit ground. What be going on here?" Elmar pointed his stick at the stallion's swollen shoulder. "She said this horse be kicked. I've seen bruises from horse kicks all my life. This be what happens when two warhorses collide at full gallop." He pursed his lips. "There's more. She got uncommon upset when I made passing mention of winged horrors. If you ever be wanting to behold eyes flash fire, you be seeing it then."

They looked at each other, then Harred shrugged and went back to applying the poultice.

As they finished, Elmar's stomach rumbled loudly. He put the sticks back into the pot, then glanced sourly at Harred. "You be enjoying your dinner with Lord Gillaon? Plenty to eat? You remember to pat your mouth with the napkin? A rhyfelwr have to do that just so."

Harred remained silent, knowing more was coming.

"We men be having fine meals of stale bread and dried meat, what with Lord Gillaon's orders that we stay around our tents and not go anywhere."

Suppressing a grin, Harred watched Elmar lead the stallion back into the stall, waiting to convey the good news of Lord Gillaon's coins in his pocket and orders to take any Rogoth warriors they could find to a tavern—when a soft voice came from behind him.

"Has High Lord Maolmin arranged stalls for our horses?"

Harred turned. The voice belonged to a petite young woman standing in the walkway. The hood of her cream-colored travel cloak was pushed back, framing a plain-featured face and raven black hair. She was not close to the Rogoth daughter's beauty, but she was comely, and something else about this one had him staring. She had a glow, an aura of serenity that pulled him.

As they gazed at each other in the soft lantern light, the maiden's hand crept up to the front of her cloak as slender fingers played along the edge. She seemed as affected as he was.

"I am Breanna."

"I am Harred."

She tilted her head slightly, then nodded at his clan dagger. "Could you be one of those foul Arshessas my father and High Lord Maolmin are so upset about?"

Harred fumbled to respond. His face felt flushed, his tongue thick and clumsy. Then he noticed the twinkle in her eyes. Could she be teasing him? Oh, my goodness.

"We are not that bad—"

"Breanna! Do we have stalls or not!" A man in a loreteller's multicolored vest led two horses through the wide doors.

"I was just asking." She raised an eyebrow at Harred. "Well, do we?"

"Yes. This way." He led them to the empty stall.

The loreteller frowned darkly when he noticed Harred's and Elmar's Arshessa daggers. He curtly refused Harred's offer to help unsaddle the horses. His frown deepened when he noticed the looks his daughter gave Harred. After the horses were unsaddled and fed, the man took Breanna firmly by the arm and led her to the inn.

Harred watched until they were swallowed by the darkness. Breanna did not walk—she floated across the ground.

"Have you ever heard such a sweet voice?"

"Huh?" Elmar squatted down to pick up the pot with the remains of the poultice.

"Her voice. Have you ever heard such a sweet one? When she spoke, I felt every word inside me."

Standing, Elmar eyed Harred with puzzlement. "You be feeling all right?"

"How old do you think?"

"That lass? Fifteen, maybe sixteen."

Harred nodded. "She's old enough."

"Old enough!" Elmar hissed. "You think she be warming your bed tonight with her father right here?" Harred fixed him with an icy stare, and Elmar held up an apologetic hand. "All right, all right. But what do you mean she be 'old enough'?"

"Old enough to stand at the Maiden Pole."

"You saw the way her father looked at us! You think Maolmin's loreteller be accepting a suit from an Arshessa, from Lord Gillaon's own rhyfelwr?"

Harred sighed. "No."

"You see her just now, she asks you about a stall, and you be ready to declare suit?"

"Not yet. But I—"

"It be finally happening!" Elmar spread both hands and lifted his face to the ceiling. "I be waiting to see if this rhyfelwr be changing you." Lowering his gaze, he regarded Harred with speculation. "It must be that fancy food you be eating. You need more dried meat and stale bread."

They walked toward the door to the inn. The warm glow inside reminded Harred of something else. "After we talk to Lord Tellan, I'll check the kitchen for a spare serving. We had a mutton dish you've got to taste to believe."

Elmar's eyes widened as he licked his lips. "Something be smelling mighty good when I walk by."

Chapter Eight

BRANOR

HIS GRACE, HIGH Lord Keeper Branor, a Keeper of Cynerice rank, dipped the quill into the inkwell resting in its round hole in his lap desk. He paused to gather his thoughts, and then finished the last paragraph. He reread the letter. Satisfied he had given the Dinari High Lord enough hints without promising anything, Branor signed his name and sanded the letter. He folded the parchment and was rummaging inside the lap desk for the wax stick when there came a sharp knock at his door.

"Enter."

The door squeaked open, revealing a pimply-faced novice. "Abbot Trahern's compliments, Your Grace. He humbly begs your presence in the front hall."

Branor frowned. He had arrived at Kepploch midafternoon and had sent a message to the abbot pleading travel weariness and proposing a morning meeting. And when a six-knot Keeper proposed, lower ranks agreed. Was this a subtle message...? No, not Trahern. The abbot was renowned for blunt speech. And the front hall was for visitors. Branor had used great precautions to keep this trip secret, but his rivals had informants, as he did. Who had learned of it? Friend or foe?

"One moment." He took the wax stick and a candle and sealed Maolmin's letter. Standing, Branor straightened his robe and gestured to the young novice to lead the way.

The front hall was in the middle of the U-shaped main

building. Constructed of gray stone with a red tile roof, the only such roof in leagues, the monastery's ground floor housed the abbot's office, the kitchen, storerooms, a scriptorium, and the huge library. Living quarters were on the second floor.

When the novice escorted Branor into the front hall, two Dinari clansmen waited impatiently at the end of a trail of muddy boot prints marring the white marble floor. Next to them stood Abbot Trahern. The abbot was well into his eighties. A few wisps of white hair covered a mostly bald dome sprinkled with age spots. His skin was thin, and spidery blue veins showed. Age had taken its physical toll, but the abbot's mind was sharp as ever.

"Greetings, Your Grace," the abbot said. "How was your trip from Shinard?"

"Wet and muddy." Branor gave his former abbot a brotherly kiss on the cheek. Trahern handed him a letter with the wax seal already broken. As he read, Branor felt an icy hand grip his heart. He glanced up. Trahern's watery blue eyes regarded him with keen interest.

Stunned, Branor turned to the warriors. "You're in service to Tellan?"

"Aye," the older of the two answered.

"And were present?"

"Aye. Both of us."

"Four winged horrors. In the light of day?"

"As real as you and the good abbot." Grim pride broke through. "We killed them."

Branor realized his mouth hung open. He closed it with a snap. Rumors surfaced now and again, but it had been centuries since a verifiable account of winged horrors. *This couldn't have come at a worst time.*

"They were after Mistress Rhiannon," the older said matter-of-factly.

The icy hand squeezed tighter. "Tellan's daughter, she must be, what, almost sixteen now?"

Both nodded. Branor quizzed them further, but as Tellan had

stated in his letter, they were adamant the creatures had come for the girl.

Why now, after years of silence?

"Begging your pardons," the older warrior said respectfully, his eyes darting between the five knots tied on the tassels of Trahern's white rope belt and the six on Branor's. "Lord Tellan was insistent we bring them that's coming as soon as possible."

Trahern nodded. "Of course." He led Branor a few steps away. "This explains this morning," he said quietly. "Several of us felt a call to special prayer. It must have been during this time." He looked quizzically at Branor. "Did you sense the same summons, Your Grace? The Eternal blessed you mightily in that area before you left us."

"Ah, yes. There did seem to be an...urgency...about that time."

"And now this letter." Trahern clasped his hands behind his back. "Can you not sense the hand of the Eternal? With infinite wisdom, he often uses one incident to accomplish many tasks."

Branor kept his expression neutral, afraid of where this was heading.

"You return after fifteen years, and your bags are hardly unpacked before Tellan is asking for our help." The abbot raised a bushy eyebrow. "Beyond the seriousness of the need, with your future plans..."

"Future plans?"

"Come, now. Our Ruling Keeper lies infirm. All realize his time is near. Soon another will tie the seventh knot. You are not the first to visit us with that in mind."

Branor nodded sagely. A majority vote of five- and six-knot Keepers was needed. With Abbot Trahern's vote secured, Branor would be only two votes shy. Additionally, the future Ruling Keeper needed the support of four of the six clan High Lords.

"So," Trahern said gently, "don't you think it best to clear this cloud from your past?"

Branor put a thoughtful frown on his face while his mind

raced. The path was fraught with danger. Tellan's grief over Eyslk's death had been a terrible thing to behold. Time could heal even the deepest of wounds, but if Tellan refused to be reconciled and if he made an issue of it, Branor's rivals would have a potent story to whisper in the right ears. On the other hand, if Tellan did accept reconciliation, Branor would be no better off than he was now.

"Perhaps this is not the time. The Rogoths must be in turmoil over this terrible attack. After meeting with you tomorrow, I plan to visit High Lord Maolmin. On my way back, I will meet with Tellan after things have quieted down."

Trahern smiled. "I received word earlier that the High Lord has arrived in Lachlann for the wool sale. You can accomplish both tasks at the same time."

"I see."

"There is more. Though Tellan has been faithful to bring his tithe every year, he neglects his children's spiritual education and has recently dismissed our tutor for their formal education. My sources tell me an Albane is being seriously considered."

Fixing him with the piercing stare that Branor remembered so well, the Abbot of Kepploch went on. "Here is a task worthy of an aspirant to the heavy burdens of the seventh knot: responding to an attack of winged horrors while healing a fifteen-year-old wound and bringing a kinsmen lord and his family closer to the Eternal's love. All laid at your feet by impeccable timing that can only come from him. Surely you must accept."

Branor had long ago learned when to cut his loses. "I am Keeper. I will respond."

"May the power of the Eternal and the covering of the Covenant be with you," Trahern finished. Then he sighed happily. "It is an astonishing sight to behold the workings of the Eternal."

Chapter Nine

LAKENNA

"LADY MERERID AND I prayed until we felt a release. I do not know how long it will last," Lakenna told Rhiannon frankly.

Four other people sat around the table in the sitting room of Lord Tellan's suite at the Bridge Across: Lord Tellan, Lady Mererid, Loreteller Girard, and Llyr, the grizzled warrior who had driven the carriage back from Inbur.

Lakenna had been surprised to learn that the man was Lord Tellan's rhyfelwr. The thick-armed, leathery-skinned man had not said a word in her presence, sitting silently through her interview with Mererid in Inbur yesterday, remaining silent during the ride to Lachlann today, and still not uttering a word tonight during Tellan's description of the winged horror attack and Mererid's recounting of the prayer on the road.

Lakenna noticed Llyr watching Rhiannon. The warrior had the weathered, ruddy look of a man much outdoors. Deep crow's-foot wrinkles surrounded his eyes. Surely the man could talk. How else could he command others?

Lakenna brought her gaze back to Rhiannon. The girl's dress was a practical woolen of a sturdy weave. Her hair, though clean, was a tangled red mane of heavy curls falling about her shoulders and down her back. Buckled around her waist was a sword enclosed in a plain leather scabbard.

The air in the room was stuffy, heavy with the odor of spicy food and a smell new to Lakenna: the oil used to sharpen steel-edged weapons. The mixture coated the inside of her throat. She would have welcomed fresh air, but the room's one glass-paned window was closed with the curtain pulled across and a blanket hanging down from the rod as well.

"Have you felt a similar...urge...to pray since arriving here at the Bridge?" Rhiannon asked.

Lakenna thought the girl's question seemed a touch too casual.

Tellan must have noticed the same. He turned to his daughter. "Did those two Arshessa..."

"No, Father. If they had I would have told you. Besides, you met them with the stallion; they are true warriors with honor."

Tellan's eyes narrowed at the interruption. His face was red, his eyebrows singed from the winged horror attack. The lines around his mouth were deep, his weariness plain. But he sat erect in his chair, arms folded, attention focused. A small scroll lay open on the table between him and Lady Mererid, with a mug resting in the middle. Both ends of the scroll curled up against it. Sheets of parchment lay in a neat pile next to it, along with a quill, an inkwell, a blotter of sand, and a block of wax.

Tellan had been angry—rightly so in Lakenna's mind—upon learning of Rhiannon's unescorted trip to the stables. Lakenna had just followed Lady Mererid into the room to tell Tellan and the others about the prayer on the road when Rhiannon barged in with her news about the horse's shoulder. Tellan had given the girl a stern lecture before going with her back to the stable. Now, the same look returned to his face.

"We need all the information we can gather," Mererid said, lightly placing her hand on her husband's arm. Mererid sat neat and composed in her chair. She had changed into a soft, rose-colored dress accented with a white border. Her hair was brushed, and it gleamed in the lantern light. And though there was no doubt Tellan was in charge, Lakenna could see that Mererid was second only to him.

"We must conclude that the horrors came after you," Mererid told Rhiannon. "Girard says our lore mentions siyyim walking the Land. Unfortunately, there is no mention of what they look like. We are treading almost blindly through this. Any incident in the stable, no matter how trivial it seemed at the time, may have bearing on these discussions."

Rhiannon nodded. "High Lord Maolmin came in after Elmar left to prepare the poultice. When he looked at me... I felt the same as when the horrors looked at me."

"How so?" Girard asked. The loreteller sat directly across the table from Rhiannon.

"His eyes. They were..." She bit her lower lip. "They reminded me of the winged horrors."

"Tell me what happened once you entered the stable," Tellan commanded.

Rhiannon did, then finished by saying, "I sensed Harred felt the same. He looked ready to engage High Lord Maolmin empty-handed."

Lakenna thought something flickered on Rhiannon's face when the girl said "Harred."

"Tell us more about Harred," Mererid urged. Her eyes met Lakenna's, and a moment of understanding passed between them.

Rhiannon's expression closed. "An Arshessa warrior. Not noble-born. He is Lord Gillaon's rhyfelwr. As I said, I was glad for Harred's presence around High Lord Maolmin." She raised her chin slightly. "Harred and Elmar both treated me with the respect due one warrior to another."

Bodies shifted in chairs. Girard cleared his throat, opened his mouth, then closed it quickly at Tellan's glare. Mererid shot a meaningful look at Llyr.

Finally, the old warrior blinked, met his lady's gaze, then rubbed a meaty hand through his hair. "I will talk to this Harred," he rumbled in a voice like an earthquake. "We'll see if he is a decorated scabbard or if he can handle steel."

"Steel," Rhiannon said flatly. She raised her chin a bit more.

Llyr glanced again at Mererid, then back at Rhiannon. He

fixed the girl with a stare hard as winter ice. "I will talk to this Arshessa tomorrow and take his measure. 'Til then, you will stay with one of us, *Mistress* Rhiannon."

Rhiannon withstood the rhyfelwr's gaze for a moment, then nodded and dropped her eyes.

Lakenna exchanged another look with Mererid. In spite of Rhiannon's apparent interest in a commoner, her stepmother seemed pleased. A faint twinkle danced in her eyes, making Lakenna think of the silver mirror set. She did not think Mererid had given it to the girl yet.

"What about High Lord Maolmin Erian?" Tellan asked. He gestured to the scroll and other parchments before him. "Our creditors have been patient, but it is time they be repaid. And the hlaford needs to be rebuilt and furnished. The Rogoth wool must sell tomorrow. Maolmin and the Sabinis merchants will strive to hinder any agreement we reach with Lord Gillaon. Was this...feeling Rhiannon had about Maolmin part of that, or could it be part of the attack by the winged horrors?"

Tellan looked at each of them. "I was caught unprepared this morning, and it was only by the grace of the Eternal that Rhiannon survived." His lips firmed, and the lines around his mouth deepened. "We will not be caught unprepared again."

The words were even, but they carried the impact of an ax hitting a tree. That, and the glint in Tellan's eyes, sent a chill through Lakenna. Home seemed far away in the mist of this hard-edged warrior atmosphere.

Mererid spoke. "Teacher, this encounter in the stables would have been while you were eating in Rhiannon's room. Did the Eternal...did you feel anything then like you felt on the road?"

"No, m'lady. But this is new to me." Lakenna noted how everyone's look turned to puzzlement. It was most disconcerting. What did they expect from her? She was awestruck with Tellan's account of the horror attack. She sat in a room with people who had been face-to-face with the Mighty Ones' creatures as had Destin Faber and Stanus Albane! Loreteller Girard said that her prayer and that of Mererid must have cut the beasts off from the Mighty Ones, allowing them to be killed.

Lakenna's mind still boggled at that. True, she had responded in faith to the Eternal's urging on the road. But at the time she had no idea it was as deadly serious as winged horrors of the night. And if the loreteller was correct, perhaps a siyyim as well! It was one thing to sit in the meetinghouses and hear Albane teachers of doctrine expound upon how the Eternal expects believers to fight the good fight of faith in the heavenlies. It was quite another to be engaged in that battle with actual lives at stake.

Now, aware that all eyes in the room rested on her, a wave of concern passed through Lakenna. It seemed the Rogoths were expecting her to issue warning of any new danger to Rhiannon.

I can't do this! You don't know what I did!

She reined in her thoughts. Lord Tellan and the others around the table waited to hear what she had to say.

"As with you, this is my first time involved in matters of this gravity. I am sure you are aware that during Stanus Albane's day, outbreaks of winged horrors of the night began occurring as they had before the Founding. It was not surprising. Keeper monasteries were riddled with drunkenness and debauchery of every description. The Keepers who worked among the people were equally ineffective. Many people in the Land returned openly to the worship of the Mighty Ones. It was proclaimed widely that the Eternal had abandoned the Covenant."

Lakenna strove to keep her voice level and matter-of-fact. "The Great Rising that Stanus Albane helped usher in resulted in a rebirth of faith, and the Mighty Ones' bid to regain dominion over the Land was beaten back. Since that time Albanes have prayed faithfully for the Covenant and the Faber dynasty. There have been no similar outbreaks of these creatures—at least in our areas." Then she could not help adding, "I assume Keepers still go about their rituals. To what effect, I do not know."

She looked around the table. "I will strive to remain open to the Eternal's leading. I will pray..." she swallowed, her insides roiling. "I will pray for Rhiannon and for all of you daily. As far as engaging the Mighty Ones, I know the teachings, but the specifics of this are new to me."

"All of us are thankful for your efforts this morning," Girard proclaimed in a deep rolling tone so surprising in a man his size. "One day soon, allow me to take you to the Kepploch Monastery. In the courtyard there is a statue of Destin Faber killing a winged horror of the night. The base of the statue contains names of more than seven score Keepers who have died in battles against the Mighty Ones and their worshipers. Five have been chiseled there this century alone. How many Albanes have died for the Eternal since Stanus' day?"

Lakenna detected neither anger nor reproach in the loreteller's voice, just statement of fact. She stole a quick glance at Tellan. His expression was unreadable. She looked back at Girard. "Our prayers have prevented any need to battle thusly. We Albanes do not—"

A sharp knock sounded. Conversation ceased. Llyr rose to his feet, scabbard held in one hand, the other gripping the sword hilt. He walked to the door. After a muffled exchange he slid the latch back and swung the heavy door open.

A Keeper strode into the room with purpose and an air of command, black robe swirling around his long strides. Lakenna thought he was in his mid-thirties. Average height and thin, his face was freshly shaved but still showing the shadow of a heavy beard. A large hooked nose gave him a rugged, angular look. The Keeper's black robe was of rich linen and finely tailored. She noticed the knots of white rope belt. Three each on the tasseled ends dangling beyond the large gold clasp. *Six knots?* Even she knew that only His Most High Excellency, the Ruling Keeper, wore seven.

Tellan's chair scraped backward as he stood. A puzzled expression furrowed his brow. As everyone else followed Tellan's example, Lakenna remained firmly in her seat. This was her first time in the same room with a Keeper, but as far as she was concerned, he was no different from anyone else.

"I am High Lord Keeper Branor. I have come in the Eternal's name for your need."

Girard's eyes widened, and his head whipped toward Tellan. The Rogoth lord's expression was a study of emotions: surprise, anger, uncertainty, and finally an inward longing that was gone in a flash. He stood ramrod straight and made no effort to welcome the Keeper.

Awkward silence filled the room. Mererid turned to Tellan, obviously puzzled at this breech in manners. When her husband remained an unmoving statue, she stepped toward the Keeper. "Our deepest gratitude, Lord Keeper, for coming—"

"What is the meaning of this?" Tellan spat. "Am I mocked?"

Mererid's hand came to her mouth. She stepped back, eyes darting between her husband and the Keeper.

Branor shook his head slowly. "Lord Tellan, fifteen years ago I wronged you. I hid behind the walls of my order instead of meeting with you so we could come to terms with the manner of Lady Eyslk's death. I deeply regret that." He lifted his hands, palms outward. "I humbly beg your forgiveness."

Tellan's face was a stone mask. But Rhiannon's eyed widened. She opened her mouth and made to step forward, but Mererid placed a hand on the girl's arm and gave a quick headshake.

Branor regarded Tellan with a level, yet pained look. "I wronged you then, and I have wronged you since by not seeking your forgiveness sooner. I ask again, will you forgive me?"

"My wife is dead because of you, and you ask forgiveness?"

Mererid's face paled. She peered at Tellan for a long moment, then her eyes dropped, and she plucked at the folds of her dress with a shaking hand.

The Keeper shook his head. "I do not ask forgiveness for Lady Eyslk's death. That is bound up in the mystery of the Eternal's purpose, and its understanding is beyond me. I ask forgiveness for not meeting with you afterwards."

When Tellan made no reply, Branor continued smoothly. "It is no accident I am here. This morning many at Kepploch were driven to their knees by the hand of the Eternal to pray. When your letter came, we realized why. We are bound together and must be one in the Eternal."

Lakenna started. *Keepers* had been praying as well? Inexplicably, she felt betrayed. Quickly she dismissed the feeling—or tried to.

"Tell me, Keeper," Tellan said, the title coming out almost as an accusation, "was a siyyim directing the horrors this morning?"

Branor's expression remained neutral. "All the accounts I have studied say that where winged horrors act with purpose, they are controlled by a siyyim."

"I would meet this siyyim . . ." Tellan's eyes flashed. " . . . this monster who sends such creatures after a young girl. Can you assist me in that?"

"I am a Keeper. I am here to see this outbreak from the protection of the Covenant contained and your daughter safe again."

"Help find the siyyim," Tellan said. "Then you and Teacher Lakenna do like this morning and allow me to meet it with weapons."

Branor looked at Lakenna. He took in her white blouse and brown skirt, and she could see "Albane" click in his mind. She returned his gaze evenly. He was not bad looking. His hairline receded slightly, but the remainder was thick and showed a hint of a wave combed straight back. For some reason, she sensed great turmoil inside the man, beyond the obvious tension with Lord Tellan. The Keeper's brow seemed permanently creased with deep worry lines, his shoulders weighted down from a heavy burden.

He hides secrets as I do.

The thought startled her. She lowered her eyes.

Branor looked back to Tellan. "Siyyim cannot be killed. They are spirit beings, powerful creatures second only to the Mighty Ones."

"Didn't Destin Faber kill all the siyyim during the battles before the Cutting of the Covenant?" Rhiannon said.

Branor turned to the girl—and stared. He blinked, then gathered himself. "My pardon, I—"

"Please, my lord husband." Mererid showed no evidence of anxiety on her face, but Lakenna heard the strain in her voice and saw that the woman's fingers were white where they gripped her dress. "Let us take seats and make introductions. High Lord Keeper Branor says he is here to help. I am sure you agree we need all we can get."

Tellan hesitated, then gestured for everyone to sit. The only free chair at the table was next to Lakenna. Branor looked at it and then at her. She kept her gaze straight ahead.

He inclined his head slightly, removed his cloak, and draped it over the back of the chair. The cloak was wool, expensive, and dyed black as his robe. Crisp linen rustled as he sat and crossed a leg over a knee. After arranging the folds of his robe, he clasped his hands in his lap. The fingers were long, the nails manicured, his palms smooth and free of calluses. A scholar's hands. Everything about him was a far cry from Loane and the other weatherworn Albane farmers and herders in the fertile valley where she had spent most of her life.

Tellan formally introduced Mererid and Rhiannon. While Girard and Llyr were presented, Rhiannon seemed barely able to sit still in her eagerness to question the Keeper—then the girl suddenly jumped in her chair and glanced at Mererid. Lakenna suppressed a wry snort. The stepmother's face remained unreadable, but Lakenna could imagine a busy foot under the table.

"And this is Lakenna Wen," Tellan said. "She has taken service as tutor. When you arrived, Keeper, we were discussing her role in the happenings this morning. From what you said, it would seem both of you were…involved." Tellan paused. "It is still unclear to me exactly how your prayers rendered the horrors vulnerable to our weapons and how long we can expect that to last. I need enlightenment. But more, we must know *why*. Why were the horrors so determined to kill the 'red-haired girl'?"

Branor pursed his lips. "First, I suggest it would be beneficial to make sure we all have the same understanding of what we face. We dare not have any among us laboring under false assumptions."

Lakenna ground her teeth. *Make sure we all have the same understanding? False assumptions? As if Albanes needed teaching from Keepers!*

The Keeper settled back into the chair and steepled his fingers. His cadence took on that of rote memory. He told of how Destin, born among the clans, had traveled to foreign lands to seek his fortune. There he encountered the teachings of the Eternal. His life was forever changed, and when he returned— full of zeal for his newfound religion and possessed of newly honed generalship skills—he led a campaign and an awakening that ended with the clans throwing off worship of the Mighty Ones of the North, South, East, and West. Although this information was basically the same as Lakenna had been taught as a young Albane, she nevertheless found herself borne along with the smoothness of Branor's voice. She noticed that she was leaning forward.

"Destin gathered the High Lords of the six clans, and together those seven men cut a covenant with the Eternal," Branor said, "pledging to rule the Land in accordance with Holy Writ and the character of the loving God they served. As Destin was crowned king, Fentuch, a holy man and the first Keeper of the Covenant, gave this utterance:

"'Thus saith the Eternal. I have made this covenant with you for the ruling of this Land. I set up one shepherd over you, my servant Destin Faber. He shall feed you, and he shall be your shepherd. And his son and his son after him, even unto one hundred generations, will they feed and protect you with this covenant of my peace. Keep this covenant, and the Mighty Ones' yoke of slavery shall be broken. The winged horror of the night and its brethren will cease out of the Land. You shall be safe in your homes and shall know that I am the Eternal. For the mountains shall depart and the hills be removed; but my kindness shall not depart from thee, neither shall this covenant of my peace be removed, saith the Eternal.'"

Branor paused. Those listening shifted in their chairs. Lakenna glanced at Rhiannon. The girl's green eyes focused on the Keeper with single-minded intensity.

Branor uncrossed his legs and leaned forward. "A covenant is a two-party contract. Each side must uphold its end. The Eternal is perfect and unchanging. His mercy endures forever. It is in *our* faithfulness to the Covenant where the problem lies. Our part details two specifics. First, the Faber dynasty. It is linked to the Covenant. 'And his son and his son after him, even unto one hundred generations.' King Balder's health is suspect, but Prince Larien is young and vigorous, and although the betrothal has ended, surely he will marry one day and produce a male heir. That is vital."

"You must not have heard about the Rite of Presentation," Mererid said.

Branor stilled. "For Larien?"

Mererid nodded. "The announcement just reached us."

"When?"

"In the fall."

The Keeper's eyes burned as he digested the news. Lakenna waited, as did the others. The room grew stuffier. Glancing at the blanket-covered window, she wished someone would open it a crack, but knew it wasn't going to happen.

"That changes everything," Branor said softly as he stared at the floor. "Whoever Larien chooses, she won't be another Sabinis."

Or Albane either, Lakenna thought. Since the Founding, every maiden marrying into the Faber dynasty had come from one of six clans. And for centuries almost exclusively from the wealthiest families of the three largest: Sabinis, Landantae, and Arshessa. Nonetheless, Lakenna found herself growing excited. The last Presentation had been two centuries ago. Maybe she would see this one. Or would it be clan members only?

Branor roused himself. He looked around the room as if seeing everyone for the first time. "Ah, yes. Back to our discussion. The inhabitants of the Land's part of the Covenant is the second component."

Tellan's face was a closed mask as he listened. The Rogoth

lord had not responded to Branor's plea for forgiveness. Lakenna wondered where that was going to lead.

Again, Branor steppled his fingertips. "We all know that worship of the Mighty Ones did not—and has not—ceased. And while the Covenant greatly hinders the Mighty Ones' power, we Keepers have long understood that their worship here in the Land can enable winged horrors and other such creatures to break past the barrier of the Covenant and rampage again."

"Albanes have long taught this," Lakenna said proudly. "More, we know that while association with pagans does not hinder a person's ability to commune with the Eternal, it does hinder that person's protection from the Mighty Ones. Those battling such manifestations must be pure and free of sin." She stopped. Then why had her prayers worked? She glanced at the Keeper. Maybe they hadn't. No, the power she had felt on the road praying with Mererid was real. Something had *happened*.

"I see," Branor said shortly. "As I was saying, after the Covenant and during the Cleansing, Keepers of the Covenant fought a long struggle against the ingrained worship of the Mighty Ones in all their different disguises. Even now, twelve centuries later, many pockets of pagan belief remain. During the past decades we Keepers have not been as vigilant in rooting them out, believing these remnants too small and insignificant to be worth pursuing."

Mererid nodded. "Just fifteen years ago, all Dinari nobles were shocked to learn that our high lord at the time had been dabbling in the ceremonies of the old gods. Either knowingly or by accident, supposedly he enabled something to break past the restraints of the Covenant."

"Supposedly!" Girard snorted. "Verified that was, m'lady. Verified by Gaelbhen, the late loreteller to the newly elected High Lord Maolmin, and brought before the loreteller assembly at the Dinari Fall Gathering that same year. It was duly investigated by three uninvolved loretellers and accepted as lore by our solemn body during the ensuing Gathering. After the reports had been given, not one of us had any doubts that something terrible had been called forth. It was only by the efforts of a group of monks sent from Kepploch, aided greatly by Maolmin himself, that it was bound and expelled from the Land. All but one of the Keepers died in the struggle."

Again, Branor stiffened. Sweat beaded his brow. He opened and closed his mouth.

Lakenna watched his distress, puzzled. "Were you there?" The words were out before she realized it.

The Keeper almost jumped in his chair. "I had already left Kepploch. I...wasn't there."

Into the ensuing silence, Rhiannon asked, "Do you believe these things can take over someone's body?"

Branor took a deep breath. "If siyyim, lilitu, or other such creatures ever inhabited people's bodies, it should not happen now. But there is disagreement on this. Since the Covenant there have been accounts of death and destruction attributed to the Mighty Ones' creatures—these attacks seem to have been human-directed."

"And the winged horrors coming after Rhiannon," Tellan stated.

"Yes, Lord Tellan," Branor said. "It is time for specifics. 'Kill red-haired girl.' Does anyone have any idea why?"

Llyr asked, "Can it have anything to do with Rhiannon's birthing prophecy? That deranged monk tried to kill her, and now winged horrors and perhaps a siyyim. There must be some connection."

"I agree," Girard said. He looked quizzically at the Keeper. "I have tried to remember what I could of that utterance. Do you still remember it, Your Grace?"

Branor remained silent. Mererid stared down at her hands clinched in her lap.

"Please?" Rhiannon asked. "May I hear it from you?"

Branor looked at the girl for a long moment, though his focus seemed far away. Finally, he closed his eyes and nodded.

"'Have I not given my word,' says the Eternal, 'that my covenant of peace will remain? Did I not say through my prophet these words: For the mountains shall depart and the hills be removed, but my kindness shall not depart from thee, neither shall this covenant of my peace be removed. This babe at the breast will be a Protectoress of the Covenant. She will be a tool in my hands to strengthen it and return its fullness to the Land while bringing the Mighty Ones and their creatures to heel again.'"

Lakenna glanced at Rhiannon. The girl's eyes were wide and round, her expression one of wonder—tinged with a touch of fear? If so, it was gone quickly. Rhiannon sat straighter in her chair while lifting her chin ever so slightly.

Mererid broke the silence. "What do those words mean to you tonight, Lord Keeper?"

Raw emotion twisted the man's features. "With all that happened after those words left my mouth, I became convinced I had erred. Surely it was not from the urging of the Eternal that I spoke, I told myself, but rather out of my own admiration for Lady Eyslk and her oft-stated desire that the babe growing in her womb be used by the Eternal."

Lakenna shifted in her chair, uncomfortable.

"And now?" Mererid probed.

Branor took a deep breath and let it out audibly. "It seems the Mighty Ones believe it. They sent a siyyim, a creature second in power only to themselves, and gave it four winged horrors of the night to kill Rhiannon." He continued almost in disbelief. "I believe the prophecy was indeed of the Eternal."

"What do I do now?" Rhiannon asked.

"What 'Protectoress of the Covenant' entails, I do not know. It may be what your mother was beginning to do before her untimely death: gathering information and encouraging a rebirth of the strong faith of Destin Faber and the Founders. It may be much more. Sometimes we get so stuck on doing the Eternal's will our way..." His voiced tailed off.

"Yes?" Rhiannon urged.

"We...we can become so focused on our way that we...don't

take the time to find what the Eternal's way might be." He swallowed. "Whatever the case, you will find that path opening before you one day, perhaps soon. The Eternal does not force anyone to follow him. You will have to choose to walk it or not. If you do so choose, it will unfold according to his timing."

"And the siyyim?" Tellan said. "Will that unfold according to the Eternal's timing, or is that in our hands?"

"All things unfold according to the Eternal's timing," Branor said. "But it has been given to us to battle the Mighty Ones' efforts to end the Covenant and reestablish their rule here in the Land."

"Is Rhiannon safe?" Tellan asked.

"I am here—for a time. Events are... I must return to Shinard." Branor tilted his head toward Lakenna. "You have said that this woman was part of this morning's effort. She must remain vigilant. You have your men and their weapons. Rhiannon is as safe as she can be until the siyyim is cast out of the Land."

"How do we find the siyyim?"

"Mainly, Lord Tellan, Rhiannon needs but walk in the Eternal's purpose." Branor smiled grimly. "If she does, the siyyim will find her."

Chapter Ten

RHIANNON

W HAT WAS SHE going to do with these? "Thank you,
Mother," Rhiannon said politely. "It is a beautiful set."
Mererid smiled. "Your father believes they come
from Aunt Serilda's estate. Please don't tell him otherwise." Mererid's expectant look continued. Teacher Lakenna stood beside
her and watched curiously as well.

Early morning light filled Rhiannon's room at the Bridge
Across, the bright shafts illuminating a multicolored rug in the
middle of the floor. A red oak wardrobe with an inlaid vine design
stood against one wall. A dresser and a ladder-backed chair were
by the window. Lakenna's bags lined one wall of the room.

When Rhiannon had awakened to sunlight beaming into
the room, Lakenna had already been up and gone, but she had
returned with Mererid to present the silver mirror set. The Albane
was dressed for the day, her waist-length hair brushed and up in
a neat bun. Mererid's hair was hastily pinned, with several loose
strands curling down about her neck. Her dress was old, surely
not what she planned to wear to the wool sale.

Still holding the silver mirror, brush, and comb, Rhiannon felt
the weight of the scabbard and sword hanging from her waist and
breathed a prayer of thanksgiving that, against her stepmother's
protests, she had brought it to Lachlann. For the sword to have
been ruined in the fire was unthinkable.

"We can hang the mirror here," Lakenna suggested brightly,
indicating a peg on the dresser by the window. "I can take the

comb and work on the worst of the tangles if you want."

Rhiannon glanced back and forth between the two women. Something was in the air. "It's time for sword drills."

"Llyr has decreed no training," Mererid said. "He is with your father, Creag, and Girard checking on the wool. We must be ready when they return to escort us to the sale."

Rhiannon suppressed a flash of irritation. Creag was with the men while she was to stay here and do her hair. Mererid would probably insist on ribbons in it as well! "I washed my hair yesterday. It's fine as it is."

Mererid's expression firmed. "The morning promises to be most difficult, Rhiannon. As the family of the lord of the Rogoth kinsmen, our station demands we present ourselves as best we can. Today will be good preparation for the Rite of Presentation."

Rhiannon ground her teeth. She would have no peace in the coming months. Mererid would be in full flood, demanding daily practice on how to walk upright and curtsy and simper and drink punch. All just to stand in line with twenty other noble girls, then spend fifteen seconds being introduced to the prince and have her hand kissed.

Mererid handed the comb to Lakenna. "Lord Gillaon and Harred will be present. Men are favorably impressed by a woman's well-groomed appearance." Mererid cocked an eyebrow. "I am sure you recognize the importance of impressing our new trading partners."

Rhiannon conceded Mererid's point. "I will wear my sword to the auction." It was half statement, half question. After her father's displeasure with the unescorted trip to the stables last night, she was on shaky ground indeed.

Frown lines crinkled Mererid's brow. She opened her mouth— but Lakenna spoke first. "May I see your sword?"

Surprised, Rhiannon slid the blade from the scabbard. "Please don't touch the metal."

Lakenna stepped forward and inspected the weapon carefully,

paying particular attention to the sharp edge. "Your sword is of superior steel."

"Of course." But Rhiannon wondered how to tell. Both Tellan and Llyr assured her it was a fine one, and she had accepted that fact without question.

"How familiar are you with the intricacies of forging steel?" Lakenna inquired.

"All Dinari, and we Rogoths in particular, demand the best weapons."

"Do you have your own smith?"

Rhiannon shook her head. She glanced at Mererid, who said, "It was commissioned to a master swordsmith here in Lachlann."

"Notice the edge where the sharpening has taken place," Lakenna said. "See the grain?"

Rhiannon looked closely and noticed a series of tiny faint lines running lengthwise along the bevel.

"This is caused by the endless folding and hammering of the hot metal during forging," Lakenna continued. "Unless the impurities in the beginning ore are removed by that process, the steel will not possess the combination of strength and flexibility needed for a weapon. And, it would pit and rust much too easily."

Rhiannon was impressed. "How does a—" Then she stopped. She had almost said, *How does a woman know this?* "How do you know this?"

"Metallurgy is one of the subjects we will study." Lakenna hung the mirror on the dresser peg, then pulled out the ladder-back chair. "We can talk more while I work on your tangles."

Rhiannon glanced warily between the two women. The issue of wearing her sword to the sale had been sidestepped for the moment. Best to save all reserves for that battle. Accepting defeat, she plopped in the chair and folded her arms across her chest.

Mererid left the room, and Phelan slipped in. His face was freshly scrubbed and his hair combed. "You're actually going to use this?" He picked up the brush and rubbed the bristles through his fingers. The dark rings that had been a fixture under his eyes for so long were gone, as was the sickly pallor to his face. "When I heard Mother and Teacher Lakenna talk about giving this to you, I knew you would set it aside." He watched with rapt attention as Lakenna went to work with the comb. "We're supposed to tell Father everything came from Aunt Serilda, but it really came from—"

"I know, Phelan." Her head jerked back as Lakenna pulled. She righted herself. "You look very handsome this morning."

He wore a white linen shirt with a cravat and bow around the neck, brown knee-length breeches, and a short cloak. It had been Creag's dress outfit the last two years. Although altered for Phelan, it hung sacklike on his small frame.

"Creag showed me how to tie the cravat." Phelan frowned. "He said I look like a dressed-up scarecrow."

"In a few months it will fit you perfectly." Rhiannon gasped as Lakenna braced herself and tugged hard.

Phelan's eyes widened. "Doesn't that hurt?"

"Some," Rhiannon admitted through gritted teeth.

"Teacher, why start at the ends like that? Why not start at the top?"

"It is best to begin at the ends, Master Phelan, and work your way up." Lakenna plucked a wad of red hair from the teeth of the comb. "Rhiannon, when was the last time you did anything to your hair other than wash it? This is going to take a while."

"She hates to do women things. Mother has to force her. Rhiannon thinks all that is—"

"Teacher," Rhiannon broke in primly, "please tell me more about steel."

They talked steel and other metals, which led to farming and plows, which led to methods of food preservation, which led to transportation and shipping—which led to the wool sale.

"Do Dinari wear swords at a festival?" Lakenna asked casually after putting the comb down.

Rhiannon frowned. "No. Only the Sabinis mercenaries standing guard over their gold."

"Will your father or Llyr wear swords?"

"No." Rhiannon checked her reflection in the mirror. Her hair did look much better. Harred would not be wearing a sword either. Best to leave hers here.

"What dress do you plan to wear?"

"This one." Rhiannon indicated what she had on. The sturdy weave held up during sword drills and did not tear when she stepped on the hem as often happened during practice sessions.

Lakenna went to the oak wardrobe and removed a pale green linen gown with a high lace neck. It was one of Mererid's. The tutor drew her hand lovingly across the gown.

A month previous, Rhiannon had been forced to stand still for a long, boring afternoon while a fat seamstress with a mouthful of pins fitted this gown and two others of Mererid's for altering. The seamstress and Mererid had talked knowledge-ably about laces, linens, fine woolens, and stockings. All the while, Creag and Phelan had been out with Llyr doing sword drills on horses.

"This one will make a more favorable impression," Lakenna said, "especially on the Arshessa."

Suddenly Rhiannon saw the dress in a new light. She hesitated a moment, then stood and unbuckled her sword belt. "Phelan, it is time for you to leave."

"Why?"

"I am going to try on this gown."

"You are?" Phelan's brow wrinkled, then he brightened. "I want to see what you look like, too."

"Master Phelan," Lakenna said, "it is proper to accord a young lady privacy when she dresses."

"Rhiannon doesn't care."

"Best for you to leave now," Rhiannon told her half-brother kindly. "I will call you in when we are finished."

Puzzlement ruled the boy's thin face as he left.

She removed the heavy wool dress, laid it across the bed, then stepped into the gown. It was lighter and hugged the contours of her body. Lakenna fluttered about, tugging and smoothing. After tying the lacing, the tutor stood back and nodded with approval. She brought the mirror.

"This green is beautiful," she said wistfully. "See how the color brings out the green of your eyes? I am anxious to see this Lord Gillaon's and Harred's faces when they see you."

Glancing down, Lakenna tapped her chin. "Those scuffed boots won't do with a gown. Let me see if Lady Mererid has a pair of slippers that will fit. And some green ribbons for your hair. I'll be right back." She handed over the mirror and hurried out.

Rhiannon walked slowly to the dresser, slid into the chair, and studied her image. Her eyes did seem more vivid. Fingering the ornate handle of the silver brush for a long moment, she picked it up and began brushing her hair.

Chapter Eleven

HARRED

ARLY MORNING FOG was a slow swirling gray cocoon that
enshrouded the stone bridge arching over the Clundy.
The swift current battered and swirled through the rock-
cluttered bed, spraying up a mist that clung damp and chill on
Harred's face.

Past the bridge, he and Lord Gillaon turned down the cobblestone street that followed the course of the river. Well away
from the bank, for fear of flooding, stood a mixture of shops,
small inns, taverns, and open-air merchant stalls that outlined
Lachlann's central square.

Normally the square would be bustling as merchants and
shop owners set out wares and produce. Not so this morning. It
was quiet and deserted, as all the day's activity would be centered
at the festival grounds. They strode briskly by a closed leather
tanner's shop and then a pottery establishment.

Lord Gillaon Tarenester was freshly shaven. He cut a dash-
ing figure in a dark blue cloak fastened at the shoulder by a
gold clasp in the shape of a tree. Chin jutting forward and blue
eyes alive with speculation, he radiated eagerness for the coming challenges. "You're certain Maolmin would have harmed the
girl," he asked, "and that she realized it as well?"

"I have no doubt, m'lord."

"Anything last night from Lord Tellan's men?"

"No, m'lord. Elmar and I checked every tavern. None were to
be found."

Gillaon grunted, then retreated into his thoughts.

Thinking of Elmar, Harred struggled unsuccessfully to smother a grin. Elmar's face after the eager first bite of spicy mutton last night had been a sight to behold. The cheese so thoughtfully brought along had not mollified his gasping brother-in-law, nor had the straight-faced explanation about the dish being a Dinari form of welcome. Harred took the muttered threats of revenge seriously and knew extra vigilance would be called for during the next few days.

Those thoughts brought back to his mind the stables and Breanna's serene features. A warm tingle washed through his body. Reluctantly, he put the loreteller's daughter from his thoughts. Not now. But later, most definitely.

They were about to round a corner when Harred heard the scuff of footsteps behind. He looked over his shoulder and saw two men stepping out from an alley. One held a wicked-looking knife, the other a long-handled cudgel. Harred whipped back, and two more men similarly armed had appeared ahead of them. Both groups sprinted toward him and Lord Gillaon.

Harred gripped Gillaon's shoulder to pull him into the street, but a third set of two came running toward them from that direction. Mentally kicking himself for not being more vigilant, Harred hustled Gillaon into a recessed door front.

"We cannot run, m'lord. Stay behind me and give me room."

Harred stepped forward, muscles loose and ready. The Sabinis merchants had known no swords would be worn to the festival and had thought Gillaon would be unprotected.

Harred smiled grimly.

Come, hirelings, and meet an Arshessa warrior.

With a flurry of pounding steps, the six were upon him. For an instant, they seemed surprised to find their prey ready to fight.

That hesitation was all Harred needed. In one smooth motion, he kicked the knife out of the hand of the first to reach him while whipping the edge of his right hand into the throat. He slid around the falling, gasping man to seize the wrist of the second, who swung a cudgel. The arm made a loud snap as Harred broke it. He leveraged the screaming ruffian into the path of the third. It was a tight tangle for a moment, and all he could manage was to knock bodies away and dodge wild swings of clubs and knife thrusts.

Breath rasping in his throat, Harred fought on instinct and training, blood singing. Time seemed to slow as he coldly calculated the most immediate threat and how best to meet it while positioning himself for the next. He felt detached, almost an observer.

He crouched and seized a dropped cudgel and used it to skillfully parry a wooden club, then cracked the wielder across the head so hard he heard bone splinter.

Another ruffian made a low sweeping knife thrust, aiming for the groin. Stepping inside the swing Harred slammed the heel of his palm up the man's nose. Warm blood spurted as nasal cartilage and bone penetrated the base of the skull. The man's knees buckled, and he went limp as a rag doll. Harred shoved him aside.

Three bodies sprawled around the recessed door front. Gillaon remained behind him, untouched. A fourth attacker crawled away, arm dragging, moaning in pain.

Harred squared off against the remaining two. "Whatever you're being paid," he growled, "it isn't worth dying for."

One ruffian eyed the other. They backed up, then turned on their heels and fled, disappearing into the heavy fog.

Lord Gillaon strode out of the doorway and lifted his cloak as he stepped disdainfully over the bodies. He gave Harred a curt nod. "As I said, your skills in this arena are formidable. Come. The true battle awaits. The wool sale is just our opening move."

The fog lay even heavier at the festival grounds. It dampened the sounds of preparations for the coming sale and blurred the shapes of merchants and their servants scurrying between colorful wagons and the open-air booths where their wares were displayed.

A few paces behind where he and Lord Gillaon waited for Lord

Tellan, a crowd of children watched wide-eyed as brightly dressed jugglers warmed up by tossing colored wooden pins back and forth. Just beyond them a troupe of puppeteers finished erecting their curtained stage and began removing puppets from travel-worn chests.

The first puppet removed was the mainstay of every show and easily recognizable. She had a round, fat face and short pigtails. She was clothed in a dress with a white apron and clutched an oversized broom. Universally dubbed Shrew Wife, her saucy comments, both pointed and veiled, always brought howls of laughter, and many dug elbows into spouses' sides.

The sun was fully above the horizon and finally beginning to burn away the mist when Harred saw the Rogoths arrive. Lord Tellan clutched a rolled parchment in one hand. He was accompanied by his heir, a youngster with a squinty expression and a self-important air; the bandy-legged loreteller; and a hard-eyed, grizzled rhyfelwr who looked as naked without a sword as Harred felt.

While Gillaon and Tellan exchanged pleasantries, Harred allowed himself to be eased aside by the other rhyfelwr, a gravel-voiced man named Llyr. They moved a few paces from the others.

"We saw bodies on the way here," Llyr rumbled.

Harred related the encounter, brief and to the point.

Llyr waited for more, then nodded. They talked generalities, but beneath it, they probed each other: two warriors instinctively assessing strengths and weaknesses. Harred decided he could best the older man now—but when the Dinari was still in his prime? Probably, but it would have pushed him.

"This goes as planned," Llyr said, "the Sabinis won't go away quietly. Stay on guard when you leave with the wool. And through the mountains."

Harred grinned like a wolf. "When you go bear hunting, sometimes the worst thing that happens is finding the bear."

Llyr's hard gaze bored in; Harred met it square on. Finally, Llyr seemed to reach a conclusion. The tension eased in his meaty shoulders. "You need anything after the sale, let me know. Your fight will be ours."

Harred nodded, aware he had passed a test of sorts. And he was more than a little pleased.

They rejoined the others. Gillaon was reading the parchment Lord Tellan had brought. Finishing, he rolled it up. "Interesting. My rhyfelwr and I will study this."

"As will I and my advisors." Tellan gave a short bow. His face glistened with a salve for his burn. "We meet in my pavilion later?"

Gillaon returned the bow, and the Rogoth party took their leave. When they were out of sight, Gillaon cursed vehemently and thrust the parchment at Harred. "Read!"

Harred struggled with the unfamiliar phrases but got the import of the proposed Sabinis contract. "Why would any Dinari agree to this, m'lord? Our price is two silvers higher."

Lord Gillaon did not reply. He paced back and forth in the wet grass, hands behind his back, clasping his leather gloves tightly. Stopping, he stared across the way to where bales of wool were stacked and knots of Dinari clansmen gathered around split-rail pens holding breeding stock for sale. Weathered sheepherders vigorously debated the merits of different bloodlines: their hardiness and resistance to disease, ease of lambing, wool quality, even carcass traits when slaughtered for meat.

Following his lord's gaze, Harred searched the grounds for Elmar. At Lord Gillaon's request, Harred had set the mountaineer mingling in the growing crowd, listening for speculations about the upcoming sale. Elmar was perfect for that role. His potbelly and ambling walk hid a keen mind; his easy smile and open manner made friends of new acquaintances within moments.

Finally, at the far edge of the gathering, Harred spotted Elmar with his foot propped on a sheep pen rail, talking and laughing easily to a group of Dinari clansmen.

Gillaon stopped his pacing. His whole body quivered with suppressed emotion. "With the price we offered and Tellan's backing, I thought we had done it. But the Sabinis have countered brilliantly. I sense High Lord Maolmin's input in this." Gillaon gestured to the parchment and fixed Harred with an anvil-hard stare. "Do you perceive the twofold approach? It is very characteristic of Maolmin. Beyond that, do you sense the subtle threat lurking? It is pure Sabinis."

As his lord's blue eyes bored into him, Harred realized these were not rhetorical questions, but that he was being tested again. His mind raced, marshalling all he had learned since being appointed rhyfelwr, all the while trying to make sense of the particulars he had just read.

"The twofold approach," he began slowly, "is vinegar in one hand and honey in the other." Gillaon's face remained unreadable as he waited for more. "Everything hinges on our partner in the Broken Stone Land," Harred continued, thinking harder than he ever had before, realizing this was more demanding than any sword bout. "We need his ships to get the wool across the Great Sea and break the Sabinis monopoly. But the Broken Stone Land worships the Mighty Ones. That is the vinegar."

Gillaon grunted. "Among the nobility it has long been understood that 'foreign goods' means pagan goods. The Sabinis have used their overseas connections to grow rich by serving as middlemen for pagan and Land trade." He snorted. "Less than a century ago Queen Cullia's kinsmen group was a minor trading house—until they began handling pagan goods, falsely claiming that they had come from lands that worship the Eternal. Ever since Destin Faber and the Founding, the Dinari have been the staunchest in not dealing with pagans."

The number of people milling about increased steadily, adding to the clamor of preparations for the festival. Merchants bustled with last-minute preparations of their wares while women waited impatiently. The younger mothers balanced little ones on their hips while toddlers tugged at their skirts. Older children ran excitedly, weaving in and out, barely managing to keep from colliding with the adults.

Gillaon pondered a moment. "This morning I asked the innkeeper about the woman Lady Mererid brought back yesterday. She is their new Albane tutor. Albanes are renowned for their determination not to deal with pagans." He cut his eyes at Harred. "Your mother's mother was an Albane, correct?"

"Aye, m'lord," Harred said, once again impressed with Gillaon's memory for seemingly minor details. "She never got over her daughter marrying my father."

"Do you see any significance with this Albane tutor?"

"No, m'lord."

"Nether do I, but the last thing we need for our plans to work is these conservative Dinari screaming that the Covenant prohibits trading with pagans."

When Gillaon went silent, Harred continued with his analysis of the Sabinis contract. "The honey is a three-year guaranteed price from a buyer they have dealt with for years, clansmen and followers of the Eternal."

"A bold move! The Sabinis, with Maolmin in the background, already control the selling of Dinari export wool. With this they tie up the source as well and prevent us from buying significant amounts for two more years!" He cocked an eyebrow at Harred. "And the threat?"

"For the next three years, the Sabinis will not buy wool without a contract."

"Exactly. If my Broken Stone merchant cheats me or the Sabinis prevent us from hauling the wool across the mountains, then I cannot repay the gold I have borrowed, and I will be ruined. Then you can be sure that Tellan and any other lords who take our offer will not be able to sell their wool for the next two years." Gillaon smiled thinly. "Their kinsmen will rise up and take their heads."

A group of young clansmen walked by. They eyed Harred and Gillaon with speculation, then strolled on, muttering among themselves. More than one looked back over his shoulder, the undercurrent of tension plain. Everyone knew that important events were afoot.

While Gillaon brooded, Harred thought of his dead grandmother, a praying woman who could quote long passages of Holy Writ from memory. With a clarity that was startling, Harred remembered an incident with her that he had not thought about in years. He must have been ten or eleven at most. One day a week, Gran baked sweet rolls for the grandchildren. That particular afternoon Harred lingered after the others left, talking to her, enjoying the warmth and smells of the hearth. Gran brought the conversation around to the Eternal and read several passages from hand-copied portions of the Holy Book. Then Harred knelt with her. They prayed, and in the Albane manner Harred swore fealty and asked the Eternal to indwell him.

After they rose to their feet and Gran wiped the tears from her eyes, a strange thing happened. Seizing his right arm, she held it aloft and intoned: "Thus saith the Eternal! 'This arm will fight for the Land as did Destin Faber. It will be a mighty tool for my purposes.'"

For a few days afterwards, Harred came by and read Holy Writ with her. Then chores and games with his friends intruded, and he stopped. Gran kept asking him to come again, but he never did. On his first day of formal warrior training, Harred had remembered that afternoon with Gran, but he had not thought of it since—until today.

He brought his focus back. All these layers to what seemed a simple wool sale still amazed him. Knowing more explanations would have to wait until another time, he asked, "What will Tellan do, m'lord?"

"Before hearing your report about the stable last night, I would have said he would have no choice but to sign the Sabinis contract. Now...I wonder." Gillaon pressed his lips together firmly; he slapped his gloves into his hand. "Much will depend on what happens between Tellan and Maolmin at the meeting."

Chapter Twelve

RHIANNON

P HELAN POPPED HIS head inside the door. "Father's back to escort us to the sale. But something is going on. Everyone is in Mother's room."

Rhiannon waited impatiently while Lakenna tied the last of the hair ribbons.

The tutor stepped back, gave one last look, and nodded. "The slippers are just right."

Although her feet were much larger than Mererid's, the doeskin slippers fit perfectly. Rhiannon's tread felt unusually light as she and Lakenna stepped across the hallway to her parents' room.

Mererid stood by the table reading a sheet of parchment. She wore her favorite gown: a dark wine velvet with a high collar of ivory lace. Her hair was swept back off her face, softly twisted behind, and held in place by a silver-topped ivory hairpin.

Tellan, Girard, Llyr, and Creag waited impatiently. High Lord Keeper Branor, dressed in Keeper black, waited as well. His cloak and robe looked clean and ironed. He must have prevailed upon one of the serving girls to launder them for him. The Keeper's eyes flickered between Mererid, Tellan, and Llyr, a faint questioning look on his features.

Rhiannon's stomach tightened at the tense atmosphere. From her father's dark expression, she realized this day—the most important day of the year—was off to a bad start. However, when Tellan's eyes rested on her, his expression brightened. "I scarce believe this is my daughter. Here stands a woman, full-grown and beautiful." He stepped toward her and gave a slight bow. "Though it is a few weeks early, may I bid *Lady* Rhiannon welcome?"

Warm pleasure infused her, momentarily damping her concern at the tension in the room.

Branor gave her a bow as well. "Lord Tellan is richly blessed to have two such beautiful women."

Flustered at the unexpected attention, Rhiannon acknowledged the Keeper's bow with a tilt of her head.

When Creag saw her, his eyebrows climbed and his jaw dropped. Then he spoiled the moment, of course. "Where is your sword? Surely you are—"

"Be quiet, Creag!" Mererid said without looking up from her reading. "I will listen to none of your and Rhiannon's bickering this day."

Tellan turned and gave a bow to Mererid. "Before we go any further, my lady wife, let me echo the Keeper's comments. With you and Rhiannon, the Eternal has indeed blessed me beyond all measure."

Mererid looked up at her husband and searched his face. "Yes, Tellan Rogoth, we are blessed with each other. No matter what happens this day, let us all cling to that."

Then Mererid lowered the parchment in her hands and gazed at Rhiannon. Her eyes moistened. "You are radiant this morning, daughter. You will do all our kinsmen proud."

Rhiannon felt her cheeks heat as she struggled again with an unfamiliar mixture of embarrassment and pleasure.

'Now," Mererid said, her focus returning to the parchment sheet. "Loreteller, rhyfelwr, I would hear your opinions on this."

Girard spoke first. "It seems straightforward. A three-year contract. If we do not accept it but sell to Lord Gillaon instead and his plan is unsuccessful, then for the next two years we will be at the mercy of the Sabinis to purchase our finest export wool at whatever price they choose to offer."

Mererid scanned the parchment again and sighed.

"The Sabinis will not bid this morning," Llyr growled, "but

guarantee a set price for three years whether the overseas markets go up or down."

"The price is the same as last year's," Girard added.

"Which was lower than the year before, which was lower than the previous year," Llyr finished.

Mererid handed the contract to Rhiannon, and she read eagerly. As the advisors had said, Clan Sabinis offered to buy all the top-grade wool the signee could produce for this year and two more at the price of two silvers per standard weight bale. She handed the parchment to Branor.

"Three years hence, when the contract expires," her father said as Branor read, "what then? With no competition, what price can we expect? That is what all our efforts with the Arshessa have been about: to receive true market value, not having these Sabinis take turns underbidding each other!" He shook his head. "I recognize High Lord Maolmin's heavy hand in this."

"Has Lord Gillaon responded?" Mererid asked.

"He consults with his rhyfelwr."

"And the other kinsmen lords? What are their thoughts?"

"They too consult with advisors and will join us when Gillaon arrives at our pavilion."

Mererid swung her cloak on with a flourish. "It seems, then, we will have many guests. The food?"

"My wife is taking care of that, m'lady" Girard said. "All will be brought soon after we arrive."

Mererid slid her arm though Tellan's and looked at the group brightly. "The coming meeting should prove most interesting."

The Rogoth party walked across the stone bridge arching over the Clundy.

"This move by the Sabinis has everyone talking," Creag informed Rhiannon importantly. They walked behind their parents, who were flanked by Llyr, Girard, and Keeper Branor. Lakenna and Phelan brought up the rear. "The contract will change the way wool is sold from now on."

"And who told you that?"

"I read it the same as you!" He frowned at her look of doubt. "Girard helped me some, but I read it! The change is plain if one thinks about it. A known price for three years? Lord Gillaon was concerned. Ask Girard. Llyr spent most his time talking to the other rhyfelwr."

Rhiannon's interest increased, but she spoke with studied casualness. "Lord Gillaon's rhyfelwr? He is young for that, don't you think?"

"Llyr doesn't seem to think so. While we were walking back to the Bridge, Girard asked Llyr what he thought after talking to—Harred?" At Rhiannon's nod, Creag went on. "Llyr said Lord Gillaon knows what he is doing and that Harred is solid."

That gave her a warm glow. They walked in silence for a moment, then Creag lowered his voice. "What did High Lord Keeper Branor say about the winged horrors last night? Are more Keepers coming? I asked Llyr, but he said Father will need to tell me."

She gave him a brief account of the night's discussion. Creag's eyes widened when he heard that Branor was the one who had given Rhiannon's birthing prophecy and widened even more when he heard about Lakenna's role in killing the horrors.

He snorted. "It was all High Lord Keeper Branor. Everyone knows that Albanes don't fight, much less their women!"

"Without Lakenna," Rhiannon hissed, angry at his smug tone, "we all would have been . . . !" She bit back the rest when Mererid glanced over her shoulder at them with a frown.

Faint tentacles of morning mist still hovered above the grass of the festival area when they arrived. The buzz of excitement increased steadily. All present were dressed in their finest. Many called out greetings and best wishes for a successful day as the Rogoth party made its way through the throng. Rhiannon held back to walk with Lakenna and Phelan. She could sense the tutor's excitement at the spectacle before them.

Merchant booths displayed all manner of expensive wares: bolts of brightly colored cloth, jewelry, glassware, oil lamps with fancy globes, leather goods, dyes, exotic spices from distant lands with unpronounceable names. All were being eagerly picked over by wives and older girls, though hardly any buying was going on at the moment. Later, once the sales had concluded at noon and gold and silver coins had traded hands, they would drag husbands and fathers back to show them the latest thing their family must have.

Noting how Lakenna's head swiveled back and forth as they walked, Rhiannon asked, "Do Albanes have festivals?"

"Yes, but not the size of this!" Lakenna gestured at the booths. "There is more here than we have at three of our festivals put together." She gave a wry grin. "Admittedly, Albanes have the deserved reputation of squeezing coins until they cry out. I guess many merchants choose more fertile fields."

"Just wait until we go to the Fall Gathering," Creag said over his shoulder. "It is three times bigger than this. Those who have been to the festival during the Raedel in Ancylar say that is ten times bigger than that."

Lakenna shook her head in amazement.

Beyond the booths were places set aside for contests of strength, agility, and other skills. Targets for archery, knife, spear, and ax throwing dotted the area. In addition, ropes ringed off spaces for engagements with wooden practice swords. That event took place in the afternoon with heavy wagering on the outcome as kinsmen and family groups backed their favorites. Rhiannon sighed, keenly missing the weight of her sword hanging from her waist.

In the very center of the fairgrounds, women and servants tended large cooking pits where sausages and thick pieces of bacon roasted. Fat drippings sizzled on the hot coals, sending up rolls of gray smoke heavy with spicy aroma. Ove, the Rogoth ancient household servant, was in her glory as she moved her spare frame about the pit, gesturing with her cane, ordering her workers about with a no-nonsense attitude and a sharp tongue. Rhiannon's stomach rumbled as they passed young boys and girls scurrying back and forth carrying wooden platters to clansmen and merchants doing business among the bales of wool.

Opposite the pits stood the pavilions of the three kinsmen lords. Their colorful banners fluttered on poles high above the throng.

"Ours is the red one on the right, the white ram with triple spiral horns," Phelan pointed out proudly to Lakenna as he held on to her hand. "The middle banner, the sky blue one with the pair of grasping lions, is the Fawr kinsmen. They are the largest in the Clundy valley, and Mother says Lady Aigneis never lets anyone forget it."

"Phelan!" Rhiannon chided.

"The black banner on the left," he went on unfazed, "the one with the red raven, belongs to the Leanons. Lord Baird is old; he and grandsire were great friends. When Lord Baird drinks too much and no women are around he curses every other word and tells better stories than Girard—"

"Phelan Rogoth!" Rhiannon said, giving him her sternest glare as they entered through the folded-back opening of the Rogoth pavilion. "That is enough!"

Lakenna winked at Rhiannon. "I do look forward to meeting all these, Master Phelan. You can tell me more later."

Carpets had been laid out to floor the pavilion. Under Girard's wife's direction, several children hustled about placing platters of food on two long tables covered with red and white linens. The platters contained steaming sausages and bacon, cheese, nuts, and loaves of dark bread. Each end of the tables held stacks of pewter plates, mugs, and pitchers of hot punch.

The first person to greet the Rogoth party as they entered was Bowyn Garbhach, a sheepherder and the head of the largest of the three family groups that made up the Rogoth kinsmen. He was the acknowledged spokesman for the other two and, as such, was always present when the wool was sold. A thick bear of a man, he possessed a large head and flat nose with widely spaced nostrils. His short-cropped hair was peppered with gray. He nodded respectfully. "M'lord, m'lady. The Eternal's blessing on you on this day."

Tellan and Mererid echoed the greeting. Mererid hurried on toward the tables.

Bowyn remained in front of Tellan. The family head's voice took on an edge that Rhiannon had not heard from the man before. "'Tis a buzz about the grounds about this Sabinis offer, m'lord." He shifted his feet and squared his shoulders. "Me and the other family heads are a'wondering how you'll be responding."

Mererid halted and turned back; a slight frown wrinkled her brow. Branor and Lakenna stopped side by side. They eyed each other, then edged apart. Lakenna moved to Rhiannon's side. Branor stood a pace from them, hands clasped behind his back.

Tellan regarded the family head calmly. "Tell me what the others are saying."

"Lord Tellan, Lady Mererid," Bowyn began gravely, as if he had not just greeted them. He raised his chin. "Lord Tellan, Lady Mererid, begging your pardons, but I'll be having a hard time explaining to my people why we did not take this offer." He removed a parchment from inside his shirt. "Once this is signed and sealed, it becomes like a letter of credit. It can be brought to any money-lender as collateral. Coins to buy more stock, clear more pastures, expand production. Many of us have children grown and married and longing for their own start. This gives them a way."

Tellan, Mererid, Girard, Branor, and Llyr exchanged looks. Looking back at Bowyn, Tellan said, "And where did that insight come from?"

Mererid moved closer until she stood shoulder to shoulder with her husband. "Yes," she said, eyes glittering, "matters of trade, letters of credit, and dealing with moneylenders normally are handled by nobles. Pray tell us, kinsman, whom do we thank for this information?"

Bowyn did not flinch. "High Lord Maolmin. One of his men

came at first light this morning and brought me to him. The High Lord read me this contract and explained about letters of credit and how they can be used." He met Mererid's gaze levelly. "It may be nobles' dealings, m'lady, and I may be naught but a simple sheepherder, but I understood it right enough."

"A simple sheepherder!" Tellan edged in front of Mererid, who took a small step back. "Always have I relied on your advice. Bowyn Garbhach's wisdom has kept me from more mistakes than I care to think about."

The tension in the family head's stance relaxed a bit, and a pleased expression flickered across his features.

While Rhiannon noted how the respect and man-to-man inflection in her father's voice was bridging the gap threatening to open between them, she recognized the glint in her father's eyes and understood well the reason. One of the sacred duties of a clan lord was to shield his kinsmen from any nobleman who might use his position to take advantage of commoners. But the reverse was equally revered, and it was a grave breach of clan protocol for Maolmin to have undermined another lord like this.

Girard's and Llyr's feelings on the matter were plain. The loreteller's mouth was a thin slash with turned-down edges. Llyr regarded Bowyn with a piercing stare that would have had a lesser man's feet shifting in a nervous fidget. Branor's face was unreadable.

But Rhiannon knew Bowyn would not be cowed easily. He had strapped on his sword innumerable times and ridden at the head of his men when Tellan called the Rogoth kinsmen out to deal with lawbreakers and other matters of clan justice.

The family head nodded gravely at the compliment. "Aye, m'lord, you've always given my opinion due consideration. That makes my duties easier. Most matters that come to me, I see solved myself. But when that's not possible and I say I'll take it before you, my people know they will receive justice."

Girard's wife had finished the food preparations. She came up to the group and stood by her husband, but then she seemed to detect the tense atmosphere and she frowned.

Bowyn scrubbed a thick hand through his hair. "Difficult times these last years. We've all felt the pinch, and the extra coins from Lord Gillaon's offer would be welcome indeed. But as followers of the Eternal, many of us have strong feelings about our wool going to the Broken Stone Land."

Lakenna suddenly stiffened as she stood beside Rhiannon. That revelation affected Branor as well. He went deadly still, and his forehead broke into small frown lines.

"We deal with Lord Gillaon Tarenester, Clan Arshessa," Tellan replied evenly. "What he does with his property after he purchases it is between him and the Eternal."

The big shepherd's eyes flicked knowingly to Branor, then back to Tellan. "High Lord Maolmin desires all Dinari to remain true to the Covenant. He is most concerned about the Arshessa and their new friendship with the pagans. Like the High Lord explained this morning, the Sabinis contract will give us a way to increase our flocks and realize extra coins while staying true to the Covenant and not angering the Eternal. That's a strong consideration."

Branor's frown deepened. He opened his mouth, then closed it.

Tellan's reserve cracked; his lips whitened and his nostrils flared, but Mererid gently put a hand on his elbow. With visible effort, the Rogoth lord regained control.

"I hear you, kinsman," he said. "First, will you help in dealing with letters of credit and moneylenders? I have not asked for your participation before because that is how my father and his father before him did. As I said, I have need of your wisdom."

Bowyn rocked back and forth on his heels as he tried unsuccessfully to keep another pleased expression off his face. "I am at your service, m'lord."

"Excellent. Now, advise me how should I deal with a family member who approached me with a matter before coming to you."

Bowyn frowned. "And who was that? Send him to me, and I will set him straight on our line of authority."

"Just so." Tellan's voice hardened. "Next, advise me how to deal with High Lord Maolmin about his interference with one of my family heads."

Bowyn's rocking ceased. He glanced from Tellan to Mererid, then Girard, Branor, and Llyr. The silence stretched. Finally, Bowyn cleared his throat. "I . . . I did not see it in that light. The High Lord requested my presence, and I went."

"In the future, if any person requests your presence before any lord—Maolmin, Gillaon, or any other lord but myself—you escort that person immediately to me. If he resists, even a warrior or nobleman, you truss him belly down on a horse and send it trotting right along. I will be responsible for the consequences." Tellan jutted his chin forward. "Fail to heed me in this, Bowyn Garbhach, and you will encounter my wrath."

Bowyn bobbed his head. "Yes, m'lord. I will—"

The large Fawr party burst noisily into the pavilion, filling it with their presence. As always, Lady Aigneis led the way. Slender and dignified in a light green gown and a necklace of emeralds and white opals, she eyed the pavilion's furnishings with a faintly disapproving air.

Tellan took no notice. "And if it is my decision to sell our Rogoth wool to Lord Gillaon for half again more than the Sabinis offer?"

Kinsmen lord and family head stood face-to-face with locked eyes. Tellan's expression was hard enough to chop wood.

Finally a slight slump came to Bowyn's shoulders, and Rhiannon knew the challenge was past. "As always, m'lord, we follow your lead."

Tellan clapped the man on the shoulder.

"Lord Tellan," Branor said, worry evident behind his eyes. "I must urge you in the strongest possible terms not to go against High Lord Maolmin in this matter—"

In came the much smaller Leanon party. Even this early, Lord Baird had his ever-present tankard. Rhiannon had rarely seen the man without it.

"Lady Mererid," Lakenna implored, reaching for the woman's

arm. "Any involvement with pagans may have ramifications for Rh—"

"Not now, Teacher," Mererid interrupted firmly, her eyes on the guests. "Duty calls. Time to discuss the Sabinis offer." She put a welcoming smile on her face. "Rhiannon, come with me. Remember," she murmured, as they made toward the front of the pavilion, "Lord Baird is oldest, so we greet him and Lady Lola first, then the Fawrs. Don't allow yourself to be flustered by Lady Aigneis's subtle insults. She is a master at it."

Rhiannon glanced through the open flap for Lord Gillaon. He needed to be here as well. Then she noticed the Arshessa lord and Harred walking around the cooking pits, heading toward the Rogoth pavilion. She felt her cheeks begin to flush. Annoyed, she made herself concentrate on searching the milling crowd for the Sabinis wool merchants or Maolmin, even as her stomach roiled at the thought of being face-to-face with the High Lord again.

That thought fell away as the two Arshessa entered. Harred was tall and hard. His piercing eyes and broad shoulders loomed above Gillaon's short, barrel-chested frame. Her stomach fluttered warmly this time.

Taking a deep breath, Rhiannon composed her features and joined Mererid in greeting their guests.

Chapter Thirteen

BRANOR

L ORD BAIRD LEANON plopped the pewter tankard on the table where the kinsmen lords and their advisors were eating. An unadorned, gray-haired man with a hard, round belly, Baird possessed a shrewd face born to command. He wiped his mouth with the back of his hand. "Four silvers for each standard-weight bale?"

"That is my offer," Lord Gillaon said. "My coin chest will be brought here at noon by my men."

Baird lifted a fat sausage link from a wooden platter and bit off half. Chewing slowly, he fixed the Arshessa lord with a penetrating gaze. "And if your wagons go tumbling off a mountain ledge on the trek across the Ardnamur Mountains, will we be seeing you next year?"

"If I buy your wool this year, I will be back to buy every bale you produce next year and the year after." Gillaon leaned forward across the table, blue eyes glittering. "This I pledge on my honor as lord of the Tarenester kinsmen of Clan Arshessa."

Branor's breath stilled in his throat. The silence around the table was profound. Everyone regarded the short, barrel-chested Arshessa with the gravity his statement deserved. The man was pledging his life and fortune—and that of all Tarenester kinsmen—that the wool would be delivered to the Broken Stone Land. And as Lord Baird had hinted, a lot could happen traveling those high peaks.

Lord Seuman Fawr belched and wiped greasy hands across

his tunic before rummaging into a pocket and bringing forth an ornate ivory toothpick.

"Well and good, Lord Gillaon; well and good," he mumbled around his probing. He had a sweaty face and bulging eyes. "Honor in business dealings is so seldom seen these days, revolving too much around ink on parchment. And we would welcome a business alliance between Clan Dinari and Clan Arshessa. However," he glanced to his wife over at the ladies' table, "I must talk with the Sabinis and, of course, High Lord Maolmin before making a decision."

Seuman squinted at the tip of the toothpick, then wiped it clean with his lips. "It has been years since our High Lord blessed us with his presence at our modest little sale here in Lachlann. Surely we should take advantage of that fact." A half smile played at the corner of his lips as he looked at Tellan. "Don't you agree, m'lord?"

Although Tellan maintained a bland expression, a fire burned behind his eyes. "I too look forward to discussing the state of wool prices with our High Lord and his Sabinis friends. Especially since we know what others can pay and still make a profit."

Gillaon nodded formally. "I will leave you gentlemen to discuss this with your High Lord and the Sabinis when they arrive." He smiled without warmth. "I will be happy to join that discussion should you ask."

Gillaon and his young rhyfelwr took their leave and walked to where the noble ladies and their attendants were gathered around another table a few paces away. Lady Mererid greeted the two Arshessa with a warm smile and started the introductions.

It took all of Branor's experience to keep his emotional turmoil off his face. It had been so clear when he left Shinard and rode here. To gain the seventh knot he needed the support first of Abbot Trahern and then of Maolmin; then with those two in hand, the Sabinis would see the handwriting on the wall and would cast their support for him as well. But the good abbot had made it clear his vote depended on this with the Rogoths being settled in a satisfactory manner.

116

Had Trahern known about this enmity between Tellan and Maolmin? Without question! And yet the abbot had let Branor ride into this without a hint of warning. *He will pay,* Branor vowed silently. But not if he didn't tie the seventh knot! He knew he could survive without Trahern's vote, but he *had* to secure Maolmin's! High Lord Keeper Nels had Clan Olablath firmly in his pocket, and the Arshessa were leaning his way. Branor already had his own clan, the Dniestear, and the Landantae on his side. Only the Dinari and the Sabinis remained uncommitted.

And, as if the stew needed more spice, a siyyim seems to be prowling.

Branor observed the other nine men standing around the table. He stood beside Girard, who was by Tellan with Llyr on his lord's left. Lord Baird was next, accompanied by his loreteller, a fragile, wizened man with rheumy eyes. Lord Seuman Fawr had brought both his loreteller and rhyfelwr. Also present was Fawr's son, Peibyn, a pimply faced youth with a mass of curly brown hair and blond stubble on his chin.

Lord Baird took a long draught from his tankard, then turned to Tellan. "Your father was like a brother to me, and you a son. He and I treated each other fairly every time we shook hands, as have you and I. May I speak to you as he would?"

"I would have it no other way, my lord."

Baird smothered a belch. "I have no love of Maolmin Erian, but it has been a puzzle to me about your continual ill will toward this man. From the moment you and I met with him to acknowledge his High Lordship right after he helped contain that ungodly pagan mess, you two have been like cur dogs stalking stiff-legged and bristled-backed around each other, begging for an excuse to tussle. I fear personal dislike fuels too much of this. Maolmin is greatly respected by the other High Lords. What is it between you two?"

Branor wondered the same. He had first met Maolmin briefly at the last Raedel. The man was impressive. Haughty to be sure, but intelligent and well spoken. He had skillfully used what clout the small Dinari clan possessed, coupled with his own strong personality, to ink agreements that had more than one High Lord grumbling afterwards. Branor felt certain that when the Dinari High Lord did finally arrive here at the Rogoth pavilion, things would get interesting.

Tellan sighed. "I have no handhold on it, Lord Baird. I feel…I *know* deep inside that the less the Rogoths have to do with Maolmin Erian, the better."

Branor's insides twisted. He felt walls closing in on him. How could he tread this quicksand between Tellan and Maolmin? For the first time in years, he found a heartfelt prayer moving within him. *Dear Eternal, show me what I must do!*

"And yet you seek to deal with the pagans of the Broken Stone Land?" Baird probed Tellan.

"I seek the best for my kinsmen and see no problem dealing with pagans one step removed to receive a fair price—instead of being cheated by clansmen who claim to follow the Eternal."

Baird took another draught. "I counsel to use Gillaon's offer to pry a higher price from the Sabinis. If they stand firm on this initial offer, then I will join you and sell to Gillaon." Baird pursed his lips, then fixed Tellan with red-rimmed eyes. "Hear me now, Tellan Rogoth, and take this to your bed tonight and wrestle with it. An ill wind blows when a kinsmen lord marks a trail that harms his High Lord at the Raedel. Much more goes on there than our wool. Maolmin makes great use of his association with the Sabinis to gain concessions on trade matters from the other clans that benefit us all. Be careful that you do not receive a silver coin in one hand while paying out a gold in the other."

As a murmur ran around the table, Branor found himself agreeing with Baird. Beyond Tellan's hindering of his clan's maneuvering at the Raedel, the thought of the Rogoths being associated with the pagan Broken Stone Land—albeit one-step removed—continued to nag.

Surprisingly, or maybe not, the Albane tutor had seemed upset about this as well. He searched the pavilion and found the woman standing away from the noble ladies' table, talking to Phelan and Creag. The older boy kept turning his head and squinting toward the men.

As Lord Baird's loreteller rambled on at great length about a minor point in the Sabinis contract, Branor let his eyes wander around the table. Most of the men looked as bored as he was. Then he noticed Peibyn Fawr ogling Rhiannon as she stood with the women. The young man's expression was that of a person with a raging thirst contemplating a dipper of cool water.

Rhiannon must have felt the scrutiny. She turned toward the men's table, caught Peibyn's gaze, and then quickly turned back to the ladies. Nervously, she raised her chin and smoothed a hand across her hip as if reaching for a sword.

Branor glanced back at the young man—and started. He could *see* inside Peibyn! A pulsing black swirled around the lad's core, radiating throughout the entire body.

Shaken, Branor looked down, his senses recoiling from the foulness. After a moment, he looked up again. The color was more vivid. Branor *knew* he saw unbridled lust and that it ruled Peibyn.

Branor glanced around the pavilion, and his eyes came to Lakenna. He found he could see inside her soul as well. A dark red wound throbbed inside the Albane tutor. The raw pain of it took Branor's breath. *How can she live with that hurt?*

Stunned, Branor realized he was seeing with spiritual eyes! Not physical appearance, but into the true self.

Even as he grappled with that revelation, something else began building. His guts roiled and a faint nausea rippled through the pit of his stomach. Sweat beaded his forehead; it seemed as if hot oil trickled over him. Something was approaching.

Concerned, he glanced again at Peibyn. But the vision was gone. The lad listened calmly to his father talk. He looked again at Lakenna, but could see her pain no more. Branor checked Rhiannon. She was eating and talking easily to Lord Gillaon and his tall, broad-shouldered rhyfelwr. As Branor watched, all three burst out laughing.

The feeling continued to build—then Branor's blood chilled.

Could this be what Keeper Alock had said in *Night Watch* about his ability to sense the approach of the Mighty Ones' creatures? Branor's pulse hammered; his nausea grew. He did not know how he *knew* evil approached, but he did.

Would the siyyim loose winged horrors in broad daylight with Rhiannon surrounded by clansmen?

Why not? The long-held belief of night-only appearances had been shattered yesterday.

And what better time than with everyone unarmed except for daggers!

He pivoted smartly away from the table and headed outside to check the sky. Striding purposefully to the front of the pavilion, he came upon the Albane woman, who was standing rigidly, dark eyes wide, slender hand gripping her throat in alarm. She looked as green around the gills as he felt.

Their gazes met, and Branor realized she was sensing the same thing.

Chapter Fourteen

RHIANNON

"A TRAGEDY ABOUT THE hlaford," Lady Aigneis said. The other women around the table murmured agreement. "But, of course, you will rebuild." Aigneis had a thin face and a long, pointed nose under which lurked the faintest hint of a mustache. She took a dainty sip of hot punch. Rings on every finger glittered. "Surely the new one will be . . . better." She raised her eyebrows in query. "If you need help with larger designs, I will be happy to send our master carpenter."

"I am sure it will be rebuilt along the same lines," Mererid said. "Already our families have promised more than adequate materials and labor." She lifted her cup to her lips. "But Tellan will not squander Rogoth resources for display."

"I see." Aigneis cast eyes on Rhiannon. "An interesting gown. So similar to the one you wore continually last year, Mererid."

Rhiannon's palm itched for her sword. She forced her fingers to unknot and hoped her faced showed a calm she was nowhere near feeling. Was she supposed to respond to that barb?

Mererid came to her rescue. "Rhiannon is growing so fast, it is impossible for the seamstress to finish a gown before remeasuring is necessary. I thought one of mine would be best." She glanced around the table. "I think it was the right choice."

"Oh, yes," gushed the wife of the Fawr loreteller. Plump with rosy cheeks and a perpetual twinkle in her eyes, it was impossible to be around her without smiling. "Rhiannon is so beautiful this morning. This gown is perfect. Surely all the young noble men at the Presentation to Prince Larien will be anxious to meet her."

Aigneis's lips tightened. She shot the woman a frosty glance, then took another sip of punch.

Lady Lola Leanons said, "Baird's nephew once removed is already interested in Rhiannon. I had thought all that boy was interested in were horses and hunting." Lola was in her late sixties and thin to the point of frailness. "And too, Aigneis, from the way your Peibyn's eyes popped out of his head when Mererid and Rhiannon greeted us, he may well be first in line to speak to Tellan after the Presentation."

Rhiannon's skin crawled remembering the formal introduction and Peibyn's eyes on her. Looking at the ladies gathered around the table, her jaws ached from the effort to keep anger off her face. Was this what she had to look forward to the rest of her life? With the overwhelming importance of the wool sale looming, why were they spending so much time on this inane discussion?

Aigneis laughed gaily. "Peibyn may show interest today. Tomorrow, someone prettier will come by and he will be off again. Certainly, many young men already talk about Rhiannon and her prowess with a sword." She arched an eyebrow. "Tell us, Mererid, does Tellan foresee that training as help or hindrance to courtship?"

That did it. "Sparring is an activity many find enjoyable, Lady Aigneis," Rhiannon said. "Of course, if it goes too far, blood may be spilled."

Aigneis's eyebrows rose to her hairline. Her cup clattered on the saucer, and punch sloshed out.

Mererid blinked with a mixture of wonder and delight.

A gurgling sound emerged from the loreteller's wife. She covered her mouth and cleared her throat several times.

"Well...I..." Aigneis sputtered, drawing to her full height, eyes flashing.

Calmly, Lady Lola took a sip of punch while giving Rhiannon a sharp look of reappraisal.

A seasoned campaigner, Aigneis rallied quickly. She smiled, and it reminded Rhiannon of winter frost. "I must—"

"Here comes Lord Gillaon," Mererid said brightly, relief plain in her voice. "Aigneis, let me introduce you and Lola. He is most charming."

Gillaon proved her correct. Smiling and radiating energy and purpose, he bowed and kissed Lola's hand, then did the same to Aigneis. He chatted with them as his sharp gaze darted around the pavilion, missing nothing. Harred stood at his right shoulder. Aigneis's eyes kept traveling across the warrior's tall frame.

"Greetings, Mistress Rhiannon," Lord Gillaon said after finishing with the other ladies. He brought her hand to his lips. "I have never seen you more beautiful."

She acknowledged his compliment with a tilt of her head. "You do me too much honor, kind sir," surprising herself as Mererid's lessons came easily off her tongue. "I pray the Eternal's blessings on the day's endeavors." Responding to his gentle pressure on her elbow, she allowed him to guide her a few steps from the table, glad to be away from Aigneis's dark glare. Harred moved with them.

Gillaon regarded her with keen interest. "I am pleased yesterday's tragic event has left no pall over you." The intensity of his stare increased. "If there is assistance we Tarenesters can lend with...anything...rest assured we will provide it." He paused. "I understand you have met my rhyfelwr, Harred Wright."

Harred nodded formally. "Mistress. How fares the stallion?"

"Much improved. We checked him before leaving the Bridge Across. Please convey my thanks again to Elmar."

"Of course."

A wave of disappointment swept her as she searched Harred's face. He did not have the same look in his eyes as had been there for that brief time last night. Had she imagined that?

Girard's wife waddled in at the head of a group of young boys and girls bearing more trays of food. Rhiannon's stomach rumbled at the smell. Girard's youngest daughter, a giggling, gapped-toothed girl, brought plates with sausage, bacon, and slices of buttered bread. Rhiannon and Harred each took a plate while Gillaon declined.

Rhiannon watched expectantly as Harred lifted a sausage, but he hesitated halfway to his mouth. He glanced at Gillaon, whose face was a blank mask. Touching the end to his tongue, Harred quickly returned the link to his plate.

"Are you sure you don't want any of this Dinari sausage, m'lord?" he deadpanned. "It is seasoned to your liking." At Gillaon's snort, they all three laughed out loud.

"Our seasoning takes getting used to," Rhiannon chuckled, more pleased than ever to be away from the ladies. "The bacon is safe."

Nonetheless, the big warrior took a small, cautious bite of the bacon before risking a larger one. After swallowing, a slow grin split his features. "I will save the sausages for Elmar. He is coming to appreciate your food."

Movement at the front of the pavilion caught her attention. High Lord Maolmin had arrived. Even with all her preparation for this moment, Rhiannon's stomach curdled as she remembered the encounter with Maolmin in the stables.

The High Lord and his party of three entered just as Branor was hurrying out—but the Keeper halted in mid-stride as if hitting a wall. He turned and regarded Maolmin with a puzzled frown.

The noise level dropped noticeably as every eye in the pavilion was drawn to the High Lord's commanding presence. Darkly handsome, his patrician face possessed an ageless quality; he could have been in his early forties or ten years older. Hesitating for a moment in silent acknowledgment of the attention, Maolmin moved toward the table where the ladies were hastily joining their kinsmen lords.

There was no High Lady at Maolmin's side. His wife had died mysteriously fifteen years previous, soon after he became High Lord. Rhiannon had heard it muttered the death had been suicide. For whatever reason, Maolmin had not remarried.

His party was small for a clan High Lord. The rhyfelwr was

a wiry, gray-haired man whose strutting walk and darting eyes reminded Rhiannon of a banty rooster. Next came the new lore-teller, dressed in the multicolored vest of his office. Rumor had it the man was as silver-tongued a storyteller as was Girard. High praise indeed. A young woman was on the loreteller's arm. From the close resemblance, Rhiannon figured her to be his daughter. She was raven-haired, small in stature, and wore an unadorned yellow gown. She moved with an understated grace that made Rhiannon envious.

Rhiannon glanced back at Harred. Irritation flashed when she saw his focus riveted on the woman. Miffed, Rhiannon looked closer at the loreteller's daughter. They were about the same age. She didn't seem all that attractive. And she was much shorter.

I'd fit better on Harred's arm...

Rhiannon raised her chin in irritation. *It does not matter where this Arshessa's interest lies! He can have that woman—or any other—once our wool is sold. That's the most important thing.*

Even so, the inward pang did not go away.

She was sick of inner turmoil! Life had seemed so simple a few weeks ago. But then the winged horror attack. And now this strange feeling for Harred and the encounter with Maolmin. Along with the tension over the wool! *Why* didn't the Eternal make everything right?

She glanced around the pavilion. Was the Eternal interested in any of this? Was he involved in the Land now as he had been during the Founding? And if he wasn't, how could she—or anyone—serve him? Or the Covenant?

It has been given to us to battle the Mighty Ones' efforts to end the Covenant and reestablish their rule here in the Land, Keeper Branor had said.

But how? When? And at what cost?

She brought her thoughts back to the coming confrontation between her father and their High Lord. Branor was back inside the pavilion and standing next to Lakenna. The Lord Keeper's mouth hung open. Lakenna's face showed growing apprehension as she followed the Dinari High Lord's progress across the pavilion.

Maolmin greeted Baird and Lola Leanons first, talked to them pleasantly for a time, then moved on and stopped in front of Tellan and Mererid. All in the pavilion held their breath while straining forward to hear. But the three had only smiles for each other. After kissing Mererid's hand and nodding formally to Tellan, Maolmin said something that elicited a burst of laughter. They chatted affably before the High Lord turned to Seuman and Aigneis Fawr. The collective sigh of relief was audible.

More movement at the front of the pavilion caught Rhiannon's eye. The three Sabinis merchants came striding in. Ryce Pleoh led the way with ponderous dignity. A large double chin spilled over his collar, and an impressive belly stuck out from the folds of his plum-colored cloak. A heavy chain of gold links fastened the cloak around his shoulders. His hairline receded sharply on both sides, leaving a narrow strip of dark hair in the middle.

Half a step behind strode Heorot Seamere. He was of late middle years with coarse white hair cut close to the scalp. The skin on his face was deeply pockmarked. He wore a cloak of dark velvet with a silver-framed emerald clasp. Sihtric Averill was last: narrow shoulders hunched, bald head scrunched down into his neck as if he expected the roof to fall at any moment.

The three merchants fell in behind Maolmin's party, greeting the lords, ladies, and advisors with a practiced combination of deference and familiarity.

Three mercenary bodyguards sauntered to a halt just inside the shade of the pavilion. The biggest one sported a three-day growth of black whiskers. Hooking his thumbs into his broad leather belt, he slowly perused the crowd. His gaze crossed Rhiannon, Gillaon, and Harred, then cut quickly back. His eyes honed in on Harred while his lips curled in a semblance of a smile, though to Rhiannon it seemed more like a wolf showing its teeth.

Then the man's eyes slid to her and remained a long, lingering moment. She felt stark naked. Peibyn's looks were one thing, but this was something beyond—an appraisal so raw and frank

126

it caused her face to heat in embarrassment. *How dare this commoner look at me like this!*

Unbidden, her hand dropped to her sword hilt—which was not there, of course! But even as her hand grasped air, she realized she would be no match for the man. If her father or Llyr saw this—but Harred had. His plate clattered onto hers as he brushed by, a low growl rumbling deep within his throat—

"Well, Mistress Rhiannon," Lord Gillaon reached a hand to restrain Harred. "It seems the business of the day is about to begin." He squeezed Harred's arm. "Agreed, rhyfelwr?"

Harred actually quivered as the mercenary turned contemptuously away and began talking to one of his fellows. Finally, the tension in Harred's body relaxed somewhat. "Yes, m'lord," he said hoarsely, hands clenching and unclenching several times. "My apol—"

"No apologies, kinsman. I saw it, too." Gillaon's voice hardened. "Just recognize the tactics and remember what we are about. That one's accounting will come another day." After Harred's reluctant nod, Gillaon turned to her. "Agreed, Mistress? Unfortunately some things must wait—"

"Lord Gillaon," Lord Baird's ancient loreteller said in a raspy voice, "my lord and lady request the pleasure of your company."

Gillaon nodded, then followed the loreteller, leaving Rhiannon and Harred standing alone in the middle of the pavilion.

In the resulting silence, she watched Harred struggle to keep from looking at the guards. Finally, she blurted, "Are all Arshessa rhyfelwrs as young as you?" then cringed at how foolish the question sounded.

Harred shook his head. "No, Mistress. Most are seasoned warriors like Llyr. Actually, this trip is my first experience as rhyfelwr. Whether I will remain so after we return home, I do not know."

Another stretch of silence. They watched Lord Gillaon talk to the Leanons and the Sabinis merchants mingling among the advisors.

When she thought Harred had regained control, she lifted her chin in the direction of the three guards. "Thank you for..." She let her voice trail away.

Harred looked full at her. His eyes twinkled as his features split into that slow grin. "You are welcome for..."

Her insides turned to mush. She foundered under a cascade of unfamiliar emotions. For some reason it was hard to breathe. Her knees seemed weak. What was happening to her?

Then she noticed how his eyes kept darting over her shoulder. Turning that way, she saw the loreteller's daughter. The woman stood quietly by her father, who was in animated conversation with Ryce Pleoh. The fat merchant's eyes traveled up and down the raven-haired maiden, taking in every contour and curve.

As Rhiannon watched, the woman glanced toward Harred, caught his eye, then quickly looked back to the discussion. The expression flickering across her face spoke volumes.

Rhiannon's inward mush coalesced into hot anger. *They can have each other! Why do I still hold this Arshessa's plate like some servant!* She turned to hand it back—

"Greetings, Mistress Rhiannon," High Lord Maolmin said, suddenly before her. "This must be Lord Gillaon's rhyfelwr. Please introduce me."

She kept from dropping the dish, but it was a near thing. Heart galloping like a runaway horse, she turned to her High Lord—and was greatly relieved not to see the same look in his eyes as had been there in the stables last night. "Greetings, High Lord," she managed, pleased at how calm her voice sounded.

Maolmin Erian radiated power. He had thick dark hair and coal black eyes that seemed to look inside her. A blue embroidered coat laced at the waist emphasized wide shoulders that appeared to be straining to burst through the garment. His hands were large and powerful with fingers easily twice as long as hers.

She introduced him to Harred, then watched the two men measure each other at a greater length than had happened at the stables. They were well matched. Where Harred was half a hand taller, Maolmin was more solid, with a grown man's heft.

Where the young Arshessa was raw strength and ability still being refined, the High Lord possessed a self-confident air that came from long experience and many vanquished foes.

Finally, Maolmin broke the staring match. "Lord Gillaon must see great potential to select such a young man for rhyfelwr."

"I believe, High Lord, it is more confidence in his own abilities."

Maolmin continued to regard Harred like an artist deciding where to place the first brush strokes on a canvas. "A Tarenester won the sword bouts handily at the last Arshessa Gathering, correct?" He cocked a dark eyebrow. "Would that skilled swordsman have been you, Harred Wright?"

Harred bore the High Lord's penetrating gaze. "I had that honor, High Lord."

"And the year before?"

"That one, too." Harred gestured deferentially. "But it is well known how you won the Dinari bouts ten years running before allowing others a chance. That is a feat of arms none is likely to surpass."

Maolmin tilted his head in acknowledgment. Then he turned back to Rhiannon and regarded her silently. "How do you feel about your family's dealings with the Broken Stone Land?" His lips twitched in what seemed amusement. "Are the Sabinis so bad that you must deal with pagans?"

"As you know," Rhiannon said carefully, "that decision lies with my father and his advisors."

The hint of a smile continued to play around Maolmin's mouth. Then, abruptly, his manner and his eyes changed. Maolmin's body seemed to swell; his black eyes rippled. "I believe you will be among those eligible to be presented to Prince Larien at our Gathering."

"Yes, High Lord," Rhiannon said, unnerved. "I will be of age by then."

"Have you been to Faber Castle?"

"No, High Lord."

"Have you met the prince?"

"I have not had that honor."

"Of course not," Maolmin stated with finality.

A chill crept into Rhiannon's bones even as sweat popped out on her forehead. She swallowed again, trying to work moisture back into her mouth. Maolmin's dark eyes bored deeper into her mind, and she felt herself drawn into—

"Mistress Rhiannon," Lakenna said shakily, stepping rudely in front of the High Lord. "I must talk to you, Mistress."

Rhiannon sagged at the release. She took a deep, shuddering breath.

The skin on the tutor's face was taut, her eyes concerned. For a commoner to interrupt two nobles talking was unheard of, and Lakenna's expression showed she was aware of that.

"Be gone, woman!" Maolmin's fingers curled like talons. "You have no part of this!"

Lakenna paid no heed. "Mistress Rhiannon, I must talk to you...alone." The tutor's mouth pressed firmly together and sweat shone on her upper lip.

Those milling about the pavilion watched with interest but politely maintained their distance. Lord Gillaon talked to Lord Baird and Lady Lola. A few paces beyond, the three Sabinis merchants had cornered Tellan, Mererid, and the two Fawrs, though Aigneis was doing most of the talking.

Branor walked up on wobbly legs and halted next to Harred. The Keeper seemed to be still struggling with an inner combination of shock and disbelief as he gazed at the High Lord.

Harred kept looking over to Gillaon, then back to Maolmin.

"I say again, woman," Maolmin growled, his eyes peering over Lakenna's shoulder at Rhiannon. "This is a clan matter. Leave us!"

As if pushed, Branor stumbled forward to stand next to Lakenna. He seemed surprised, then shook himself. "High Lord," he said, gently easing Lakenna aside. He turned to face Maolmin. "It is a pleasure to see you again. May you walk in the Eternal's light."

As she looked over Branor's shoulder, Rhiannon could have

sworn something *moved* inside Maolmin's eyes. The black orbs finally left her face and rested on the Keeper.

A warm hand enclosed hers. It was Lakenna, who smiled and gave an encouraging squeeze. Then the tutor's lips firmed, and she turned to Maolmin and Branor.

Clan High Lord and High Lord Keeper stood face-to-face. Harred stepped back, a puzzled frown creasing his features as his eyes darted back and forth between the two men.

Maolmin was again the cultured noble. "Greetings, Your Grace. I heard a rumor this morning that a six-knot Keeper was in Lachlann—staying in one of Tellan's rooms." His expression hardened. "But I discounted it since I received no notice of such an august visit."

"I came for private consultation with Abbot Trahern. You are aware a major change looms." Branor's hand toyed with the knots on his belt. "After the abbot, my plans were to call on you—in a purely unofficial capacity, of course. You are aware of how much..." Branor swallowed, "...of the rewards an early commitment can reap."

Maolmin studied the Keeper. "I must deal with Lord Tellan's association with agents of the pagan Broken Stone Land. I am sure you agree that is an ominous development. I will have your support in taking sense to Tellan, correct?"

"Pagan?" Puzzlement joined the mixture of emotions dancing across Branor's face. Then, seemingly to himself, "Why would that—"

"Keeper," Tellan broke in, "is there a problem?" He had left Mererid with the merchants and the Fawrs and made his way across the pavilion.

As if in a daze, Branor's head swiveled to Tellan, back to Maolmin, then back to Tellan. The Keeper's mouth opened and closed twice before a word came out. "Problem?" he croaked. Beads of sweat popped out on his forehead, and a nauseated look appeared. "I am sure there must be a way out of this...dilemma."

"Yes," Maolmin almost purred. "Surely the three of us can

reach an understanding that does not violate the Covenant."

Tellan's faced hardened. "Is that why you meddle with one of my family heads behind my back?"

A smile played on the corners of Maolmin's lips. "I was acting more as a follower of the Eternal than as High Lord. As such, I felt I could take a few liberties. Now that High Lord Keeper Branor is here, he can address that aspect of this treacherous deal with Lord Gillaon."

While Branor gaped at Maolmin in bewilderment, Rhiannon's heart thumped madly at the way her father and Maolmin regarded each other. If looks were swords, both men would be bleeding. From the light blazing in Tellan's eyes, she had real fear he verged on launching himself at Maolmin.

The High Lord waited, a faint smirk on his lips, huge hands relaxed at his side. His blue coat swelled, and Rhiannon could almost hear the seams popping.

Harred must have sensed the same. He took a half step backward, right hand groping for a sword hilt as his eyes darted between the two men.

Then a thought struck Rhiannon. Could this be the High Lord's plan? Was this the reason behind last night in the stables and now—to goad Tellan into an unheard-of personal attack on his High Lord? Then all Rogoth lands and titles would be forfeit.

Thankfully, Girard and Llyr appeared at Tellan's side.

"Easy, m'lord," Llyr warned in a low voice.

"Yes, m'lord," Girard murmured. "You cannot do this."

Tellan came back from the brink. The light in his eyes dimmed a bit. He took a deep breath.

Rhiannon let out her pent-up breath as well. She noticed everyone crowded shoulder to shoulder around them, watching and listening.

Maolmin smiled. "Lord Tellan, I am curious. Why do you seek to go against both my wishes and our clan's long-standing obedience to the Covenant and begin trading with the Broken Stone Land?" He shook his head sadly. "Even before Destin Faber, the

Dinari and the Broken Stone peoples were rivals. Our ancestors worshiped the Mighty One of the North while theirs followed the Lady of the West—as they do to this day."

Branor's eyes widened. He regarded Maolmin in puzzlement.

Tellan said, "I have seen how the Sabinis do business." He lifted a hand to the three merchants, who were standing nearby. "Across the Great Sea they trade regularly with pagans, including those from the Broken Stone Land, and yet you do not accuse them of breaking the Covenant. The Sabinis and their friends grow richer while my kinsmen grow poorer. I will have no more of that."

Maolmin's face darkened. "What do you mean?"

"As kinsmen lord, my duty requires me to seek the best offer I can. Ask your Sabinis friends to explain why Lord Gillaon can pay two silvers more than they and then transport the wool across the Ardnamur Mountains instead of barging it down the Clundy River, and still make a profit."

Maolmin turned to the Sabinis.

Ryce Pleoh stepped forward. He gave a greasy smile. "Markets go up and down, as I am sure my lords are aware. We are at the mercy of overseas demand." His pig eyes darted among the three sets of kinsmen lords and their advisors. "Droughts, floods, wars, rumors of wars, pestilence—all these can drive prices down. Many times we have sold at a loss due to factors beyond our control. Worse, ships set sail and are never heard from again." He looked directly at Lord Gillaon. "After such setbacks, those who overextend themselves by paying too much for their goods go bankrupt."

"I have pledged my honor," the barrel-chested Arshessa stated coldly, "that I will be back next year and the year after. Against that, you offer parchment and ink."

"One's honor lasts only as far as the grave."

Gillaon's hand dropped to his clan dagger. "Is that a threat, Sabinis?"

Raising his hands in mock apology, the fat merchant said, "You misunderstand me, m'lord. I simply meant even honor has its limits." He turned back to Tellan. "By joining our resources, we three can spread risks that honor may not be able to withstand. If the markets are down, we lose money; if they are up, we realize a better profit as our reward." Ryce pursed his fat lips and looked meaningfully at Tellan. "Without this contract the price we can pay and the amount we purchase next year will be volatile."

Lord Baird Leanon had been drinking steadily, his lined face growing more flushed by the moment. Finally, he thrust his pewter tankard at Ryce, causing a cupful of mead to slosh out and splatter the carpet. "I hear a threat woven into those fine words, don't I just." At Ryce's protest, Baird growled, "Don't be insulting my intelligence, Sabinis. We understand what you are saying."

He lifted the tankard, drained it, then wiped his mouth with the back of his hand. Then he pointed a bony finger at Sihtric Averill. "Let us say I decide not to sign your contract, and that Lord Gillaon's proposal with the Broken Stone Land proves unsatisfactory. And further, for reasons beyond your control, next year you cannot give us a fair price or even purchase our wool at all." The lines around the kinsmen lord's mouth deepened; his eyes flattened. "In that case, Sabinis, I would ask how you plan to get the wagonloads of wool you do purchase out of these highlands."

Sihtric Averill stepped forward. He regarded Baird, his nose wrinkling as though smelling something rotten. "We depend on kinsmen lords to maintain safe passage through their lands—and for High Lords to deal with any not fulfilling their historic duty." The weasel-faced merchant's mouth quirked. "We are confident High Lord Maolmin will not be found lacking should his authority be challenged."

All faces turned to Maolmin. The High Lord pulled his eyes away from where Branor and Lakenna stood next to each other talking—or rather, Lakenna was whispering to Branor, who still wore a dazed expression.

Maolmin seemed distracted for a few heartbeats, then brought his focus back to the discussion. "This has strayed from my purpose from coming. Let me state my position, then I will leave you to strike your deals." He paused and gathered his thoughts, and when he spoke, Rhiannon was struck by the difference between this manner and the much more ominous one she had just seen.

"Beyond the Covenant," he began, "I ask everyone to consider the balance of power between the six clans. We Dinari must ally ourselves with a larger, stronger clan or risk domination by the others. Hard choices must be made. This contract with the Sabinis meets with my approval. It will bring greater prosperity to each kinsmen group while benefiting the clan as a whole at the Raedel. And I say again," he looked quickly at Tellan and then the others standing around him, "it allows us to remain under the covering of the Covenant."

With that, the High Lord and his party took their leave.

To Rhiannon, the sale an hourglass later proved blessedly anticlimactic. When the three Sabinis wool merchants remained firm on their initial offer, her father and Bard Leanon accepted Lord Gillaon's offer of four silvers per standard weight bale. Maolmin watched silently, his face set like stone. Seuman Fawr, after much hemming and hawing, sold to the Sabinis.

Chapter Fifteen

HARRED

THE WAGON MASTER maneuvered the quid to the other side of his mouth, then spat a streak of dark liquid onto the grass. "Tell your Lord Gillaon that nobody loads wool until the day after the sale. That way everybody has a chance to enjoy the fair. His wool will be right here tomorrow."

It was past noon. Groups of empty wagons dotted the area farthest from the activities. Hobbled mules grazed the hillsides, enjoying a rare day of rest. Harred and Elmar stood beside the wagon.

"You'll haul it then?" Harred asked, trying to keep the elation off his face.

They had done it: the wool was theirs! At least the Rogoth and Leanon wool. More importantly, the Sabinis monopoly was broken. Now Harred had to arrange to transport the wool safely to Lord Gillaon's hlaford and then across the Ardnamur Mountains to the Broken Stone merchants. Accomplish those two tasks satisfactorily, and surely the position of rhyfelwr would be his permanently. Harred fervently hoped so. After being by Lord Gillaon's side these days, the role of a common warrior would never be satisfactory again.

The wagon master raised a ham-sized hand. "Didn't say nothing about hauling." He propped a muddy boot on the spoke of a wooden wheel, worked his quid, and spat another liquid streak. "Never been to Arshessa land, much less across the Ardnamurs—"

"Not all the way. Only about half."

"I heard you the first time." He cocked an eyebrow. "What will we haul back? Can't make money hauling one way empty."

"Furs and amber. Silks. Some jewelry and precious stones. You will receive a tenth."

Greed flared in the wagon master's eyes. "You have the King's License for all that?"

Harred answered the way Lord Gillaon had instructed if the question was asked. "Your job is to haul the wool and then return with the other. The rest is in our hands."

"You have a guide for the mountains?"

"We be passing through areas I hunted as a boy," Elmar said.

The wagon master chewed furiously, lost in thought. His face was the color of old leather; deep crow's-feet wrinkles surrounded his eyes. "We'll be a long way from anywhere in those mountains. A lot can happen."

"My men and I will be with you every step, there and back," Harred said.

The wagon master spat and chewed.

In the distance, Harred heard the din of happy clansmen. Their wool was sold, and the fair was in full swing. Eager buyers crowded merchants. Horse races and contests of strength and skill were underway. Acrobats, jugglers, acting troupes, and puppeteers plied their specialties as well.

Struggling to keep his features blank, Harred waited impatiently while the wagon master continued his contemplation of Lord Gillaon's offer. If this one refused, then it was to do all over again with someone else—and that much longer before he tracked down Breanna in the crowd.

He had to find out why she had taken his breath away at the Rogoth pavilion. Never had a woman affected him like this. How could she so easily remove from his mind all thoughts of Rhiannon, who was clearly the more physically attractive of the two? He wanted to pick Breanna up, bring her face level with his, and gaze into those warm dark eyes from now until the sun went down—

The wagon master pushed away from the wheel and stood straight. "Tell your Lord Gillaon he has a deal. We will start loading his wool at first light."

"She be so short," Elmar said, head swiveling as they both dodged a group of running, giggling children, "we could walk right by and never know. You sure she be here and not back at the inn?"

"She's here," Harred stated with more confidence than he felt. They had checked the merchant booths, the sword bouts and archery area, and the cooking pits. Nothing.

"You eat anything yet?" Elmar half trotted to keep up with Harred's long strides.

"Not enough to matter. You wouldn't believe all that was going on inside that pavilion. I understood about a third of it." Harred kept scanning the crowd. There!—no, it was a young girl about Breanna's size wearing a yellow dress.

"Have one of these." Elmar unrolled a cloth containing two fat links of sausage.

Harred took one. Elmar took the other but waited expectantly.

"Are they any good?" Harred asked, as if he didn't know what would happen if he bit into it.

"As good as your mother's," Elmar said with exaggerated innocence.

"You've tried them?" Try as he might, Harred's lips begin to twitch into a smile.

Elmar realized it wasn't going to work. "These Dinari," he snorted in disgust. "You've never seen such laughter. My mouth still be burning."

They came to a large crowd standing in a semicircle around the puppet stage. Shrew Wife was onstage by herself, grousing loudly about her husband. The crowd roared at a particularly tart comment.

"I'll look to the left," Harred said. "You take the right." They scanned the crowd once, then again. Breanna was not among the puppet watchers.

"If they be at the inn, packing to leave..." Elmar said.

Harred sighed. She had to be here among the crowd where he could talk to her without her father intervening. At the inn, that would be next to impossible.

Then it hit him. "Have you noticed any loretellers?"

They found the loretellers in a quiet area behind the sprawling Fawr pavilion. Four loretellers, Breanna's father included, sat in a row of chairs listening to apprentice loretellers. A smallish crowd had gathered behind the chairs to listen, but Breanna was not among them. Harred slapped his leg in frustration. At least when he did find her, she would be away from her father.

Then movement at the back of the Fawr pavilion caught his eye. Breanna entered carrying a tray of food and a mug. Watching her approach, Harred was again struck by the smooth grace of her movements.

As Breanna came closer, her gaze came to rest on him. She smiled full at him, and Harred felt the impact down to his toes. She stopped behind her father's chair, handed the food and drink over his shoulder, then stood directly behind him.

A new apprentice got up and began the familiar tale of Destin and Meagarea at the first Rite of Presentation:

> Unmarried when he took the throne, Destin knew he needed a queen and a male heir. He summoned all six High Lords. "Choose from among your noble women those you think suitable for a queen. Look not for comeliness alone. Seek maidens of pure heart and high intelligence who love the Eternal as I do..."

Breanna eased back a step and caught Harred's eye. Lowering her gaze, she made her way toward the edge of the small gathering.

Harred moved to join her. His feet hardly seemed to touch the ground. His heart pounded; his mouth was dry. How could a young woman—girl, really—have this effect on him? He sensed she possessed a sweet nature, but what had twisted her around his heart like no female before?

> When you have gathered these maidens, I will come and have you present them...

He halted before her, and Breanna's dark eyes searched his face. With her head tilted up to his height, her expression had an openness, a questioning wrapped in vulnerability.

> I will trust the Eternal to show me the one he has prepared...

Again, Harred found himself tongue-tied. This was his chance, perhaps his only chance. But with her before him, he faltered. This was not the way of courtship. But something rare and precious was happening, and he could not ride away without an effort. She knew nothing of him and his family. Or he of hers. What to do? Something inside urged total honesty. And for the first time with a female, he found himself doing just that.

He stepped to her and led her a small distance back from the gathering. "I looked everywhere. I feared I would never see you again. Then it came to me about the loretellers."

"I knew you would come." Breanna continued to regard him with that same open vulnerability. "During my prayers this morning, I felt strongly this day would not end without us talking."

Harred's heart surged. He should have tried honesty sooner. He heard himself saying, "I intend to ask your father's permission to bring suit." Then he cringed inwardly, afraid she would think he was too forward.

But Breanna simply nodded. She cocked her head sideways. "Do you serve the Eternal, Harred Wright?"

For a moment, he was unnerved. "When I was a boy," he

began, "my grandmother and I prayed. I bowed the knee to the Eternal and, uh..." he groped to remember the phrases, "asked him to indwell me. I pledged my life...I pledged to serve him."

Breanna's liquid black eyes searched his face. "My mother says once the Eternal puts his mark on a person, it cannot be removed. His presence seemed particularly strong on you in the stable. I have wondered what happened before my father and I came in."

"High Lord Maolmin had just left. He was talking to Lord Tellan's daughter...I interrupted them." *And came within a heartbeat of being run through*, he finished silently, still in awe of how fast the man had whirled and drawn his sword.

At the mention of Maolmin, a shadow crossed Breanna's features. "My father has changed so much since accepting the High Lord's offer. Mother begged him not to, but he went against her wishes. She cannot bear to be in Maolmin's presence. That is why I accompanied my father on this trip."

Then Harred realized how quiet it had become. He turned back to the loretellers.

Breanna's father, Abel, was striding toward them. Beside him waddled Ryce Pleoh, the big-bellied Sabinis merchant. The crowd had turned around and was watching with open curiosity.

"Leave this Arshessa!" Abel demanded, his thin face pinched. "And come with me. Now!"

Angered at the tone, Harred stepped between Breanna and her father. "I hear concern in your voice, loreteller. Do you fear I seek to dishonor you daughter?"

The look on Harred's face halted Ryce in his tracks.

Abel came two strides further—but no closer. "Breanna. Now!"

As Breanna stepped around and went to her father, Harred raised his voice until it carried to the rest watching and listening. "The reason I ask, Loreteller Abel, is to make sure before we leave this place that honor has been satisfied. If you have ought against me, state it now before these witnesses that I might respond in like manner."

Ryce fingered his cloak and sneered. Abel was opening his

mouth when the bandy-legged Rogoth loreteller hurried up.

"I am Girard, Lord Tellan's loreteller. Is there a problem...Harred, I believe it is?" He turned to face the loretellers and other people coming. Elmar's was the only friendly face. "This Arshessa is here under Rogoth covering," Girard said. "If there be ought against him, Lord Tellan will see justice done." Then under his breath to Harred, "If there is, I'll have your guts for bowstrings."

"I have treated the maiden with honor, loreteller."

Girard studied him long and hard. Then, seemingly satisfied, he spoke formally. "Loreteller Abel Caemhan, have you fear this man has harmed your daughter in action or word?"

Abel looked like he could have bitten a nail in half, but he turned to Breanna and followed the time-honored formula: "Breanna en Erian de Caemhan, do you have ought against this man? If so, state it plainly and know he will not be able to touch you now or ever."

"No, Father," Breanna said quietly, eyes downcast. "He was telling me he wanted to present suit. I would be hon—"

"Enough." Abel turned to his fellow loretellers. "Be it known that I have accepted bride price for my daughter from Ryce Pleoh. She will meet him at the Maiden Pole during the Dinari Presentation Gathering and there be married."

Breanna's expression showed surprise. Abel took his daughter by the elbow, and they left. Ryce smirked at Harred and followed.

Harred felt as if a mule had kicked him. This frog-eyed, sow-bellied Sabinis would carry Breanna to the bridal bed? A delicious heat begin to build. *Not while I draw breath. But what can I do?* Heartbroken, he watched her walk away.

The rest of the people drifted off to other activities. Girard remained with Harred and Elmar.

Girard said, "My sympathies, clansman. Breanna seems a rare one."

You don't know the half of it, Harred thought with deep sadness.

Her father had spoken, and Harred knew he stood little or no chance to change that decision.

Or did he?

"Loreteller, does Dinari honor allow for a *Wifan-er-Weal*?"

Girard's eyes widened, then narrowed. "Be not hasty, clansman. It has been generations since a *Wifan-er-Weal* was allowed."

"My great-uncle fought one for his wife. She was Landantae. Clan rivalry made that the only way."

"With Breanna, there will be ramifications."

"How so? Is Dinari lore that different?"

"I will explain." Girard's voice deepened as he took on the familiar loreteller cadence: "*Wifan-er-Weal* is from the Old Tongue and translates roughly as 'Marriage-or-Death.' This trial by personal combat takes place when two clansmen present suit for the same maiden. If she and her father agree on the same suitor, then the other is driven from the Maiden Pole by stoning. If, however, the maiden chooses one suitor while her father declares for the other, then our lore allows the maiden's choice to demand a *Wifan-er-Weal* to settle the matter."

"It is the same with Arshessa," Harred said.

"Undoubtedly. Among Dinari, the next step is for the maiden to reaffirm her assent. If she refuses, that ends it, and she marries her father's choice. Only if she agrees and her other suitor does not withdraw does the combat take place."

Girard spread the fingers on one hand. "Anyone demanding a *Wifan-er-Weal* must vanquish five warriors, one after the other without pause. The maiden's kinsmen lord is in charge and chooses the first three warriors. They must come from the father's kinsmen group, and since the bride price is equally divided among those three families, many vie to be chosen. The original suitor or his designate, as I am sure will happen with Ryce Pleoh, is the fourth." The loreteller paused, then went on with more gravity. "The fifth must be the maiden's kinsmen lord."

"In personal combat," Harred said, "all rank is left behind once swords are drawn."

144

"Of course," Girard agreed. "Typically, if the suitor makes it that far, the kinsmen lord steps aside and the rite is over." The loreteller's expression firmed. "Hear me out. If you decide to attend our Gathering and bring suit for Breanna Caemhan, understand that once her father became High Lord's Maolmin's loreteller, the Caemhans transferred their fealty to Maolmin, and he—Maolmin—is now their kinsmen lord."

Harred's stomach turned, remembering the unbelievable quickness in the stable and the *power* that had rolled off the man in the Rogoth pavilion.

"Given the fact," Girard was saying, "that the maiden will be going against his own loreteller's wishes, coupled with his well-known association with the Sabinis in general and Ryce Pleoh in particular, I do not see Maolmin Erian stepping aside."

Girard regarded Harred frankly. "Examine yourself, son. Do you know this woman well enough to risk death? Do you know that you are truly compatible, or is this merely the wishes of youth rushing in your heads?" He shook his head and sighed. "If Breanna agrees to a *Wifan-er-Weal*, and your skill is such that you vanquish the first four warriors, know that your fifth and last opponent will be the man universally acknowledged as the greatest swordsman alive."

Chapter Sixteen

BRANOR

THE OUTLINE OF the distant hills began to separate from the gray sky as dawn fought its age-old struggle against darkness. With exquisite slowness, the rugged landscape around Kepploch unveiled itself.

The first landmark the watcher recognized was the pale streak of the lane winding up the steep slope to the monastery's front gate. On either side scattered throughout the meadow indistinct shapes, with etiologies heretofore limited only by the watcher's imagination, revealed themselves as half-buried boulders thrusting through the grass. In the sky above, the growing light brushed vivid shades of yellow and rose-red on the low-hanging clouds as morning claimed its triumph.

High Lord Keeper Branor sat on a simple three-legged stool before the open window of his second-floor room, chin on hands and elbows on knees, watching this daily rite of nature unfold.

It was deathly quiet. Two turns of the glass previous, perched on the same stool and looking out the same open window, he had heard the coughs, throat clearing, and scuffs of leather-soled sandals on the flagstone path below as the monks of Kepploch made their way through the inner courtyard to the chapel. Morning prayers would be over soon, and the monks would be returning to the courtyard to file into the dining hall and break their fast.

Branor's stomach growled, but he ignored it. A large covered tray with food and a silver pitcher sat on the writing desk behind him. Delivered to his room last night shortly after his arrival back from Lachlann, it remained untouched where the novice had placed it.

After the encounter with Maolmin at the wool sale, Branor had realized he had to distance himself from the Rogoths to have any chance at the High Lord's endorsement. Mind still reeling from all that had happened, Branor had told Tellan that Rhiannon was safe enough for the moment, and then he had fled back to Kepploch and the solitude of his room.

Stark and unadorned, with a white plaster ceiling and dark wood paneling, it was perfect for contemplation. The narrow bed—its feather mattress the only concession to his rank—had a chest at its foot and wall hooks on either side for clothes. The writing desk and its stool were the only other furniture.

It had been a dark night of soul-searching. A night for harsh truths. Now, in the early light of day, Branor needed more of...something.

Any moment now a novice would be knocking on his door to relay Abbot Trahern's invitation to join the brethren in the dining hall. Branor ground his teeth. Trahern would also inquire, ever so politely, about yesterday's events.

Branor stood abruptly, muscles stiff, joints creaking. Removing his cloak from its hook, he threw it across his shoulders, walked to the door, and pulled it open. After checking both ways to make sure the hallway was empty, he headed to the stairs, boots loud on the polished wooden floor.

Boots, not sandals. Another marker—as if he needed more—of just how far removed he was from his days here at Kepploch. He could not remember the last time he had been awake two glasses before dawn, much less up that early to *pray*.

Descending the stairs, he hurried across the marble floor of the front hall, out the arched entrance, and down the walkway to the ironbound gate. He lifted the metal latch and pulled the gate open with a rusty squeak of hinges.

A stiff breeze billowed out his cloak and molded his robe

around his legs as he headed up and over the nearest ridge. At the bottom bubbled a small stream. He stepped nimbly across on exposed stones. A few paces beyond rose a knoll crowned by a circle of trees. The knoll had been a favorite meeting place of seven monks, of whom he had been the acknowledged leader.

"The Mighty Seven" they had called themselves, eager in their youth and foolishness for opportunities to take on the Mighty Ones. Branor had just tied the third knot and become the teacher of novices—five of whom had joined his effort to rediscover the outpouring of spiritual power that had occurred during Destin Faber's time. The seventh member had been a much older monk. Narlan his name was.

Besides Branor, Narlan was now the only one of the seven still alive—if the monk's current existence could be called that. Narlan was a mumbling shell of a man with a mind damaged during the encounter with the siyyim called forth by the former Dinari High Lord. Upon arriving the day before yesterday, Branor had seen the monk wandering about the monastery in an awkward, quick-stepping walk while carrying on a never-ending, disjointed conversation with himself. Thankfully, Narlan had given no evidence he'd recognized Branor.

Breathing heavily—yet another marker of his fifteen-year journey—Branor crested the top of the knoll. The circle of trees was taller than he remembered, the shadows long in the early morning sun. Birds flittered about from limb to limb, making wing noises and chirping.

He stood silently, soaking in the peace of the place, seeing the faces of the five dead novices. Their excitement of those early meetings had been contagious. Each new nugget unearthed from their study was endlessly discussed and debated. With Lady Eyslk's help, they obtained clan writings dating back to the Founding. They spent hours sifting through them and other old writings—some Eternal-based, some pagan—learning about the Mighty Ones and lesser demons: siyyim, lilitu, rabisu, and how it seemed that the lesser beings served the greater.

Of all the accounts in Kepploch's library about encounters against the creatures of the Mighty Ones, the Mighty Seven's favorite was the six-hundred-year-old *Night Watch*. Keeper Alock's simple words written in the beauty of the Old Tongue had held them enthralled.

While no record was ever found of his entering the Order, it seemed Alock spent his adult life in the fertile valleys of the Olablath clan traveling a circuit of farming villages doing the work of Keepers: blessing marriages, dedicating babes, comforting the sick, burying the dead, and educating those who expressed a desire to know more of the Eternal. Then a group of pagan worshipers who had gathered at an ancient shrine were somehow able to call forth the Mighty One of the East. An outbreak of winged horrors followed. For weeks the families who remained faithful to the Eternal lived in terror as the creatures destroyed their homes once darkness fell.

Alock beseeched the Eternal. The Eternal answered with a call to battle. With fear and trembling, the peasant Keeper and a few faithful followers marched into the night and met the enemy. Alock's fantastic tale of supernatural endowments that flowed through him as they fought desperately with farming tools and makeshift weapons seemed taken straight from the legends of Destin Faber and his anointed sword, *Asunder*. And as in the battles of the Founding, Alock's engagements with the East's fanatical, self-mutilating worshipers were fights unto death. In the moonlit fields, no quarter was asked or given.

After the defeat of the Mighty One of the East and the disappearance of the horrors, Alock rejoiced that most of the pagan worshipers repented, returned to the Eternal, and remained faithful. In the treatise's last sentence, the Keeper stated the greatest joy he had ever known was in being faithful to the Eternal's call to carry his light into the face of that darkness.

Brave words and even braver deeds. How Branor's blood had soared when he'd read them years ago, believing he was called to such a duty.

He sighed inwardly as the morning sun warmed the knoll. Those days seemed a lifetime ago. The battles he fought now were far subtler, though just as profound in their way. Certainly the weapons employed were far different from the crude farm implements Alock's peasants used.

How many more balls can I continue to juggle? I must have Maolmin's support! But how can I ally with the overwhelming foulness I saw in him—

Taking a deep breath, Branor reestablished control. He had dealt with clan lords and even fellow high-ranking Keepers who could tie the truth in knots, sell it to three different rivals, and make each think he was receiving a precious gift. His main rival for Ruling Keeper was a master at it, and Maolmin fit that description as well. Branor had no problem with that and welcomed the exchange of wits and hard bargaining Maolmin was known for. It was this other...aspect...of the High Lord that had kept Branor awake all night.

Fifteen years with every move planned. Everything focused and in subjection to the bright shining light of his ambition. Every small victory providing more fuel for the next one; every pitfall avoided providing more experience to sidestep the next one. Fifteen years without a major mistake—and Maolmin Erian the last victory needed.

Why was I given what must have been the lost gift of spiritual discernment those few moments? What am I to do with that insight? How can I use it to gain the seventh knot?

He had no answer to those questions. He had come too far to stop now. Nonetheless, he had the sense of being in a vice while someone slowly tightened the screw. A few more turns, and all of Branor's carefully laid plans would shatter like a clay pot squeezed in the vice.

And there was Rhiannon and winged horrors of the night! That had to be tangled up with the girl's birthing prophecy. She was about to come of age. Was that the reason for the sudden return of evil after no known attempts since her birth? This could become a major distraction. A great temptation to protect the daughter to honor the mother's memory. *Is that why Trahern thought he could maneuver me into responding?*

Then Branor fought mounting disgust at his cynicism. *Have I degenerated this far?*

No, truth said, Trahern was correct to suggest I go. With all that study, he knows I am the best prepared—or the least poorly equipped—to respond to Rhiannon's need. What is going to happen with that? How long will it take?

That Albane tutor seems to know what she is about. She sensed the same thing about Maolmin. An Albane...?

He shook himself. *Deal with one problem at a time.*

He gazed at the circle of trees and grass on top of the knoll. It was the same, yet different. The grass in the open middle was only a handsbreadth tall, but it was the undergrowth, or rather the lack of it, that struck him the most. No brush or vines grew around the base of the tree trunks. No fallen branches or leaves marred the pristine purity of the scene. Clearly someone was expending a great deal of effort with a scythe, ax, and rake to keep this area clean.

And flowers. Branor noticed an area at the edge of the trees bursting with color. Red, gold, yellow, pink. Walking closer, he noticed the lush foliage of the plants in addition to their flowers. Someone must be carrying water and compost up the knoll for the distinct groupings outlined with rocks—

Five groups of flowers.

Branor felt as if a cold hand gripped his heart. For nights on end after hearing the manner of their deaths he had woken from nightmares, drenched with sweat and his heart pounding. Those dreams still visited him occasionally even now.

The Mighty Seven's last few meetings here on the knoll had been different. His zeal had been draining away. He had been afraid to admit to himself—much less to the other six—an inward questioning of the ultimate worth of their quest. Where was the power? Surely after their hard work the Eternal would pour out his power and send them forth to battle evil as he did Destin Faber and the Founders. The Land still had many pockets of pagan worship. The need was there.

Gradually, Branor had seen his hubris, realizing that he, at least, had been saying, in effect: "See me, Eternal? See how hard I have labored? Now, bless me with your power!" Frustration had turned into anger when it did not happen as quickly as Branor thought it should. Then came the final blow.

A visiting monk had appeared, asking to study with the group. But it had been they who had become the students. The new monk's knowledge of the Mighty Ones and their worship and the supernatural creatures that did their bidding had the ring of truth. He had quickly become such a valued member of the group that Branor had asked him to come and pray during Eyslk's difficult labor. And then . . . that night. It was grief over that beautiful lady's death that had driven Branor away from Keploch, so he had not been there when the five others had died . . .

Branor disciplined his thoughts. The present had problems enough without borrowing from the past. But then, as had happened several times during the night, the last conversation he had had with Abbot Trahern before leaving Keploch all those years ago bubbled up in Branor's mind.

"The Eternal has placed a special call on you, Branor. I have no doubt he will use you greatly. But know this: Those the Eternal calls for great purposes, he first breaks. That way they know to rely on his strength instead of their own." The abbot had raised his bushy eyebrows, compassion in his eyes. "Do not run from your breaking, Branor. The longer you run, the harsher it will be."

If this trap he found himself in now wasn't a type of breaking, then Branor missed his guess. He had survived his flaws and miscalculations to rise to the point where the seventh knot was almost within his grasp . . .

Someone was coming up the knoll. Branor turned and was not surprised to see Narlan trudge over the top carrying a water bucket in each hand. The bottom of his robe was soaked and the hem was covered with dirt and bits of grass. His face was a mask of determination as he half-stumbled, half-walked across the grass toward Branor and the flowers. Water sloshed out of the buckets with each step.

Ignoring Branor, Narlan set the buckets down at the leftmost group and used his hands to pour water lovingly around each plant. After ladling out the contents of both buckets on that group, he stood quietly, head bowed.

Feeling like an intruder, Branor came up and reached down for the buckets. "Here, I will fetch the next—"

A gaunt, long-fingered hand caught his arm, and he was jerked up with surprising strength. Angered, Branor opened his mouth—but the retort died stillborn at the incensed gleam in Narlan's eyes.

"Don't you dare!" Narlan hissed. "You were not there!" A vein pulsed prominently on his forehead. "You, our leader, whom the Eternal called and gifted for that battle! The summons came from the High Lord requesting our help. He feared a great evil was loose in the Land again. We six were sent to determine the level of need." Narlan's mouth worked wordlessly before he continued. "When we arrived, suddenly it was before us. We were thrown into battle without you, our teacher who had—"

"Enough!" Branor spat hoarsely. He jerked his arm free. "I will hear no more of this!" But his feet remained planted in the grass. Cold dread froze his breath as again and again the faces of those young novices flashed before his eyes. All killed during the effort to bind the siyyim. All killed except Narlan, who had been damaged in the mind. Disaster had been averted only by—

Maolmin Erian!

Branor's stomach heaved and hot acid seared his throat. He swayed, dumbfounded at how blind he had been. *Why didn't I put it together sooner?*

But in the next breath, he knew the answer: He hadn't wanted to see it. He hadn't dared face the consequences of acting on what he seen *inside* Maolmin at Lachlann. He had been too busy thinking about his own advancement.

O dear Eternal, he wept inwardly, haunted by the specter of those poor, unprepared youngsters coming face-to-face with the unbound *evil* inside—

His mind reeled as the full impact washed over him. Maolmin was indwelt by a siyyim! That's how it had been vanquished—by taking up habitation inside him! A siyyim had sent winged horrors to kill Rhiannon! *That* was the reason for the tension between Maolmin and Rhiannon at the pavilion! *That* was the reason the Albane tutor had moved rudely between them and stubbornly refused to stand aside until Branor had finally given in to what had seemed a steady push from an unseen hand and stepped between them himself! All the while wondering desperately how to salvage—

"Thus saith the Eternal!"

Branor started. Narlan stood straight and tall, his eyes full of a holy fire.

"Hear the word of the Eternal, you who strut so proudly with your six knots while your fingers itch to tie the seventh! Woe to you who takes the Eternal's purpose and twists it for your own advancement. While you feed your ambition, the Covenant weakens and so the Mighty Ones stir, seeking to reestablish their rule upon the Land."

Narlan flung out his arm, his index finger almost touching Branor's breast. "To every person come moments to decide, clear forks in the road. This day the Eternal places such a fork before you. Will you continue to walk the path of your ambition? Will you strive to call evil good while trying to mold darkness into light?"

The words cut Branor to his joints, penetrating to the very marrow of his bones. Part of him wanted to run and hide, but a deeper part demanded he stay.

Narlan lowered his finger. "Or will you give your ambition to the Eternal and seek his purpose so you can become a vessel to pour his love and protection into the lives of his people?"

Something slammed Branor's knees. Dimly, he realized it was the ground. He swayed back and forth, barely able to remain upright.

Narlan turned his palms outward and finished softly: "A desperate battle for the soul of the Land looms. Mighty warriors are needed. The decision lies before you. Choose you which path you will tread."

Grass blades cut Branor's face and dirt filled his mouth, muffling the sound of his bitter weeping. Tears ran hot on his skin as the ruin of fifteen years lay in shattered pieces around his prostrate body.

Chapter Seventeen

LARBOW

THE SUN WAS down in Inbur, and the Three Sisters Tavern held a lively crowd. A minstrel strummed a lyre and sang in a high-pitched raspy voice barely heard above the talk and laughter. The aroma of roasting lamb floated from the kitchen. Serving maids in ankle-length dresses and white aprons wove through the blue haze of pipe smoke, bringing food and drink to a steady stream of new patrons. Which was the reason Larbow had specified this hour.

He watched the two Sabinis merchants make their way to a corner table. The fat one pulled out a dowel-backed chair and settled ponderously into it. The older, white-haired merchant remained standing. Heorot Seamere glanced around the crowded room, his pockmarked face shouting to any who cared to notice that he was looking for someone.

Larbow sighed. White Hair should know better. But clansmen understood nothing of this. And so much the better. If they did, it would have hindered Larbow's ability to pick them clean and then melt away unnoticed while stupid clan warriors scurried like yapping dogs unsure of the scent.

Lifting his mug to his lips but not drinking, Larbow followed the fat one's eyes across the room to a table where two men in dark brown leathers sat with barely touched mugs. One of them, a large man with coarse features and a heavy beard shadow, met the merchant's gaze and shrugged slightly.

Just so. Larbow had marked the two as bodyguards the moment

they had sauntered in a bare quarter glass previous. Quarter of a turn! Not enough time to get a feel for the surroundings. Larbow had been here a full glass before the agreed upon time.

He made eye contact with an attractive young woman three tables down. She wore a deep blue linen dress with a high lace collar. The man sitting next to her had on a wool coat expensive enough for a prosperous tradesman. Holding the woman's gaze, Larbow raised a forefinger from the mug held before him, then cut his eyes back to the coarse-featured man's table. Nattily signaled confirmation by bringing a silk handkerchief to her lips. She turned to her companion and whispered in his ear. He smiled and placed his hand on hers.

Should anything happen while Larbow talked with the Sabinis, and the two bodyguards moved to intervene, Nattily and her erstwhile husband would bring out their blades and have both bellies slit open before the strongmen knew what happened.

That three quarters of a glass may get you killed, clansmen.

Not that Larbow expected trouble. His father—may the Wind Giver receive his spirit—had dealt with the white-haired Sabinis several profitable times in the Land. But this excursion from the Rosada homelands was final training for Nattily and two new raiders: the one posing as her husband and a fuzz-cheeked youth who looked three years younger than his last name day. Accordingly, Larbow decreed tonight's meeting done with more attention to detail than the situation warranted. The youth was outside watching the street with an older Rosada warrior.

A serving maid scurried by with a tray perched on her shoulder and a pitcher in her other hand. She stopped at Nattily's table, slid off two steaming pewter-ware plates and a loaf of bread, refilled each mug, and hurried back to the kitchen. Nattily removed a linen bundle from her leather bag, unwrapped forks and spoons, and she and her companion began eating with proper Land manners.

Perhaps too proper for a tavern, Larbow decided even as he grunted overall approval. Later, at the inn across town, all would gather to discuss tonight's meeting. This minor detail and a few others would be discussed as they followed the maxim of Rosada raiders since time immemorial: we become trees in their forest.

Larbow glanced at the tavern doors. One of the two outside would step in and signal if the Sabinis brought more armed men beyond these two. Not an easy task to spot them. Inbur's streets remained crowded after sundown, and even stupid clan warriors could filter in unseen. The city was a busy trading center and staging area for caravans and wagon trains traveling the Spice Road.

Larbow checked the front door again, then back to the Sabinis merchants, who had just been served. The short fat one attacked his food with relish, his attention on the plate. White Hair only picked at his food and continued to glance around the common room. His gaze passed the table with the two bodyguards—then whipped back to the fat one. White Hair whispered curtly to his companion. Fat One answered while continuing to eat. White Hair's mouth firmed, not pleased.

So Heorot Seamere had not known the bodyguards would be present. Larbow breathed easier. White Hair had been the sole go-between for all of Larbow's father's dealings with the trading house, and in the pigeon-brought message requesting this meeting no mention had been made of a second Sabinis.

Larbow drummed his fingers on the scarred surface of the table. This was his first time as *chwaer*, family head and raid leader, and he was determined that tonight go smoothly. What to do? When the two Sabinis entered the tavern, they had moved easily and without the stiffness and subtle distance strangers—or adversaries—maintained. White Hair knew the "abort meeting" signal: a hand brought to the throat while giving a cough.

While Larbow pondered, the tavern door opened and Decart came in, his weathered face deeply lined and his thinning hair more gray than black. Like Larbow, he wore the thick wool pants and leather vest common among wagon drivers. Instead of giving a hand signal, Decart came straight to Larbow's table and slid his lean frame into a chair.

"Only the one driving the carriage. Same man you and I watched last meeting. He put feedbags on the horses and stays with them."

Larbow nodded, feeling better about the situation. Decart was his father's younger brother and had been raiding when Larbow was still a suckling babe. By rights, the older Rosada should be the new chwaer. But Decart had firmly refused after his brother's death, maintaining his nephew was best for the position. The other heads of the extended family readily agreed.

"Two guards inside." Larbow indicated which table.

Decart turned to watch a serving girl move through the room and let his gaze flicker past the men. Looking back at Larbow, he lifted an eyebrow. "You want me to stay here or go back outside?"

"Stay a moment. What do you make of the fat one's presence?" Larbow knew that was the reason his uncle had come to the table instead of signaling and silently blessed him for the consideration.

Decart pursed his lips. "Like me, White Hair grows old. He will introduce you to the younger one, and that is who you will deal with from now on."

That squared with Larbow's thoughts. "Go back outside with Chant. Nattily and Tam can handle anything here."

Larbow rose from his chair and walked to the far side of the common room to approach the Sabinis table from a different direction. Decart would remain and not leave until Larbow sat with the merchants. After checking the crowd one last time and seeing no one paying any attention to him, Larbow made his way to the clansmen's table.

"I am Larbow, son of Lugal, whose spirit now rides with the Wind Giver."

A moment's confusion flickered across White Hair's ravaged face.

Strange, Larbow thought. *It's as if he doesn't know who Wind Giver is. Barbarian. These ignorant clansmen call Wind Giver by a different name, the Eternal, but it is the same God. Which is more than could be said for the Broken Stone Land pagans who bow the knee to demons!*

Finally recognition appeared on White Hair's face. "Greetings, Larbow, son of Lugal. I am Heorot Seamere, Clan Sabinis. Your father was a great man and leader. You resemble him strongly. I will miss him." In Rosada fashion, the clansman lowered his face for five heartbeats of silence.

The fat one shoveled another mouthful of lamb and chewed noisily, eyes darting from Heorot to Larbow then back to Heorot. Belatedly, he stopped chewing but did not bow his head in sorrow.

Heorot raised his head and gestured to an empty chair. "Join us, Larbow, son of Lugal. May we each be blessed by the other's company."

Keeping the anger off his face at the fat one's insult, Larbow settled stiffly into the chair. *They are only stupid clansmen.* His father had told him how this Heorot Seamere had been shockingly ignorant of civilized ways. But with great patience, Lugal had educated the merchant, who proved a willing and apt pupil. White Hair had progressed to the point where he could travel unescorted through Rosada territory and live. Would this new one be the same?

Demeanor solemn, Heorot said, "How fares your mother?"

"She grieves, but her health is fine."

"Were I Rosada, after her time of mourning, I would tie five horses to your tent post for the right to court her. Her smile is as the sun breaking over the mountaintops and bestows even more warmth."

This merchant had learned well. "Three horses would do her great honor. I will tell her of your words."

Heorot formally introduced Ryce Pleoh, and then gave a thin smile. "My partner is in awe of the Rosadas' fearsome reputation. My apology for the two at the other table. No disrespect was intended."

Larbow nodded acceptance, then looked at Ryce. The merchant tore a chunk of bread from the loaf. Sopping it in meat juice, he stuffed the piece into his mouth. Folds of fat hid most of the man's

161

eyes, but what Larbow could see was hard and calculating.

"My apology," Ryce mumbled around his chewing, tone flat and at odds with the words.

Larbow bristled outwardly. Time to start this one's training. He turned stiffly to Heorot. "Twice this man you brought uninvited has insulted me. Only my family's past association with your house keeps me from slitting his fat throat. Is Ryce Pleoh a fool, or is this deliberate?"

"I beg your indulgence." Heorot's hands were clinched as they remained in plain view on top of the table. "My intention is to have him take my place for these meetings. But my partner has not been himself since paying betrothal price a fortnight ago at the wool sale." Though his words were addressed to Larbow, White Hair looked straight at his fellow clansman and made no effort to hide his anger. "Unless he comes to his senses, I fear I will have to find another to treat with you Rosada."

Ryce's chewing had ceased abruptly at Larbow's threat, and the merchant's jaw had dropped steadily during Heorot's speech until now his mouth hung wide open. Blinking, he closed it with a snap. His pig eyes darted between Larbow and Heorot. "Since this meeting is in our territory," he said, "I thought precautions on our part would be in order."

"We Rosada are responsible for the security of all meetings. You can bring guards for your travel." Larbow's voice hardened. "But come to the chosen place alone."

Ryce nodded. "I will not make that mistake again." He looked down at his plate, swallowed, and then pushed it away. "The reason for this meeting is most pressing. And while it is a sudden request, Heorot is confident you are capable. A certain Arshessa lord has developed aspirations beyond his means. We intend to send a clear message about the consequences of treading on our trade."

A quarter of a glass later, Larbow had drawn out all the two Sabinis knew about Lord Gillaon Tarenester, his young rhyfelwr, and the wagons of wool scheduled to head across the Ardnamur

Mountains once the snow melted in the passes. More information was needed, but that would be gathered with an immediate trip into Arshessa territory.

White Hair passed a leather bag of gold under the table. "Attack where many eyes will see. That much again when we hear accounts of the wool burning."

Larbow nodded, pleased at the bag's heft. "And the Tarenester warriors and wagon drivers?"

Ryce stiffened. "The rhyfelwr also has aspirations beyond his means. Kill him for sure. The others only as necessary."

Watching the man's eyes go flat and reptilian, Larbow made a quick reassessment. *Never will I turn my back on this one.*

He checked Nattily and Tam. They had finished their meal and awaited a signal from him. Time to leave while the tavern remained crowded.

Larbow said politely, "The Wind Giver's blessing on your betrothal. May your chosen present you strong sons."

Heorot chuckled. "He has been thinking about that—but only the begetting, not the birthing." He snorted. "The maiden's father proved as canny a bargainer as his daughter was desirable. In spite of mine and another's counsel, Ryce allowed lust to overcome good sense and agreed to an outlandish sum. Every day since, he has continually bemoaned the loss of his gold and the time he must wait until he...enjoys the girl's tender company."

Ryce shot Heorot a sour look. Pulling back his plate, the fat clansman cut another piece of meat and shoved it into his mouth.

Larbow stood and brushed imaginary crumbs from this shirt, signaling Nattily and Tam "all clear." Then he wove through the noisy crowd toward the door, mind racing.

At first light, he would send a pigeon to request every available raider. By the time they arrived, in groups of twos and threes, the mountain passes would be open, the wagon's trail would be thoroughly scouted, and Larbow would have a plan ready.

The raid would be a fitting start to his time as chwaer.

Chapter Eighteen

RHIANNON

S HE PARRIED THE sword thrust with a flick of her wrists and slid forward, careful to keep her weight centered between her feet. Her sword hilt was slick with sweat. A damp strand of hair had worked loose from her leather headband and waved irritatingly in front of her eyes. She ignored it. Using her legs and back muscles she swung with a firm two-handed grip and rolled her wrists in preparation to—

Her blade was met with enough force to vibrate her arms. She winced as a wooden blade thudded into her ribs. Even through the protection of the heavy quilted vest, the blow hurt.

"You're dead!" Creag whooped, sweaty face glowing in triumph. He lowered his practice sword. "You're still leaving your side exposed with that maneuver. I wasn't strong enough before, but now I am and—"

"A warrior does not gloat, Master Creag." Llyr turned to her, frowning. "Mistress, how many times have I told you about the hole left in your guard with that counter? You must batter the opponent's blade down far enough so that he cannot recover before you thrust. That will no longer work with Master Creag. He is thirteen and coming into his strength."

Fighting the urge to rub her side, she tucked the wayward strand of hair behind her ear and regarded her half-brother with new eyes. Creag had grown and now stood only a half a hand shorter than her. His arms were more muscular and his shoulders wider than she remembered. And although she would die before admitting it, the gap between their skill level was narrowing at an alarming rate—as her throbbing ribs proved.

It was morning, and until today the weather had been unseasonably cool for late spring. That had been a blessing these last few days as workers toiled steadily on building the new hlaford. Rhiannon, Mererid, Lakenna, and Ove, the house servant, slept in the pavilion, now erected several paces from the main stable where Tellan and the boys slept.

At first staying in the pavilion had been an adventure. But now the close confines and inconveniences of tent living were getting on the women's nerves. Rhiannon longed for the privacy of a room to herself again—and the security of solid walls and a roof over her head.

Increasingly, her sleep was restless, with frequent wakenings from murky and fearful dreams. She could not shake the pervading sense that the Mighty Ones were gathering strength.

Maybe it was the aftermath of last week's thunderstorm. The rain and gusting winds had blown down one side of the pavilion and had torn a rent in the old fabric. Startling awake at the noise, Rhiannon had first thought winged horrors were upon her again. Heart pounding, she had groped for her sword, which she kept beside her even during the night, and had the steel blade halfway out of the scabbard before she'd realized what was happening. It was a wild, wet time as the women scrambled up and fled to the stables. Halfway there Ove fell and lay unseen in the downpour until Creag and Phelan got the stable lanterns lit and everyone realized the old servant was not present. Tellan dashed out to scoop her up and came running back with her in his arms, both of them soaked. Ove's lips were blue, her teeth chattering. The next morning she had awakened with a fever, and she still had a deep, racking cough.

Rhiannon fingered the hilt of the practice sword. If a thunderstorm could wreak such havoc on the pavilion, what could winged horrors do? Warriors stood guard from dusk to dawn, bows strung and nocked. But night after night had passed with no winged horrors appearing. Life was rapidly returning to normal.

The weeks of tension leading up to the wool sale were gone, as were many of the money worries Tellan and Mererid had always grappled with. Though grumbles still came from a few kinsmen about dealing with Lord Gillaon and the Broken Stone Land, most were glad for the extra coin. The busy time of culling and separating the herds was almost done. Next week the herds would be driven to the high summer pastures.

"That is all for you, Mistress," Llyr announced, looking up at the sun. "Your lady mother awaits." His weathered face came close to a smile. "M'lady made it plain yesterday that I have been keeping you too long."

Rhiannon bit back a plea for one more try at Creag. Mererid had butted in, and that was that. Her stepmother was using the coming Presentation as a potent weapon in her campaign against Rhiannon's training. *It won't work. I'll just do more drills at night.*

Harred could teach me...

She put him from her mind. Harred had *that girl.*

Creag and Phelan engaged with wooden swords as she peeled off the wool-padded vest and hung it on a line stretched between two poles outside the armory. Wood clacked as Creag defended against Phelan's spirited attack. Since Lakenna had come, Creag actually looked forward to the afternoon sessions. Rhiannon had to admit that his whole attitude was changing. He was almost bearable to be around for short periods. And Phelan. He devoured everything Lakenna put in front of him.

"Mistress, a moment, if you please," Llyr rumbled as her brothers continued to flail at each other. The old rhyfelwr took her practice sword and placed it in the rack with the others. The skin on his forearms was a crisscross of faint white scars from old cuts.

Before he could speak a group of men came into the armory, talking and joking among themselves. Her father struggled to keep eight warriors in full-time service, and they spent most of their day training Rogoth horses for sale. Beyond those eight, Tellan maintained a reserve of twenty trained kinsmen who received a small stipend to drill with Llyr one morning a week, and today was the day. In addition to swords, each man had a bow in a leather holder on his shoulders and a quiver full of arrows around his waist. Since the winged horror attack, their training was placing more emphasis on archery.

Llyr motioned to her, and she followed him out of range of the warriors' hearing. They walked a ways on the hard-packed dirt surrounding the armory. It and the two stables, the main one and a smaller foaling stable, resided on the second of three ridges rising from the valley floor. The structures, constructed mainly of rock gathered from the countryside, were sturdy and functional. The hlaford, its privy, smokehouse, and an underground root cellar rested on the uppermost ridge. Corrals for horse training and sheep pens comprised the broad lower ridge.

Even an untrained eye could see what a strong defensive position this was. Any attacker would have to fight up the steep slopes and take each ridge in succession. Not an enviable task.

But that means nothing to winged horrors—

She waited on Llyr to speak. Since returning from Lachlann, she had noticed subtle differences in the way her father's rhyfelwr treated her. They were having more of these one-on-one conversations—which thankfully were not about becoming more ladylike, as Mererid harped on morning, noon, and night.

Rhiannon recognized what her stepmother and Lakenna had done in Lachlann, using Harred—who only cared for someone else—to get her to primp and simper and drink punch while making inane conversation to a group of poison-mouthed ladies. Well, Lady Aigneis, anyway. But no more. High Lord Keeper Branor had confirmed it. She was to be "Protectoress of the Covenant" and fight winged horrors and siyyim.

Rhiannon lightly flexed her sore muscles. Next time the Mighty Ones' creatures came, she would be ready.

Her father strode up and joined them. Like his men, Tellan

wore leather breeches and simple wool tunic. Normally he made appearances at these weekly training sessions every third or fourth time, but since the winged horror attack he was here at every one. His face had healed from the burn. His eyebrows were almost back to their normal thickness.

Tellan and Llyr exchanged a glance.

Something's coming, Rhiannon thought.

Llyr cleared his throat. "For your time in training, you are as good with a sword as I have seen. But you see what is happening in your bouts with Master Creag." The rhyfelwr folded thick arms across his chest. "Every day you grow more like your mother. Lady Eyslk was tall and lean and possessed a wiry strength that kept her going at the end of a long day when even Lord Tellan flagged."

Tellan nodded. "Like your mother, your full-grown strength will be of a different type than a man's strength. From now on, we will concentrate on other aspects of what it means to be a warrior."

Rhiannon relaxed. "For a minute I thought you were going to say something else." She looked at her wooden blade in the rack. "Speaking of which, what do you think about forging me a sword with a longer, thinner blade, the better to thrust for a horror's eyes?"

A long moment passed before Tellan answered. "Interesting idea. I will talk to the master smith next time I am in Lachlann."

By his expression she could tell they hadn't got to his real reason for talking. Mererid had been busy.

"Daughter," Tellan said, "whatever your future as Protectoress of the Covenant, you are being called to lead, not draw steel. The men who bow the knee to you will expect some knowledge about tactics and other fighting skills, but it is their job to wield weapons when and where you bid them."

"I take pride in my skills, Father. What I am learning will enable me to personally lead their training."

"Your father is a master swordsman." Llyr said. "But ask yourself: is that why we Rogoth kinsmen will follow him to the ends of the earth—or is there another reason?"

Rhiannon chewed the inside of her lip. The rhyfelwr spoke truth. Her father did not need a sword strapped around his waist to lead.

Tellan's eyes probed her gently, lovingly. "Have you noticed the difference in Creag now that he is beginning to hold his own against you? If he was in your service and you wanted him to become the best warrior he could be, how would you go about it? Best him continually? Wound his pride? Or encourage him—lead him—to grow better each day?"

"I will think on this," she managed.

"Good." He turned to Llyr. "Prepare the men for inspection."

Aware that she was going to receive Mererid's sternest frown and a lecture for being late, Rhiannon lingered and watched her father move among the men of the reserve. He checked swords, bows, arrows, and other gear, and asked about wives and newborn babes or commiserated with another about the loss of a loved one.

He stopped in front a pudgy, round-faced kinsman only a year older than Rhiannon. Tellan examined the youth's bowstring and frowned. He took the bow, slid an arrow from the quiver, notched and drew the shaft back to his ear and let fly. The arrow flew barely half the distance expected.

Dead silence reigned among the men as Tellan turned slowly back. Instead of anger or open derision at the lad's failure to maintain his gear in suitable condition, Tellan's expression showed sadness tinged with disappointment. "I had a better opinion of you than this, Larris Werfl. Your father served me with distinction, and I never found him lacking. This string is old and frayed. If a fellow clansmen had been standing shoulder to shoulder with you, depending on your bow for his life, you would have let him down."

Larris's face paled. He swayed, a stricken look on his features. For a moment, Rhiannon thought he might faint. After a moment, Larris opened his mouth, but nothing came out. Swallowing, he managed to croak. "I've been meaning to prepare new strings,

Lord Tellan, but you know how Da's been sick and all the extra work that I've—"

"When swords are drawn there are no excuses, only deeds." Placing both hands on his hips, Tellan fixed the lad with an anvil-hard stare. "Go home and take care of your father. Think about what it means to be a Rogoth warrior. If you decide to seek service again as a reserve, present yourself to Llyr. When he is satisfied, your place will be waiting."

Larris wilted. His head dropped, and he swallowed several times. Finally, he nodded and trudged off.

Before he got out of hearing range, Tellan addressed the remaining men. "Larris Werfl comes from good stock. He will be back." A murmur of agreement came from the warriors.

Rhiannon looked at the young clansman. Larris raised his head slightly, and his shoulders showed he felt a trifle less dejected. When she looked back to her father, she found Llyr's eyes boring into her. The rhyfelwr held her gaze for a long moment. Finally, she nodded to herself and he returned the nod, satisfied.

She hurried to meet Mererid.

"A lady does not clump, Rhiannon. She glides." Mererid placed the board on her head and demonstrated. "Chin level, shoulders square, and imagine a broom handle running through your middle and into the ground." Mererid moved regally across the rugs placed in a line outside the pavilion. The sun shone brightly, and the air smelled of grass and flowers. "The rear foot moves in toward the front foot, but does not touch, and then moves out and forward. That gives just the right amount of sway." Mererid turned and came back. The board stayed on as if was glued. "Now, try again."

Blank-faced, Rhiannon took the board and positioned it on her head. She didn't know which was worse, walking or sitting and rising gracefully as they had just spent forever doing before Mererid got out the hated board again.

Rhiannon made it all of four steps before it tumbled off.

Mererid's lips tightened. "I have watched you doing sword drills. You move like a cat. If Llyr told you it would make you a better warrior, by now you'd be able to put a goblet of water on that board, walk thirty paces, turn around, and come back without spilling a drop."

"Because that is where my future lies. Not this."

"Your future lies with a husband and running his household."

"But my prophecy..."

Mererid raised a hand. "If you are indeed to battle the Mighty Ones' creatures, your husband will have to provide the funds for men and weapons. You must serve your husband even as you serve the Eternal's purpose."

"The Eternal will provide what I need."

"Most likely he will provide a husband to meet those needs."

So, Rhiannon realized, the latest tactic was twofold: a frontal assault about a husband coupled with a rear action of sending her father to talk after sword practice. "I won't marry. I will be too busy."

"No one will follow a woman alone in this world. Your husband and his station will determine your resources. That is a fact every woman must accept." Mererid nodded to the board in Rhiannon's hand. "The Dinari Presentation is the time to attract the best—and richest—suitor for you."

"Maolmin will never include me, not after Father went against his wishes at the wool sale."

"We don't know that. And even if he doesn't, you will be there and be seen—and you will present yourself in a matter worthy of your mother's memory."

Things were serious indeed for Mererid to mention Eyslk. All mementos pertaining to her were long gone. Not even a portrait remained. Rhiannon had mentioned that to Lakenna the other day in Ove's hearing. The old servant brought the silver hand mirror and said, "Look. Here is your mother's face."

Rhiannon stared at the board in her hands. "Are we through for today?"

"We will continue until you walk to the end of the rugs with that board balanced on your head."

Rhiannon sighed audibly.

Color bloomed on Mererid's cheeks. "Your father and I have talked. If you do not attend to my lessons and Lakenna's with the same diligence you show Llyr, your sword training will stop until she and I are satisfied."

Lakenna, too? Rhiannon felt betrayed. "If I were born a man, none of this would matter. I could fight winged horrors anytime I wanted to!"

Mererid's face whitened. She opened her mouth—then reestablished control. She turned abruptly and stared up the ridge at the hlaford. Carpenters worked on the second story. The spaces left for the windows being built were twice as big as the previous ones, and each bedroom had two of them.

Rhiannon waited. Protectoress of the Covenant. What does that mean? It must lie with the last half of the Covenant:

> Keep this covenant and the Mighty Ones' yoke of slavery shall be broken. The winged horror of the night and its brethren will cease out of the Land. They shall devour you no longer. You shall be safe in your Land and shall know that I am the Eternal.

But the more she tried to fathom that part of the Covenant, the more the first half kept nagging her:

> I have made this covenant with you for the ruling of this Land. I set up one shepherd over you, my servant Destin Faber. He shall feed you, and he shall be your shepherd. And his son and his son after him, even unto one hundred generations, will they feed and protect you with this covenant of my peace.

She felt Maolmin's dark eyes bore into her again. *"Have you been to Faber Castle?"*

173

"No, High Lord."

"Have you met the prince?"

"I have not had that honor."

"Of course not."

She had not told anyone about that part of her conversation with Maolmin. Nor about the wrongness that had rolled off the man. From the way Tellan's eyes had blazed during his confrontation with the High Lord, Rhiannon knew her father had been a knife's edge away from a physical attack and the disastrous consequences that would have entailed.

But what to do?

An old clan maxim came to her: "Pray. Sharpen your sword. Then pray some more."

Besides, she cared nothing for Faber Castle or Prince Larien. As Protectoress of the Covenant, she would have other things to do. Much more important things.

She had begun to read Holy Writ again. The more she read, the more she wanted to read. Her prayers had resumed. And she had questions for Lakenna. The tutor's strong faith should help uncover what the future held. Every day the feeling built that the Eternal was finally about to make something of her birthing prophecy. Rhiannon contemplated her hands and the calluses from gripping the sword hilt. Surely, the prophecy would entail her... But in her mind she kept hearing what Keeper Branor had said in the room at Lachlann:

We can become so focused on our way that we don't take the time to find what the Eternal's way might be.

Irritated, she shoved that nagging thought aside. Who better to understand what should be done than the one called to do it?

Finally, Mererid turned back. Her features had softened. "I understand your frustration, Rhiannon. But you are a woman. A beautiful young woman who will make a wonderful wife and mother." She took both of Rhiannon's hands in hers. "You will not be as hindered as you may think." Her eyes twinkled. "Can you think of anything I really wanted that did not come to pass?

Anything that your lord father refused me, flatly and forever?"

In spite of herself, Rhiannon chuckled.

"I'll make you a deal." Mererid held up the board. "Walk to the end of these rugs like I know you can, and we will sit and I will share some of my secrets until time for lessons with Lakenna."

Rhiannon couldn't be bought that easily. But Llyr had always taught her that there was nothing wrong with a momentary retreat to regather one's forces. Rhiannon forced a smile. She took the board, placed it on her head, and glided down the rugs. Mererid had raised an unintended point. Moving this smoothly should indeed help in swordplay.

Chapter Nineteen

HARRED

"GET ON!" THE man flicked the reins smartly across the mule's rump. "Get on, now!"

The mule paid no heed. It stood two-thirds of the way across a one-lane bridge spanning a stream in full spate from snowmelt. In contrast to the bone-chilling water two spans below, the mule dripped sweat. Its head drooped and its sides heaved as it sucked the mountain air.

No wonder, Harred thought as he reined in his black gelding, Coal. The rickety wagon behind the mule looked overloaded. Its canvas-covered contents rose head-high behind the two riders on the seat: a man and an older girl, his daughter perhaps.

Rising stiffly, the man took a long-handled whip from a holder on the side of the wagon and cracked the leather tip above his mule's head. "Get on, I say!"

The mule remained still. Its nostrils flared, and the sweat made more dark splotches on the hand-hewed planks.

Harred waited for the exhausted mule to gather its strength and pull the wagon the last few feet to clear the way. Behind him on the narrow trail bordered by steep-rising bare rock stretched twenty-eight wagons that contained Lord Gillaon's wool—and Harred's future as rhyfelwr.

It was a turn of the glass before dusk and the full night that descended so quickly at these elevations. The wagon train was in sight of Maude, the westernmost town in Arshessa territory. Harred intended to spend the night there and take on final supplies before heading into the higher regions of the Ardnamur Mountains. The white-capped peaks towered in the western sky. But the passes were open. Elmar had scouted ahead and had rejoined them mid-afternoon with that welcome news.

Now, trail-worn and needing a shave, Elmar eased his dun mare up beside Harred. They watched the little drama on the bridge. The man cracked the whip with increasing fury but with the same results.

Ard Gand, the grizzled wagon master, climbed down from the first wagon and ambled up. Harred and Elmar dismounted and stretched their legs.

Tilting his head toward the bridge, Elmar grinned. "If Lord Gillaon be here, know what be happening about now?"

Harred and Ard chuckled. The kinsmen lord had been a caged bear until the wagons had finally left the sprawling Tarenester hlaford only three days after arriving from Lachlann. "We must have the wool through the passes before the Sabinis organize an attack!" he had said.

Knowing another test loomed, Harred had worked day and night to have everything ready in half the time Ard had predicted.

On the bridge the man flung the whip down in disgust and clambered off the wagon. He stalked to the mule's face and, with arms waving, he loudly began to curse it.

Ard spat a stream of tabac juice and lifted an eyebrow at Harred, silently asking which of them should handle this. Since they were still in Arshessa territory and this might be a fellow clansman, Harred sighed and took a step toward the bridge.

Movement from behind caught his eye. He turned and saw a group of horsemen edging between the line of waiting wool wagons and the steep confines of the trail. They were well-mounted, lean men. Each led a packhorse laden with fur. Undoubtedly a company of trappers coming down after the long mountain winter to trade in Maude.

Instinctively checking for weapons, Harred noted only a long-bladed knife on each man's belt. No concern there. Then he hesitated. Lord Gillaon's words came to him again.

On the trail, overreact to anything that happens. Ninety-ninety times out of a hundred, it will be just that: overreaction. But on the hundredth, you and your men will be ready.

Harred chewed the inside of his lip. For one of these trappers to ride ahead to see what was causing the delay was understandable. But it was a bit rude for all to do so. The trappers had doubtless endured a long, hard, womanless winter. With Maude's taverns and serving wrenches virtually in sight, they had perhaps decided it would be too long a wait for twenty-eight wagons to cross ahead of them. *Or perhaps not.*

Since they were still in Arshessa territory, Harred, Elmar, and the other eighteen Tarenester warriors had put their swords and scabbards away in bundles or strapped on saddles along with unstrung bows and quivers of arrows.

Stepping back to Coal, Harred slid his sword and scabbard off the saddle and buckled it on.

The act was not lost on Ard. "Trouble?"

Harred gave a quick headshake. "Trying to think like Lord Gillaon. He stays two or three moves ahead." Harred caught Elmar's eye. "Talk to the trappers. I have no problem with them going first once the bridge is clear." He smiled without humor. "But there's a difference between accepting a gracious offer and demanding to be let past."

Elmar nodded. He went to his mare, buckled on his sword, and walked to where the first trapper had reined in his horse beside the lead wagon.

Harred checked the line of wagons. As trained, the other warriors stationed between each wagon dismounted and did the same. Harred grunted approval. Good preparation for tomorrow when they left Arshessa lands and things became more serious.

He strode to the bridge. The sky remained cloudless. Steep granite wet with snowmelt bordered the trail, which narrowed toward the bridge. The raging, rock-strewn stream below it made the air damp and cool.

The man on the bridge gave no heed to Harred's approach. Glaring bug-eyed at his recalcitrant mule, he showered it with colorful and inventive curses. Harred was impressed. He listened with half an ear while checking out the older girl waiting patiently on wagon seat. Dressed in a much-mended wool skirt and a white blouse with frayed cuffs, she had dark, expressive eyes that were focused over his head at the wool wagons.

"Da," she said, "this nice man and his friends prepare to help us." She had a faint accent and put a slight emphasis on *prepare*.

Da's cursing stopped mid-phrase—which disappointed Harred. He was wondering how much longer the father could continue without repeating himself. The man darted a quick glance at Harred's waist. Turning, he stared pointedly at Harred's sword. "Why bring sticker? Mercy. Don't need. Mercy me, no."

He cursed much better than he talked, Harred decided. Da looked in his late-thirties. He was whip-thin and stood easily on the balls of his feet. And while Harred's instincts said the man would be lightning quick in a fight, Da's expression seemed befuddled.

Harred looked at the mule and said gently, "Looks like this one's had a long day."

Da drew himself to his full height, indignant. "Stubborn, he is. Stubborn!"

"And exhausted. Unhitch him; we'll bring one of ours."

The man winced as if Harred's words had been body blows. Straight-backed indignation turned into cringing fear. He pressed his back into the mule and spread his arms protectively.

"I *was* unhitching him! Mercy!" Unaccountably, the man's face crumbled. Tears flowed freely as he wailed, "I didn't know until it was too late! I tried. Mercy knows I did!"

Bewildered, Harred glanced at the daughter, who had climbed down. She gave a sad smile when she halted on Harred's other side. She was taller than Breanna, but most women were. Their dark eyes were similar, but this one did not have Breanna's glow. . . . He pushed that aside.

"Two years ago," she said, "on a day much like today, a group of Landantae clansmen followed us home from Maude. They had been drinking and made...inappropriate suggestions to me as I waited in the wagon while Da purchased supplies. Fortunately, some Arshessa clansmen were passing by on the street and over-heard. They came to my defense, upbraided the Landantae, and made them apologize."

Landantae! Harred growled silently. *Typical.*

"I made no mention of the encounter after Da loaded the wagon because I feared that although my father is a peaceful man, he would seek satisfaction." Her eyes continued to search Harred's face as she stepped closer. "And I knew my wrong had been righted by the noble Arshessa."

Just so, Harred thought, pleased.

She lowered her gaze. "The Landantae thought otherwise. Unbeknown to us, they followed us back to our farm an hour's ride hence. I went inside while Da took the mule and wagon to the barn. When...when Da heard my screams, he came running, and they gave him a sword blow to the head and left him for dead." Her voice was expressionless. "After they...fin-ished...they rode away. I nursed Da as best I could, but...." She shrugged sadly. "As you see, he is not himself. And the sight of a sword..."

Harred nodded. *Poor girl.* "Did you receive justice?"

Her father began dancing about while pointing at Harred. "He draws it! Mercy! Have mercy!"

Startled, Harred eased his white-knuckled grip off his hilt. He lifted both hands chest high. That mollified Da somewhat. He slowed his prancing and stopped an arm's length away. The daughter eased closer while fingering the top button on her blouse. Harred's gaze was drawn—

Then came the sharp call of the red-tailed pheasant.

Recognizing Elmar's version of the warning all Tarenester warriors were taught to imitate, Harred stepped back and cut his eyes to the wool wagons. The narrow trail was even more crowded. A warrior itch built in him when he noted a trapper sitting directly behind each Tarenester stationed between the first several wagons.

"Stay here—"

Da lunged at him with a short-bladed knife held low and competently.

Harred had been correct. The man *was* lightning fast. If not for the step back at Elmar's call, it would have been all over.

Reflexes and years of training took over. Harred pivoted smoothly while whipping his right forearm down to deflect the thrust. Then he brought his arm up and over, trapping Da's wrist between Harred's bicep and forearm. The pressure caused the knife to fall free and clatter on the wooden bridge. Harred bore down further to break Da's arm—but the daughter had an identical knife! The steel flashed in the late afternoon sun as it swept at his belly.

Desperate, Harred kicked. The tough boot leather caught the sharp blade square on and sent the girl's knife arcing into the rushing stream below. But the kick loosened his grip on Da. Twisting like a weasel, the man broke free and tried to gouge Harred's eyes.

Harred blocked with his left arm and countered with a powerful right fist to the midsection that lifted the man off his feet.

Da *oofed* and stumbled backward before collapsing by the mule's rear feet, moaning and out of it.

Behind came the clash of steel amid Elmar's bellow, "To arms, men! To arms!"

The girl on the bridge produced another knife and waited by her father, eyes glittering challenge. Harred stepped to disarm her and join the fight for the wool, but the wagon's canvas covering flew back and out poured men gripping long curved swords!

Harred drew his sword, the worn hilt familiar and comforting. He skipped back to the front of the mule, blood singing. Attackers dropped light-footed onto the planks, three on each side of the wagon. The narrow bridge and long drop to the raging water below forced each side to come single-file. And Da blocked one side. He had struggled to one knee, white-faced, with both arms wrapped around his stomach. The daughter had a handful of shirt and was tugging him out of the way. The lead swordsman slowed to lend a helping hand.

Harred lunged to the other side, sword a blur. He noted surprise on the first man's face who was clearly not expecting such an out-numbered foe to attack. Surprise went red in a spray of blood. Harred shoved the dead man back into the second, who had been spaced too close. Before number two could free his sword arm, Harred slammed the weighted end of his hilt down on the skull and shoved that crumbling attacker back into the third—but this one had time to prepare. He retreated halfway down the wagon's length, sword ready.

Harred hesitated half a heartbeat at the mule's rump to recalculate. Six had become four. The three swordsmen on the other side had pulled Da out the way. One was clambering over the wagon tongue to join the fight while the other two raced around the mule's front. What to do? Engage the one straddling the tongue? An easy kill, but then attackers would be front and rear—Harred leaped over the bodies at his feet and charged the third attacker.

Swords clashed as the man gave good account of himself. But his curved blade was thinner, more useful for horse-born attack. Harred's superior strength and heavier blade quickly sent the man tumbling into the stream below.

Scurrying on beyond the wagon, he thought about continuing to the other side to engage without the restrictions of the bridge, but decided against it. The narrow confines favored him. Turning around, he waited in the middle of the bridge, his sword-point held low.

Shouts and howls came from the long line of wool wagons. The shrill neighs of horses rose above the din of steel meeting steel as Harred's men, aided by Ard and his drivers, fought to protect the precious cargo. But that was in Elmar's capable hands. Harred's fight was here on the bridge.

The remaining attackers gathered at the rear of the wagon. Three pairs of eyes regarded him, dark and merciless. Da shuffled up, hunched over with one arm cradling his middle. The daughter stood with a hand on his shoulder.

Da spat a curt order. As one, the three swordsmen moved forward. Boots scuffed lightly on the worn timbers as the men formed into an inverted V with the two in front spaced two arm's length apart and the third in the middle a step behind. Harred had hoped they would be foolish enough to come three abreast. The formation coming at him was designed to keep an opponent funneled into the middle where he could be flanked and all three attackers could engage and stay out of each other's way. He had faced this scenario many times in training—and died more often that not.

Harred held up a pleading hand. "You can have the wool. You can have it all. Just let me live."

The three came on, focused and deliberate. Their curved blades glinted in the late afternoon sun.

"I can be ransomed." Smiling sickly, Harred slammed his sword back into the scabbard and held out both hands. "See? No need to fight. Alive, I'm worth five golds. Maybe ten." He stared hopefully over their shoulders at Da. "That's right! Ten golds." Harred allowed his body to sag in relief as if Da had nodded assent. "Agreed! Ten golds."

The two in front did not slow, but their sword points lowered just a fraction. The one in the rear faltered and darted a quick glance over his shoulder—

Harred leaped straight into the V as his sword left the scabbard in a silver arc. He was past the front two before they could recover, and he engaged the third, who stumbled away bleeding from a long cut to the shoulder. The front two turned and came at him with swords whistling in the mountain air. Growling in vexation, the bleeding one rejoined the fray a second later.

Things got very busy indeed. These people were not clan warriors, but they knew the use of a sword. They came at him with deadly skill and single-minded purpose. Harred fought as desperately as he ever had, striving to keep three blades away while preventing them from reforming their V.

As it did for him in these situations, time slowed. He operated within a bubble of icy calm, a quiet cocoon where every move flowed out of the one before and set up the one coming—and the one after that. The different feel of steel meeting flesh or meeting steel communicated success or failure even as his eyes sought the next opening. Thrust, counter, pivot, and parry, his sword seemed alive as he used every possible combination of the seven basic forms he had been taught. This was what he had been born to do! And he gloried in it.

He drove two of them back and then focused on the one with the wounded shoulder. Parry, slice, thrust. Three became two. Harred's sword blurred as it danced between the other two. Lunge, pivot, parry—and parry again! Block and thrust.

Only one remained.

And quickly, none.

Harred paused for a deep breath, then trotted across the blood-spattered planks, wondering if two more deaths awaited before he could join Elmar and the others. But Da was in no shape to fight. The daughter had picked up a sword dropped by one of the first three. Bravely, she moved to meet him, only to be held back by Da. Harred watched them warily as he trotted by on the other side of the wagon, but they remained still. Their glares, however, spoke volumes.

Beyond the bridge, the battle for the wool raged full force. The front two wagons had been set ablaze. They burned busily, billowing black greasy smoke. Harred could smell the lamp oil that had been used to set them afire. Those wagons' mules brayed in panic while Ard and a handful of his drivers struggled to cut the rigging loose. The next three wagons bore burned patches amid the top-most bales, but the flames had not taken hold. Unmanned horses milled about, dragging reins. Three trappers and one Tarenester lay unmoving on the trail.

Elmar and the rest of the warriors swirled among the trappers in the narrow confines between the wagons and the rocky cliffs. Guiding his mare with his knees, Elmar fought with a grace that belied his bulk as he met an attacker. Swords rang, and the man slumped on his saddle, blood pouring from his side. Following Elmar's lead, the other Tarenester warriors surged forward.

Before Harred could mount Coal and join them, a shrill horn blast came from the bridge. Turning back, Harred saw the daughter standing on the wagon seat blowing a small horn that gave out a surprising loud sound. Another man had ridden up with two saddled horses. He had dismounted and was helping Da climb painfully on the back of one. The daughter blew two more blasts, then jumped down and vaulted nimbly on the back of her horse. All three wheeled and galloped away with Da in the middle being braced by the other two.

Down the line of wool wagons, the din faded as the attackers heeded the signal and withdrew.

That night, after wounds were tended and the mules rubbed down and fed, all gathered around a huge campfire and assessed the damage. Three Tarenesters had given their lives protecting their kinsmen lord's wool; four others had sustained wounds severe enough to prevent them from continuing the journey. Two of Ard's drivers were dead, and two were wounded. Two wagons had been lost with all their wool. Eight more bales on other wagons were burned beyond redemption. One panicked mule had broken a leg in the rigging and had had to be put out of its misery. A bad enough state of affairs, but not nearly as bad as it could have been.

After the others bedded down, Harred, Elmar, and Ard remained by the campfire.

"We were very, very lucky," Harred said.

Ard threw more branches on the fire. "Luck had its part. But you did yours by having Elmar check them trappers." He looked at Elmar. "What tipped you?"

Harred's brother-in-law shrugged. "They didn't feel right. Their faces be not winter-worn nor showing even a touch of frostbite. The horses not shaggy-haired enough after a winter in these mountains. The furs be cheap, not worth selling. When I smelled lamp oil and saw a torch sticking out from a bedroll, it all came together."

Harred told them about Da and the daughter.

"Rosada tribesmen," Ard pronounced.

"I thought those days long gone," Harred said.

"Some still cling to the old ways." As the wood crackled and popped, Ard chewed tabac and recounted tales of his family's experiences from the days before the treaty and the Rosada princess who had married into the Faber dynasty.

Harred listened and learned. During warrior training the Tarenester loreteller had told of the Rosada and their tactics. Harred had listened with half an ear then. Tonight, he determined that upon returning from the mountains and making his report to Lord Gillaon, the old loreteller would be the first person he'd seek out.

A rhyfelwr could learn much from these people and their well-thought-out preparations: the trappers; the beaten circle of hoof prints on the other side of the bridge where the mule had been galloped round and round; Da and the daughter's rehearsed antics to allay any suspicion; the excellent location for an ambush.

Finally, Ard rose stiffly to his feet and turned in. Elmar remained, quiet and waiting.

Harred stared into the campfire as the flames turned to red coals. "I had no idea being rhyfelwr would be this demanding."

Elmar smiled softly. "It be like the first days of training. Muscles be mighty sore, but they toughen and strengthen."

"Six months ago, my biggest concern was the sword bouts at the next Gathering. Now Rosada, and dealing face-to-face with Broken Stone merchants. Pagans." Harred sighed. "Gran must be turning in her Albane grave."

Elmar picked up a stick and poked the coals. "Last year, when she be on her deathbed, she called me to her side. We talked about you."

Harred straightened. "You never told me that."

"Time not be right. Tonight seems to be. She say, 'You take care of my Harred.' I tell her it probably be the other way around. She say, 'He is destined for great things, only the Eternal knows what. He is preparing Harred, training him.' Then she raise up and grab my arm, fierce-like. 'You stay with him, Elmar. Help him. Guard his back. Bigger things are coming for you both. Bigger than you can know.'" Elmar stared into the fire. "The next morning, she be gone."

They sat silent, remembering a great woman. The coals went from red to gray.

"Gillaon be having his eye on you for a while," Elmar said. "Remember traveling to our last Gathering? He be talking to you about the swords bouts and the men you be facing and what you think be their strengths and weakness. Then casual like, he'd ask if you think Duncan's courtship of Katharine be successful?"

"Anyone could see they were not suited for each other. You and I talked about that more than once."

"Aye. But most be surprised when he started calling on Donia instead." Elmar stirred the ashes. "Remember Gillaon asking you about that trader from Ancylar and if you thought he be honest?"

"The moment I saw that one, I knew he was wrong. You did, too."

"Aye. But Gillaon defended him and kept demanding reasons why you be feeling that way."

"I had no reason, only what my gut was telling me." Harred shifted to look full at his brother-in-law. "And the next time the trader came, he was caught with rigged scales."

"I'll bet my next three meals Lord Gillaon already knew. He be wanting to see what you thought." Elmar rose to his feet and brushed off his pants. "I don't know how your Gran knew, but this rhyfelwr be coming for a while."

"Gillaon asked you plenty of questions, too."

"He be testing me, same as you." Elmar yawned as he headed to his blankets. "And here I be, saving your hide."

Harred chuckled, feeling better. He remained by the dying fire a while longer, alone with his thoughts.

Overreact to anything that happens. Ninety-ninety times out of a hundred, it will be just that: overreaction. But when the hundredth time comes, you and your men will be ready.

Remembering the burning fire in Da's dark eyes, Harred tucked the day's lessons away and vowed never to be caught like that again.

Hours to the east and many lengths off the road in a sheltered cove of trees, those same dark eyes also stared into a campfire. Around him, wrapped in blankets on the cold grass, shivered the surviving raiders that had come from his family group. More than half were wounded. One had given his spirit to the Wind Giver during the ride here and now lay buried a stone's throw from the fire. At least one more seemed likely to join him in the morning. The others would live. Decart had washed their wounds, packed them with salve, and then wrapped them in boiled linen strips. Nattily had brewed a draught for pain that allowed most to sleep, although some still moaned softly.

Larbow refused the draught, preferring the sharp pain of torn and bruised stomach muscles to remind him of his failure. The Arshessa wagons had appeared much sooner than anyone had thought possible—days before all the raiders needed had arrived. But lying hidden along the trail with Decart and seeing how the stupid clan warriors were not even wearing their swords, Larbow had decided the ambush would work. It should have. Why had they suddenly donned swords? And what had tipped the one who had talked to Ren, who next to Decart was their most experienced raider? Ren could not say because he had been among the first to fall. Thankfully, Decart had not fallen as well. Ancient Rosada tactics demanded either the chwaer, the leader, or the second in command, as Decart had been today, to stay removed from the fray and thus be able to gather the broken strands of failure and reweave them into a new rope. Decart had done that by appearing with horses for Larbow and Nattily and telling her to sound the withdrawal before total disaster had occurred.

Eleven Rosada—eleven!—remained at the bridge. Six alone by the big rhyfelwr the fat Sabinis wanted killed. The warning of the bird signal should not have mattered. Larbow's knifepoint had been almost at his shirt when he had *moved*. Never had he faced such quickness! Three of his best blades had cornered him on the bridge, yet it had been like a wolf among little lambs.

Larbow shifted in anger—and gasped as white-hot pain shot through his belly. He stared into the flames, welcoming the agony, allowing it to deepen his vow for revenge.

One fine tomorrow, warrior, he thought. *One fine tomorrow, we will meet again.*

Chapter Twenty

LAKENNA

"Of course, doing more than your sums is important," Lakenna told them matter-of-factly. "Say that you want to increase the size of your flocks. You borrow thirty gold coins from a moneylender for three years at 18 percent interest. How much new wool must you produce to make the first year's payment?"

Five students were arrayed before her on stools. A long plank served as a makeshift writing surface. They met under a felt awning stretched from one side of the foaling stable. A temporary arrangement, as were many things until the hlaford was finished.

Although her contract called for her to teach no more than five children besides Rhiannon and her two brothers, at Lakenna's urging Lord Tellan had agreed to triple that number in the fall. The current five had lessons in the morning. Most of the older youth Lakenna taught rose well before dawn to do morning chores before making the trek to the hlaford for their two hours with Lakenna. More than once, Lakenna had pointed out their sacrifice to learn as a stern rebuke to Rhiannon about her lack of interest.

It was pleasant in the open air, the morning bright and sunny, almost hot. Birds chattered, and the roses around the hlaford were in full glory. Surprised at the variety of the roses the Dinari highlands produced, Lakenna had begun making plans for a large garden. Rhiannon, Creag, Phelan, and the other students had brought a cartload of river rocks to enclose the area.

Waiting for a response, Lakenna absently waved a fly from her face. Three of the four boys' faces wrinkled in confusion, grappling to understand the question, much less the answer. But the fourth, an older lad named Rahl Digon, was with her, as was the lone girl, Vanora Garbhach.

Rahl had a strong build and an unruly mass of dark hair. He was undergoing warrior training with Llyr. Rahl's father had died, and his mother scrimped out a living with her sewing and Rahl's herding. His inclusion with the five was due to Lord Tellan's direct order. After the first day of lessons and seeing the lad's potential, Lakenna had raised her already high opinion of her employer.

"Let's see," Rahl said slowly as he worked the problem in his head. "That will be five and a half gold for interest, then ten coins to repay one-third of the loan. Fifteen and a half gold due the first year."

"Which is too much." Vanora folded her arms. "The money-lender takes the profit needed to live on. My father does not like moneylenders and says that is why it is best to work through Lord Tellan to increase our flocks."

Lakenna suppressed a pleased smile. At Tellan's request, she had spent a session with Bowyn Garbhach, Vanora's father, and the other family heads to demonstrate the harsh math of interest rates.

"Better to buy more ewes with money you have saved," Vanora said. She was Bowyn's youngest child and only daughter. She had waist-length, mahogany-colored hair and sparkling brown eyes to go along with the ripening curves of young womanhood. As Lakenna had learned of clan custom, the maiden's unbound hair signified that her parents deemed her not ready for courtship. Still, it was plain as the nose on a face that she and Rahl were besotted with each other.

Rahl looked meaningfully at Vanora. "In addition to coins, warriors in service receive five ewes a year."

Vanora returned his look while slowly wrapping a strand of

hair around her finger. The air between them almost shimmered with heat. She opened her mouth—

"That is all for today," Lakenna said brightly. *Best to head this off.* "As you know, this is the last day of lessons; we will resume when the sheep return from the summer pastures. Although this has been a short session, I am pleased with the progress you five have made."

The twins, Jaime and Catel Colemon, grinned. They were twelve. Jaime had fair skin and reddish blond hair; Catel was dark complexioned and had black hair. The two did not look like brothers, much less twins. Their father was the Colemon family head and had pledged half the materials for the new building.

Terr Luwin was ten and painfully shy. He was the only child of the Jon Luwin, the third family head of the Rogoth kinsmen. Jon was an accomplished furniture maker, and he and his apprentices had orders from all over the highlands. He had promised a desk and chair for Lakenna.

The boys scrambled up when Serous, Lord Tellan's head herdsmen, walked under the awning. Every day this week, he had collected the four boys to help in the extra work needed to cull and separate the sheep into different herds for the summer.

Serous nodded formally. "Morning, Teacher." Then he asked the same question he had every day. "My boys learning?" Not *these* boys; *my* boys. And they took pride in it.

The four held their breath as they waited her response.

"A good day of school," Lakenna said.

All smiled; Vanora, too.

Serous nodded solemnly. His weathered face was a mass of fine wrinkles; his fingers were crooked at odd angles from swollen joints. As Lakenna understood the Rogoth hierarchy, the head herdsman ranked just below Girard and Llyr and was on equal footing with family heads like Bowyn Garbhach. Serous was always overly polite to her without any hint of insult; it was his way of showing respect.

The more Lakenna was around the man, the more she liked him. His dry wit and practical wisdom cut straight to the heart of any matter, and she was impressed with the easy authority with which he handled his herders.

"These are the most eager students I have had." She raised her eyebrows and looked their way. "I will depend on them to help with the new students when we start again." That brought five pleased smiles.

Serous grunted approval. Then he sidled up to her and lowered his voice. "You'll be remembering to pray for us herders up there in the high pastures?"

Surprised, she turned to face him.

Faded blue eyes regarded her solemnly. "Strange things have happened up there off and on—even before any of this with the old hlaford and Mistress Rhiannon." Serous worked his tongue around his two upper teeth. "I know she'll be here with you, but don't forget us herders. Come nightfall, it'll be strong comfort knowing a believer like you is praying for us."

Her stomach twisted. "Yes. I . . . I will do so daily."

Relief mixed with pleasure lit up the man's lined face. He called to the boys, and they headed toward the path that snaked along the stream meandering through the valley floor.

"Been talking to Llyr," Serous told Rahl as they walked away. "He mentioned some things he wants you to work on. Time was, before my joints swelled, there wasn't a hair's difference between Llyr and me. Bring your practice sword with you next week. By the time we get back, I'll have you ready to acquit yourself well." The head herdsman's voice trailed away in the distance.

Vanora watched them go. The breeze ruffled her long hair, and the sunlight sparked off the new locket around her neck. She and all the boys but Rahl had new clothes and footwear. Signs of freshly spent money brought by Tellan's agreement with Lord Gillaon and the Broken Stone Land—and a source of nagging unease to Lakenna.

She *knew* the deal was a danger to Rhiannon—but how to

convince Lord Tellan of that when all evidence thus far seemed to prove otherwise? It had certainly brought more prosperity, and the Rogoth kinsmen needed it. And there had been no further attacks since the wool sale.

"Rahl will be working directly with Serous," Vanora said with a touch of pride. "Master Phelan will be with them. Serous wants Rahl to help train him." She frowned prettily. "Women can't go. The summer pastures, I mean. I'm as good a herder as any of them, but I can't go to the high pastures."

Lakenna regarded the maiden. It was best she stayed here under her father's eye. That was probably why girls weren't allowed to go. Too many opportunities for—

Oh, enough of this! Just because Loane and I failed doesn't mean Vanora and Rahl will, too.

"I will work with Mistress Rhiannon and Master Creag each morning during the summer," Lakenna said as Vanora prepared to leave. "But my afternoons will be free. I plan to catalog the different varieties of roses and plant one of each in the new garden. Would you like to help?"

"Oh, yes!" Vanora's brown eyes lit up. "I know where bushes stand several cubits high and so thick you have to walk around them. And colors! Red, pink, white, and yellow. After the herders leave next week, I can show them to you."

"I look forward to it."

Wearing an ear-to-ear smile, Vanora took her leave. Her family lands lay a good hourglass's walk in the opposite direction of Serous and the boys.

Living among clansmen was not what Lakenna had expected. To her, as a non-clan inhabitant of the Land, clansmen had always seemed secretive, guarding both their centuries-old trade advantages and precious clan lore with fanatical devotion.

Nonetheless, Lakenna found clansmen—the Rogoths, anyway—to be just like her close-knit Albane community. True, her role in the winged horror attack had helped them accept her readily. But the longer Lakenna was here, the more she suspected that Serous's quick endorsement of her had smoothed her set-tling in. Still, it was amusing to encounter red faces and half-finished sentences when someone mentioned something in her hearing that had to be part of secret clan lore.

Albanes were found in all six clans, but most were women who had married into a clan or were the offspring of such marriages. That seemed to be the only way to become a clan member: marriage or birth, although there were stories of adults being made clan members. Lakenna had no idea how that happened.

She sighed. Marriage. A husband. Home and hearth. All things she did not have—and might never experience. She pondered her lack of attraction to men. Though she did not possess the beauty of Rhiannon or Vanora, Lakenna knew she was not totally unattractive. Growing up, many of her female friends and a few boys had mentioned how expressive her eyes were. And some had noticed her thick hair.

Loane in particular had been fascinated with it. The one time she had unpinned it in his presence, his eyes had widened in wonderment as the heavy waves cascaded about her neck and shoulders. He had reached for her like a man beholding the most precious thing imaginable. She had stepped into his arms, exult-ing in his desire for her...

I cannot allow these thoughts. I must try harder! A true Albane could do so.

A true Albane. Like she used to be.

She walked to the edge of the awning and looked uphill at the soon-to-be-completed hlaford, knowing what a relief it would be for Mererid to move in and get her family back in order.

Day by day, Lakenna grew closer to Lady Mererid. Beyond the tight quarters of the pavilion and their common agenda of the children's education, Lakenna recognized the noblewoman's loneliness and hunger for companionship.

The rich farmlands of Lakenna's home were densely popu-lated compared to the far-flung homesteads here in the rugged highlands. The Fawr kinsmen were south of Lachlann, with Lord

Seuman and Lady Aigneis's hlaford more than half a day's ride—
which Mererid maintained was a blessing. Lady Iola Leanon was
two hours' ride north, but Mererid said the two of them, while
friendly, had never been close. That had been shared last night
during an after-supper walk that was becoming a nightly ritual
for the two of them.

Lakenna's mouth firmed as she realized it was past time for
lessons. She turned back toward the stables. Then she noticed
Creag and Phelan coming, leather folders under their arms. She
glanced toward the pavilion. No sign of Rhiannon. Lakenna suppressed a sigh. Late again.

For the hundredth time since arriving, Lakenna pondered
her role with Rhiannon. Despite the girl's tendency to give short
shrift to her lessons, Lakenna could see something changing: if
not yet an eagerness to learn, at least a noticeable improvement.

Creag's progress was most satisfying. By this time next year, he
would be where he should be compared to others his age.

Phelan was a delight. The boy possessed a mind like parched
earth, soaking up every drop of knowledge poured out and eager
for more.

She looked to the pavilion again. *What does Protectoress of the
Covenant entail? And how can I bring Rhiannon closer to the Eternal
when I feel farther from him than I ever have?*

She realized how sheltered her twenty-five years had been
within the cocoon of the Albane community. The stories of Destin Faber and Stanus Albane's encounters with the Mighty Ones'
creatures were told frequently, both for their own sake and to
illustrate points of doctrine. At the end of every Albane meeting,
it was standard practice to offer up prayer binding the Mighty
Ones and their creatures. All took pride in the fact there had
been no outbreaks of winged horrors in Albane settlements in
living memory.

Those thoughts brought up Serous's request for prayer. Here
at the Rogoth hlaford she was surrounded by respect, both for
her position as tutor and for her part in defeating the winged

197

horrors. Yet deep inside Lakenna knew she was an imposter in the spiritual battles that undoubtedly must be fought if Rhiannon was to fulfill her birthing prophecy.

Could prayer bind a clan High Lord? And if it couldn't, then what?

How she wanted to talk to someone about her insight concerning Maolmin. But aware of the privileged position a High Lord held within his clan, and fearing she might run afoul of some code of clan honor, she had not done so. As the budding relationship with Mererid continued, perhaps an opportunity would present itself.

I need to talk to that Keeper. I am sure he sensed the same thing about Maolmin! But Branor had disappeared immediately after the wool sale, and as far as anyone knew, he was still behind Kepploch's walls.

Although it stuck in her craw, she remembered the relief that had flooded though her when Branor had edged her aside so he could come to grips with Maolmin, one nobleman to another. As a commoner and non-clan member, she knew she had been risking much by stepping between the High Lord and Rhiannon. But *something* had to be done. That she had actually done so, in spite of... everything, still amazed her. Her boldness must have come from the Eternal.

Lakenna neatened a stack of cheap parchment. Every day it grew harder to make herself pray even a short morning prayer. She felt a hindrance, a heaviness. And when she did pray she felt the sense of a gathering storm that lingered long after she rose from her knees.

Creag and Phelan stepped under the shade of the awning. Each greeted her, took a stool, and removed parchments from his leather folder. She put them to work on their handwriting.

Finally, Rhiannon rushed in with her smooth, long-legged stride, red mane flowing behind her. "I was sketching a design for a new type of sword to fight winged horrors."

"Swords!" Creag set down his quill. "You need bows and arrows against winged horrors."

Rhiannon plopped her folder next to him on the plank. "Not

if they are astride you like they were Father and me! The new sword will—"

"Father's sword got chewed up. If *he* couldn't kill one with a sword, what makes you—"

"That was before Teacher Lakenna began praying," Rhiannon replied loftily. "If they come again, things will be different."

Lakenna's stomach rippled. "That is quite enough about winged horrors," she said. "Mistress Rhiannon, take out the map we are making. I want you to finish drawing out the course of the Clundy River from its beginning here in the highlands to its mouth at Shinard. Master Creag, listen to Master Phelan repeat the multiplication tables and tell me if he makes a mistake."

As the three went to work, Lakenna gnawed her lower lip. It seemed everyone from Rhiannon to Lord Tellan to Serous and his herders remained confident in her ability to keep the winged horrors from drawing power from the Mighty Ones.

Her failure loomed ever larger. What did they think, that she was an anointed prayer warrior like the Founders? Able to stand in the gap and pray the fire of heaven down? That she would find herself clothed in supernatural armor and a flaming sword in her hands to battle siyyim and even the dread Mighty Ones as Destin Faber did with *Asunder*?

He and Stanus Albane were pure, unsullied believers, giants of the faith. I am a woman alone, a sinner with innocent blood on my hands. I came here to escape, and here I am in the midst of it! Dear Eternal, take this burden from me!

"Teacher?" Rhiannon asked.

"Yes?"

"What do you think 'Protectoress of the Covenant' means?"

Creag groaned, but Lakenna almost jumped. A cold barb stabbed her heart. She found herself giving the only answer she could: "Tonight before bed let us read and discuss scripture, seeking to learn what it meant to serve the Eternal in general and some hint of what 'Protectoress of the Covenant' might entail specifically."

Rhiannon smiled. "I would like that."

Feeling an impostor, Lakenna returned the smile. "Back to work."

As Phelan finished reciting his multiplication tables, Rhiannon looked up from her map. "Phelan, would you open the geography text and read me the distances between Ancylar, Strath, and Shinard?"

"I'll do it," Creag said.

Frown lines creased Rhiannon's brow. She opened her mouth, then closed it.

Creag opened the heavy leather-bound book and turned the pages. "From Ancylar to Strath: thirty-eight leagues."

Rhiannon dipped her quill in the ink and entered the numbers. "And from Strath to Shinard?"

Creag started at the page. His lips firmed. "Eighteen leagues . . . I think."

"No," Phelan interjected. "It's much farther than that." He reached for the book. "Here, let me—"

"I can read it!" Creag fumed. He blinked, looked away from the page, then back. "From Strath to Shinard is . . ." He set his jaw and began yet again.

Rhiannon raised her head, her expression thoughtful as she watched Creag's distress.

"Why can't I do this!" Creag looked close to tears. "I must be stupid!"

"You're as smart as Phelan," Rhiannon said quietly, setting down her quill. "You just learn differently, that's all."

Creag's jaw dropped open. Phelan's eyes almost popped out of his head as he looked at his sister, astonished. Stunned silence reigned under the awning.

Creag regarded Rhiannon warily. "What do you mean?"

"Since Teacher Lakenna has come, you're getting better every day."

Lakenna found her mouth open as well. What was this?

"You found the distance from Ancylar to Strath," Rhiannon went on. "What happened after that?"

"The words moved and I couldn't find them." He looked down. "How can you keep them straight?"

"What do you mean, 'the words moved'?" Phelan snorted. "They're written on the page."

"I have an idea." Rhiannon took two pieces of writing parchment and placed them over the page so only one line was uncovered. "Read this line."

Creag did so perfectly. Rhiannon moved the sheets to uncover the next line only. Creag read it perfectly. With mounting excitement for them both, she did half the page that way.

Creag took the sheets from his sister and read on. "I can read as good as you and Phelan!"

Stunned, tears came to Lakenna's eyes. *I should have thought of this!*

Rhiannon nodded solemnly. "It won't be long before you're reading better than me."

"I'm getting better in sword drills, too!"

Rhiannon's eyes flashed green fire. "That was luck!"

"You heard Llyr say how I'm—"

"Tomorrow I will touch you every time—"

"Tomorrow I'll hit you twice as hard—"

"Back to work!" Lakenna demanded, regaining control.

Rhiannon flounced her head and returned to the map, muttering under her breath. Creag went back to the book, face aglow. Phelan's eyes flicked from one to the other, puzzled. Finally, he picked up his quill and started writing.

Once everyone was back on task, Lakenna walked to the edge of the awning, pleased with the solution to Creag's reading problem but still a bit chagrined that she hadn't seen it herself. No matter. The important thing was that nothing would hold the boy back now.

She glanced back at Rhiannon. The girl bent over the plank, carefully labeling the map. Long, elegant fingers gripped the quill, her beautiful face a study of concentration, unlined with the burdens of life.

Rhiannon remained an enigma, the exchange with Creag a perfect example. One moment she was a young woman who showed signs of maturity and leadership that were startling, and then the next she reverted to immature squabbling with her brother.

Lakenna sighed and looked out on the peaceful landscape. The scenery was breathtaking. The blue smudge of the towering Ardnamur Mountains dominated the west; immediately to the north rose the smaller Fea range, though their proximity made them seem larger.

Then, without warning, a powerful sense of foreboding washed over Lakenna, much more potent than during her brief prayer this morning. Somehow she knew she was sensing the Mighty Ones stirring. Before her eyes, the landscape changed.

Northward, where High Lord Maolmin resided, the sky seemed to darken and pulse with flashes of lightning. Westward, behind the Ardnamur Mountains, the sky turned an angry purple and black. Another presence brooded there, restless and sure of its power.

Chapter Twenty-one

HARRED

WHITE-CAPPED PEAKS TOWERED all around them, glittering in the green-blue sky. In the Ardnamur Mountains, winter always released its grip with reluctance, but this year it had lingered well past the norm. Patches of dirty snow remained under the spreading branches of the evergreens. Small clusters of red flowers bravely bloomed on both sides of the road. A raucous birdcall rose and fell from the high forest, echoing among the bare rocks outlining the narrow wagon trail.

Harred reined up and scanned both sides of the tract, all senses alerted. But he heard only rodents of various kinds scurrying amid the underbrush. He checked his horse. Coal waited patiently, ears relaxed, unconcerned. Harred breathed easier. There had been no further attacks since Maude, but he was taking no chances.

A stone's throw to his right—north—a granite cliff rose straight up for several hundred paces to a wide, treeless shelf of stone where they were to meet the Broken Stone party. Elmar had scouted ahead yesterday and confirmed their presence.

It was an hourglass till dusk. The rendezvous was supposed to have taken place at noon today, but the wagons' progress had been slowed by a long stretch of mud and clay sucking on the wheels. Frequent rests had been necessary for the mules. Their flaring nostrils and heaving sides showed the strain of the hard going in the thin air.

Harred nudged Coal up by the front wagon. "Elmar says the

ground turns rocky and it's good footing once we start up to the meeting place."

Ard nodded. "Be glad to get out of this accursed muck." He lifted his eyes to the sheer cliff. "The mules will need a full night's rest before heading up there." His cheek bulged as he maneuvered his wad of tabac from one side to the other. He spat a dark liquid stream, then wiped his mouth with a meaty hand. "Come first light, I'll be wanting a saddle horse to ride the trail and see if there's need to double hitch."

"Elmar rode it this morning. He said normal rigging should do."

Ard spat again. "Elmar's a good man, and he knows these mountains. But it won't be his wagons and mules sliding off that cliff if he's wrong." He cocked a bushy eyebrow. "Don't imagine Lord Gillaon will be too happy, neither."

Harred grunted agreement. "I'll ride with you."

He was learning everything he could from the wagon master. If tomorrow went well on this trip, Gillaon had told Harred he would want to send another shipment of goods before the autumn snows closed the passes. Without the bulky bales of wool, ten or so farm wagons fitted with heavier axles would suffice.

It took another half glass of trudging through the mud around the base of the cliff before they came to where the narrow road began the winding ascent to the meeting place.

Harred called halt for camp. The drivers pulled the wagons close together, unhitched their teams, and began rubbing them down. Harred sent four of his men out for first watch, then put the rest to building cook fires and hauling water from a nearby stream.

After finishing the rubdown, the drivers put hobbles and feedbags on the mules. Once the animals had finished the grain and the bags were removed, they would graze on the grass between the road and the forest.

It was deep twilight, and the smell of cooking mingled with the scent of evergreen and damp earth when Elmar came riding in from the west. Dismounting with a groan, he ambled stiffly up to Harred's fire. The mountaineer had a three-day stubble of beard, and his face was etched with weariness. "Nothing be moving but tree rats and half-starved deer."

Harred nodded. He took a wooden bowl and filled it with stew from the steaming pot hanging over the fire. "Here."

A spoon materialized in Elmar's hand. He took the bowl, sat down, and took an appreciative sniff. He dipped out a steaming spoonful and blew to cool it. "My papa and uncles dealt with Broken Stone smugg—*traders*—off and on. Tomorrow, we best keep one hand on our coin purses and the other close to our knives."

"Lord Gillaon spent some time talking to me about that."

After testing the spoon's contents with his tongue, Elmar blew on it some more. He had lost weight from long days in the saddle and trail food. "Does Lord Gillaon think we be having any trouble?"

"He says they are as eager for this as we are. The advantages for both sides are too great. Still . . ."

The night before you arrive, camp early if necessary, Gillaon had said. *You and Elmar make yourselves presentable. Wash and shave. Bring new shirts and pants and keep them clean. Never enter negotiations tired and dirty. Puts you at a disadvantage. They will be traveling lighter and will most likely be there first, rested and clean, wits about them. You must not allow them to gain the upper hand.*

Elmar finished the bowl and filled it again from the pot.

Harred stood and stretched saddle-stiff muscles. He looked up at the outline of the cliff and swallowed down his nervousness. The meeting with the pagans would be another test. Hopefully he would pass it as he had the others since becoming rhyfelwr.

What had Gillaon said way back at the Bridge Across? *Think upon this as a different type of battle, fought with different weapons.* Just so.

"When you're finished eating," Harred said, "we need to heat water to bathe and shave, then unpack those new clothes."

The wagons creaked slowly uphill. The roadbed, though damp, was rocky and firm. The incline remained acceptable as the narrow track zigzagged across the face of the cliff and finally reached their destination.

The shelf of rock was covered with lush grass. The level clearing was not large, five hundred paces in circumference at the most. The mountainside bordered two sides and the hillside dropped away on the third. The Broken Stone wagons were arrayed straight ahead on the west side of the road that continued to the Cyodan Pass, a day's journey deeper in the wilds of the Ardnamurs. Several paces from the wagons stood a large white tent on the grassy turf of the shelf, and a smaller blue tent beside it. Atop the larger tent's center pole fluttered the universally recognized trading banner: a red field with a narrow white stripe in the middle.

Harred remained mounted as the wagons lumbered up behind him. His eyes swept the pagan encampment. The shelf was grassy but treeless, and he saw no place for warriors to be concealed. Small groups of men lounged around campfires whose smoke hung in thin wisps close to the ground. When the men saw the Tarenester party, they began to bustle about, unhobbling mules and picking up harnesses.

Movement came from the large tent as well. The figure of a man emerged and strode across the grass toward Harred. Harred caught Elmar's eye, and they dismounted.

Wait for this Thoven to greet you, Gillaon had said. *Who he sends will be informative. If it is his older white-haired retainer I have met with, it will show respect among equals. Someone else, and it will show he deems us inferior.*

The messenger neared. It was a lad sixteen years of age at the most. He wore pants and a plain, knee-length cotton tunic. Stopping five paces away, he spoke in a high-pitched piping voice without proper greeting or a bow. "You are later than expected. My master is anxious to be done here. Bring your wagons alongside ours to transfer the bales."

Opening move. A sharp, probing attack.

206

"It has been a long trek," Harred said. "I will be ready to meet at noon to make these arrangements."

"After the wool is loaded," the servant continued as if Harred had not spoken, "my master wants to see you."

Harred warmed to the task. "I am rhyfelwr and advisor to Lord Gillaon Tarenester, Clan Arshessa." Assuming his most fierce scowl, he strode three steps forward. "Am I *summoned*?"

The young man's face whitened, and he took a step backwards. He squared thin shoulders and tugged his tunic. "Er...no, m'lord...er, ah..."

"I am no nobleman. Rhyfelwr will do."

"Yes, ah, rhyfelwr. My master is most anxious to—"

"I am sure your master does not want this to end before it begins. As we are new to each other's ways, I will ignore the insult of this greeting. At noon, let us begin afresh." He placed fists on his hips and let his gaze drill into the messenger. "If this is repeated, I will see honor satisfied."

Eyeing him warily, the servant gave a slight bow. "I will inform my master." He pivoted smartly and retraced his steps back to the tent. Though his gait was steady, he seemed ready to break into a run.

Elmar gave Harred an appraising glance. "Aye, this agrees with you. If I hadn't been aware of your underlying gentle nature, I'd swear you be about to rip that one's liver out and eat it raw."

Harred blinked. "That bad?"

"Your face be something to behold." He snorted. "Get your eyes to flash fire like that Rogoth daughter does, and you'll never have to draw a sword again."

The small red flowers Harred had noticed on the trail bloomed in broad swaths across the grassy shelf. He and Elmar were being escorted to the trading tent by Keto, the white-haired retainer. Arriving at the Tarenester wagons just before noon, Keto had been gracious and apologetic "for any misunderstanding."

Keto was reed thin and moved with an ease that belied his white hair and wrinkled skin. His silk tunic was richly embroidered with unrecognizable symbols. Around his neck were a gold chain and an emerald the size of a pigeon egg, a display of wealth at odds with the mountain wilds around them. If it was meant to awe, Harred had to admit it was working. He found himself even more apprehensive about dealing with the Broken Stone merchant waiting inside.

He and Elmar were plainly dressed in new wool shirts and leather pants, boots freshly polished. Keto's lined face had shown momentarily surprise when he saw they wore no arms.

Do not wear swords. Broken Stone warriors clank around with weapons hanging all over them. By going unarmed you will make them seem overly frightened. Besides, if they plan treachery you're dead men anyway.

Nonetheless, Harred had two throwing daggers inside each boot and a thick-bladed knife strapped to his back under the shirt. Elmar was similarly armed.

As the three of them neared the tent, Harred's gaze was drawn to the red flowers again, and despite everything, thoughts of Breanna flooded his senses. Tingling warmth enveloped him. He saw her in the stable, her dark eyes wide with a mixture of wonder and questioning; he saw her during the loreteller meeting and the way she had tilted her head: "Do you serve the Eternal, Harred Wright?"

Yes, indeed. Here is a bouquet of flowers I picked for you while proving myself as rhyfelwr. Even in the mist of dealing with incredibly rich pagans, your image was ever before me.

Harred told himself for the hundredth time to forget the loreteller's daughter. Her father would refuse his suit, making a *Wifan-er-Weal* the only way. He'd take his chances against any four handpicked Dinari—but then to face Maolmin Erian? Not after seeing him move in the stables and being in his presence at the Rogoth pavilion.

He reviewed in his mind Lord Gillaon's instructions. Keto's

appearance signaled success during the opening skirmish. Harred knew his true test—if there was to be one—awaited him now.

The breeze picked up and snapped the red and white trading banner against its pole. The Broken Stone wagons stood ready, mules hitched, drivers waiting.

A message, that. Good. No one wants this wool heading west more than Harred did. He smiled grimly. *As long as the original agreement is adhered to.*

They came to the front of the tent. Keto pulled back its opening flap and ushered them inside.

Thick rugs covered the grass. In the center a small brazier burned some type of aromatic wood. Faint tentacles of smoke rose to escape through a flap in the roof. Assorted bags, cushions, and small chests were arranged next to the sides. At the back of the tent stood a small table and two chairs.

The Broken Stone merchant stood waiting beside the brazier. He was an impressive figure. Almost as tall as Harred and broader across the shoulders, he gave the impression of immense physical strength. He was clean-shaven except for a large mustache drooping below his mouth. His green leather vest and black cloak were clean and well made, although decidedly plainer than Keto's flashy attire. The merchant's face was impassive as he watched them enter. Four warriors stood quietly to his side. Identically dressed in quilted vests and dark gray leather pants, each had a long, curved sword hanging naked from a broad belt, along with several knives. They carefully kept hands away from the hilts.

The Broken Stone merchant strode toward them with a smile that did not reach his eyes. He halted two paces from Harred and Elmar and gave the slightest of bows. Although his voice was quiet, his deep bass filled the tent. "I am Thoven Vlaeska. It is an honor to receive you. I have been looking forward to our meeting with keen anticipation."

"The pleasure is ours," Harred replied smoothly, just as he'd rehearsed with Lord Gillaon. He formally introduced himself and Elmar. "Lord Gillaon sends both his greetings and his hopes that this will be the first transaction of a long and fruitful association."

The faintest of frowns crossed Thoven's face. "I am here to meet Lord Gillaon."

"With the uncertainties of the King's Licenses he thought it best to send me in his stead. As rhyfelwr, I am familiar with the details of the agreement reached last year."

"You speak for Gillaon?" Thoven demanded, his eyes intent.

As the power of that gaze rested on him, Harred felt that the pagan was looking inside him somehow, assessing his strengths and weaknesses in a way disturbingly familiar. He gathered himself and managed to reply. "I am empowered to carry out the agreement."

Thoven's eyes bored into him a moment longer, then the merchant seemed to reach a decision. "With your permission, I will have Keto and his men inspect the wool."

Elmar went with Keto and the four warriors, leaving Harred alone with the merchant.

"Please, sit." Thoven indicated the table and chairs. "Food will be brought soon. We can talk while we wait."

Harred pulled a chair and sat. *Now it begins.*

Thoven settled into the other chair and crossed a leg. As big as he was, he somehow gave the impression of a larger presence. "Was Maolmin as much a problem as we feared?"

"He opposed the sale, but Lord Gillaon's price and Lord Tellan's support made the difference."

"How did Maolmin react to the prospect of his wool coming west?"

Although the merchant's face remained bland, Harred sensed an underlying anticipation. Again Gillaon's coaching returned to him.

With Clan Sabinis squeezing us harder every year, I have been in communication with Thoven for some time, trying to import goods through the Broken Stone Land. From the beginning, he demanded Dinari wool. It is a prize export to be sure, but I sense a desire to damage Maolmin. See if you can find out more about that.

"The High Lord," Harred said, choosing his words carefully, "was concerned that dealing with pagans would violate the Covenant."

Thoven barked a laugh. "Of course." He looked inquiringly at Harred. "Tell me, clansman, where does this Covenant mention not to trade with those who worship the Lady of the West?"

Harred's silence was answer enough. According to legend, when Destin Faber united the six clans and cut the Covenant with the Eternal, many of the defeated worshipers of the Mighty Ones left the Land. In the western area, where the Landantae clan and Harred's Arshessa clan dominated, the pagans had crossed these Ardnamur Mountains and settled in the Broken Stone Land beyond.

Finally he said, "It does say: 'Keep this covenant and the Mighty Ones' yoke of slavery shall be broken.'"

Thoven uncrossed his legs and leaned his arms on the table. His hands were large, his fingers long and powerful. Waiting for the merchant to speak, Harred understood what nagged him about the man. Thoven sounded like Maolmin. Not with voice or accent, but the same sureness, the same unruffled command. And something was similar about the two men's eyes.

"Frankly," Thoven said, "the yoke you are under is the Sabinis control of the Faber throne. They use that interpretation of the Covenant to shackle competitors. My people and others across the Great Sea—'pagans,' all—have dealt quietly with the Sabinis for years." He shook his head. "The Faber dynasty totters. Lord Gillaon sees this clearly. Your king is invalid, allowing Cullia to profane her oath by aiding her clan in squeezing her subjects dry." He paused. "Would Lord Gillaon dare import without permits if the crown was not so weak?"

Harred had to concede that point. Still, the Covenant and its link to the Faber dynasty was the bedrock all six clans stood on. Or did they? Maybe it was words only. Harred knew that many in the Land still worshiped the old gods. How much did they communicate with and profit from their Broken Stone and overseas counterparts? The more he learned about higher-level clan dealings, the more it seemed the Covenant was ignored when trade and profit were concerned.

The front flap opened, and a young woman entered carrying a tray with a pitcher and two goblets. Harred almost gasped. She was the most exquisite woman he had ever seen. The Rogoth daughter—Rhiannon—was a rare beauty, but this woman belonged in another category altogether.

As she glided toward the table, the impact of her perfection was breathtaking. Her oval face was fine-featured and accented by high cheekbones and a thin nose. Elegant eyebrows and upward slanting, almond-shaped eyes gave her face an exotic cast. She had full red lips and hair as yellow as honey gathered atop her head in a jeweled clasp. Soft curls swayed against her neck and shoulders. A blue gown with many folds covered her demurely from neck to feet and yet somehow managed to draw attention to certain curves.

Something very male stirred inside Harred. With a strength that rocked him he desired to posses this young woman. To be able to hold such beauty. To feel her softness.

No, no. He tore his eyes away. *She is bait being dangled. Watch yourself.*

She set the tray on the table, took the pitcher, filled the goblets, and placed them in front of the two men. She went about her task with practiced movements and downcast eyes. Finished, she glanced at Thoven.

"Thank you, Zoe," he said. "You may leave now. I will send for you later."

She bowed her head in acknowledgment. Then she lifted her face and looked straight at Harred. Those tilted, almond-shaped eyes enveloped him like a lover's embrace. Her smoldering gaze promised erotic pleasures only dreamed of.

Harred could only gape. His blood surged hotly. Once more he was seized with the desire to possess this exquisite creature.

As suddenly as it appeared, Zoe's raw sexuality vanished.

Smiling faintly, she turned and left the tent, a picture of demure femininity.

Harred had to will himself not to get up and follow her. Teetering before a volcanic abyss, he flailed inwardly for some landmark to help him regain his center. What was happening here?

Mercifully, Breanna flooded his senses again. He clung to her like a drowning man thrown a rope. He clung to her goodness. Her purity. Breanna became a beacon beckoning him into a sheltered harbor and away from the storm of emotions that threatened to engulf him.

Taking a deep breath, he brought his focus back to the wool. When he did, he noticed the Broken Stone merchant watching him like a hawk, eyes hard and calculating before a bland mask reappeared.

Harred had entered the tent prepared to use his wits and Gillaon's training to see that the original agreement was adhered to. And then Zoe was thrown at him. Why? To befuddle him before Thoven reneged on the agreement? Again, why? No, Zoe could not have been meant for him. Perhaps for Lord Gillaon?

As it turned out, he was wrong on all counts.

"Prince Larien seeks a bride," Thoven said softly. He traced a finger lightly around the rim of the goblet. "The Rite of Presentation is perfect for Zoe. The rewards of being allied with the new princess—and future queen—will be enormous."

Harred swallowed, mind whirling at the implications. "Only clan nobility will be presented."

"You have had foreign queens before. The latest was the Rosada princess, Natachasa de Delgurre."

The Rosada. Again, Harred saw Da's burning eyes. But Harred could deal with Rosada; they at least worshiped the same God. This now was something entirely different. "That was to seal a treaty that ended generations of Rosada raids." Harred shook his head. "No Broken Stone woman could hope to—"

"Zoe is from Costos. The island has large numbers who worship the Eternal." Thoven smiled without humor. "But with her Broken Stone ties, Zoe will be an instrument to return our two countries to the relationship we enjoyed before the Faber dynasty." The merchant's mouth firmed. "We must reach agreement on this before discussing Lord Gillaon's wool."

Harred sat straighter in his chair. "What is there to discuss?"

"A small favor between partners. Zoe returns with you, and Lord Gillaon takes her to the Arshessa Presentation. Lady Ouveau, the chief advisor to the queen, is...a friend of a friend. She will see that Zoe is introduced to the prince." Thoven's lips quirked. "Zoe is capable of proceeding from there."

Wrongness twisted Harred's stomach. Cold sweat trickled down his back.

Thoven's eyes flashed. "The Faber dynasty is at its lowest ebb. New blood is needed. I say again, the rewards will be beyond your imagining."

It was unnaturally quiet inside the tent. Outside, Harred heard the braying of mules and the jingle of harnesses as wagons moved.

He took a deep breath. How he longed to be out of this chair, to stand before his opponent with the familiar heft of his sword in his hand.

Why did he keep thinking of this man as an adversary like Maolmin? Lord Gillaon had warned him that the Broken Stone merchant moved in the highest circles of nobility and government. A person to be taken with the utmost seriousness. Harred believed it.

What to do about Zoe? If she was from Costos, it was possible, though by no means certain, that she served the Eternal. More likely she did not. A *pagan*—albeit a secret one—as princess and ultimately queen? Would Gillaon go along with this?

No, though Gillaon's own lust might be stirred up by Zoe, he would see this woman for what she was: poisoned bait dangled in an effort to—what? Take the throne? End the Covenant? Both?

Harred's mind reeled. He could not make a decision like this. Suddenly he realized this was his lord's true reason for not coming. Cannily, Gillaon must have feared something like this: a demand carefully wrapped and presented. Gillaon had borrowed beyond his limit to buy the wool and was vulnerable to pressure from the Broken Stone merchant. If Thoven did not take the wool, who would? The Sabinis controlled all Land harbors and shipping. Gillaon would be unable to export the wool to the lucrative markets across the Great Sea. He would be ruined. But by sending a young rhyfelwr not empowered to deal beyond the wool agreement, Gillaon would deflect any such pressure.

Harred struggled to keep the relief off his face. Here was his way out. A way around the wrongness roiling his guts. "I am under strict orders to sell the wool and purchase the return goods only," he said. "I will relay your request to Lord Gillaon. He requests another load of amber and other jewels later in the summer while the passes remain open. When we return, I will bring his answer."

Thoven frowned fiercely. "That is too long! Another will have to see this done, and Lord Gillaon will lose the reward." He glared at Harred. "You risk much. A man of Lord Gillaon's talents is wasted as a mere kinsmen lord. He is capable of more—much more. When he understands what he has lost with this opportunity he will not be pleased." Thoven waited expectantly.

The implications of all this continued to batter Harred. Six months ago he was a simple warrior. Now he found himself in the middle of a plot to place a pagan queen on the throne—at the very least, and perhaps to end the Faber dynasty and the Covenant as well.

"I do not have the authority to make this kind of decision," he replied truthfully.

Thoven hissed in disgust. He stood angrily to his feet.

Harred rose as well. "And the wool?"

Thoven ignored the question. "I will prepare a letter outlining our conversation for you to give Lord Gillaon. Though this opportunity has passed him by, there will be more." The cold promise in the merchant's voice sent a shiver down Harred's spine.

"And the wool?" Harred repeated dangerously. Weary of this war of words, his hand edged toward the knife strapped to his back. If Thoven reneged on the agreement, Harred was ready to kill him, then walk outside and signal Elmar and the Tarenester men to arms. The emerald Keto wore should come close to repaying Gillaon's debt.

Thoven watched him as if reading his thoughts.

"Easy, warrior. If it is top-grade Dinari wool, as I am sure it is, then I will pay eight silvers per bale as promised. And we have brought ample wares for your trip back. Return here two months from today, and Keto will meet you with more amber and jewels." His eyes glowed. "But hear me! Tell Gillaon that if we are to continue beyond that, he must bring triple the number of Dinari bales next year. I will pay a gold per bale. Triple it again, and it will be a gold and two silvers."

Thoven smiled, and Harred felt another chill. "Let us see how Maolmin and the North counter that."

Chapter Twenty-two

LAKENNA

"AFTER THE MAIDEN Pole," Creag explained, "the kinsmen gather for music and dancing and singing—"

"And scenes and skits," Phelan broke in while Ove set out his bowl. "I like that the best."

"This time I will help Girard tell *The High Lord's Horn*." Creag took a loaf of bread from the wooden platter, tore it in two, and handed Rhiannon the decidedly smaller piece.

Lakenna watched approvingly as Rhiannon bit back a retort and then thanked him. It was Rhiannon's sixteenth birthing day celebration. Everyone in the pavilion seemed in high spirits. In the morning, Serous and his herders and Phelan would begin driving the sheep to the high pastures. It had long been Lord Tellan and Lady Mererid's custom to combine Rhiannon's birthday with a feast for the departing herders, their families, and the three family heads.

The tables were arranged in a huge U with the people seated according to rank. The Rogoths sat at the head table with Girard, Llyr, and their wives. And Lakenna. Serous and the three family heads and their wives sat on the sides closest to the Rogoths. The other herders and their families stretched further down the table.

Lakenna wore a new gray wool dress that Mererid had presented to her before the feast. Even with the plain stitching and no lace, it was the finest Lakenna had ever possessed. Mererid wore a dark yellow dress with a narrow band of ivory lace outlining the bodice. The skirt was wide and flowing. Rhiannon looked stunning in the green linen she had worn at the wool sale. Surprisingly—or maybe not—it was no struggle to get her to wear it tonight.

Tellan stood. He looked distinguished in a high-collar dark blue coat, white shirt, and brown breeches. His black hair was oiled and combed. The happy babble died down into an expectant silence. He turned to his daughter. "Today, Rhiannon de Murdeen en Rogoth, you come of age." He stopped, eyes misting. "Henceforth you will be addressed as Lady—" He cleared his throat. "You will be addressed as Lady Rhiannon." His voice thickened. "And that you are. A beautiful and noble young lady with whom I am most pleased."

Lakenna glanced at Mererid. Her stepmother's smile was sincere and loving. She handed Tellan a requin, the woven leather band that clan maidens wore encircling their hair and forehead to signify that they were ready for courtship and betrothal.

Tellan's face was a mixture of emotions as he placed the requin on his daughter's head. "The man who takes this off, Lady Rhiannon, will be blessed indeed."

Rhiannon sat misty-eyed while her father and Mererid, then Girard, Llyr, Serous, and the three family heads took turns congratulating her.

That done, the banquet began. Ove shuffled stiffly around, filling bowls.

During the meal Mererid patted her lips with a linen napkin. "Normally, Teacher, the three kinsmen groups here in the Clundy River valley hold a Maiden Pole together. But with the Presentation for Prince Larien upon us, High Lord Maolmin has announced his Erian kinsmen will hold their Maiden Pole the morning of the Presentation. He invites all Dinari to join them. We have not had a clan-wide Pole in years."

"Remember Loreteller Abel's daughter, Breanna?" Girard asked. "She was the one who accompanied him at Lachlann. The girl is betrothed to Ryce Pleoh and will be married at the ceremony."

He paused and lifted an eyebrow. "I have heard her bride price is ten gold coins."

Everyone was stunned. From talks with Vanora, Lakenna knew that two gold coins were normal; five was high. Ten seemed extraordinary for a commoner, even for the daughter of a high-ranking advisor.

"Ten golds," Mererid said slowly, "would purchase a fancy carriage, four horses to pull it, and still leave coins left over."

Bowyn Garbhach cleared his throat. "M'lord, after the insult the High Lord has shown by not including Mistress—I mean to say *Lady* Rhiannon—in those to be presented, me and the other heads are in agreement that we should hold our own Pole as always."

Murmurs of assent came from all.

"The Rogoth kinsmen will attend the Dinari Maiden Pole and the Presentation," Tellan stated flatly.

"Most assuredly," Mererid agreed.

Lakenna glanced at Rhiannon. The young woman's face held relief—with perhaps a touch of sadness. What was that about?

"But enough of this," Mererid said determinedly. "Back to our food."

"Teacher," Phelan said as he pulled up the bowl of white sauce and spooned on a layer, "after the Maiden Pole is over, you have to hear Lord Baird tell *A Serving Maid's Dilemma*, especially if things have been going for a while and he has emptied several tankards."

Tellan lowered his spoon, opened his mouth as if to protest, then closed it. His face was carefully neutral.

Mererid took a sip of hot tea. "Lord Baird can tell any story he wants to his kinsmen. With *ours*, your father will see that the good lord maintains a proper tongue in his head." A smile played at the corners of her lips.

Phelan's expression was guileless. "But Mother, no one enjoys Lord Baird's stories more than Father. Last time, he laughed so hard he had tears—"

"Phelan," Tellan growled, though Lakenna noted the twinkle

in his eyes, "do you seek to land on my bad side?"

"No, sire."

"Then attend your bowl while your brother informs Teacher Lakenna of the wonders of our Pole."

Everyone laughed.

Rhiannon passed the bowl of white sauce. Lakenna hesitated, then put a tiny dab on the tip of her spoon and mixed it thoroughly into her stew.

"It is more than songs and music," Creag said.

Lakenna took a small bite of stew, then a quick bite of bread. Fire on her tongue caused beads of sweat to pop out on her brow. How could anyone get used to such spices? She reached for the cheese.

"More than anything, the Maiden Pole is when we acknowledge to each other that we are..." Creag's face reddened. He looked around and then mumbled, "That we are kinsmen."

"The Maiden Pole is for clan members only," Mererid said.

"I see," Lakenna said into the silence.

"A member of another clan can come, but it is rare."

"Of course." Lakenna glanced at Vanora, the maiden so besotted with Rahl, who was sitting at the end of the table. All the girl talked about was betrothals and Rahl, and the Maiden Pole and Rahl. And the two gold coins Rahl had saved for her bride price. Even though Bowyn had not given his assent, Lakenna had assumed they would be betrothed at the ceremony and that she would be there to see her two students. Now, strangely, Vanora seemed to be fighting a smile.

Girard said, "But rest assured all Dinari clansmen will be at the Presentation. None would dare miss it."

Silence reigned once more. Lakenna's face heated. Should she leave? Surely they were aware that this was making her feel excluded.

Serous, the head herdsmen, was watching her. He seemed to be considering something. Finally he stood and spoke. "I have watched Lakenna Wen since she has come. Everything she has touched is better. She has poured herself into my boys. They read and do sums. Her prayers helped save Lord Tellan and Mistress—*Lady* Rhiannon from the winged horrors. I stand for Lakenna Wen."

No, Lakenna breathed inwardly. *Not my prayers.*

Bowyn Garbhach spoke. "Like Serous, I have watched Lakenna Wen. Vanora learns and grows. At Lakenna's urging and for the same pay more children will learn in the fall. My family sleeps safer because of her."

You don't know. If you did . . .

Bowyn came to his feet. "I stand for Lakenna Wen."

Jon Luwin, the furniture maker and family head, rose. "I stand for Lakenna Wen."

"I stand for Lakenna Wen," said Bar Colemon, the third family head.

Llyr came smoothly to his feet and rumbled, "I stand for Lakenna Wen."

Tears trickled down her cheeks. She didn't understand totally, but she had an idea.

Girard confirmed it. "Lord Tellan, five Rogoth kinsmen, true Dinari all, stand for Lakenna Wen. What say you?"

Tellan rose to his feet. "Do these five stand of their own free will and accord?"

"We do, m'lord."

"Do any here have ought against Lakenna Wen?" Tellan waited, his eyes searching the pavilion.

Only me. Through tear-filled eyes, Lakenna looked at the five good men. *I was tested and found wanting.*

Tellan nodded. "I am satisfied." He turned to her. "Lakenna Wen, the Rogoth kinsmen, and through us, Clan Dinari, offer you a place among us. This is more than attendance at the Pole, Teacher. This is entrance into our clan we offer. If you accept, know that our homes and hearths will be ever open to you. Your enemies will be our enemies. We will stand shoulder to shoulder with you should they attack you in word or deed." He gestured to the other men standing. "More importantly, by standing for you, these five pledge that should you find yourself unable to repay any obligation, moral or financial, they will take that debt upon themselves."

She covered her face with her hands. *No!* Sobs tore through her. *I am unworthy of this.*

"Lakenna Wen, do you accept our offer?"

I cannot. O dear Eternal, how can I?

"Lakenna Wen, do you accept our offer?"

She opened her mouth to refuse, but it came out, "Yes! Yes. Help me be worthy of this."

Rhiannon came to her side and took Lakenna's hands. "Having you as part of my family is the best birthing day gift I can think of."

Strong arms enveloped her. It was Mererid. "Welcome, sister. Welcome."

Lakenna buried her face in that good woman's bosom and wept.

Later, after the congratulations and birthing day celebrations had ended and everyone had left, Lakenna helped Mererid bathe and wash her hair. Afterwards the noble lady put on a dab of perfume after her bath. Lakenna knew what that meant. When she was dressed, they walked as they had done for weeks now.

The moon was half full and cast a silvery light on the stream as it snaked across the valley floor. The current swirled and bubbled around exposed rocks, the sound soothing to Lakenna as she and Mererid walked along the hard-packed dirt trail that followed the twists and turns of the bank.

As usual, conversation was dominated by the coming Rite of Presentation and their united purpose to drag Rhiannon kicking and screaming into womanhood.

"After the wool sale to Gillaon," Mererid said, "I knew Maolmin would not include Rhiannon among those presented to Prince Larien. An understandable retaliation, but of no lasting import. Clan Dinari is the smallest and poorest of the six clans. In twelve hundred years, no Faber has chosen a Dinari. Accordingly, we are always 'honored' by being first. The royal party will only spend one day in Lachlann, our southernmost town of sufficient size, before leaving for the Presentations that will matter."

She smiled wryly. "One can only imagine the maneuvering and infighting going on among the other clans to choose the most eligible of their maidens. By now, Cullia should have found someone suitable, giving her time to wring as much gold and trade concessions as possible from the girl's kinsmen group and High Lord before the announcement."

Lakenna stopped walking. "I thought it would be like when Destin saw Meagarea and the Eternal turned their hearts to each other . . ." Her words trailed off at the noble lady's snort.

"Would that it was so. A great story. I never tire of hearing it or seeing it portrayed in skits. We should pray it will happen like that this fall." She looked up at the star-strewn sky and hugged herself. "But, no. King Balder is invalid with some mysterious aliment and rarely leaves Faber Castle. Cullia rules the Land, and she understands power like no queen in generations. I don't know all that happened to cause Larien's betrothal to be broken and this Rite of Presentation declared, but undoubtedly the Sabinis maiden must have had eyes on the throne, which would have threatened Cullia. Rumors had the girl's father busy making deals for when Balder dies."

They continued on their walk.

"Prince Larien is said to care little for governing," Mererid said. "With King Balder's condition worsening and Larien's coronation not far off, Cullia's purpose is to find a complacent girl from a high-ranking family who will look pretty during royal functions, produce a male heir, and leave the ruling of the Land to her. Our purpose," Mererid finished as they headed back up the ridges to the pavilion, "is to have Rhiannon seen by all, act like the noble young maiden she is, and attract a better match than we could expect otherwise."

As they passed the stables, Lakenna heard stomping of feet and soft whickers from horses. The lantern light was still shining. Mererid left her and went to say goodnight to Tellan and the boys.

Rhiannon and Ove were already abed when Lakenna eased back inside the pavilion, trying not to stumble over chests or the wash stand. After hanging her blouse and skirt on pegs driven into a tent pole next to her pallet, she slipped into her cotton nightdress and crawled under the light wool blanket.

It was much later when Mererid returned. The noble lady hummed a faint tune as she undressed—for what Lakenna felt sure was the second time that night.

Why am I not undressing for a husband instead of lying here, alone, where an evil beyond my wildest imagining walks on two legs and stalks a young woman?

She was twenty-five! Years beyond the age to be married. Time was slipping away. Would she ever know the pleasure of a warm body next to hers every night? Of his hands upon her and hers upon his? Of a babe suckling at her breast—

Enough! I am still Albane, and I will not harbor these feelings.

Finally, Lakenna tumbled into a restless sleep...

In her dream she stood on a plain with Rhiannon behind her. High Lord Maolmin strode out of a misty gray veil and came toward them, huge hands balled into fists. He wore a black cloak that did not swing as he walked. His eyes were terrible, unforgiving, two black orbs pulsing with arrogant power. Behind him the gray mist rolled, concealing weird shapes, waiting, patient and evil. One shape—a winged horror—reared and flapped its long, pointed wings. The mist flowed into eddies and swirls.

Confident in her spiritual authority, she watched Maolmin approach. This should be easy. She was Lakenna Wen, Albane of Albanes. She had been faithful all her life, attending every meeting as a child with her parents, and had been just as faithful as an adult. No one could quote more Holy Writ from memory than she could. No one could equal her in debates on doctrine. Everyone pointed to her as an example of what a virtuous woman should be. Surely demons would flee before her.

She flung out a finger. "You are bound, foul demon!"

The movement of the strange shapes in the mist stopped. She could feel them straining to hear, pensive. But her words had no effect on Maolmin. He came on, unfazed. With every step he loomed larger, more menacing.

Full of righteousness indignation, she thundered, "I bind you! In the Eternal's name and by the Covenant, you are bound!"

"You can't bind me!" he hissed. "You are full of sin! The worst kind of sin!"

She reeled, the truth of his accusation a body blow. Words of faith died in her mouth. Her proud notion of herself crumbled into dust, and she wanted to curl into a ball and weep.

Maolmin smirked. He was head and shoulders above her now. Coal black eyes peered down into her very core.

"With Loane, and then the herbs from Old Tanny. You knew it was sin, but you did it anyway. And what is more, you still lust for a man! Let one beckon you to his bed, and you will unpin your hair and scamper eagerly—"

She bolted upright in her pallet, cotton gown damp with sweat. Dry-mouthed, she pulled the thin blanket around her shoulders and got up. She stumbled though the dark interior of the pavilion. She drew back the front flap and walked a few paces into the night.

The moon had set and the stars were thick in the sky. Sweat poured off her. She shrugged off the blanket and let it puddle around her feet.

Her failure was a millstone upon her neck. She was a hypocrite in every Holy Writ session with Rhiannon. She, Lakenna Wen, who for years had eagerly pointed out the barest hint of such in other's life, was the worst hypocrite imaginable. She, Lakenna Wen, had deliberately committed the most grievous of sins. Not once, but twice.

She fought to keep tears back as the memories came. A fortnight before her expected wedding date, she had gone to meet Loane at their cottage he was constructing. The fireplace was finished, and Loane wanted her opinion on a red oak slab he had found for the mantel. They stood before the hearth, envisioning what it would look like, the smell of wood shavings and wet mortar a pleasing mixture that somehow declared a bright future for the two of them.

It had been so natural when he slid his arm around her waist, and she responded by laying her head on his shoulder, content. Then he turned and pulled her to him, arms strong and pleasing as she was crushed against his chest, his mouth on hers. Although they both knew they should stop, they allowed it to continue. The back part of her mind calculated that with only a fortnight remaining, it would not matter, and so Lakenna gave in to the body hunger she had kept tightly wrapped for years. She stepped back from his embrace, unpinned her hair, and it had happened.

Afterward, it was awkward and embarrassing as they silently rearranged clothing and brushed off the dust and wood shavings.

Then, beyond all knowing, a week later Loane was dead of lung fever. Two months after that, Lakenna finally faced what she had been growing more sure of with each passing day. Sleepless nights and nauseated mornings followed, until...

Until, with mounting desperation, she made a visit to Old Tanny, the herbalist living on the outskirts of the village, and came back with the root of blue cotash and instructions on how to brew the tea.

Lakenna did so, then stared at the cup—and stared. Eventually, she picked it up, held it in trembling hands for a long moment—and finally drank. It worked like Old Tanny said it would. The other herbal preparations and teas sent for afterwards had worked too, easing the discomfort and other bodily aspects.

But Lakenna had discovered a much deeper stain, one that all the herbs in the world could never take away.

I am Dinari now, but nothing can change what I have done.

Even so, Loane and Old Tanny were behind her. Somehow, with enough effort, she would learn to live with it.

Not so for Maolmin's second accusation from the dream.

She did still long for a man. She had fought those longings for years—as she had done tonight. But how she yearned for a husband. For companionship, for the security of a home hearth, and, yes, for sexual intimacy. To be sated and hum a happy tune like Mererid had.

Lakenna turned and regarded the pavilion where Rhiannon slept. *Of what help to her is a sinner beset by such desires!*

She listened to her own heartbeat, which was loud in the stillness of the night. Never had she felt more alone. Her distance from the Eternal seemed a huge chasm.

By day, Lord Tellan and Llyr drilled the warriors at an increased pace, and everyone was confident that, should the Mighty Ones' creatures come again, the Rogoths would be ready. But what about the other part of the battle? *Will I be able to stand in the gap again? How can I pray as I did before?*

The night air chilled her sweat-drenched gown, and cold pierced her skin and seeped into her soul. Shivering, she reached down and drew the blanket back over her head and shoulders. She peered out to the north and then to the west. Evil was on the move in both directions, and she had no doubt of its destination.

She lifted her gaze heavenward. Tears filled her eyes.

Dear Eternal, forgive my sin.

Chapter Twenty-three

BRANOR

SOUTH THE WIND blew from Salmand, the city of the Dinari High Lord. Though it was high summer, the wind carried a chill as it billowed down the crags of the Fea Mountains and across green pastures dotted with sheep. Hardened sheepherders shivered when it passed and tightened their grip on staffs. Sheep raised heads from grazing, uneasy. Lambs scurried pell-mell back to their mothers.

The wind ripped the surface of small ponds and clear lakes and added more velocity to snowmelt streams bubbling downhill. It blew down the narrow road toward Lachlann, raising dust and scattering small pebbles. It eddied and swirled around the high walls of Kepploch Monastery, then gathered itself and sped toward the Rogoth lands.

The skin prickled between Branor's shoulder blades as he strode across the inner courtyard on the way to meet with Abbot Trahern.

Two gardener monks straightened from their labor. They stared at each other for a moment, then shrugged and returned to their weeding of the flowerbeds that lined the walkways. All were in bloom with pleasing colors of red, yellow, pink, and blue. Rosebushes with blood red petals circled a pool in which yellow and orange fish swam beneath water lilies. Rising from the middle of the pool was a statue of Destin Faber with his sword hilt deep in the chest of a roaring winged horror. On the base of the statue were chiseled the names of Keeper monks killed through the centuries battling outbreaks of the Mighty Ones' creatures.

Branor halted and looked over the east wall of the monastery toward the Rogoth lands. Whatever he had felt before must have been his imagination. He was not ready for it to be anything but imagination. He swallowed hard and strode on.

He walked under the columned walkway surrounding the courtyard, leaving the flowers and sunshine behind. The hallway to abbot's office was hung with colorful tapestries. Tightly woven rugs covered the stone floor. Chests and cabinets of polished wood held plates and platters, bowls and cups as fine as anything he had seen in the hlafords of high-ranking clan lords.

As usual, Keeper Ubie, Trahern's ancient and irascible secretary, perched on a stool in front of a slant-top desk. And as usual, Ubie did not deign to acknowledge Branor's entrance.

Suppressing a sigh, Branor stopped in front of the desk. "I am here to see the abbot."

The secretary's face was hollow cheeked, and tufts of white hair grew on the bridge of his nose and from his earlobes. His fingers were ink-stained and his hands dotted with age spots. As usual, he pretended not to hear the request, remaining engrossed in shuffling the parchments before him.

Branor smiled. *The Eternal gives me opportunity to practice my rediscovered humility. But if I weren't such a recently broken man, I'd jerk this pompous bag of bones off that stool, give him a good kick in the backside, and then count how many times he bounced—*

"Yes, Your Grace?" Ubie peered up with rheumy eyes and pursed lips. "What did you say?"

Branor's toes twitched. "As I have twice a week since I have been here, I have come to talk with Abbot Trahern."

Not changing his expression, the secretary managed to convey affront as he set the parchments aside. He slowly lifted the hinged top of the desk and rummaged in the underlying compartment. Bringing out a leather-bound ledger, he dipped a quill into ink and with great deliberation jotted down a notation. Finally he creaked off the stool and shuffled to the abbot's door.

Branor had needed Kepploch's slow pace these past weeks. Needed the peace to regain his focus on the Eternal. And to be reconciled to a new future.

He was still surprised at his lack of tension. His ambition had been a burden he carried for so long that only in its absence was he able to understand what a crushing weight it had become. He still felt fragile, numb at the sudden change. Overnight he had gone from years of examining everything he did for its further-ance of his ultimate goal to...nothing. Quest abandoned. When he had been so close.

Or had he really been so near his goal?

The closer he got to the seventh knot, the greater the obsta-cles. With the benefit of weeks of contemplation, he now real-ized how the effort to surmount those obstacles had molded him into a different person. He had moved his boundary line of what was acceptable. The changes had been subtle. Tiny nudges to the barrier along the way, punctuated with substantial reposition-ing to crush stubborn rivals. All easily excused in the stress of competition.

Until the encounter with Maolmin and the realization of the horrendous leap that required.

After Branor's breaking, days of weeping had followed. And sleep. Deep, healing sleep. In that time he rediscovered prayer and meditation on scripture. He had long talks with Trahern. The abbot's wisdom and spiritual insight were giving Branor the mortar to put the shattered pieces of his life back together.

During the past few days, Branor had sensed the process coming to, if not a conclusion, then an ending of sorts. He rec-ognized his growing irritability with life at Kepploch as further confirmation. He'd needed the slow pace, but now it was time to get moving again.

After Ubie announced him and the day's session got under-way, Trahern agreed.

"It is time," the abbot declared, tapping his finger on the pol-ished wooden surface of his desk. "The urgency increases every day." When Branor made no reply, Trahern cocked a bushy eyebrow. "Many of the brothers feel stirrings in the heavenlies. Don't you?"

"Yes. More every day." Branor shifted uncomfortably in the chair, surprised at the fear rippling through him. "But I am not able to face Maolmin."

"Of course *you* are not able! None of us can face the Mighty Ones and their creatures in our own strength. The Founders certainly couldn't. It was only by the Eternal's power that they triumphed. Nothing has changed in twelve centuries. The Covenant still covers the Land. The Mighty Ones are defeated foes. It seems they need to be reminded of that fact." Those faded blue eyes studied Branor deeply. "The Eternal called you to this battle years ago. His call still rests upon you today."

"How can that be when I turned my back on him to pursue my own agenda? I would think I had forfeited any call he might have once graced me with."

Trahern's face softened. "But he never turned his back on you."

"All those years wasted."

"Not necessarily. Worms have eaten a part, but edible fruit remains. You claim that the Dinari High Lord harbors a siyyim—" he raised a hand when Branor stiffened, "and I believe you. But if demons indwell nobles, then what better weapon to engage that threat than High Lord Keeper Branor, a man possessing knowledge of higher-level clan politics as do few in our order? In his infinite wisdom, the Eternal allowed you to learn and gather experience. When the time was right, he separated you from the pack, knocked you to your knees, and then put his foot firmly on your neck until you surrendered."

Trahern turned to look through the window at the inner courtyard. "Now, to the future." He steepled his fingers. "Without question you are linked to the Rogoth girl. Whatever 'Protectoress of the Covenant' entails, the Eternal expects you to see this matter to its conclusion. The Mighty Ones are stirring. You need to be at the Rogoth hlaford."

Branor swallowed. "I am not ready. I need more time."

Trahern went on without heed. "You returned to us a rusted, pitted sword that had been banged against brick walls of intrigue and used as a tool to pry boulders out of the path of ambition." He brought his gaze from the window and fixed Branor with a level look. "These last weeks you have gone through a refining fire. You are retempered for your original purpose as a weapon in the Master's hand." He smiled gently. "Times and places are not for us to determine. When the Eternal calls, we obey."

The librarian brought the leather folder containing *Night Watch,* the ancient book in the Old Tongue. Branor took it and went to a small desk next to a window that caught the morning light.

The monastery's library held dozens of accounts collected through the centuries of encounters with the Mighty Ones' creatures. During his first time here at Kepploch, Branor had studied those writings. Many were hearsay and rumors finally written down months—more often years—after the fact: sightings of large, winged creatures flying overhead; herds of sheep and cattle ravaged; unexplained cottage or manor burnings with no survivors. The majority seemed embellished fairy tales cut whole cloth from the legends surrounding Destin Faber and the Founding.

More than one account read exactly like the winged horror attack on Rhiannon, however. This made Branor wonder how many more of the seemingly farfetched accounts were true as well.

An even dozen of the library's accounts were penned by Keepers detailing encounters of verified outbreaks. Branor had concentrated on those during these last days. Of them all, the six-hundred-year-old *Night Watch* seemed to speak the clearest. In it, not only was Keeper Alock called upon to quell an outbreak of winged horrors, but also the peasant monk and his faithful helpers had contended face-to-face against a demonized pagan priestess.

Branor settled down at the small table, opened the folder, and gently thumbed through the yellow, brittle sheets containing the blocky characters of Old Tongue. The manuscript had been written by Alock's replacement, Keeper Devitt. Devitt was the youngest son of a minor clan noble and well educated, as his writing indicated. Why this young Keeper had been sent to replace the aged and dying Alock was a matter of speculation. Having dealt with Keepers from noble families with too many sons, Branor was certain Devitt's superiors had done so for punishment and humbling.

Branor found the passage that had been nagging him. The ink was faded but was still legible. He mentally translated:

> The last two days I have feared the end is near for Alock, and I despaired of finishing this account. But he has rallied. The old crone who faithfully tends to him woke me at first light saying that Alock requested I bring my parchments and ink. Upon my arrival, I found him even more shrunken but alert and propped up on the narrow bed under two layers of quilts. He lifted a hand and motioned me to bring the stool next to the bed. Without waiting for me to arrange my materials he started exactly where he had stopped at the end of our last session. As before, I have striven to maintain the essence of Alock's account while taking the liberty to correct his atrocious grammar. I resume his narration:
>
> Night belonged to the horrors. Come sundown, true believers huddled in their homes, doors barred, curtains over windows to keep any trace of light from showing. The beasts seemed to hate any light. They went into a frenzy and attacked any fire or person carrying a lantern.
>
> A dwelling—always one belonging to staunch believers—would be attacked at night. We would find the smoking ruins. It was awful picking up the remains for proper burial.

I kept beseeching the Eternal for insight. And, praise his name, he answered with a vision. I saw that during those attacks the horrors were like a pack of trained hounds under control of their master. I saw the creatures linked to that master, who directed them like a wagon master with horses hitched to a wagon. And I knew who that master was.

Talladin was built on a limestone ridge above the Verrin River. Several abandoned hill forts dotted the area. They dated back to before Destin's time. In their superstitions, many of the people believed one of the forts was a sacred shrine to the Lady of the East, that accursed Mighty One. During certain nights, many of the people—even some who worshiped the Eternal the rest of the year—would go to that shrine and participate in vile worship directed by some high priestess.

Oh, I knew who the priestess was. Supposedly it was a hereditary office, handed down from mother to daughter. She and her fellow pagans sought to keep it a secret from all but the initiated. Some aftermath of the Cleansing, I suppose. Until the outbreak, this high priestess had seemed a harmless sort. She and her followers would dance about, sometimes naked, mumbling their incantations and other gibberish, beseeching the Lady of the East to grant them favor. Worshipers would leave offerings of food and drink, coins and jewelry, and carved wooden human figures meant to represent a sick person in an effort to receive healing. But my vision clearly identified the high priestess as the one directly controlling the winged horrors.

I called the true believers together and told them what we must do. At first, most refused. I kept after them until they realized this was their only hope. Otherwise their homes and loved ones could well be the next attacked. Many of their friends had already bowed the knee to the Lady of the East to safeguard themselves. And the number was growing. The whole area was taken by fear.

I heard rumors of nightly ceremonies at the hill fort shrine. At sundown, I divided my people. The men and older boys I took with me. The women, children, and older folks stayed behind and prayed for binding of the horrors and a covering over us.

We set out for the shrine. We had no proper weapons like Destin and the Founders. Only hay sickles, hoes, sticks, and clubs fashioned from tree limbs.

That first time we surprised the pagans. They had set out no guards, so sure were they of their security. The high priestess was not there. I learned later that she was at another shrine two days' distance, leading that area back into pagan practices.

At our arrival and my declaration that we were claiming the hill for the Eternal, the lower priestesses ran about in a panic, screeching spells and incantations to call forth something, but to no avail. I sternly admonished those worshipers present to repent and go home. I recognized many of them, although in their shame, they tried to hide their faces from me.

Once everyone fled, we gathered every pagan implement and offering we could find and burned them. Then we marched back. We encountered no horrors that night. For the next four nights Talladin lived in peace.

Then the high priestess returned.

Branor looked up from the parchment. He said a prayer of protection over Rhiannon, then returned to his reading.

The directed attacks resumed. Three families were killed the first night, two more the second. I called my people together, divided them as before, and marched back to the hill shrine.

I will always remember how quiet it was. Nothing moved in the fields. No sound of night creatures. Crickets, frogs, owls were all strangely silent.

We marched unmolested up the hill. The high

priestess seemed to be waiting for us. This was not the same woman. Oh, she looked the same, but she was different. Transformed. The other priestesses were there as well, standing a few steps behind her. I saw no worshipers that night.

The high priestess stood before me in her white robe, hands on her hips. All manner of clacking bracelets encircled her arms and wrists. She wore a heavy gold necklace with jewels of many colors. I could hardly stand to look her in the face. Her eyes were terrible.

I gathered my courage and told her that I bound her power and reclaimed the shrine for the Eternal. I will never forget her laugh. It was evil, arrogant. I tell you frankly, it sent chills running down my spine.

The jewels on her necklace glowed. She sneered and drew a sharp knife from her belt and cut a long slice down her left arm. As the blood dripped, she spouted some chant—and horrors descended upon us.

As the fight swirled around me, I found myself seeing with different eyes. The demon indwelling the high priestess held a number of reins. The reins were attached to the flying horrors, and the demon controlled their attack as a coachman directs a team of horses. Another, thicker rein ran from the demon back into the mist. I could vaguely see a larger demon holding that rein. An even thicker rein ran from the larger demon into a mass of swirling, black and red clouds. I ignored all that and focused on the demon before me.

I had a rope in my hands. I ran forward and bound the demon. But with a flex of its muscles, it broke the bonds.

"Your rope is frayed, little man," it sneered. "It cannot bind me. And your covering has holes." The demon struck me, and I found myself back on the hill, seeing normally, the vision gone.

It was a rout. A sickle in the hands of a hay cutter can be an awesome weapon. But the sharp blades only bounced off the horrors. Three of my men were burned to death; many others received deep cuts from claws and broken bones from those cruel wings.

I know now that the prayers of the wives and others hindered the horrors just enough to allow our escape.

The rest of that night and the next day I lay on my face before the Eternal, begging for an answer. Praise his name, he answered. He gave me to understand what "frayed rope" and "holes in our covering" referred to. Like moths eating away at cloth, my people's involvement in pagan practices, which many of them saw as harmless tradition—feast days, ceremonies with pagan foundations, charms, amulets and the like—were eating away at our ability to confront the pagan evil.

I brought this before my people and had them renounce all involvement with pagans. They examined their homes and barns and removed all objects that may have had pagan origins. We built a huge fire and burned everything. To a person, all wept tears of repentance and renewed their fealty to the Eternal and the Covenant. As night was falling, we joined in one accord and had a powerful time of prayer.

Then we marched back to the shrine.

Branor stopped. *I fear Tellan's involvement with the Broken Stone Land is similar. And the demon that Alock faced must rank lower than a siyyim. How can we bind Maolmin, a siyyim and a clan High Lord?*

He shivered, remembering the feeling in the courtyard.

Have I overstayed my time here at Kepploch? I am not ready for this. I need more time.

We were in the middle of the wheat field that surrounded the hill shrine when I begin to have chills and a strong sense of nausea. I called a halt and told my men to form a circle and prepare for an attack.

Even horses cannot outrun winged horrors. You must stand and defeat them, or they will fly you down.

As we waited, I rejoiced that our cleansing earlier in the day and our prayers must have put a holy fear in the pagans. Why else would they strive to keep us from their sacred hill? But that joy was short-lived. A flock of the creatures came winging out of the night sky. They were smaller than those of the first attack, but they came at us in a killing rage.

Again, I found myself seeing with different eyes. I held a triple-strand rope, and I knew with certainty it could not be broken. I grasped the reins of the horrors and followed them until I came to the demon. I could feel the strengthening of our prayer warriors flowing into me.

"You will not have these people!" I screamed at the demon. "The Eternal rules here, and you will bow the knee!"

It turned to flee, but I was upon it and bound it. Immediately the reins running to the horrors disappeared, and I found myself back in the bloodied wheat field.

The creatures were even smaller now and had lost their ability to fly. Our long-bladed sickles, pitchforks, and sharpened hoes penetrated their flesh. One man was killed, ripped open by a claw. But soon the horrors not killed ran away, wounded and bleeding.

We rejoiced in our triumph over the Mighty Ones' creatures, but the battle was not over. The high priestess and her followers fell upon us. The high priestess stood at the edge of the fighting. Her face was not so terrible, and her presence did not seem so imposing. She took her knife and cut herself again and again. Holding her bleeding arms high, she whirled in the moonlight, chanting and urging her fighters to a greater frenzy.

Though the power of the Eternal filled us and we sensed his desire that these pagans be redeemed, they gave us no choice. Both sides knew what was at stake.

My people did not waver. Under the covering of their

wives' and daughters' prayers, the men fought for their families. They fought for a future where their children could walk in the Eternal's light. They fought not to live huddled in darkness, fearing every sound of the night. They fought those linked to that brooding evil, and no quarter was asked or given.

When it was over, the surviving pagans had fled in disarray and we had reclaimed the night.

Most who had bowed the knee to the Lady of the East repented. They returned to the one true God and have remained faithful. To this day, Talladin and surrounding areas are free of winged horrors of the night.

The greatest joy I have ever known was being faithful to the Eternal's call to carry his light into the face of that darkness.

The narration ended, and Keeper Devitt's words took over.

These are the true and faithful words of Keeper Alock, spoken in his final days. In truth, I despaired of finishing this account before his death. But he rallied to complete his chronicle.

After his final words Alock closed his eyes and breathed his last. The events following his death bear relevance to his chronicle, so I take the liberty of extending the account.

It was only when the old woman who cared for him began to lovingly stroke his stilled face, silent tears running down her cheeks, that I realized Alock had gone to the Eternal.

Finally, she leaned forward and gently kissed the old man's forehead before pulling the quilt over his face. For the first time, I noticed the mass of scars running the length of her arms and realized who she was—or rather who she had been twenty years ago.

Each night since the funeral and the huge crowd of mourners, I have talked to Tia, the name the old woman took after she sought out Alock weeks after the above events. He cast out the demon indwelling her and brought her into the Eternal's family.

Her story is beyond belief. Many times I find the short hairs rising on the back of my neck while she stares into the fire and calmly talks about her days as high priestess of the Lady of the East.

I respectfully submit Alock's account, which I call Night Watch. When time allows, Tia's story will follow. At this point, we have only scratched the surface, and my duties to the people of Talladin are taking more and more of my time.

Branor remained seated at the table for a long time, immersed in the faith and raw courage of Keeper Alock and his fellow peasants. Branor wondered, as had many before him, what became of Tia's story. No trace of it had ever been found.

Finally, he returned the parchments to the leather folder and placed the folder on the librarian's desk. Returning through the colorful inner courtyard, Branor stopped at Destin's statue. The late morning sun was pleasant on his face. The air was thick with the scent of flowers. Bees buzzed and butterflies flitted from bloom to bloom. It was hard to believe that great evil lurked over the horizon.

Branor's eye was drawn to the names chiseled in the granite base, especially the five newest ones. He knew them all so well. He swallowed, remembering that stomach-turning foulness indwelling Maolmin.

The sun had moved across the sky before Branor left the courtyard and returned to his room. He crawled into his bed and was asleep within moments.

It was dusk when he startled awake, fuzzy and disorientated from the lengthy slumber. He made use of the chamber pot, then washed his face. He went to the window and looked toward the Fea Mountains.

A strong sense of foreboding swept over him. He said another prayer of protection for Rhiannon—and his breath caught. His stomach churned with nausea, and he felt beads of sweat popping out on his forehead. The oppressive sensation grew.

Dear Eternal, what am I to do? I am not ready for this! Help me!

Suddenly the presence of the Eternal filled the room, and the foreboding fled. Branor found it impossible to stand. He slid facedown onto the wooden floor. It seemed as if warm oil poured over him. Peace and acceptance and love flowed as the powerful manifestation continued. For an unknown time he wept unashamedly, immersed in indescribable joy.

Finally, from the recesses of his spirit, he heard these words:

Pray. Pray. Fight the good fight of faith. The Mighty Ones plot to end the Covenant. What warriors will stand in the gap and fight this fight of faith? Whom shall I send with my sword and my armor to battle the evil that covets the Land?

Prostrate on the floor, his bones afire with the power of the Eternal, Branor's answer surged from the depths of his soul:

I am a Keeper. I will respond.

Though the particulars were unknown to him, he knew a battle was joined at that moment. On a spiritual plane he suddenly came to grips with *them*, determined to protect Rhiannon. But somehow he sensed she was safe. Puzzled, he continued to battle but felt a hindrance like gooey mud that weakened his attack.

The need grew rapidly. Desperately, he rallied and threw himself back into the fray with renewed vigor—and encountered the same hindrance. He kept at it, but despair mounted as he realized it was not going to be enough.

Then another presence joined the battle.

The effect was immediate. The two spirit warriors knew of one another somehow, and together they mounted a decidedly stronger assault. Hand in hand, they slogged through the mire and hammered at the enemy until they opened a crack in its shield.

Chapter Twenty-four

SEROUS

THE SHEEP WERE finally bedded down.

The sun had slid behind the peaks long before, marching shadows across the high meadow until time gave way to what Serous stoutly maintained was the best time of the day: dusk.

Breathing deeply, Serous let go the demands of the long day and savored the moment as he looked down the slope at the bowl-like meadow where the sheep's dirty white wool blended into the gray light. Dawn had its beauty, truth said, but not like this. Dawn never gave the barest of tingles like he felt now in the velvet air. The old herdsman drew in another slow breath. There it was again: a softness as day faded gently into night.

His tired eyes roamed up and down the meadow, lingering on the small pond in the middle. A beautiful scene.

Good grazing here for another day. Then we'll split the herd into three groups and move to the smaller pastures higher up.

Ripples of movement appeared among the flock. The animals milled about in a growing wave of unease.

Must be a wolf slinking around, hoping to find a stray lamb run off from the protection of the herd.

"Rahl, that fire started?" Serous asked, eyes still on the herd. The sheep settled down somewhat, but there was still too much movement.

Rahl was on his hands and knees, striking flint and steel above a ball of dried grass. He blew gently to coax along the tiny flame.

243

After putting a few twigs across the burning grass, he stood and brushed off his pants.

"It's going. I'll have your tea brewing soon."

"Later on the tea. First, take a walk about the herd. Stay fifty paces from them. My joints are a-telling me to look sharp for wolves."

That was not true, the joints part anyway. For years everyone had sworn by what the various twinges of Serous's swollen joints could foretell. He used that fact shamelessly as axle grease for his orders, as he did now to make Rahl's scouting among uneven terrain in fading light a bit easier to accept. If Serous's joints truly warned him, he would send one or both of the older, more experienced men.

After a moment's thought he added, "Take Master Phelan with you."

"I'll bring the bow." Phelan rummaged among the gear. "If we see a wolf, I'll shoot it and we can skin it—"

"Easy now, master archer. And how will you be a-seeing anything in this light? You'd trip and stick an arrowhead through yourself most likely. Then Lord Tellan be taking a skinning knife to my hide, and fittingly so." Serous put a gnarled hand on the noble lad's shoulder. "Go with Rahl. He'll show you how to look."

Serous smothered a grin at the resignation flitting across Rahl's face.

The two lads picked up their staffs and strode down the rocky path to the herd below. Phelan's piping voice faded slowly into the growing dark as they hurried on.

The youngest Rogoth had a hardier soul than his size and frailness would indicate. His nonstop questions had irritated Serous to no end the first day until it dawned on him that they showed an insight and desire to learn.

Serous stooped down painfully and added more twigs to the fire while the other two herders pulled provisions from their bags.

"Talk the hills flat, can Master Phelan," Mil chuckled. He was Rahl's uncle and had a thick black beard shot with gray. Taking out a long-stemmed pipe and a twist of tabac from a pocket in his tattered leather vest, he filled the bowl, tamped it down, then took a burning twig from the fire and got the pipe going. Blowing out a blue plume of smoke, he removed a knife from a ram's horn sheath that hung from a belt around his waist and began to peel a potato. "But, truth said, rather Master Phelan than his brother. When it comes to Master Creag, what I say is: pray the Eternal grants Lord Tellan a long life."

Adwr grunted in agreement. He lifted a bucket with a frayed rope handle and poured water into a soot-blackened pot. Bald except for a fringe of white hair, Adwr was an outstanding cook and took great pride in that fact, which was the reason Serous always included the man with his herd for the summer, ignoring the grumbling of the other groups of herders. After all, being head herder had more than its share of headaches; having the best cook was only proper.

They camped on a shelf of land that jutted above the meadow to the height of four men. It afforded a good view of the herd below. The stars were out. The easily recognizable constellation Shepherd's Crook dominated the northern sky. The Crook's tip contained Mother's Eye, the brightest star in the night sky. As long as a man kept it directly ahead, he headed due north.

Last week, Serous's group and the other one, overseen by Bowyn Garbhach, the head of the largest family group, grazed through a series of narrow low meadows encircling the Fea Mountains, smaller brothers to the towering Ardnamur range to the west. Tomorrow, the two herds would move into the Fea themselves and break into even smaller herds; this was necessitated by the decreasing size of suitable pasturelands.

This season away from wives and mothers was a time when boys became men as they shared the rigors, loneliness, and occasional mercies of shepherding. A time when fathers, uncles, and other men passed along the accumulated wisdom of being clansmen, of raising sheep, of honor, of all it meant to be Dinari.

The fire blazed nicely now. Adwr removed three small pouches of spices from a larger bag and sprinkled a portion of each into the pot. He sniffed the water, then added a pinch more from one. With the fresh supplies delivered yesterday, he was preparing everyone's favorite, potach stew.

The other two herders with Serous's group had left some time ago to invite Bowyn and his herders to make the short walk over and eat. All would be arriving within a turn of the glass. The stew would take longer to be ready, but the wait would give everyone time to visit.

"Last summer I took Creag with me one night to walk about the herd," Adwr said, retying the pouches and putting them away. Pulling at the hairs on an earlobe, he snorted. "That boy thrashed about, stumbling and tripping over his feet the whole time. Made more noise than a herd of wild boars. Next morning he had scrapes all over from the falling. From then on we kept Master Stumble-foot by the fire after dark. Thank the Eternal it was several days before Lord Tellan come riding up. By then the lad had healed."

Serous added more branches to the fire, then took a flat stone and pounded two metal rods into the ground on either side of the flames. Each rod had a hook for a crossbar to hang the pots.

Mil sliced the peeled potatoes into the spiced water while Adwr took a knife and a flat board and chopped a handful of wild onions and a clove of garlic. He scraped that mixture into a pot of salted beef that had soaked most of the afternoon. Serous's stomach rumbled.

"When we fitted the rafters for the hlaford," Mil said as he reached for another potato, "instead of waiting for the carpenter to mark the angle for the notches, Master Creag declares he can do it. Says he had watched during the last cottage raising. So he takes the compass and awl and proceeds to..."

Serous listened with half an ear, thinking his boy Rahl was going to need a cottage raising of his own come the fall.

Bowyn Garbhach's daughter, Vanora, had dogged Rahl's foot-steps around the hlaford during the send-off to the summer pas-tures, then walked by his side down the trail until it was time for everyone but the herders to turn back. The lass's mahogany-colored hair had been loose and unbound as a maiden not ready for betrothal should be.

Yesterday, Vanora—her hair and forehead encircled with a requin—came with the wives and older children on the daylong trek to bring supplies to the herders. She went straight to Rahl and presented him a bag bulging with fresh baked goods.

A statement, that.

Serous sighed. The woman had decided, and Rahl had about as much chance as a plucked goose ready for basting. Not that the lad cared. In a year or two, he might, but not now. When he had taken the bag from Vanora, the two had stared a hole in each other.

Good as done. He wondered if Bowyn would say something to Rahl tonight after they ate. Bowyn knew Rahl was solid. Serous pounded down the second rod and snorted wryly to himself. If Bowyn didn't bring it up, he could rest assured one of his men would. Too good an opportunity to rib the lad to pass up.

Serous attached the hanging bar between the two rods and grunted, remembering fondly those nights beneath the layers of quilts as he and his late wife learned of each other. He sighed. Things had changed after the little ones had started coming.

"Three rafters ruined," Mil said, scratching his chin through his beard. "When Lord Tellan saw it, he—"

As one, the three ceased their talk and looked toward the meadow, instincts alert, though it was too dark to see the flock. The sheep were uneasy again, their bleating not panic-stricken but carrying a decided edge.

Serous stepped away from the crackling of the fire. Turning his good ear toward the meadow, he opened his mouth slightly to aid hearing; every fiber concentrated on sensing his surroundings.

At first, it was more felt than heard, faint, but growing stronger. Rhythmic. A steady beat that reminded him of the night—

His blood froze. Wings! Big ones! An icy barb twisted his guts. *Not again. Not with young Phelan out there!*

Serous reached for his staff. "Adwr, light a torch! Mil, string that bow and bring the quiver." Not waiting, he lumbered down the slope as quickly as sore knees allowed, dry-mouthed, heart thudding.

Halfway down the path his boot caught a protruding rock and he tumbled, staff spinning away. The impact with the ground jarred the breath from his lungs in an explosive *oof!* Stars flashed before his eyes as he skittered and rolled downhill. Finally, he came to a dazed halt at the bottom of the slope.

Raw pain sliced every joint; blackness threatened to overwhelm him. Biting back a whimper, he fought the agony and came to hands and knees, mind curdling at the specter of having to stand before Lord Tellan with the news that Phelan—

Strong hands grasped him under the arms and lifted him to his feet. "Here you go," Mil said. He wore the strung bow across one shoulder, the quiver around his waist. He maintained his grip as Serous wavered back and forth. "Sit you down now. Adwr and I'll see to the sheep."

"I'm fine." Serous jerked his arm loose. But the ground tilted, and he stumbled. Mil reached out to steady him again. "I'm fine, I said!" Serous hissed testily even as every joint screamed in protest and the night sky spun. "Listen. What do you hear?"

The urgency in his voice hit home. Mil and Adwr paused, eyes unfocused as they concentrated. The burning torch Adwr held sputtered and threw a wavering circle of light around the three of them. The sheep's bleating was an ever-increasing chorus echoing back and forth across the dark reaches of the bowl-shaped meadow.

Adwr shook his head. "I can't tell where the wolves stalk. The whole herd seems—"

"Not wolves! Your ears hear better than mine. Is there something in the air?"

"The air?" Mil echoed, puzzled.

"Aye." The icy barb in Serous's gut grew colder. "Like the night the hlaford burned. Do you hear their wings again?"

Adwr's eyes widened; his head swiveled back and forth as he searched the darkness. He looked ready to drop the torch and run.

Mil shrugged the bow off his shoulder and fumbled to nock an arrow. But his hands trembled so violently he dropped the shaft and had to stoop to retrieve it.

Serous ground his back teeth. *A bunch of old women!*

But even as the thought came, he knew it was not fair. Neither of these two had undergone warrior training as Rahl was doing now nor faced armed foes as he himself had. Mil and Adwr were sheepherders, and before that night in the spring it had been generations since Rogoth kinsmen had faced anything like winged horrors of the night.

Heart thudding and tongue swirling around his two upper teeth, Serous moved into the dark meadow. He skirted around the edges of the milling flock. Adwr and Mil followed close behind.

After a moment whatever it was seemed to pass, and the sheep calmed. Serous continued to walk and listen. Nothing. He breathed easier. But where were the two lads? Which way had they gone: left or right?

He was drawing a breath to holler them up when the night changed again. The darkness became heavier, even more menacing.

Serous stopped—and Adwr bumped into his back, the torch's flame painfully close. Irritably, Serous motioned the man back and listened into the night.

Was that wings again or only his thudding heart?

No, I hear it. A rhythmic beating, circling, coming closer!

The sheep in the center of the meadow broke and fled as two large objects dropped out of the sky with a flurry of wings. Landing, they lunged into the mist of the terrified herd with astonishing speed.

"Winged horrors!" Serous bellowed. "Rahl, if you hear me, protect Master Phelan! He is in your care! Stay away from the horrors. Leave them to us!"

Adwr moaned. He dropped the torch and turned to run.

But with a strength and quickness Serous had thought long gone, he grabbed the herder's tunic and jerked him back. "You worthless piece of dog dropping! We showed these things our backsides last time, but never again! We stay and protect Master Phelan and our lord's sheep!"

"We can't fight that!" the bald-headed herder whined, round-eyed. He struggled vainly to pry Serous's grip loose. "You heard Lord Tellan say we would have been fools. Only anointed warriors can kill—"

"I'm a warrior, and so is Rahl," Serous interrupted, giving the lad a position not yet earned. "I'll show you and Mil how to kill these beasts." He pulled the herder closer until their noses almost touched. Spittle ran unchecked down the man's chin. His fear was a sour stench. "You do as I say, Adwr Enit, or I'll slit your belly open and leave your worthless carcass for the vultures!" He let the man go. "Now pick up that torch. You and Mil come with me."

Reluctantly, Adwr did as ordered, as did Mil. They followed Serous into the swirling melee where the two horrors rampaged among the sheep.

Serous had spent a night talking with the three who had killed the beasts on the ride back to Lachlann. After complimenting them on their bravery and skill—justifiably—Serous had carefully pointed out that he and the herders at the hlaford had faced the horrors in black night, unarmed, completely unprepared for creatures right out of a loreteller's story and without the prayers of the new tutor. That established, he had picked their brains about the attack on the road, determined that if he and his herders were confronted again, they would give a better account of themselves.

"Best time is when those things go still and start that belching movement before breathing fire," Nerth had declared with the authority of having killed one single-handedly. "But here's the thing: I was close enough to smell 'em when I loosed. Get that close and miss, you're roasted meat for sure."

As they approached the winged horrors, Serous reminded

the two herders of that information, even as he mentally kicked himself for not demanding more archery practice. But with Mil trembling so violently that the nocked arrow clattered against the bow like a child's rattle, all the practice in the world would have been useless.

The nearer of the two beasts fed noisily on a fresh kill. To Serous's eye, this one was smaller than those that had attacked the hlaford. Nonetheless, it was still a fearsome sight.

It was twice the size of a full-grown horse. With its wings folded it seemed all legs, neck, and teeth. Its rear legs were heavily muscled. The feet had three toes with wicked-looking talons as long as a man's foot, which now gripped the half-eaten carcass. The horror's tail served as a third leg for balance while the narrow tip moved on the ground like a cat's tail, curling in pleasure as the creature ate. A ridge of knobby bumps ran from the top of the wedge-shaped head down the middle of the surprisingly long snout. And its eyes—the vulnerable eyes—were deeply recessed below a prominent ridge of bone and much smaller than Serous had hoped.

He took a deep breath, careful to keep his voice level. "Adwr, run forward and wave the torch to get its attention. If it starts that stomach heaving, lay the torch on the ground and duck to the side. Mil will use the light to aim for the eye."

Adwr's jaw dropped. He turned to regard Serous as if the old man had lost his mind. "Uh...I, uh..."

"I'll do it!" Phelan piped out eagerly, appearing suddenly out of the darkness into the light.

Snatching the torch from Adwr's hand, the lad trotted straight toward the horror, then stopped about ten paces from it and began waving the burning brand over his head in a slow arc. He seemed especially tiny before the beast's looming bulk.

Up close, the light revealed a greenish-gray hide splotched with darker hues that made the horror's outline hard to distinguish from the shadows. It truly seemed one with the night.

With a powerful twist of its head, the beast ripped a shoulder and forelimb from the bloodied carcass. Jaw muscles rippled and bones crunched between sharp teeth as the horror eyed the man-child balefully. The tip of its tail began to lash in agitation.

Phelan lowered the torch. "Hear me, winged horror of the night! I am Master Phelan de Murdeen en Rogoth, Clan Dinari. Leave our sheep alone and fly away while you can!"

The horror gulped the leg down and hissed menacingly. Yellow eyes pulsed with fury. The wings behind its back rippled in agitation. Then, with its head remaining almost motionless, it began the stomach belching and neck rippling the warriors had mentioned.

"See that, Mil!" Serous turned to the wide-eyed herder cowering behind him. "Get yourself up here and shoot the eye!" Quickly to Master Phelan: "You've done it, lad. Now drop the torch and run!"

The ball behind the horror's jaw increased steadily, but the youngster gave no heed. Calmly, he pointed the burning brand at the beast, and with gravity beyond his years, intoned: "Destin Faber hunted and killed your kind. When I become a man, so will I."

Serous's mind boggled. He lumbered stiffly ahead, whipsawed between rage at the fool child and admiration for the courage displayed. *Dear Eternal, help me keep this one alive to see that day!* Tingling warmth descended upon him; the pain in his joints disappeared. He shot forward as if shoved.

The horror's broad wings unfurled threateningly. The head swung down and the jaws opened.

Moving faster than he had in years, Serous reached Phelan and scooped the lad into his arms. "Drop the torch!"

He rolled them both sideways just as a jagged tongue of flame erupted from the beast's mouth. It crackled forth with astonishing speed and slammed into the ground where the lad had been standing, curling and blackening the grass in a wide circle.

Intense heat crinkled the skin on Serous's face, and for a moment there was no air to breathe. The night brightened, casting stark shadows as the fireball billowed skyward.

The horror lunged ahead with an ear-shattering roar. Its churning feet showered dirt and grass over Serous where he huddled over Phelan, barely an arm's length from the creature's path.

A heavy oily musk lingered in the beast's wake. Strong in Serous's nostrils, it was more than a smell. It penetrated deeply like a plunge into cold water and brought an awareness of rotted vegetation, of corruption, of pure, malevolent evil that sent shivers up and down his spine.

How is this happening? Serous fretted while Phelan squirmed with surprising strength to break free. *Why are we herders always facing these things alone! Where is Lakenna? Safely asleep in the Rogoth hlaford undoubtedly. And that six-knot Keeper! Where is he? Most likely rubbing shoulders with High Lords and rich merchants, leaving a cripple like me to deal with the Mighty Ones' creatures.*

The horror skidded to a halt a few paces beyond, wings beating for balance. Its right hip was within spitting distance from Mil and Adwr. Hissing angrily, the beast swung its head back and forth as it searched.

Mil's bow wavered like a sapling in a winter storm, but he drew full and loosed. At that range, the powerful bow could drive a broadhead point three fingers deep into an oak plank. Tonight, the arrow sped to the side of the horror's jaw, quivered at the impact, then bounced off harmlessly.

But the blow caught the beast's attention. It pivoted nimbly about to face the two herders. Opening its mouth to reveal a double row of sharp teeth, it roared its rage.

Bravely, Mil fumbled to nock another arrow, but Adwr let out a blood-curdling shriek and bolted. His motion drew the horror's attention away from the trembling bowman.

Adwr ran, legs pumping, arms flailing. He looked back over his shoulder with bulging eyes and so did not see the second winged horror crouching in his path, the ball behind its jaw huge. Though smaller than the first beast, the fire this one spewed out was far more impressive.

A sheet of flame engulfed Adwr and turned him into a grotesque human torch, illuminating the meadow. His agonized shrieks echoed throughout the night and went on and on.

The hair rose on the back of Serous's neck as the inhuman wails hammered the core of his being, conveying a height of unimaginable agony. Bile rose in his throat as he watched helplessly while Adwr staggered about. In the macabre light Serous could see Rahl. The lad's face twisted in revulsion as he watched Adwr's plight. Then he bent over and vomited.

Mercifully, the shrieks finally ceased. Adwr dropped to his knees, then fell face forward to the ground and remained still. The flames on his blackened body flickered and died.

The stench of burning meat clogged Serous's throat, and he gagged as well. He wiped his mouth with the back of his hand—and realized that Phelan was gone!

Casting about, Serous saw the lad retrieve the burning brand, then wave it in front of the first horror to divert its attention from Mil's efforts to notch another arrow.

The first horror! Serous ground his back teeth. *This ten-year-old is keeping his wits better than I am!*

Mil drew and loosed—to no effect that Serous could see.

"Rahl!" Serous shouted. "Come with me!" Then he sprinted where Mil and Phelan were frantically dodging an open-mouthed lunge of the angry beast. As he ran, Serous searched the night for signs of the second horror. But it was nowhere to be seen. It had disappeared back into the darkness and the bleating sheep.

Still retching, Rahl stumbled after Serous, determinedly not looking at the corpse smoldering a few paces away.

Again Phelan got the beast's attention. Waving the torch, the youngster darted in quick as a stable fly, then scampered nimbly aside when, with a low growl, the horror turned and lunged. Its teeth snapped loudly, missing Phelan by a hair.

Once more Mil drew and shot. This time the arrowhead penetrated a finger's length into the beast's upper neck.

With a bellow of surprise, the horror jumped straight up.

Landing, it swung its head and caught Mil a glancing blow on his leg. The herder cartwheeled through the air, and the bow and arrows spun into the night.

"Find the bow, Rahl!" Serous called out. "And some arrows! Help him, Phelan! I'll keep the monster off you." Then he wondered how he was going to do it. He didn't even have his staff, not that it would have done much good.

But instead of continuing the battle, the horror dropped its head and whimpered in pain. Dark blood dripped from the arrow shaft. The beast seemed confused.

Serous's blood surged. Undoubtedly this thing was not used to having the prey it encountered stay and fight. *Not only fight,* Serous thought proudly, *but also hurt it—*

Understanding flooded over him. He sagged with relief. *Somebody's praying!*

He ran around the horror to Phelan and Rahl. With the light from the torch, they had found the bow and a handful of arrows.

Rahl took the bow and nocked an arrow.

"Aim for the heart, lad, and keep shooting," Serous panted. "The arrows will penetrate now."

Splatters of vomit stained Rahl's tunic. His face had lines not there at dusk, but his expression was a study in determination. Steady as a rock, he drew, aimed, and loosed.

The arrow buried a handsbreadth into the horror's chest.

Quickly, Phelan handed Rahl another arrow. Over and over Rahl smoothly nocked, drew, and fired, taking the next arrow from Phelan as if they had practiced for months. Each arrow penetrated deeper into the beast than the previous one.

The horror died with the fifth arrow. It crumbled inward and turned to dust.

Serous took the torch from Phelan and searched for the second horror, but he sensed that the beast had fled. The sheep were calming down.

Then he heard Mil's moans and found the herder a few paces

away. His right leg was twisted at an impossible angle. His face was white in pain against the black beard, but his leg and bruises seemed to be his only injuries from the ordeal.

Phelan and Rahl joined them.

"I wish the one that...killed Adwr was still here," Rahl said grimly, his mouth a straight line. "I have enough arrows for it."

Serous listened into the night toward the other herd. Faintly, he heard the now familiar sounds of horrors bellowing and sheep bleating.

His blood chilled as he realized horrors were attacking Bowyn's herd.

Chapter Twenty-five

RHIANNON

RHIANNON GAVE ONE last tug on the girth strap, then turned and lifted the bridle off the peg. She slipped the bit into Nineve's mouth and fitted the top over the ears. Taking the reins, she led the prancing filly out of the stable.

Grim-faced Rogoth warriors bustled about under Llyr's watchful eye, securing weapons and tying down supplies on pack mules. All wore swords on their belts and carried quivers bristling with arrows and strung bows on their shoulders. Their leather vests had hundreds of small steel discs tied on with rawhide strings: poor man's chain mail.

Puddles dotted the dirt after last night's hard rain. The gray false dawn was clear and cool with a nip in the air that hinted of the autumn to come, making Rhiannon glad for her cloak and leather vest.

Yesterday one of the herders had brought news of the attack and Phelan's safety. Tellan had been a growling bear, wanting to gallop off immediately, but he'd forced himself to wait for the reserve warriors to be called in and supplies gathered.

Now in the dim light he stood impatiently and talked to Mererid, Creag, and Girard. A group of herder wives and families gathered a few paces away, concern evident in their faces.

Tellan and Girard came to Rhiannon. "I want you with me when I talk to the kinsmen," Tellan said, tilting his head toward the wives and families. "Girard informs me that everyone is convinced this is tied in with your prophecy. I think it will be good for them to see your involvement and concern."

Rhiannon nodded.

Loreteller Girard smiled at her. "Know, m'lady, that no Rogoth harbors you ill will. On the contrary, most kinsmen seem to be taking pride in your prophecy. They see both the tutor's presence and the High Lord Keeper's arrival as further evidence of the Eternal's hand in the matter."

"Thank you, Girard."

Rhiannon and her father stepped around the puddles as they walked the short distance to the families. As he had many times in the past, Tellan instructed her: "We are their kinsmen nobility. They give us their fealty and their honor; we give them protection and our respect. In times like this they look to us for reassurance. We need to show concern and determination, but never fear. Whatever the outcome, we must make it better than they could have resolved on their own." His mouth firmed. "If nobility cannot do that, we have no reason for existence."

Cora Garbhach stepped forward and dipped a short curtsy. She was a stout woman with a sharp-nosed, handsome face. Her hair was drawn into a bun shot with gray. She gathered the ends of her shawl in hands red and rough from labor. "M'lord, m'lady. The Eternal's blessing on you and the warriors. We're praying for Master Phelan and the others."

Tellan nodded solemnly. "If anyone can keep both men and sheep together and safe, it'll be Bowyn Garbhach and Serous Caillen. No two better men in these highlands."

Cora tilted her head in acknowledgment. Then her eyes took in Rhiannon's sword and riding garb. Her brow knitted, and her mouth turned down in disapproval. "You're going? With the warriors...?"

"Lady Rhiannon will ride by my side." Tellan did not raise his voice, but his tone cut like a knife.

The woman's frown vanished. "Of course, m'lord. I meant no disrespect." Still, she radiated disapproval.

"How is Willa?" Rhiannon asked into the resulting silence. Willa was Adwr's widow.

"Numb, m'lady." Cora looked relieved at the change of subject though her gaze lingered on the sword. "She is most appreciative of yours and Lady Mererid's visit yesterday. After you left, we were able to get a sleeping draught down her. She'll be abed 'til noon. Her daughter should be here by then."

Rhiannon looked at Vanora, who stood next to Rahl's mother. Their look of concern mirrored her fear. Keeping her features smooth, Rhiannon told them, "I know Phelan is safe with Rahl. Both Teacher Lakenna and High Lord Keeper Branor think no further attacks have occurred."

Vanora blinked back tears.

Rahl's mother, a plump woman with a kindly face, nodded bravely even as her chin quivered. "Like Lord Tellan says, m'lady, Serous and Bowyn will keep everybody together till you and our men get there and deal with these evil creatures." She shot a quick glance at Cora, then looked back to Rhiannon. "Teacher Lakenna was not the only one praying night before last." Murmurs of agreement came from the others. "The Eternal woke many of us up to pray. We know Teacher Lakenna and the Keeper will be with you." Her voice strengthened. "But you'll be riding under our prayers as well, Lady Rhiannon, both for this and for your prophecy."

Another wave of agreement came with many nodding heads.

Tears came to Rhiannon's eyes. She did not trust herself to speak. "Thank you," she managed finally. "Whatever the prophecy entails, I will strive to be faithful."

Rhiannon and her father took their leave and hurried to mount up. Lakenna and Branor stepped forward. The Keeper wore his black rope and a thick winter cloak. His boots shone with fresh polish. Lakenna wore her customary white blouse, a blue cloak of heavy wool, and one of Rhiannon' split skirts. The two of them had altered that skirt and another one like it for Lakenna during the night's frantic preparations.

Night before last, Lakenna had startled the entire family after rising from her knees from what she described as another call to prayer similar to the one on the road to Lachlann. She said this one had seemed much more difficult, and without the assistance of some unknown partner, it might have failed. Since the hlaford and the immediate area were quiet, everyone's first thought had been for Phelan and the sheep. Those fears had been confirmed at the herder's arrival the next day.

Then, upon Branor's arrival at the hlaford late yesterday afternoon, he had related a prayer battle exactly like Lakenna's. At first, both Albane and Keeper had seemed relieved to discover the identity of their fellow spiritual warrior. But not for long. Things had quickly chilled since that initial revelation.

Now, however, they seemed in one accord as Lakenna spoke first. "M'lord, before we leave, there is a matter of grave urgency that Bra—...that High Lord Keeper Branor and I feel we must share with your family and your advisors."

Tellan frowned fiercely. "Be quick. We have delayed long enough."

Branor and the tutor stepped inside the sables. Rhiannon, Tellan, Mererid, Creag, Llyr, and Girard followed.

Branor and Lakenna described in detail their prayer battle on the night of the attack. Then, with each one helping the other put words to such a difficult subject, the two startled everyone— all but Rhiannon, anyway—by declaring they believed a siyyim indwelt Maolmin Erian.

Tellan received that revelation more calmly than Rhiannon would have thought, if a face hard enough to chop wood was calm. He stood with arms folded across his chest. Mererid stood straight-backed by his side, her fingers drumming on her leg as she digested the implications of what it would mean if the supreme leader of their clan were truly indwelt by a demon. Girard and Llyr stood on Tellan's other side. The loreteller was ashen-faced. He put a hand over his eyes and moaned. Llyr nodded to himself as he stared at the ground.

Finally, Tellan spoke into the silence. "Rhiannon, is this what you felt in the stable at Lachlann?"

She loved him for that. "Yes, Father. In the stable and then in the pavilion, I sensed the same... *wrongness* about the High Lord."

More silence. Outside, the day brightened. Rhiannon was as anxious as anyone to be gone, but this had to be settled.

She was also wrestling with a new and insistent feeling that she needed to bow the knee to the Eternal. It confused her. She had done that years ago at the ceremony at Kepploch. Why should more be necessary? She was as ready as she could be to be Protectoress of the Covenant. Still, the more she read Holy Writ and talked to Lakenna and Branor, the more it seemed that she had to, well, *surrender* to the Eternal. It was as if the faith she'd had as a child had served her well, but, like a young girl's dress, she'd outgrown it and must now decide if she wanted a new one fitted for her, a mature faith that could look hard at the Eternal's ways—accepting that she would never understand everything—and embrace it nevertheless.

"Lord Tellan," Branor was saying, "I have thought long and hard over this matter and have discussed it with Abbot Trahern. If true, this explains your continual ill will toward Maolmin."

"Of course!" Mererid looked at her husband. "All who know you have wondered at that. Lord Baird and I have talked of it many times." She frowned. "But why only Tellan? The other kinsmen lords have no such feelings about Maolmin."

"Rhiannon's father is her first line of defense," Lakenna said. "Though Lord Tellan may not have understood why, the Eternal was ensuring Rhiannon's protection."

Tellan's face darkened. "You're saying Maolmin is a threat to Rhiannon?"

"Yes," Lakenna and Branor replied as one. They looked at each other, then back to Tellan.

"How great a threat?"

Keeper and Albane exchanged another glance. It was Branor

who answered. "A deadly threat, my lord. The siyyim inside him must be seeking Rhiannon's death so the prophecy will go unfulfilled."

"Then why did he send winged horrors to attack the sheep a day's journey distance?" Rhiannon asked.

"To draw us away," Llyr rumbled. "Maolmin expects us to gather most of our men, gallop off to protect the sheep, and leave you here."

Tellan swept his arm across the courtyard and the men and horses assembled there. "Which is exactly what we had planned to do!"

Branor related what he had learned from his reading about that outbreak centuries before, about how the Mighty Ones' creatures seemed to be controlled by a siyyim.

"Keeper Alock noticed that the directed attacks ceased when the high priestess, or more specifically the demon inside her, was out of the general area. From what your herder has told us, the recent attack on the sheep must have been undirected, while the previous one on the road must have been directed." Branor paused. "If Maolmin is attempting to draw away Rhiannon's physical protection, he must be planning to come here and direct another attack himself."

"Not Maolmin," Girard said, "it'll be his rhyfelwr, Lomas Erian." Everyone turned to look at the short loreteller. "Lomas will be in Lachlann tomorrow to check on preparations for the Presentation. It was to be Abel Caemhan, Maolmin's loreteller." Girard rubbed his chin. "The other loretellers and I were to meet with Abel and decide who was to speak at the Presentation. But last week, Abel sent a letter asking me to make those choices in his place. It seems Abel's sister lost her husband during a sudden outbreak of lung fever. Since she lives in the Ardnamur Mountains, Abel and his family were leaving immediately so they could be back in time for his daughter, Breanna, to participate in the Maiden Pole ceremony. Lomas is coming to Lachlann instead."

"The Albanes have teachings that say lesser demons, like a

rabisu, serve the greater demons," Lakenna said slowly. "Perhaps Lomas is indwelt by one of those."

Branor nodded. "Rabisu are said to be male and bloodthirsty. Lilitu are female and are depicted as very sexual. It is said they . . ." His voice tailed off. "Discussion for another time. I agree with Lakenna. If Lomas harbors a rabisu or lilitu, it could direct the winged horrors even without Maolmin's presence."

"So where does this leave us?" Mererid asked. "How do we send enough men to bring Phelan back safely and still defend Rhiannon? Not to mention us here at the hlaford."

"By me still riding with father," Rhiannon said, determined to ignore her thudding heart and clammy palms. Her father and Mererid frowned mightily, but she hurried on. "With my training I will be an asset, not a liability. Tomorrow Girard can ensure that Lomas knows I have left in the midst of twenty-five Rogoth warriors. There will be no reason to attack here. Besides, if winged horrors do find me, don't you think it's better to face them in the open and not trapped inside a burning building?"

Tellan pondered. The etched lines around his mouth cast deep shadows on his face. Finally, he raised an eyebrow at Llyr.

"I would prefer to face them in the open," the rhyfelwr said. "And I'd feel better having Rhiannon with us."

"How do we handle Lomas?"

Llyr gave Tellan a look. "Girard tells Lomas that if anything happens to the hlaford—anything—then I'll find a reason to call him out on a matter of honor and kill him."

The two locked eyes for a moment. Tellan nodded slightly, then turned to Girard. "At first light, you ride into Lachlann and give Lomas this message from Llyr."

"I will go with Girard," Mererid declared firmly, "and deliver Llyr's message myself." Her eyes flashed. "These *things* slink around and attack children and unarmed herders. I want Lomas and Maolmin to know that we are prepared and ready." She looked at Tellan, her eyes fierce as a mother bear defending her cubs. "Would that we could deliver the same warning to Maolmin himself."

263

"Why not?" Lakenna asked, puzzled.

"By honored tradition," Rhiannon explained, "the six clan High Lords are protected against attack on their person or property, or being called out on matters of honor like the challenge to which Llyr refers. In the event of an unprovoked attack, all kinsmen lords unite and march on the traitor and strip away title and lands."

"We'll be treading on dangerous ground to even challenge a High Lord's rhyfelwr," Girard said. "If Maolmin chooses to make an issue of it, I fear the Loreteller Assembly will decree it would be the same as attacking the High Lord himself." He sighed. "Unfortunately, Maolmin—and the siyyim, if one truly dwells in him—are protected by clan lore. We would have to prove to a majority of kinsmen lords that Maolmin is what you say he is. Can you do that?"

Branor and Lakenna shook their heads.

"But there is one thing more, Lord Tellan," Branor said. "I . . . we fear your association with Lord Gillaon and the Broken Stone Land might be hindering our ability to pray for protection."

Tellan's face darkened. "Explain."

Again, the two looked at each other. "Something is," Lakenna began. "I . . . we think—"

"This stretches things too far," Tellan said. "Worship of the Mighty Ones, I can see. But we are far from that. Trade is trade, and coin is coin."

"We don't understand it," Lakenna said. "We are new at this and uncertain on many things . . ."

Tellan clenched his jaw. "Until you are, continue to pray. We will keep our bows strung and our swords sharp. Mount up."

Rhiannon gave Mererid a quick hug and hurried out with the others.

A groom brought out Munin, Phelan's gelding, and gave the reins to Lakenna. The tutor eyed the horse uncertainly, as if trying to decide which end to mount.

"You'll do fine," Rhiannon assured her. "Munin taught me how to ride. He'll do the same for you."

Lakenna looked unconvinced. "I could ride in the carriage. It could carry part of the supplies."

"The terrain is much too steep and rocky. A carriage would never last."

"I am a tireless walker," Lakenna stated with faint hope as she continued to eye the saddle. It was the highest-cantled saddle they had, something that would to give her a more secure seat.

Rhiannon found herself smiling for the first time since the news of the attack. "We will be riding fast, alternating between a trot and a canter."

"Trot?" The tutor swallowed. "Canter?" She looked anew at Munin, her expression one of growing doubt.

"As we discussed at length last night," Keeper Branor said as he mounted easily his long-legged bay mare, "it makes perfect sense for you to remain here with Mererid and Creag while I accompany Rhiannon and Lord Tellan." He shifted in the saddle to arrange the black robe around his legs. Though freshly shaven, his face still had a dark beard shadow. "If another attack comes, we can pray together in the same manner as we did night before last."

Lakenna's expression firmed. She patted Munin on the neck. "M'lady, show me how to mount."

Rhiannon helped the tutor mount and showed her how to hold the reins. Moving around to mount Nineve, Rhiannon caught Creag's gaze and knew he was furious about being left behind. She stepped close to him. "It is a measure of Father's confidence that he trusts you to protect Mother. Besides, you are the heir; you must carry on if he does not return."

Creag thought that through and seemed somewhat mollified.

Llyr and the others mounted. Rhiannon's filly danced around skittishly as Rhiannon took the reins and mounted, careful to keep her sword out of the way.

Rhiannon nudged Nineve closer to Creag. "I'd feel better if you and your sword were by my side. But I know what a comfort that sword is for Mother."

"Indeed," Mererid said. She placed a hand on the boy's shoulder while giving Rhiannon a look of approval. Creag brightened and wished Rhiannon safe journey.

A touch of pink showed in the eastern sky. Tellan gave Mererid a formal bow, charged Creag to protect his mother, then mounted easily his stallion and rode to the head of the column of the warriors.

They made an impressive column, Rhiannon thought. Twenty-five men with various types of metal helmets, swords, strung bows, and quivers bristling with arrows lined up behind the Rogoth banner: a white ram with triple spiral horns on a red field. More than half wore chain mail, treasured heirlooms handed down from father to son. Four pack mules and five spare mounts were hitched head to tail at the rear of the column. Rhiannon noted that the mules were being handled by Larris Werfl, the young man her father had sent home for not maintaining his gear. As Tellan had predicted, Larris had satisfied Llyr and regained his place in the reserve.

Llyr rapped out an order, and three riders galloped ahead to a serve as scouts.

Rhiannon joined Lakenna and Branor in the middle of the column.

"Stay between Rhiannon and me," Branor advised Lakenna. "We will keep you in the saddle."

"I'll be fine," the tutor declared. She patted Munin's neck—then her head jerked back as the gelding leaped to follow the horses ahead. Eyes wide in alarm, Lakenna seized the saddle horn in a death grip as Tellan led them out at a fast canter toward the Fea Mountains.

They were several turns of the glass from home, the horses in a ground-eating trot, when Rhiannon felt the first tingle. It felt like a chill running up her spine. She shrugged it off.

The sun was high in the cloudless sky. The land was all uphill, rolling crests covered with a carpet of tough grass dotted with clumps of rank bitterweed. Groves of trees became more scattered as they traveled higher.

Lakenna was hanging on determinedly. Both hands still gripped the pommel of her saddle as she bounced about on the leather seat. Rhiannon could only imagine the agony the tutor was going to suffer in the next day or two.

Branor, an experienced horseman, rode smoothly. His mare, however, was not used to such a pace over uneven terrain; she was well lathered and her nostrils were flaring when Tellan finally called halt for a short break.

After helping Lakenna step down, Rhiannon loosened Munin's and Nineve's girths. Groaning, Lakenna wobbled away, knelt in a patch of grass in front of a rock, and began massaging the inside of her thighs.

Tellan rode down the column, checking horses and men as they dismounted, eyes missing nothing. When he saw Branor's mare, he snorted. "You should have listened to me, Keeper, and left her at the hlaford. Unsaddle her. I'll send you one of our spare mounts, a sturdy Rogoth horse that'll carry you at this pace all day and not be blowing like this one."

Branor nodded sheepishly and began uncinching his saddle.

Rhiannon felt it again: a strong tingle between her shoulder blades. Shivering, she felt the hairs on her arms rise.

Branor froze. He turned and looked at Lakenna. The tutor rose to her feet, face concerned.

"What is this I am feeling?" Rhiannon asked, afraid that she knew.

"The presence of the Mighty Ones' creatures," Branor answered as he dropped his saddle to the ground. He regarded her with interest. "You are sensing this, too?"

She nodded. Then her stomach twisted up in a sick knot. Branor grimaced as well. Hands on hips, he scanned the horizon. The sky was empty. No birds flew. It was deathly quiet, punctuated by an occasional snort from a horse and the creak of gear as the men checked their mounts and the straps on the pack mules.

The feeling passed.

Branor sighed, looked back at Lakenna again—and frowned. The tutor was turning in a complete circle, searching the sky. Finally, Branor cleared his throat. "Ah, Teacher?"

Lakenna still studied the sky. "Yes. They are further away somehow. Still, we'd best inform Lord Tellan."

Rhiannon watched Branor chew his lower lip in indecision. He looked about to speak again when a young warrior led up a shaggy-haired gelding.

He handed the reins to Branor, then picked up the saddle. With practiced ease, he placed it on the horse's back and cinched it tight. He took Branor's mare. "I'll try to give her a quick rub-down before we mount back up." The young man led the sweating horse to the rear of the column.

Branor rubbed the muzzle of his new mount, then looked toward Lakenna again.

The tutor must have felt his scrutiny. She turned to face him. "Yes?" Her voice was cool. Rhiannon could barely hear it.

Branor stepped toward Lakenna. "Are you . . . in pain?"

At first, Lakenna seemed puzzled. Then the skin around her mouth and eyes whitened. "What do you mean?"

Branor gave a half shrug. "Sometimes I . . . I have been able to—just on occasions, you understand . . ." He stopped and fumbled for words. "I have read of similar giftings in the time of Destin Faber and the Founders. Recently, I have been able to see things inside people. Twice I have sensed a deep wound in you—"

"I am fine!" Lakenna hissed. Stiff-backed with indignation, she grabbed the edges of her cloak and strode to Munin. Picking up the reins, she whirled back around. "The spiritual gifts operate strongly among Albanes. I do not seek Keeper insights into my fail— . . . into my . . ." Her face twisted, and for a moment Rhiannon thought the tutor verged on tears.

"No, no," Branor pleaded. "You misunderstand me. I only wanted to—"

His words died as another cold ripple twisted through Rhiannon. This one was much stronger than the other two. Something vile raised the hackles on the back of her neck. Her stomach flopped one more time. She detected the hint of some foul odor. All her senses screamed that something was here that should not be.

She eyed Branor and Lakenna. They stood still as statues, faces pensive.

Rhiannon's blood chilled when a dark spot high in the sky caught her eye. Though the distance was great, the unfurled wings and long neck were unmistakable.

"Father!"

They galloped down the rocky trail in a jostling bunch. Rhiannon, Lakenna, and Branor rode near the front with Tellan. Llyr had dropped back among the column, and Rhiannon heard his deep voice above the pounding hooves as he ordered the men to spread out.

Three horrors circled above them now, gliding effortlessly above the green foliage and blue granite peaks of the lower Fea Mountains. The beasts stayed well out of bow range but never out of sight.

Tellan searched the sky. "They know where we're going," he growled. One hand gripped the reins; the other was white-knuckled around his sword hilt. "Unless the herds have been scattered, Serous and Phelan should be over the next series of ridges. If the beasts are going to attack us, it would be better to do so before we join with the herders." The lines around his mouth deepened. "Unless..."

Rhiannon swallowed. *Unless they are already dead*, she finished. She too gripped her sword hilt with one hand in an effort to keep the scabbard from banging into Nineve's side. Lakenna was not bouncing in the saddle as much. The hard gallop the horses were in, while much faster than a trot, was a smoother gait.

Two warriors rode in front of them and one on either side. All carried bows with nocked arrows. The four were the best archers the Rogoths had.

"How sure are you," Tellan asked as they galloped, "that these things have not attacked the sheep again?"

Branor shortened his reins to hold back his fresh mount and glanced at Lakenna. "Not sure at all." When she nodded agreement, he continued. "We were called to intense prayer the day before yesterday and have not been since. We felt their nearness today before they appeared, but that is all."

"Are you two praying like you did?" Tellan lifted his chin skywards. "Will our arrows penetrate these things?"

A guilty look flashed across Lakenna's face. "I pray continually. But the same hindrance I felt before is still there."

Tellan halted their charge to allow the reserve to catch up.

Lakenna's expression firmed. "I am certain your association with the Broken Stone Land pagans is influencing this somehow and placing Rhiannon in greater risk. Like this Keeper Alock that Branor has told us about, Stanus Albane was adamant that all who enter into spiritual warfare must renounce any taint of the Mighty Ones."

Tellan scowled. "We are cheated for years by clansmen who only *claim* to follow the Eternal, who themselves trade with pagans, and it is fine. When finally we receive a fair price, it is wrong?"

"I don't understand all the ramifications, m'lord," Lakenna said, gripping her reins tightly. "The Covenant protects us, but dealing with pagans seems to remove that covering somehow and greatly weakens our ability to fight the evil of the Mighty Ones."

"If you are correct about Maolmin, then why was he so upset about my dealing with the Broken Stone? His displeasure seemed to go beyond any potential harm with his bargaining with the other clans. If indeed being associated with pagans weakens us and strengthens him, he should have been pleased."

Branor brought his eyes down from the circling horrors. "At the wool sale, remember how the High Lord mentioned that the Dinari used to serve the Mighty One of the North and that the

Broken Stone Land still worships the Lady of the West? We know that in the time before the Covenant the Mighty Ones fought continually among themselves for supremacy. Most likely those rivalries exist today. It makes a certain sense that the siyyim inside Maolmin serves the North." He regarded Tellan frankly. "The more the Dinari deal with the Broken Stone Land, the more it must strengthen the West."

"And dealing with Maolmin and the Sabinis strengthens the North? Bah, Keeper! You talk in circles."

"Like Lakenna, I do not understand it all. This much I do know: the Land resides under the protection of the Covenant, and as long as the Faber dynasty remains intact and the inhabitants overall remain faithful, the Mighty Ones are bound by it." He lifted his chin to the winged horrors. "But more evil is loose in the Land than we have encountered in generations. At least one High Lord is indwelt by a siyyim, and who knows how far the Mighty Ones' grip extends among the nobility." Branor gestured to Rhiannon. "Your daughter has been called to protect the Covenant and to lead a rebirth of its fullness. And yet you have become a partner with the very evil she will be fighting." Branor straightened in the saddle. "I ask you formally to renounce this agreement with Lord Gillaon and his Broken Stone partner."

Tellan urged his mount into a gallop again and the group followed, armor and tack jingling and clapping. "You pray so we can kill these things," he said. "I will deal with trade matters."

"Our prayers are hinder—"

"*Later*, Keeper! Even if I should desire to break those trade agreements, I can hardly do so here and now."

They pounded around a bend in the trail. Before them rose a high ridge with many half-buried boulders. On the other side of the ridge, Serous, Phelan, and the sheep were supposed to be waiting.

Rhiannon looked up—and startled when she realized the three horrors were lower. More, their wings were tucked.

They were diving straight at them.

271

Chapter Twenty-six

LAKENNA

"**D**ISMOUNT!" TELLAN ORDERED as he pulled his stallion into a skidding stop. Munin came to a smooth stop without Lakenna doing anything but what she had been doing since this agonizing day began—holding on with both hands.

She glanced up quickly. The three horrors were dropping toward them at an alarming rate. They were much the way she had pictured them from descriptions and images on tapestries: sleek bodies, pointed wings like a hawk, long serpentine necks, wedge-shaped heads. Sunlight sparkled off their smooth skin. In spite of her thudding heart and the nausea in the pit of her stomach, she found the diving horrors strangely beautiful—

Strong hands lifted her out of the saddle and set her unceremoniously on the ground. "Come, Teacher," Branor said. "We must pray."

Warriors scrambled all around them. Every fifth man held his horse and four of his mates' horses. Men jammed arrows in the ground next to their feet for quick access, then stood and faced the oncoming beasts, bows in hand, arrows nocked and ready.

Rhiannon! Lakenna worried. *Where is she?* Then she saw the girl surrounded by the four who had ridden at the head of the column—the four best Rogoth archers. Rhiannon had drawn her sword. She held it in both hands, point up, her eyes on the horrors that were hurtling closer!

Branor's hand almost crushed hers. "Teacher, I need help!"

273

he gasped. "It is much worse than before." His brow knitted in concentration.

Chagrined, she joined him in prayer—

And was shocked at the *barrier* she slammed into. All morning as she had prayed, or tried to, she had felt it growing: a hindrance like slogging through dank, foul-smelling water. Now, she could sense that thing she needed to come to grips with—*but she could not get to it!*

She felt Branor hammering away desperately even as she redoubled her efforts. They made painfully slow progress, and Lakenna knew they needed more help. She opened her eyes and looked at Rhiannon. The girl had sensed the approach of the beasts. Lakenna opened her mouth to ask Rhiannon to join them when the diving horrors let loose a series of ear-piercing screeches that shattered the morning.

Pandemonium broke loose. Horses reared, eyes wide in terror. Many broke free from their holders and dashed among the warriors. The men who managed to keep a grip on the reins were dragged into the milling mass of bodies and trampling hooves.

Fast-moving shadows obscured the sky. The horrors broke off their dive and spiraled over them, shrieking. The wind of the horrors' wings beat at Lakenna. A bolting horse slammed against her side. She lost her hold on Branor's hand as they both were knocked to the ground. Screams from the circling beasts added to the neighing of terrified horses.

"Loose!" Tellan bellowed as he drew his sword. "On your feet, men. Draw and loose!"

Lakenna came to her hands and knees, gasping for breath, mind spinning. Looking up, she saw the horrors at treetop level, wings beating furiously. A ragged volley of arrows sped up. A chill passed through her when she saw them bounce harmlessly off the light-colored underbellies.

Our prayers aren't working this time! What are we to do?

Two horrors banked lower, no more than the height of two men above the ground. With jaws parted, each spewed forth a long, jagged tongue of flame. Two lines of fire ran across the green grass at amazing speed. Caught by surprise, warriors rolled and cartwheeled out of the way. Two men ran smack into each other. Stunned, they were unable to dodge the line of flame that washed over them. Clothes afire, they ran screaming until tackled by quick-thinking companions and rolled in the dirt to douse the flames.

The third horror swooped down and unfolded its long rear legs to land in the mist of the scrambling mass. Screeching, it darted forward cat-quick and seized a hapless victim between its jaws. The man's scream was abruptly silenced with a sickening crunch of bones. The beast flung the body away, then turned back with wings unfurled for balance and a huge ball bulging behind the head. Lakenna watched numbly as its head lowered and the mouth opened to reveal a double row of bloodstained teeth. Men broke and ran.

"The eyes," Tellan directed, sprinting up. He grabbed a fleeing bowman and spun him around. "Stand and shoot! Aim for the eyes!"

His presence rallied them. At almost point-blank range, the warriors stood, drew bowstrings back and sent arm-long shafts toward the beast. At least one found its mark. The horror jerked up with a blood-curdling scream, a feathered end of an arrow in one eye.

Men scrambled to avoid being crushed as the beast collapsed. A shaft of fire billowed out its mouth at it hit the ground, blackening the grass. The body seemed to shimmer for a moment, then crumbled inward to become a cloud of dust scattered in the wind of wings as the other two horrors beat upward in the sky and disappeared over the ridge.

Coming shakily to her feet, Lakenna gave a quick glance at the twisted body of the warrior and wanted to cry. *More deaths will follow unless we can overcome this hindrance.*

Everyone stood still for a long moment. Then all began talking at once: loud, relieved. Several debated hotly whose shot had hit the eye.

"Enough!" Llyr's voice cut through the babble like a dash of cold water. He limped up from the area where most of the trampling from the loose horses had taken place. "I'll hear no arguing over this. Neither will I hear arguing over who turned backsides to these things, intending to leave poor Dar unavenged before Lord Tellan rallied us." His eyes were fierce enough to bore holes in wood. The men hung their heads and avoided the rhyfelwr's gaze.

Llyr let the uncomfortable silence last a moment longer. "Still," he continued in an even tone, "we did ourselves proud. We killed one and ran the others off. Not bad. Next time, if we can handle the horses better, not one of these things will fly away." The men raised their heads and squared their shoulders. "I want ten men to stand guard with bows. Those of you who have horses, go round up those that broke loose. The rest see to those that got burned or come with me to tend to Dar."

Everyone moved smartly to obey. Once the body was wrapped in a blanket, the Keeper left to say rites. Lakenna followed and stood at the back of the gathering, feeling out of place. Rhiannon stood next to her father in front of the wrapped body. After Branor finished, Tellan said a few words. Dar's body was tied on to his horse to be brought back and buried.

By the time the stray horses were brought back, it was past noon. Tellan ordered a quick meal.

Lakenna was not hungry. She took a blanket and folded it several times to make a pad. Placing it in front of a chest-high rock covered with brown moss, she sat down and winced. She fought the urge to rub her buttocks. Soon she was going to have to get back in that saddle.

"Undirected," a low voice said.

Lakenna started. "What?"

Branor gathered his black robe and sat down cross-legged in front of her. "This attack. It must've been undirected. The horrors acted like wild beasts. If a demon had been directing them, they would not have stopped." He regarded her frankly, his dark eyes alive as he worried with it. "We did no good just now. If they attack at night, and you and I cannot fight past that barrier, this will seem like an afternoon stroll."

She had no answer to that. Then she noticed he was looking at her that way again! *I don't need this!* She steeled herself and returned his look evenly.

His eyes dropped. He pulled at a blade of grass. "I spoke out of turn about the hurt I see in you. This is new to me. I only want to be of help, if you will allow it."

Anger flared. "I do not need Keeper help! We Albanes have people who can see my..." She looked away.

"Sin," he finished softly.

"I am indwelt by the Eternal," she said firmly. "I am forgiven." Unaccountably, tears flooded her eyes. "I am." She wiped her eyes. "I don't need anything from you."

"Whatever you have done, I have done much worse." Branor leaned toward her, his eyes sad. "Many years ago, the wisest man I know told me that those the Eternal calls for great duties, he first breaks. That way they know to rely on his strength and not their own." His voice thickened. "I ran from my breaking, and five good men are dead because of it. When I was forced to face that—forgiven though I was—it broke something in me." He paused. "I sense a similar running in you."

As she struggled to keep her face bland, the bitter taste of Old Tanny's herbal tea flooded her mouth. She swallowed twice in an effort to be rid of it.

He gestured to where Rhiannon stood talking to her father and Llyr. "Her prophecy is about the Covenant. I fear some problem within the Faber dynasty has weakened the protection of the Covenant to allow the Mighty Ones to loose so many winged horrors." He shook his head. "This is far beyond any Keeper-Albane rivalry. Great events are afoot, and the Eternal has placed you and me in the very center of it."

Branor's look of compassion deepened. "Please stop running, dear woman. Too much is at stake. Something very powerful happens when one believer looks another in the face and confesses sin. Whether with me or someone else, do whatever is necessary to keep from bearing that burden any longer."

Lakenna sat stiff as the rock she leaned against. What would people think of her if she confessed as Branor suggested? She did not have beauty like Rhiannon or position like Branor. Being admired as an Albane of Albanes was what she had clung to all the years of no suitors and diminishing prospects. If she admitted that she had willfully committed the most grievous of sins, she could no longer wear that badge. What would be left?

Only a sinner saved by the unearned love of the Eternal. Isn't that what true *Albanes believe?*

She wasn't ready for this right now.

"Tell me what you felt during our prayer," Branor inquired.

"I could sense . . ." Lakenna said slowly, grateful for the change of subject as she searched for words to explain the unworldly. "I sensed the demon—perhaps—anyway, whatever we needed to bind. But I could *not* get to it."

Branor grunted. "For me it was like a bad dream where I knew I had to reach something, but my legs and arms felt like lead."

"I didn't encounter that the first time." She pondered. "This hindrance the last two times must be the effect of Tellan's alliance with the pagans." Discernment surged, and she understood with a clarity that was startling. Her words tumbled out as she tried to keep pace with her new insight. "We're fighting through the West's presence! Tellan's agreement with the Broken Stone Land has tied him to the West, and now we're having to wade through that to get to the North!"

"Of course," Branor said softly. "Just as the North, through Maolmin, is seeking to prevent Rhiannon from walking in the prophecy, the West, through this wool deal, is seeking the same. And all of it is coming to a head just when Rhiannon is stepping into adulthood."

Men began kicking out cook fires and tying gear back on horses. Branor came to his feet and held out a hand. Lakenna took it and felt his strength as he pulled her up. They both turned and looked for Rhiannon. She was tightening Munin's girth.

Lakenna gritted her teeth and began walking determinedly toward that unbelievably hard saddle.

"I wonder," Branor said quietly as he walked beside her, "how many more will have to die before Tellan is convinced of the danger he has brought to his daughter?"

They crested the ridge, and Lakenna sagged with relief. Down the slope, masses of sheep covered the huge meadow as it stretched into the distance. Shepherds moved calmly among the herd.

Beside her, Rhiannon exhaled audibly. She nudged Nineve into a canter down the steep slope. Munin plunged on right beside the filly. Lakenna's eyes went wide, and her mouth opened in a wordless cry as she pitched perilously over the gelding's neck. Rhiannon reached out a hand and righted her. Reining up on Lakenna's other side, Branor put his free hand on a shoulder as well. Somehow, the three of them made it to the bottom with the tutor still in the saddle.

Lakenna took a deep shuddering breath. "M'lady, please help me down, or I fear I will split in half."

Before Rhiannon could comply, they heard a shout and saw Phelan running toward them from the far side of the meadow, waving his arms and jumping with joy.

A low moan escaped Lakenna's lips as they broke into a canter toward the running boy. Tellan beat them all. The stallion flew across the meadow, scattering sheep in all directions. Coming to a skidding stop a few paces from the boy, Tellan jumped off and Phelan leaped into his arms.

Rhiannon kept checking the sky. It was clear and cloudless. The sheep were calm, except where horses plowed through them. "Do you sense anything?" she asked Branor and Lakenna.

Branor said no. Lakenna just shook her head, watching the decreasing distance to Phelan like a thirsty person eyeing a glass of water. They pulled up at father and son. Rhiannon jumped off Nineve and gave Phelan a bone-crushing hug while Branor helped Lakenna down.

"Rahl and I killed a winged horror!" he announced excitedly as he broke the embrace. "It was easy. Well, once Teacher Lakenna started praying anyway." He frowned. "Adwr was killed. But he ran. If he had stayed by Mil—" He broke off when he saw Lakenna. "Teacher!" He ran to her. "We could tell when you started praying. What took you so long? I want you to teach me how to pray like that because—"

"Phelan!" Tellan broke in, smiling. "Later. Now, tell me: have there been other attacks?"

"No, sire. Just the one. They did attack both our groups, but at the same time."

"Any herders injured other than Mil?"

"One of Bowyn's men sliced his palm with an arrowhead. They only had one horror. They killed it. We had two, but one got away."

Lakenna exchanged a worried frown with Branor. They both understood the numbers. So many winged horrors. Were more arriving every day? How many more were there in all?

A gentle breeze ruffled her hair, bringing the now-familiar smell of sheep. The sun was warm on her face. Glancing at the grass, Lakenna saw it had been grazed down to the dirt. The sheep had to be moved to fresh pastures.

Serous came striding up. "Greetings, m'lord. Been a right interesting few days. Master Phelan proved himself a true Rogoth. Proud I am of him."

As Tellan asked about the men and sheep, Lakenna kept wondering what was different about the head herder. He had always been unflappable, but now she sensed a solidity, a calmness about the old man that had not been present before. Then it hit her. His hands! The joints were normal, not red and swollen. And his walk. That was what had first piqued her curiosity. Serous had stridden up smoothly, without his characteristic stiff shuffle.

Rhiannon had seen it, too. "Serous," she blurted, "what happened to your hands?"

"The Eternal healed me, m'lady." He regarded his hands solemnly. "I prayed for help so I could protect Master Phelan." He held up his hands and wiggled his fingers and lifted his knees. "The Eternal answered by freeing me to move." He nodded to Lakenna and Branor. "Grateful we herders are for your prayers. Without them, we couldn't have stopped those things. Shooting an arrow into a horror's eye by torchlight is nigh on impossible."

Lakenna cast a worried glance at the sky. Only a few turns of the glass remained until sundown.

Chapter Twenty-seven

RHIANNON

THEY DROVE THE sheep as fast as they dared toward another meadow with good grass and water. Rhiannon, Lakenna, and Branor rode with Tellan and Phelan, who was on a spare mount chattering away learnedly about sheep herding and winged horror slaying. Mil, his leg splinted, rode in a makeshift litter along with the two bandaged burn victims.

The sky remained empty of all life. Rhiannon had mixed feelings about that. Remembering the ride back to Lachlann, she knew that the total lack of birds could be ominous. All during the afternoon, she had watched the sky with Lakenna and Branor, alert to any outward or inward warning of the Mighty Ones' creatures. The lower the sun sank, the more the north wind picked up.

They stopped with twilight falling. Llyr divided his men into four groups. Serous and Bowyn did the same. Two groups would spend half the night protecting the camp and patrolling among the sheep while the other two groups slept. They would switch at midnight.

Phelan did not last long once he ate in front of the fire. He managed to tell Rhiannon even more about his adventure before his eyelids grew heavy. She made a mat for him with a folded blanket and tucked a second around him. After kissing his forehead, she smoothed his hair and told him how proud she was of him. He smiled happily and was asleep before she straightened up.

She added a few branches to the fire and began oiling her

sword. Lakenna sat across the flames, picking at her food.

The attack had unnerved Rhiannon more than she wanted to admit. Such a helpless feeling watching the arrows bounce off the horrors. It reminded her again of that first attack on the road, something she hadn't really dealt with in her mind. And then there was the difficultly she'd felt in praying. She had tried to join Branor and Lakenna, but didn't think she'd helped. She had to face it: in the moment of need she'd been useless. Protectoress of the Covenant? She couldn't even protect Nineve.

The inward nagging built again, telling her to surrender. Surrender her will, her plans, her hopes to the Eternal and trust him for the outcome. Almost like Lakenna and Branor wanted Tellan to give up the trade agreement. Rhiannon suddenly understood his dilemma in a new light.

Around the other fires, the warriors and herders scheduled for the midnight watch ate and talked among themselves, bows and quivers within easy reach. Each fire had a supply of unlit torches stacked nearby.

Tellan and Llyr rode in from stationing the early watch. As they dismounted, Branor walked up to them. The three engaged in an intense conversation. Rhiannon had no doubt what it was about.

Rhiannon drew the oilcloth across the shiny steel. How could her father renounce the agreement with the Broken Stone people? If they did not sell their export wool to Lord Gillaon, then the only other buyer was Clan Sabinis. And without a contract, the best the Rogoths could expect from Ryce Pleoh and the other two would be a ruinously low price.

But if winged horrors continued attacking the sheep or the hlaford or the homes of Rogoth kinsmen, then what? How many winged horrors were there? True, three of the beasts had been killed in the last three days. But two kinsmen were dead, two had severe burns, and one had a broken leg. A rate of exchange that could not continue. Tellan was responsible for his kinsmen. Something had to change.

She folded the rag and put it in a leather pouch. Full dark had fallen, and the temperature was dropping steadily. She pulled her cloak tighter around her shoulders.

Serous brought an armload of branches for the fire. Though his face was still a mass of fine lines and wrinkles, he moved with the spry step of a man thirty years younger. "Mark my words, m'lady," he said as he placed a few branches on the fire. "It'll be an early winter." A shadow crossed his weathered features, but then he brightened and flexed his joints. "But that'll be no problem now!"

"I haven't seen Rahl," Rhiannon said. "I promised his mother and Vanora that I would check on him."

"He's out for the first watch with Bowyn. Best not to mention Vanora's concern where the other herders might hear." Serous grinned. "The lad's being ribbed bad enough as it is." Putting both hands on his hips, he looked up at the stars, sniffed the night air, and grunted. "No doubt about it, an early winter. Wouldn't be surprised if there's snow on the ground for the Presentation and the Maiden Pole ceremony." He eyed Lakenna. "Teacher? Anything I can do for you?"

Lakenna, startled, looked up. "Pardon? Oh, no. Thank you, though, Serous."

He nodded and took his leave. The tutor resumed her contemplation of her bowl of stew. The fresh wood hissed and popped in the fire.

Watching sparks dance and weave in the updraft, Rhiannon chewed the inside of her lower lip.

Have you met the prince?

…as long as the Faber dynasty remains intact…

…you will find that path opening before you one day. The Eternal does not force anyone to follow him. You will have to choose to walk it or not. If you do so choose, it will unfold according to his timing.

Could it be? Was there something in all this to connect her with…with the prince? Or was she being some starry-eyed twit? If there *were* some connection—protectoress and prince—the implications would be mind-boggling.

Rhiannon stilled. If she were going to be responsible in some way for the Covenant, didn't *she* have to change as well? And quit ignoring the nagging inward voice that kept telling her to surrender? Surrender what? But she knew. Branor had told her that night in Lachlann. *We can become so focused on our way that we don't take the time to find what the Eternal's way might be.* She had to surrender her desires and allow the Eternal's will to be done. It sounded simple, yet it was so hard.

Rhiannon saw that her father and Llyr had finished their conversation with Branor. Llyr moved among the camp, talking and encouraging the men.

Now was the time. "Teacher?"

Lakenna started again. Her face seemed pensive, worried. "Yes?"

"I need to talk to you and Branor. And my father."

She led them to the two men. Rhiannon stuttered around at first, trying to get it out. All three watched her patiently. Finally, she found the words.

"It is time for me to...surrender. To the Eternal, I mean. I have been determined to walk in my prophecy my way, through my hopes and desires. I have been afraid to admit to any weakness, afraid to let the Eternal have his way with my life."

She paused. Branor nodded encouragingly. Lakenna nodded, too, but her eyes contemplated the ground. Tellan folded his arms across his chest and waited. The etched lines around his mouth proclaimed the strain of the long day.

Rhiannon took the plunge. She dropped to one knee. "Before you as witnesses, I bow the knee to the Eternal. I give my life to him. I give my prophecy to him. And my future to him. When he opens the door, I will walk through it. I will open no door on my own. This I pledge of my own free will and accord."

A huge weight left her shoulders.

When she rose, Branor hugged her. Lakenna did so next, then abruptly turned away with her head down and hurried back to the fire. Tellan regarded her with a mixture of pride and curiosity.

Then he hugged her strongly. They walked arm in arm to the fire and sat opposite Lakenna.

Rhiannon dipped her father out a bowl of stew. A part of her wanted to ask about his thoughts on renouncing the agreement after the talk with Branor, but her heart was too full of thankful prayers to do anything but send them upward.

Lakenna stood rooted by the fire, with a white-knuckled grip on the edges of her cloak. The firelight flickered across her pensive face. She took a few steps, hesitated, glanced at Rhiannon, then raised her chin resolutely and walked to Branor. After conversing a short moment, they stepped to the far edge of the light cast by the campfires.

Lakenna talked at length. Branor listened and nodded a few times. Lakenna stopped and began pulling nervously at the edge of her cloak. Branor waited patiently, face neutral.

Finally, Lakenna spoke again, then buried her face in her hands. A soulful keening came, and deep, shuddering sobs racked her body. She swayed back and forth before crumpling to her knees.

Alarmed, Rhiannon rose. Her father reached out a hand to stay her.

Branor knelt and wrapped Lakenna tightly in his arms. His lips moved in prayer as tears streamed unchecked down his face as well.

"No, daughter," Tellan said gently. "Whatever this is, let it remain between them. Mererid and I have long known something eats away at our tutor. Hopefully, this will help her."

Rhiannon sat down and tried to keep her eyes away. She of all people understood what Lakenna was feeling right now, though it had never occurred to her that the tutor might need to surrender, too. Perhaps surrender was not just a one-time event. Perhaps it was something you simply had to keep doing so long as you served the Eternal.

The fire had burned down to red coals when Lakenna returned. The front of her blouse was wet, but her face was more at peace than Rhiannon had ever seen. She gave Rhiannon a hug, the first one ever, then crawled under her blanket and went to sleep.

Giving one last look of the star-filled sky, Rhiannon pulled up her own blanket and fell into a fitful sleep.

She came awake suddenly, completely. The moon was up, a thin crescent just past the new moon. Wide-eyed under her blanket, Rhiannon listened for the slightest sound. Other than her father's soft snoring, it was quiet—dead quiet.

Then something like a douse of cold water washed over her. She sat up, her stomach turning in a way that was now frighteningly familiar. On the other side of the fire, Lakenna stirred and propped up on an elbow. Her long hair rippled across the wool blanket like a dark cloud as she searched the sky.

Another wave came, then another and yet another. Nauseated, Rhiannon reached over and shook her father. "Father!" she gasped. "Winged horrors."

Tellan kicked off his blanket and rolled to his feet, sword in hand. "Where?" he asked as he jammed on his boots.

"I don't know." Her stomach churned again. Then twice more. Cold sweat beaded her forehead as she drew her sword. Her heart hammered wildly.

"Lord Tellan!" Branor stumbled into view, hair tousled. "Call your men to arms! Many horrors approach. Many!"

"To arms, Rogoths!" Tellan bellowed. "Light torches!" The camp exploded like a disturbed anthill. Men poked torches into the hot coals while others grabbed bows and slung on quivers. Soon, torches threw enough circles of light to illuminate the entire camp. Warriors searched the sky, arrows nocked, bows half drawn.

The horses whinnied nervously. Several pawed and snorted. But beyond that, it remained strangely quiet. Branor and Lakenna joined hands and bowed their heads.

"Llyr!" Tellan rapped out. "Send a man to warn the herders."

The rhyfelwr did so, then returned, face concerned. "Keeper?

Teacher? Will our arrows penetrate, or will it be like yesterday?"

Branor opened his eyes. His unshaved beard was a dark shadow across his jowls, the lines around his mouth deep from the strain. "It is still there."

Lakenna moaned. "I sense him. But I cannot get to him!"

Llyr gave Tellan a frank look. "If we can only kill these things with an eye shot, we may have made a terrible mistake telling Maolmin's rhyfelwr that Lady Rhiannon is with us. It may be best to put her and an escort on fresh horses and send them galloping home."

"And if they can sense Rhiannon and follow her?" Branor asked.

Tellan's brow knitted, wrestling with it.

Part of Rhiannon said, *Yes! Let me run!* Angry at herself, she shoved that aside. "My place is here, Father. I will stay and fight." Cold sweat ran down her sides. She had to clamp her teeth to keep them from chattering.

"Rhiannon stays with me," Tellan decided.

"Lord Tellan," Branor pleaded, "I say again, our inability to bind the horrors must be directly related to your agreement with the pagans of the Broken Stone Land. Many lives will be lost if we cannot bind these beasts so they can be killed with weapons. Even if we survive this night, there will be more attacks. Renounce this association. Trust the Eternal. He will provide."

"How can I, Keeper? Shall I shout to the wind and hope I am heard by all parties to the agreement?"

"In your heart, m'lord," Branor said. "Annul the agreement now, in your heart, and it may be enough. You can deal with the parchments later."

A *rightness* surged inside Rhiannon, and she knew she had to speak. "Please, Father. I believe he and Lakenna are correct. I ask you not for my sake, but for our kinsmen."

Tellan pondered a moment longer, then turned and looked at her. His eyes were full of love. He took a deep breath and spoke in a raised voice. "I, Tellan Rogoth, kinsmen lord of the Rogoth kinsmen, do hereby renounce any and all associations with Lord Gillaon Tarenester and his Broken Stone partner. I beseech the Eternal for help in our time of trouble."

Tears came. Rhiannon hugged him—just as a series of shrill screeches split the darkness.

Startled, Rhiannon glanced up into the sudden wind and saw the underside of a winged horror. Its rear legs were extended, and wickedly sharp talons descended straight at her!

Tellan threw her to the ground and rolled them both sideways. Swirling gusts of sparks blew from the fire and stung her face. The horror landed with a thud that shook the ground. Lakenna fell at the impact. All around came the twang of bowstrings and shouts mingled with the guttural hissing of more and more horrors—perhaps a dozen of them—as they plummeted down into the midst of the camp, mouths spewing fire.

Lakenna struggled to her hands and knees. "Yes!" she cried. Her lips began moving silently, face fierce and determined as she prayed.

Branor staggered backward from the same wing buffeting. Righting himself, he closed his eyes and grunted like a warrior swinging a sword. "You are bound, foul demon! Bow the knee to the Eternal!"

Rhiannon stopped rolling five strides to the side of the beast. She rose, sword in hand. Sounds of pain and fear and battle swirled all around her. The horror swung its head back and forth, searching. When it saw her, it bellowed and wheeled about with the elegance of a snake. Yellow eyes pulsed with raw fury. Its rank, decaying smell filled her nostrils.

Tellan lunged, sword stabbing for the near eye. Almost contemptuously, the horror swung a wing forward to cover its face like a shield. Tellan's thrust bounced off the leathery surface and did not leave a mark. Whipping the wing back, the beast knocked him sprawling.

Then, open-mouthed and terrible, it bounded straight at her.

She ducked just under the snapping jaws, but the sharp

teeth caught the hem of her cloak and she was jerked off the ground. Swinging back and forth, choking on the chain clasp, she watched helplessly as one front claw grabbed for her. But her dangling movement swung her out of reach, and one talon only slashed through her dress, missing her flesh. She was swinging toward the other front claw when the clasp chain broke, and she tumbled back to the ground, stunned. Somehow she maintained her grip on her sword as she scrambled away.

The horror roared its frustration and bounded at her again, rear feet churning. Rhiannon turned to face it. It was something out of a nightmare. The monstrous head, with its long snout and ridge of knobs, was right before her. She lunged at an eye, knee bent, sword straight, wrist locked. Caught by surprise, the horror twisted its head to the side. Her point hit a bare finger's thickness below the lower lid but did not penetrate. The shock of the impact traveled down her arm and almost tore the hilt from her grasp.

The wedge-shaped head flew back and crashed into her side. She skittered across the hard ground, and the creature rushed upon her. Everything melted into a mass of slashing teeth, talons, and fear; swishing wings, the powerful stink of oily musk, and desperate, mind-numbing fear.

She found herself flat on her back, bruised and battered, staring up at the underside of the horror as the head darted down for another bite at her.

Then suddenly...she sensed the same *shift* as had happened during that first attack months ago.

The beast hesitated right above her, its breath hot and fetid in her nostrils. With mounting hope Rhiannon thrust upward. She drove her sword hilt-deep into the soft tissue between the mandibles of the jaw. The sharp blade penetrated through the beast's tongue, the roof of the mouth, and into the base of the brain. Hot blood streamed down her hand and arm and splattered her face and hair.

The horror lurched away with a muted, closed-mouthed moan

that turned into a death rattle as it collapsed a few paces beyond.

"Aim for their hearts, lads," Serous bellowed above the clamor. "They've been bound! Give them cold steel and watch 'em die!"

It was over quickly after that. A few horrors fled back into the night sky, wings beating franticly. Most died from a hail of arrows, their bodies crumbling quickly into dust.

Tellan helped her to her feet and wrapped his arms tightly around her. His face was bruised. Blood ran from a deep cut above his eyebrow. He checked her head to toe. "Your arm is bloodied. Are you all right?"

She nodded, still in a daze. "Not my blood." Ignoring the pain that racked her body, she walked weak-legged to the pile of dust that had been the horror. She bent down and picked up her sword. The blade seemed unharmed. Her hands trembled a bit, but she managed to slide it back into the scabbard. She took a deep breath and looked at her father.

"Come, my lady warrior," he said with quiet pride, "we must see to the needs of our men."

Tears verged, but she struggled to hold them back. Squaring her shoulders and determined to project a calm she was nowhere near feeling, she went with him to do their duty.

Amazingly, they found that only one warrior had been killed in the mêlée. Another warrior and a herder had suffered burns. Phelan was incensed at the Rogoth warriors who had kept him out of the fight.

Rites were said over the dead man. Burns, cuts, and bruises were tended to, and the camp was put back into some semblance of order.

Tellan, Rhiannon, Llyr, Lakenna, and Branor sat around the fire and tried to come to grips with all that had happened.

"When you were doing your part," Tellan said to Lakenna and Branor, "did you see Maolmin?"

As had become usual when discussing these matters, the two looked at each other. Lakenna answered first. "I don't think so. This time I could clearly see the demon controlling the horrors.

We were able to go straight to it and bind it with a rope that was in our hands."

"In the distance," Branor said, then stopped himself. "*Distance* is not exactly correct, but it is as close as I can come to describing it. In the *distance*, I felt another presence lurking. Much larger and more powerful than the demon Lakenna and I were binding."

"Much more powerful," Lakenna agreed. "The demon we encountered here tonight must have been Lomas. When I prayed during the very first attack on the road to Lachlann, it was against a larger presence. With all that we have learned since then, I believe that stronger force was the siyyim inside Maolmin. I think all I did then was surprise him enough that he lost contact with the horrors, and that rendered them vulnerable."

Llyr poked a stick in the fire. "Can you *get* to the siyyim now and bind it?"

"Not unless he gets directly involved, as he was careful not to do tonight," Branor said.

"Explain," Tellan demanded. "I renounced my partnership— did that make no difference?"

"It made all the difference, m'lord," Branor said. "Had you not done so, the battle would have...ended differently."

Tellan fumed. "Then why can you not get to Maolmin?"

"It is a matter of free will." Branor paused, gathering his thoughts. "We know that the Eternal does not force anyone to follow him. He respects our will. He will love us, hound us, pursue us, and close doors in our faces, but he will never force us to go against our will. Once we do turn our will to him, he overwhelms us with his presence and love. Unfortunately, it works the same way for Maolmin.

"It is obvious now that Sim Anwar, the former Dinari High Lord, was not the one dabbling in ceremonies of the old gods. It was Maolmin. He called the siyyim forth. He freely chose to welcome it into his mind and soul. Now that it is inside Maolmin, we cannot go against the man's free will. In order for us to get at him, he will have to become directly engaged in the battle somehow, as he was when he first used the winged horrors and Lakenna was able to come against him." Branor shrugged. "If he continues to do as he did tonight, keeping a lesser demon between himself and us, we will be stymied in the spirit realm."

Silence ensued.

"So," Llyr growled finally, "our High Lord can use both his demonic power and the power of his position to harm Rhiannon, and there is nothing we can do about it short of convincing a majority of Dinari kinsmen lords that he is unfit."

"Is there any way," Branor asked Tellan, "to get around this protection of the High Lord?"

"Well," Tellan said, "there is one way. Maolmin would have to accept a challenge to personal combat. In such duels all rank and privileges are left behind."

Lakenna clearly did not understand the ensuing silence. Perplexed, she looked around the fire until her gaze rested on Llyr.

He met her eyes and answered, "Maolmin won the Dinari sword bouts three years running before he became High Lord. After that, he won seven more years with no one even coming close to matching his level of skill. I faced him the year before and the year after he became High Lord. The one before, I was a bit past my prime, but not much. Maolmin defeated me, but he had to work at it." Llyr shook his head grimly. "The year after, it was over in less than ten heartbeats. I have never faced such strength and speed and power."

"Even so," Lakenna pressed, "this may be the only way to deal with Maolmin's threat to Rhiannon."

"If we could find a reason to issue a challenge for personal combat," Llyr said, "it would take a very special swordsman indeed to face Maolmin. Personal challenges are fights to the death."

Lakenna stared into the fire. "We must set ourselves to pray for the Eternal to provide such an opportunity and for that warrior to be sent forth."

Chapter Twenty-eight

HARRED

ENOS RILYN WAS built like a boar, and he had the manners of a stag in rut. Gravy dribbled down his chin and bits of cheese decorated his green satin doublet. It was rumored that this jewel merchant from Clan Landantae had gotten his start by selling loot accumulated from earlier days as a highwayman. Harred could believe it.

Enos took another loaf from the wooden platter in front of him, sawed out a trencher, and waited as a serving girl ladled in a dipper of stew. Picking up a spoon, he took a huge mouthful and chewed noisily. He was not a man for small bites.

They were in the common room of the best inn in Maude, the village where the wool train had been attacked. Not hungry, Harred only picked at his food.

A Rosada spice merchant named Decart sat across the table, next to Enos, eating with impeccable manners. Although in late middle years, with black hair shot with gray, the spice merchant was still lean and hard. He was dressed in a light blue silk coat and had sun-darkened skin and brooding eyes.

Harred ran his fingers across the scarred surface of the white pine table varnished with years of accumulated grease and glanced at the other two occupied tables in the common room. In the far corner, enshrouded in a fog of blue smoke from their long-stemmed pipes, two elderly men hunched over a game of Kings and Queens. The sound of their pieces slapping down on the wooden board mingled with the clank of spoons at the other occupied table. At the other

table a tired mother in travel-stained clothes cradled a nursing babe
in one arm and ate with her free hand. Her husband and young son
leaned over their bowls and shoveled food into their mouths with
the single-mindedness of the famished.

Enos followed Harred's gaze. "Running from the fever, most
like," he declared around his chewing. "The whole area from
Denoch to Balliolium is said to be involved for weeks now." He
took a long draught from his mug and belched. With a wide
mouth and no chin, his face reminded Harred of a frog's. "Any
more best hurry. Bad storm brewing higher up. The passes will
be closed soon. Everybody's been predicting an early winter.
Looks like they're correct."

Enos had just bought all the amber Harred had brought back
from the second trading trip with Lord Gillaon's Broken Stone
partner. Clan Sabinis tightly controlled amber's import into the
Land, and its price was exorbitant. The cold seashores and for-
ests of the Broken Stone Land provided the substance in abundance. Lord Gillaon's eyes always gleamed when he discussed
the potential profit from that one item alone.

On this second trip Keto, Thoven's retainer, had met Harred at
the same mountain plateau. Besides the amber, Harred had purchased silks, fine porcelains, fur, and perfumes. All available in
the Land only though Sabinis merchants—until now. Elmar and
the warriors guarded the Tarenester wagons, which were camped
at the outskirts of the village.

Decart brought the conversation around to business. "I sell
you everything, yes?"

With the money from the sale of amber to Enos, Harred was
authorized to buy spices from Decart. The import of spices, like
many other valuable items, was otherwise tightly controlled by
Clan Sabinis.

"What do you have?"

"Spices of the highest quality and variety." The merchant removed
a folded sheet of parchment from his vest and slid it over to Harred.
"This is what I have in my three wagons, and the price."

Scanning the list, Harred struggled to keep his face expressionless. He figured a minimum twenty-gold-coin profit per wagon. When he glanced up, he found Decart watching him closely. Something about that gaze tugged at Harred's mind, but his thoughts were reeling at the immense profits.

The spice merchant smiled, but it did not reach those piercing eyes. "We do business, yes?"

"Yes. We do business. And next spring, we meet here again?"

"Next spring I will come to Lord Gillaon's hlaford with ten, maybe twelve wagons. The same price. You buy everything, yes?"

"Yes."

Decart nodded. He held Harred's gaze. "One fine tomorrow." He rose and took his leave.

Enos brushed crumbs from his belly, rose ponderously to his feet, and promised to return for more amber next year.

The innkeeper bustled forward while wiping his hands on a dirty white apron. "Weather be turning. First snow of the season coming. Not a night to be sleeping out." He smiled hopefully. "Five coppers and you gentlemen be dry and warm tonight. By morning, best be leaving these mountains or you be staying until the storm passes."

Elmar had talked about little else on the trail. The last two days he had kept sniffing the wind and growling that they needed to hurry to the lower regions.

Enos dug into a leather pouch and dropped coins for the three meals into the innkeeper's outstretched hand. "One room."

The coins disappeared under the innkeeper's white apron. "And you, warrior?"

"I sleep with the wagons," Harred said. Something about the spice merchant kept skittering around Harred's mind as the innkeeper escorted him to the door.

"Not a night to be on the trail," the innkeeper was saying. "A family stayed here a few nights ago, traveling to bring back kin from the fever area. The wife and grown daughter be sweet and loving. A fine catch, that one. If I were but a young man..." He sighed. "The father be a loreteller and a prickly sort. Didn't take kindly to my warning about how quickly the weather can turn this time of year. Still, he left coins to reserve two rooms for their return. They intended to be here yesterday." He shook his head. "You would think any Dinari be more aware of winter storms and be listening to my advice."

Harred froze. "A Dinari loreteller? You say he had a grown daughter?"

The innkeeper tsked. "The loreteller be a hard man to deal with. I hope his family be safe and not caught in this storm."

"Their names!" Harred's voice strengthened. "What were their names?"

"Caemhan, it was. Abel Caemhan. He be the loreteller to the Dinari High Lord."

"You be killing these horses, we don't slow down," Elmar warned.

Harred paid no heed. He glanced at the roiling mass of fast-moving gray clouds that hid the sky and encompassed the granite peaks towering above them. It was well past dawn, but the narrow mountain trail remained dark and foreboding. The wind gusted, bringing a few snowflakes, and the temperature dropped steadily.

"How much farther we be searching?"

"As long as it takes." Breanna was out there. Harred felt it in every bone in his body.

Elmar sniffed deeply and shook his head. "This storm we be riding into be a bad one."

"You sure this is the trail to Balliolium?"

"My daddy and I be hunting this area since I could sit a horse. This be the only trail between Maude and Balliolium wide enough for a wagon."

They had left Maude near midnight. Elmar and the innkeeper had both failed to dissuade Harred from leaving. A strong gust came howling down the trail, blowing leaves and snowflakes, startling the pack mule tied to the back of Elmar's saddle. The mule carried all the heavy cloaks and blankets the innkeeper could spare. Harred's pack mule carried food, horse feed, and a supply of medicinal herbs. The Tarenester warriors had been left in Maude to guard the wagons.

Tugging the wide-eyed pack mule forward, Elmar groused, "How do we know the Caemhans not be safe and snug in Balliolium?"

Harred surveyed the rugged landscape. "They're out here. I can feel her."

Elmar raised his eyebrows but remained silent. They trotted on, straight into the gloom of the approaching storm.

Half a glass later it was much colder. Snow was beginning to cover the trail, and the wind was biting through Harred's cloak.

"This thing be right at us." Elmar pointed down a ridge to his left as his cloak billowed out in the stiffening wind. "There be a cave not far from here. My papa and I camped there for years to smoke elk meat. We always left a supply of wood."

Harred nudged his horse into a faster trot. "A bit more." Somehow he knew that Breanna was in mortal danger from this brewing killer storm. He could feel her more strongly then ever.

Around the next bend they caught whiffs of wood smoke. A little farther on and they came upon a boy carrying an armload of branches and struggling against the cold wind.

The boy might have been eight. He looked up, eyes wide with surprise when Harred and Elmar cantered up through the falling snow. "Can you help us?" he called out. "My family is over this way. Our wagon axle broke yesterday."

Harred jumped from the saddle and came to the boy. "Breanna and Loreteller Abel—are they with your family?"

Feldan nodded. His jaw was shivering. "How did you know? Uncle Abel broke his leg."

"We will help you, son," Harred said. He took the bundle of firewood and gave it to Elmar. Then he put Feldan into the saddle with him atop Coal.

"Our wagon axle broke yesterday," Feldan said as they started off in the direction the boy pointed. "My cousin Breanna and I were helping Uncle Abel lever the end up so he could put on a new one, when...my end slipped and the wagon dropped and caught his leg. We got it off, but his leg was all twisted." The lad's voice cracked and the words spilled out in a rush. "Now it's swollen bad and Aunt Cyndae says a storm is coming and we need plenty of wood..."

"We're here to help, lad," Harred said. "You're going to be all right now. Just hang on." Harred dug his heels into Coal's side.

Harred and Elmar spotted the disabled wagon through the falling snow. They galloped to it and found Abel propped up next to the wagon. The wind whipped the flames of a small fire over which a pot steamed. A light dusting of snow covered the wagon and the bundles on the ground. The sky continued to darken.

Feldon slid off from behind Harred and ran to the woman kneeling beside Abel. A young girl snuggled in the woman's lap, wrapped within the folds of a cloak. On the other side of the fire sat another person, face concealed within the deep hood of a cloak. The figure stood, turned to Harred, and pulled back the hood. The wind whipped Breanna's hair around her face as her dark eyes fixed Harred with an unblinking stare.

Patting Abel's arm, his wife rose, listened to Feldon's report, squeezed the lad's shoulder, and then approached Harred and Elmar. She moved with an understated grace that reminded Harred very much of her daughter.

This was an attractive, self-possessed woman, but the dark smudges under her eyes and deep lines etched around her mouth told of the burdens she bore. As the wind molded her cloak to her body, her brown eyes searched Harred's face, clearly attempting to assess the character of the young man who stood before her. "I am Cyndae," she said with a shiver in her voice, "wife of Loreteller Abel de Erian en Caemhan of Clan Dinari. May the blessing of the Eternal be on you for responding to our need."

"I am Harred de Tarenester en Wright, and this ugly one behind me is Elmar de Tarenester en Stuegin. We are of Clan Arshessa, and we stand ready to help."

A wave of relief passed across Cyndae's face. She closed her eyes and nodded gratefully.

Elmar dismounted and strode through the swirling snowflakes. "Dame Caemhan, I be sure the next two, three days, these mountains be trying to kill us. It be too exposed here on the trail. If we like to be breathing when this storm ends, we need to move to shelter."

Cyndae brushed strands of hair from her face. "This has been an ill-fated trip. We would have been much lower by now except for this accident. Let me bring you to my husband. His leg pains him greatly. Fortunately, I have paste of poppy, and the tea from it has eased him."

As she and Elmar went to Abel, Harred made his way though the swirling snow to Breanna. She watched his approach with a solemn expression. Snowflakes dotted her tangled black hair, mimicking a spray of white flowers. She had a smudge of ash across one cheek, and her lips were chapped and peeling from the wind.

He halted before her. Though disheveled and wrapped inside the heavy cloak, she filled his world.

"I knew you would come," she said simply. Her eyes seemed to be memorizing every contour of his face.

His throat closed, and for a moment he did not trust himself to speak. "I knew that you knew," he managed finally.

Her eyes teared. Then, with visible effort, Breanna steeled herself. Without another word, she turned and walked to where Elmar and Cyndae were tending to her father.

Abel Caemhan was drifting in and out of consciousness, the skin of his face taut.

Elmar squatted down beside him, lifted the blanket, and frowned when he saw how the swollen leg was stretching the breeches tight. He took his dagger and slit the fabric, revealing the bruised skin beneath. His frown deepened. "When we get him to shelter, I will make a brown moss and tangleweed poultice for his leg. After that brings the swelling down, we can set and splint it." He glanced up at Cyndae. "Best you give him more swallows of that tea. Moving him now be bad, but to stay here be worse."

Working with urgency, Cyndae, Breanna, and the two young ones gathered what could be brought of their supplies and placed them on the pack mule. Harred and Elmar made a litter from two saplings and a blanket, reinforced it with leather reins from the wagon, and placed Abel on it.

Elmar and Harred lifted the litter and led the group through the heavy snow toward the cave across the next ravine. Cyndae and the young girl rode double on Harred's gelding with the pack mule's lead line tied to rings in the rear of the saddle. Breanna rode Elmar's dun mare, a small, graceful hand reaching out from the cloak to grasp the reins. Bringing up the rear was Feldon, bareback on the Caemhan's wagon mule, his teeth chattering from the cold. Within moments, the disabled wagon was swallowed behind them in the gloom of the storm.

They reached the cave half a glass later. By the time they set the litter down inside the mouth of the cave, Abel was white-faced with pain and awake enough to recognize Harred. The loreteller made no effort to hide his displeasure. Harred ignored him and went out with Elmar while the Caemhans brought in supplies. Cyndae unwrapped a hot coal she'd brought from the other fire and started a fire with the dry wood that, thankfully, was still there.

Harred helped Elmar cut several green saplings to weave a frame for a barrier to enclose the mouth of the cave. Then Harred took the ax and told Feldon to come with him to gather firewood. While they worked, the lad told Harred that his mother had come down with lung fever right before Abel and his family arrived. She had lingered for two more days before finally succumbing, and that had delayed the Caemhans' return. The boy appeared numb when he spoke about his mother. His father had died weeks before. Harred realized this wasn't just a friendly trip with his aunt and uncle—the boy and his sister were going to live with Breanna's family now.

Every time Harred brought wood inside the cave and stacked

it next to the fire, he felt Abel's eyes boring into him. Swallowing his anger, Harred told Feldon to bring in more dead wood, and went to bring the horses and mules into the back of the cave. That done, he went to help Elmar finish the panel.

It was snowing heavily now. The wind numbed exposed flesh in mere moments as they stood outside the cave mouth pounding the sharpened ends of the frame into the ground and wedged the bottom with rocks. Fighting the gusts, Harred helped Elmar stretch two of the blankets across the frame so they could stuff moss and leaves between them to give a bit more protection from the wind.

Breanna came out carrying a wooden bucket with a rope handle. She set it down, filled it with snow, and lugged it back. She and Harred exchanged a long look as she edged by the frame. Turning back to work, he found his brother-in-law's eyes on him.

"More maidens than I've got fingers be hoping you approach them at the next *Arshessa* Maiden Pole," Elmar said softly. "That's where you best be looking."

Harred sighed. "Breanna's different somehow."

"Yes! She be different because her bride price be already paid, remember? Besides, you see how Abel be acting. He'd as soon gut himself as be agreeing to a suit from you."

"I know." Harred stared into the cave where Breanna was emptying the snow into a pot over the fire. "But there is a way. Maybe."

"A way to have a foot of Dinari steel be driven through you." Elmar wove a rawhide string around the saplings and through the holes he'd stabbed in the blankets with his knife. "This between you and her, it be beyond my ken. You be talking to her two times, and you already risked dying for her once." He gripped the blanket tightly as a particularly strong gust threatened to snatch it loose. "And that maybe still happen if you be taking that path."

Harred grinned. "How could I be in danger with you guarding my back?"

"There'll be no back guarding at a *Wifan-er-Weal*. Stop this foolishness now. Maolmin Erian still be her kinsmen lord, right? It be the next thing to suicide to face that man. Particularly since he'd only be fighting you after he be watching you fight four of the best warriors the Dinari have and seeing your technique." He gave Harred a level look. "You be something special with a sword in your hands, but facing Maolmin Erian be an act any sane man should fear..." Elmar's voice tailed off when Breanna returned with the bucket to gather more snow to melt.

"I'll be back," Harred said as he went to help her. Elmar's answer was lost in the wind.

Snow swirled, making it difficult to see. Breanna smiled at him when he approached. She allowed him to pack the bucket for her but then refused to let him carry it back. "You need to help Elmar." She gripped the rope handle and made for the cave.

"You knew I was coming today," Harred said.

She paused and lowered the bucket into the snow to rest. "Yes. It was...certain somehow." She peeked at him then looked away. "I could feel you out there. I don't know how, but I knew you were looking for me. I..." She looked him straight on. "I wanted you to find me."

Harred felt the impact of her direct gaze. She had kept it shielded from him since the wool sale. How he'd yearned for those eyes to engulf him once more. And here they were.

"I came for you here," he said into her eyes. "Know that I will come for you one more time."

She tilted her head, puzzled. "When?"

"Lachlann. The Dinari Maiden Pole. I will voice my suit for you, and when your father refuses, I will fight the *Wifan-er-Weal*."

Emotions chased each other across her face. Confusion, realization, and something that looked entirely like longing. But then it was gone, and her features hardened. She shook her head. "That cannot be. Must not be." She grabbed the bucket and headed toward the cave.

Harred watched her go, the cold seeping into his legs and through his spine. Then he trudged back and helped Elmar finish the frame.

Within the turn of a glass, the wild storm winds hit with

impressive fury, shrieking and moaning. With everyone huddled under two blankets apiece, Elmar kept only a small fire burning, constantly cautioning them to husband the firewood and watching every new piece thrown on the flames with the eyes of a jealous lover.

"Better to be a little cold now," he warned. "Later, if this be bad as I fear, we burn more wood for a bigger fire."

The fire was adequate for the game of eyes Harred and Breanna played with each other across the flames. He and Elmar sat huddled on the hard clay floor with their backs to the woven sapling panel. Eddies of sharp cold still filtered in and chilled their backs.

The Caemhans were on the other side of the fire, with Abel propped up against the far wall, his broken leg stuck out straight before him. Since Elmar and Harred had set him down inside the cave he had adamantly refused any more of the poppy tea, perhaps determined to remain clearheaded. Earlier he had held a long, whispered conversation with Cyndae. Afterward the mother had looked knowingly at her daughter, then at Harred, and had smiled sadly.

Now Cyndae seemed to have picked up on what was happening between Breanna and Harred. Her worried eyes cut back and forth between the two of them, then at her husband.

"Clansman Stuegin," she said warmly to Elmar as she rocked her sister's little girl to sleep in her lap, "I have never heard of this brown moss and tangleweed poultice you are preparing. Are they found only in these mountains?"

At the sound of her mother's voice breaking the silence, Breanna lowered her eyes from Harred's, who cleared his throat and looked into the fire.

Gripping a pot of warm water between his knees, Elmar used the handle of his skinning knife to make a paste of the shredded mass of herbs from the supplies he had brought. "Be calling me Elmar. And yes—"

"I think it will be best to use proper modes of address," Abel said. Feldon gave his uncle a puzzled look at the cold tone.

"These are Lord Gillaon's men," Abel went on, "and less than cordial relations exist between our kinsmen at the moment. More," he said, giving Harred a sharp look, "Breanna will be betrothed at the Dinari Presentation. Her bride price has been paid, and I will tolerate no interference with that."

Elmar peered up from the pot and locked eyes with Abel. "I tell you this because you must not rightly hear Harred—Lord Gillaon's rhyfelwr—when we first be at your wagon." Elmar's voice was dangerously soft. "He gave his word that we be ready to help you and your family. That be meaning, Loreteller, that he and I be putting aside clan rivalries and such until we be a-seeing you and your family safe out of these mountains." He tapped the lip of the pot with his knife to emphasize his next words. "You be mentioning betrothals and bride prices. Can it be you question our honor? That you feel the need to protect your daughter from us after we give our word that we be here to help you and have risked our lives to do so?"

Harred glanced quickly at Breanna, who caught his look then dropped her eyes to her lap.

The silence lengthened.

Abel swallowed. "I...er...of course I do not question your honor. This is difficult and—"

"What be difficult about your wife calling me Elmar and believing we will respect your daughter?"

It dawned on Harred that he *was* a rhyfelwr, an advisor equal to a loreteller, and it was time to start acting like it. "Can we wash this pot clean and start a fresh stew?" he said earnestly. "Until we leave these mountains I am Harred, he is Elmar, you are Abel, and your wife is Cyndae. Agreed?" he said with a touch of command in his voice. *And your daughter is an angel straight from heaven.*

Abel exchanged glances with Cyndae, then nodded. "Yes, I agree."

Cyndae tried again. "Elmar...please tell me about this poultice. It is brown moss and what?"

The tension eased as she and Elmar talked about healing

herbs and their uses. Cyndae was well versed on the subject and related several uses Elmar had not known.

Harred watched Abel. The man's face was still tight with anger or pain or both. Suppressing a sigh, Harred let his eyes drift again toward Breanna as the wind and snow roared outside.

She sat calm and neat, hands folded in her lap, staring into the fire, the flickering light playing across her features. As if feeling his eyes upon her, she looked up at him. The hint of sadness, of loss, in her gaze twisted his heart.

Glancing toward Elmar, Harred caught Cyndae's gaze. She smiled ever so slightly while almost imperceptibly shaking her head, silently communicating the impossibility of any future between him and her daughter.

The wind howled the rest of the day and into the night. Elmar and Cyndae applied the poultice to Abel's leg. Then everyone pulled blankets over their heads and tried to sleep.

Long after darkness fell, Harred remained huddled underneath his blanket, arms wrapped around his legs, knees pulled to his chin, staring into the fire.

The storm lasted until mid-afternoon the next day. Overnight the poultice had reduced the swelling. So, with Abel full of poppy tea, Elmar set the fracture and applied a splint to the leg.

The following morning dawned clear and bitter cold with a stiff north wind. Harred and Elmar ventured out and led the horses and mules through hip-deep snow to a sheltered area where the animals were able to paw down to the dried grass below.

Thawing out back inside the cave, Harred kept finding Breanna's dark eyes resting on him, and a warm tremor coursed through his body each time it happened.

Cyndae proved to be a skillful cook. She took the supplies brought from their wagon and prepared mouth-watering meals. Every time Breanna brought Harred his plate, her hand managed to brush his. Her touch sent tingles through him. The first time it happened, he almost dropped his plate. Both Elmar and Cyndae were aware of this interplay, but Abel, full of poppy tea—Harred suspected Cyndae of deliberately keeping him so—remained unsuspecting.

The next day, the wind was less frigid. The morning after that, Elmar declared it safe to leave.

When they left the cave, the whole world seemed coated with white. The powdery snow had softened every angle and covered the landscape as if an infant's blanket had been laid over it. A crow called from far away, its caw echoing across the hillside. Feldon led the way with his horse breaking through the fresh snow. Cyndae cradled the young girl, and Breanna followed, their horses and the mules packing down the trail for Harred and Elmar as they carried Abel in the litter.

It was a cold, wet, slow, and exhausting struggle, with frequent stops for both the lead horse and for the two Arshessas to rest. That night they made camp under a dense tangle of berry vines and mountain laurel over which the snow had formed a heavy roof.

A little before noon the next day they were overtaken by a small group of travelers heading in the same direction. Abel was taken out of the litter and placed in their wagon. By nightfall they were back in Maude.

With the rest of the Caemhans following, Harred and Elmar carried Abel up the stairs of the inn. Knowing that the date for the Dinari Presentation was approaching, Abel was anxious to be traveling on. He had contracted with the wagon owners to take them straight to Dinari territory. He had told his family to be ready to leave at first light. Harred and Elmar set Abel on a bed and turned to go. Breanna gave Harred a weary smile, then disappeared behind the closing door.

Elmar clomped away on the plank floor, but Harred stood there, numb. Under Abel's watchful eyes there had been little opportunity to talk to Breanna on the trail, and last night he had been too exhausted to do anything but eat before falling into a dreamless sleep. Now he longed desperately for *something* from her before they parted. He had ridden out to save her from certain death, after all, and had saved her extended family in the process. Surely he could take away some token of her esteem. Something to acknowledge the mysterious connection they seemed to share.

Finally, he shook himself and went to his and Elmar's room and collapsed into bed.

The next morning, he and Elmar ate in the common room. At least Elmar ate. Harred sighed and pushed his food around as he kept checking the stairs for the Caemhans. He had heard voices inside their room as he'd passed on the way downstairs, so he knew they had not left.

Elmar sopped the last bit of gravy with a chunk of bread and popped it into his mouth. Eyeing Harred's plate, he asked, "You be eating that or stirring it?"

Harred sighed and slid it over. Elmar ate with relish. Harred glanced at the stairs again, then took a sip of from his mug and sighed.

Finishing Harred's plate, Elmar regarded his brother-in-law. "Let her go," he said softly. "She be spoken for. You just be tying yourself in knots. Many other beauties be wanting a man like you. You still be Lord Gillaon's rhyfelwr and the wagons not back safe yet, are they?"

Harred sighed again. Elmar spoke truth. Still...

Finally, Harred came to his feet. "Let's go check on the horses."

When they returned from the stables the Caemhans were outside the inn waiting for the wagon to be loaded. While two men lifted Abel onto the back and situated him comfortably, Cyndae motioned to Harred and Elmar and led them a few paces away.

"I was hoping to see you before we left," she said, "so I could express my undying gratitude. Without your assistance, we would surely not have survived. Elmar, thanks to you Abel's leg is mending, and I believe he will walk without a limp."

Elmar was pleased. "I be your servant, m'lady. And I say Abel be like me. He be married to a better woman than he has any right to."

Cyndae smiled, and Harred was struck by how much Breanna's smile was like her mother's.

At that moment Breanna came up to them. "I need to say good-bye, too, Mother."

Cyndae looked at her daughter closely, then turned back to Harred. "Well, young man, I am sure we will never see each other again," she said meaningfully. "I wish you the Eternal's protection on your way home."

"As I do for all of you."

"Cyndae! Breanna!" Abel shouted. "We must be leaving."

Cyndae nodded. "Do not linger, Breanna." She gave Harred a sad smile, then climbed into the wagon and helped Felton and his sister get situated in the back next to Abel.

Breanna and Harred stood on the wooden sidewalk. Elmar cleared his throat and paced away. People edged by them, hurrying about their business. The steady wind molded Breanna's cloak to her petite frame. Her black hair framed her face. Her dark eyes were moist as her lips parted in an unspoken good-bye. Her look was so poignant, so full of unspoken pathos and longing, that it seared into Harred's core.

He heard himself saying, "Do you serve the Eternal, Breanna Caemhan?"

She smiled at the memory, then lowered her gaze. "Always."

"Do you long to join with a man who follows the Eternal as you do?" Harred pushed aside the mental image of the wagons of pagan goods he had brought back this summer.

Breanna lifted her face and regarded him with liquid eyes. "Is Harred Wright such a man?"

As had happened when he had talked with her after the wool sale, something inside him urged total honesty. "I can be . . . with your help."

310

"Breanna!" Abel shouted. "We leave!"

Breanna closed her eyes and her lips moved silently. After a long moment, she opened her eyes again. She studied Harred's face with the intensity he was coming to recognize. He felt her searching his eyes, questioning, wondering.

"Sometimes I sense the Eternal's guidance," she said slowly. "And sometimes I think I sense it but am proven wrong. In you I *believe* I sense his purposes. For you and...perhaps...for us."

Harred took her hand. "I will come for—"

She covered his mouth with her fingers. How sublime they felt on his skin. "But I could be wrong, Harred de Tarenester en Wright, Clan Arshessa." She dropped her hand and regarded him thoughtfully. Then she seemed to come to a conclusion. She leaned to his ear and spoke in a whisper. "If you come for me at the Pole, I will not refuse you. We will trust the Eternal."

"Breanna!" Abel shouted. "In the wagon now!"

Quick as a breeze Breanna gave Harred a kiss on the cheek. Then she was into the wagon, and the driver carried them off.

Pulse racing, Harred watched them jostle down the snow-packed street. Breanna did not face him. He watched her black hair blow in the cold wind. The wagon rounded a bend in the road and was lost from sight.

Harred stood there watching the empty road. Elmar approached and waited patiently.

"After we return," Harred said finally, "I will visit the Dinari Gathering and there present suit for Breanna Caemhan, daughter of Loreteller Abel Caemhan. If Abel refuses my suit, as I am sure he will, then I will demand a *Wifan-er-Weal*."

Elmar let his breath out slowly. He put his hand on Harred's shoulder. "May the Eternal have mercy on us all."

311

Chapter Twenty-nine

RHIANNON

THE COLUMN MADE an impressive sight, harnesses gleaming, banners fluttering. A full hundred king's guards, well mounted and freshly shaven, wearing yellow tabards and dark blue cloaks, led the way into the fairgrounds on the outskirts of Lachlann. Cloak clasps, sword hilts, freshly polished boots, silver ornaments on bridles, even the bits in the horses' mouths, shone brightly in the late morning sun.

Behind them, on a prancing white stallion whose coat glistened like freshly fallen snow, rode a young man in the same attire as the guards but with rows of gold cord with long tassels attached to the shoulders.

"Is that him?" Lakenna asked.

"That is our prince," Branor confirmed. "Prince Larien Faber."

The crowd of Dinari clansmen, gathered for the Maiden Pole ceremony, let out a cheer. At the noise, the white stallion broke into a hopping canter. Though Larien was too far away for Rhiannon to see his face clearly, she could tell he rode well. He was tall and strong and bore himself regally. He reined in the excited horse with practiced ease, keeping it just ahead of the queen's carriage.

The carriage was constructed of black oak with gold fittings and was pulled by four high-stepping blood red horses with black manes and tails. All four had matching white stocking feet and a full blaze on their faces. The Faber emblem, a naked sword lying across an open scroll of Holy Writ, fluttered from all four corners of the highly varnished equipage. The blue and yellow curtains were closed, affording the crowd no view of their queen. Nonetheless, they cheered her passing, though with noticeably less volume than for Larien.

Lakenna turned to Rhiannon and Branor. "Do you sense it . . . him?"

"Maolmin," Branor said, nodding. "Continually."

Rhiannon certainly did. It was the same faint nausea she'd felt previously. And if that weren't enough, her stomach held enough butterflies for every maiden about to go to the Pole.

When the carriages of royal advisors and attendants paraded by, Rhiannon, Lakenna, and Branor looked at each other in surprise.

"Another?" Lakenna said. "Do you feel this new presence?"

Branor turned to watch the advisors as their carriages trailed behind the queen's. "At least one. Perhaps more. It must be someone close to the throne." He shook his head slightly. "Unfortunately, it doesn't surprise me."

"What are we to do?" Rhiannon asked.

"That will be in the Eternal's hands," Branor said. "We must simply hold ourselves ready for whatever may come."

Last came the supply wagons, servants, and grooms with strings of remounts. The column made toward the roped-off royal area prepared by the advance party that had arrived yesterday in two score sturdy supply wagons. The workers and servants had erected a dozen large and colorful pavilions. Rhiannon had been astounded to see two blacksmiths in that advance party. They had set up anvils and a small furnace and had hammered away all yesterday, reshoeing horses and mules and repairing other items necessary for the royal workers as they erected the pavilions, all of which dwarfed those of the Dinari kinsmen lords, even Maolmin's.

Lakenna said, "The wealth necessary for such a contingent is beyond my ken."

Rhiannon was thinking the same. "I thought the advance party to be most of it. But this is twice as big."

Branor smiled kindly.

Watching the long line of carriages and wagons, Rhiannon felt the ground shift beneath her feet. She had known her clan was the smallest and poorest of the six, but now she understood how *much* poorer they were. And why no queen had ever come from Clan Dinari. *I have been a foolish little girl, dreaming little girl dreams!*

She raised her chin and reached for her absent sword hilt. *I have faced and killed winged horrors. That is how I will walk in my prophecy. And...there is always Harred.* Her gloom lifted. Though she had scarcely seen Harred since the wool sale, he had loomed large in her memory. *He is better for me anyway. We will be two warriors, shoulder to shoulder, his sword and mine, as we face the Mighty Ones.*

She brought her thoughts back to the coming Maiden Pole ceremony. She stood with her family, Lakenna, and Branor in the area roped off around the Pole. A tall tree had been felled, limbed, and erected in the middle of a grassy field. Everyone waited anxiously for this beautiful, centuries-old spectacle where clansmen and women publicly announced their betrothal. Many, if not most, of those eligible would be married before sunset.

More Dinari packed the area than Rhiannon had ever seen before. The participating maidens were conspicuous in their white gowns, the requins in their hair, and the colorful Maiden Staffs in the crook of their arm.

"Why the walking sticks?" Lakenna asked.

"Maiden Staffs," Rhiannon said. "They're heirlooms handed down from mother to daughter. They are decorated with clan and family emblems. It's for her to drive away unwanted suitors." She laughed at Lakenna's look of alarm. "I've never seen that happen. In most cases formalities and bride prices are settled long before today. As with Vanora and Rahl."

Rhiannon searched among the maidens and saw Vanora. The bride-to-be's face was aglow. Last night, Mererid, Rhiannon, and Lakenna had made a visit to the Garbhach tent. Vanora had been a bundle of nerves but eager for the ceremony and her approaching marriage. Cora Garbhach and Mererid had given the bride-to-be some frank—and most informative—advice about the wedding night that left had Vanora, Rhiannon, and even Lakenna red-faced and giggling.

The royal column arrived at their pavilions and began to dismount and unload. Rhiannon eyed Maolmin's pavilion, which was closest to the royal area. The Presentation was scheduled to begin after the Maiden Pole ceremony concluded.

But I am not to be presented, Rhiannon chided herself again. *And surely the siyyim will do everything possible to keep the prince from seeing me! Time to put away childish dreams.*

Overhead, a few dingy clouds begin building as the Dinari waited for the commencement of their first clan-wide Maiden Pole event in years. The Pole and the Presentation were two separate events, though this time they were being held during the same festival. As the Pole was a clan event, the royal family would not be attending, so there was no need to wait for them.

A breeze out of the north fluttered hems of dresses and rippled cloaks. With the damp air and dropping temperature, Rhiannon was glad she had chosen her heavier cloak.

The Maiden Pole ceremony started. The line of maidens moved with long, flowing strides, making a complete circle around the Pole. Then they stopped and faced the crowd, Maiden Staffs still resting in the crook of their arms.

Now it was the young Dinari men's turn. They stepped out from the throng and formed a second circle around the first. The inner maiden circle, white and fluttering as the breeze freshened and threatened rain, remained still. The outer suitor circle, composed mostly of young men wearing homespun brown and gray wools, moved slowly around. The two sides nodded formally to each other as the men passed by.

Rhiannon nudged Lakenna. "For Rahl and Vanora, this is the end of courtship. But it can also be a beginning. If a man sees a girl he would like to know better, the emblems on her Maiden

Staff tell him whom to approach later to discuss formal courtship. That's if she doesn't end up betrothed to someone else now at the Pole!"

The men completed their circuit and halted. Those maidens so inclined grounded their staffs to acknowledge willingness to receive suits. Suitors milled around until each one stopped in front of his chosen girl, a circlet of woven flowers in hand. The rest of the young clansmen and maidens returned to the crowd.

Rhiannon had been focused on Vanora and Rahl, but when the movement around the Pole cleared and only the serious suitors remained, she saw Ryce Pleoh, the fat Sabinis merchant, standing in front of Breanna Caemhan, the loreteller's daughter with the astounding bride price.

Then movement from the crowd caught Rhiannon's eye. A tall, wide-shouldered, dark-haired man stepped over the rope fence and into the Pole area. It was Harred! He wore a full cloak, buttoned closed; only his hands and a circlet of flowers were visible.

It was so wonderful to see him. Had he come looking for her? But then Rhiannon's heart twisted. Of course not. From his set gaze and determined stride she suddenly understood where he was headed. Straight to Breanna. *Foolish dreams, indeed.* No Presentation. No Harred. It was too much to bear.

But even as she rode out the inward pang, she felt a curious sense of freedom arising. Everything seemed stripped away. Now, finally, there was nothing left to hold her back. She bowed her head. *Dear Eternal, forgive me for not surrendering all to you. My prophecy is in your hands. I am ready now. When you open the door, I will step through it.*

Harred walked calmly toward Ryce Pleoh and Breanna. The maiden brought her hand to her mouth, eyes wide and round as the Arshessa approached. The fat Sabinis merchant's puzzled frown grew rapidly into anger.

Recognizing Harred and what was happening, Abel Caemhan burst out from the crowd and limped on crutches and his splinted leg to his daughter. He beat Harred's more stately approach and propped himself in front of Breanna and Ryce, arms folded across his chest, his thin face a mask of fury.

A hush descended on the crowd. Everyone began edging forward, eager to hear this confrontation between an obviously love-stricken suitor and an angry father. Rhiannon and the rest of the Rogoth party were carried along with the press.

"I will accept no suit from you!" Abel hissed through clenched teeth. "Leave now! Persist, and your blood will not be on my hands!" People were much closer now, those in front being shoved forward by anxious ones behind as they strained to see and hear.

Harred's eyes never left Breanna's face. His words carried clearly to all. "I, Harred de Tarenester en Wright, Clan Arshessa, bring suit for Breanna de Erian en Caemhan, Clan Dinari. I promise to love, protect, and provide for her as long as I have breath in my body. This I pledge of my own free will before the Eternal and before these witnesses."

The skin on Abel's face tightened and his lips turned white. Gasps came from the Erian kinsmen as they realized a hated Tarenester was among them. "I refuse your suit!" Abel replied icily. "I find it an insult to my clan, my family, and my daughter."

Angry cries of agreement came from the Erian kinsmen as they pressed forward even closer. Their mood was turning ugly, the air thick with hostility.

Harred remained calm and resolute. "Loreteller Abel, I respect your wishes as father in this matter and will withdraw." He nodded formally and walked back to the edge of the crowd.

"Could it be?" Branor cut his eyes to Lakenna and Rhiannon. "Prepare yourself."

Though Branor's outward appearance remained calm, Rhiannon sensed a change in him. Now he reminded her of her of father's stallion: saddled and bridled, muscles rippling, ready to charge into battle at the touch of the master's hand.

Lakenna gave the Keeper a puzzled frown, then nodded.

Rhiannon touched her arm. "Prepare for what?"

318

"For battle on the spirit plane," Lakenna whispered into her ear. "We need Maolmin to be personally engaged so we may bind the siyyim inside him. Branor believes we may receive our wish."

Once Harred stepped back over the rope the ceremony continued. Each maiden leaned her staff forward. Her suitor placed his woven circlet of flowers on her staff on a hook near the top and stepped forward to remove the requin from her head. Breanna's face remained a blank mask as Ryce removed her requin. Silently she removed Ryce's wreath and placed it on her head.

Then the new couples made a procession around the crowd to the shouted cries of congratulations and ribald comments from family and friends. Together they strode to the spot where High Lord Maolmin and the other kinsmen lords waited to finish the ceremony. Rhiannon followed her family and the crowd to watch.

Bowyn Garbhach and his wife, along with Rahl's mother, all dressed in their finest, stood proudly in front of their children. Serous stood close to Rahl, along with Rahl's uncle Mil, proud as any father. Vanora was stunning in her white gown, flowers encircling her mahogany hair. Her eyes sparkled as she regarded Rahl. He returned her look, his expression one of wonder as if scant believing this marvelous creature on his arm would soon be his to have and to hold.

Tellan and Mererid congratulated the couple. Then, in his most formal voice, Tellan intoned, "Bowyn Garbhach, I see that Rahl Digon brings suit for your daughter, Vanora. What say you?"

Bowyn tugged nervously at his tunic. "Lord Tellan, Lady Mererid, I find Rahl Digon worthy of Vanora." Bowyn turned to face Rahl. The father's lip quivered; he cleared his throat and took a deep breath. "Vanora is a fine woman, Rahl. She comes to you a virgin, precious and eager to make for you a home and hearth—as her mother has done for me. Treat Vanora with love and provide for her, and you will be blessed beyond your imagining." His mouth firmed and he gave the lad a level look. "Raise your hand against her, and though she bears your name, you will answer to me."

Rahl nodded and placed his hand over Vanora's.

Bowyn went on, voice breaking slightly. "Rahl Digon, I give my blessing to this union and place Vanora under your covering. May the Eternal's light shine on both of you."

Vanora's mother reached out and hugged her daughter, and tears of joy flowed from them both. Next, Rahl's mother embraced Vanora warmly, and then everyone waited for the other kinsmen groups to finish.

Finally, High Lord Maolmin stepped into the open area and raised his hands for quiet. Slowly, the happy babble died down. Maolmin waited a moment longer before thundering, "Does any clansmen present have reason to keep these couples from saying vows?"

Harred stepped forward, this time accompanied by Elmar, the fellow Tarenester kinsman whom Rhiannon remembered from the stables at Lachlann. "I have reason!" Harred declared.

The crowd gasped.

The two Arshessa clansmen walked to within a few paces of Maolmin. Harred slipped out of his cloak and handed it to Elmar. Strapped to Harred's side was his sword. He loosened the straps and shifted the scabbard around to where it hung normally.

He looked straight at Maolmin. "I demand a *Wifan-er-Weal* for the right of Breanna Caemhan's hand in marriage."

Chapter Thirty

HARRED

"EVERYBODY BE KEEPING their distance," Elmar told Harred softly from behind. "Still, you be neck deep now."

Harred nodded. Earlier, when he had tried to talk Elmar out of accompanying him, his brother-in-law had snorted. "I promised your Gran I be guarding your back."

Ryce waddled angrily toward them. His mercenary bodyguard followed a half step behind—the same dark-jowled guard from Lachlann. Though more battle ready than he had ever been, Harred felt an additional surge when he realized this man might well be part of the ordeal ahead.

"You seek to outbid the bride price?" Ryce demanded, halting in front of Harred. His lip curled. "Don't bother; it is more than you will see in several years."

"I am Harred de Tarenester en Wright, Clan Arshessa. Who addresses me without proper greeting?"

The guard stepped forward, hand on the hilt of his sword, coarse features taut with anger. "Watch your mouth, Arshessa, or I will spill your guts on the dirt!"

Harred's gaze never left Ryce. "I see a clan dagger but am greeted with the manners of a tavern wretch. I ask again, who addresses me?"

The guard reached for his sword.

"Stay your hand!" Maolmin roared. "I will handle this!"

Muttering darkly under his breath, the guard stepped back.

Tall and distinguished, his black cloak thrown back over

321

wide shoulders, Maolmin was the very image of a clan noble. He placed both hands on his hips and regarded Harred with a heavy look of disapproval.

For a moment Harred found himself wilting under that piercing gaze—then he rallied. The die was cast. If Breanna turned her back on him, so be it. But he was going to see that she had that chance.

A man now stood beside Maolmin: his short and wiry rhyfelwr Lomas. The man's sharp gaze took Harred in. As their eyes met, one warrior to another, Harred recognized pure bloodlust. Lomas chomped his teeth in anticipation. Would he cross swords with Lomas today, too? *Well,* Harred thought, *I never imagined this was going to be easy.*

The High Lord spoke in a flat, precise voice. "A *Wifan-er-Weal*, marriage or death, has not been done in generations and for good reason. Marriage is properly handled between families, with calm deliberation and not with swords." He shook his head. "Leave us, Harred Wright, and find a good wife from among your own clan."

Lomas frowned. He turned to Maolmin.

Harred had been afraid Maolmin would take this approach. "Do you Dinari no longer give heed to loretellers, High Lord? Do your loretellers stand around the fires and recount the glories of the past simply to tickle your ears, or do they tell their stories to remind you of the traditions we all stand on?"

Maolmin's eyes narrowed, but Harred pressed on. "Call forth the Dinari loretellers and tell them you turn your back on the sacred honor of your ancestors. Have Abel Caemhan name your lineage and their deeds. See if you do not have the blood running in your veins of at least one man who stood as I am standing today and fought a *Wifan-er-Weal* for his wife. We Tarenesters have three!"

Seeing the High Lord waver, Harred played his next card. "You are Breanna's kinsmen lord. I am the Arshessa sword champion two years running. Are you refusing," Harred sneered, "because you fear you will have to face me?"

Maolmin's countenance changed. His face darkened and his whole body seemed to swell. Everything about him became icy steel. Lomas sensed the change and turned to Harred hungrily.

"Very well, boy," Maolmin said. "If the maiden agrees, you will have your *Wifan-er-Weal.*" The High Lord's black eyes pulsed, and Harred had to fight to keep from taking a step backwards. "I hope your reputation is justified. If you are still standing after the fourth warrior has fallen, it will give me more pleasure than anything I have done in a long time to carve you up a piece at a time."

Maolmin turned to Breanna, who stood beside Cyndae and Abel, a stunned expression on her face. "Refuse this man's suit, and we will drive him from our Gathering," Maolmin said. "But know this, girl! If you accept, you will be removing yourself from the covering of your suitor, Ryce Pleoh, and coming under mine. Then when this Arshessa lies dead in the dirt I will be the one to decide your future. Make your decision."

Breanna's eyes widened, and her lips parted as everyone looked at her.

Harred's heart hammered inside his chest. He waited, not daring to breathe. If she refused his suit, the odds of Elmar and him leaving the Gathering unharmed would be slim. Though he stood on the ancient lore of the clans, more than anything he stood on that last talk with Breanna in the mountains. He risked all on that talk.

The struggle going on inside Breanna was evident. She gazed straight ahead, eyes unfocused, as she digested Maolmin's statement.

Finally, she blinked and looked at Harred, her expression unreadable. She turned slowly to her mother. Cyndae's face was a mixture of compassion and concern.

Breanna opened her mouth in a silent plea of understanding. Then she ripped off Ryce's wreath and threw it to the ground. The crowd gasped and Ryce's pig eyes bulged. Breanna laid her Maiden Staff in the crook of her arm, walked to the Pole, and turned around. She grounded her staff, chin held high as the damp breeze lifted her hair.

Pure white joy surged through Harred. He wanted to lift his face and hands to the sky and bellow in triumph! Taking a deep breath, he reined in those emotions and tried to save that savage energy for the trial to come.

With a derisive growl, Maolmin stormed away to make preparations for the rite. Ryce gave Harred a long, challenging look of contempt, then whirled around and followed Maolmin, the guard on his heels. Lomas lingered a moment. He showed Harred his teeth like a wild animal, then turned away to follow Maolmin.

Abel wavered on his crutch, stunned and ashen-faced. Cyndae took his hand and pulled at him. Then rage twisted his features. He opened his mouth, but she shushed him and led him reluctantly away.

Elmar let his breath out audibly, then stepped up and whispered in Harred's ear. "You don't be making it through this, can I be taking Coal?"

Harred snorted and relaxed a tad. Elmar squeezed his shoulder and stepped forward to act as his second. It was the second's task to examine the swords of the five opponents and make sure they wore no armor or protection of any kind.

The crowd cheered as High Lord Maolmin returned with four men walking single file behind him. Next paraded the Dinari loretellers, dressed in the traditional decorated vests denoting their position. Harred knew that, to a man, each loreteller was blessing his good fortune to be a witness to the first *Wifan-er-Weal* in generations.

Girard stepped forward and waited for the crowd to quiet. He was in his glory as he sent his rich voice projecting out to the assembly with the traditional opening of his office.

"Clansmen and kinsmen! Turn your hearts and ears to me! Today we hearken back to our past. Before our Maiden Pole comes Harred Wright of Clan Arshessa. He brings suit for Breanna Caemhan of our Erian kinsmen. Her father, Loreteller Abel, has refused this suit, but as Breanna has signaled her acceptance of this suit by grounding her staff, High Lord Maolmin has agreed to Harred's demand for a *Wifan-er-Weal*."

A wave of murmuring swept the crowd. Girard stepped forward several strides and turned slowly as he scanned the faces. He lifted his arms dramatically, asking for quiet. "Clansmen and kinsmen! Be it known that Breanna de Erian en Caemhan no longer resides under her suitor's covering. She now is under High Lord Maolmin's authority, and should Harred fail in this trial, there she will remain."

Every eye turned to Breanna standing alone by the large pole.

Girard paused, then thundered, "Harred must vanquish all five warriors, one after the other, without rest or succor of any kind. Then he must walk to Breanna Caemhan unassisted. The moment his right hand touches her right hand, they will be lawfully wed before the Eternal and all men, and the *Wifan-er-Weal* will end."

Watching it unfold, Branor was struck by how alone the Arshessa warrior and the maiden looked. She, tiny under the Pole, staff grounded, family and kinsmen left behind to accept Harred's suit; he, straight and tall in the open with only his sword strapped to his waist to protect himself. The crowd around them was comprised mostly of Erian kinsmen, Abel's folk, and they clearly were against the Arshessa.

You are not as alone as you may think, warrior.

Branor's mouth firmed. Harred had handled himself well thus far, and his reputation as a warrior had reached even Branor's ears, but was he good enough to get through the first four opponents? He had to be if he was to cross swords with Maolmin and thus make the High Lord vulnerable to spiritual intervention. But would Harred survive the ordeal?

The Keeper's blood pounded; his muscles twitched. He looked at Lakenna. She squared her shoulders and swallowed nervously.

Like him, she was ready for battle of a different kind. Branor opened his mouth to speak to her—

And found himself somewhere else.

Harred and Breanna gazed at each other across the short distance separating them. A solid covering of gray clouds hid the sun now, and the wind scattered a few fat drops of rain. An angry buzz came continually from the crowd; it seethed as a living thing. Harred barely noticed. Breanna's white dress rippled in the freshening breeze, and the red ribbons in her hair fluttered. He nodded minutely. She returned it with a quick, brave smile.

While Elmar inspected each of the five swords, Harred ran his eye over the men and smiled grimly to himself. Maolmin had chosen with cunning. The first two were large and heavily muscled. These would be arm-jarring slashers, thrown at him first to wear him down. From the way the third one moved, Harred realized the man was pure swordsman and would be a worthy and dangerous foe. Not surprisingly, the fourth in line was the Sabinis guard. Ryce Pleoh had wisely decided he had no place with warriors. The guard met Harred's eyes, swallowed, then looked down. His hand played nervously across the hilt of his sword, bravado gone.

Harred wondered why Maolmin had not chosen Lomas, his rhyfelwr, as one of Harred's opponents. The man, who now stood beside his lord, had seemed like a wild animal that couldn't wait to get at Harred. Such rage could be used against an opponent.

Finally Harred studied Maolmin. He knew with iron certainty that there lay his true challenge. The High Lord had shed his cloak and wore only breeches and a white linen shirt, sleeves rolled up, top buttons undone to give free movement to his massive chest. The sword in his hands seemed small though Harred knew it was larger than the one he carried. Unlike the guard, Maolmin returned Harred's scrutiny with the flat-eyed challenge of a predator. Seeing that, Harred realized why Lomas wasn't included. Maolmin wanted it all for himself. Harred wondered how much he would have left when he faced Maolmin. By then the High Lord would have watched him meet four foes, ample opportunity to access technique and tendencies.

Maolmin strode forward. "On your honor, Harred Wright, does your sword and clothing meet the demands of personal combat?"

"Aye, High Lord."

Elmar finished checking the other swords and clothing. He nodded his acceptance and moved aside.

Harred gripped the pommel of his sword and approached. "I come to bring suit for Breanna Caemhan, to ask her to be my wife, the keeper of my hearth, and the mother of my children. Who stands in my way?"

The first opponent stepped forward. Thick-necked, with shoulders like a bull, he held a broadsword upright in massive fists. "I am Tay Erian. You have been found unworthy of her. Withdraw or die!"

Harred's blade sang as it left the scabbard.

Chapter Thirty-one

LAKENNA

AN UNNATURAL FOG covered everything. With spiritual eyes Lakenna could see shapes and murky images moving around her and Branor, but she could not identify them. From within the blanketing mist came anxious mutterings tinged with anger and more than a little fear.

Slowly the gray veil parted, and the shapes became less obscure. She and Branor stood in a central square surrounded by buildings. A dull glow shed light but produced no shadows. The leaden sky above pressed down, cloudless and oppressive. The structures seemed wrong, the corners at odd angles. The windows sagged like melted wax. The distance ended too soon, fading into a blur. The air was unpleasant and held a hint of spoiled meat mixed with swamp mud.

She stepped forward, her shoes bumping on the dusty, uneven cobblestone pavement. Her footing felt solid, and yet the ground seemed tilted at odd angles. Everything looked weathered. Faded. The plaster on the buildings cracked and peeled. The wooden casements outlining the doors and windows looked ready to crumble at a touch.

She saw Branor moving beside her and took comfort in that. They continued downward on the flat, yet uneven pavement. The effect was disconcerting. Her insides quaked. Then out of the corner of her eye she saw movement. She whirled to look. Nothing. But the stone buildings loomed taller and closer. How did that happen? Turning to Branor, she saw he was staring tense-shouldered to his other side.

"Where are we?" she whispered.

He glanced back at her, his face pensive. "The heavenlies? The spirit world?" He looked around, nodding to himself. "It must be. Legends tell of Destin fighting here during the Founding, of course. We Keepers have accounts of this happening to some after the Covenant. Accounts of fighting and..." His voice trailed off.

"Albanes, too." She placed a hand on his arm. "Some teachings maintain that if you are..." Now her voice trailed off, too.

Branor nodded gravely. "If you are harmed here, it will affect you when you return."

Lakenna stared at the wrongness all around them. "Destin had *Asunder* and armor." She gestured to their clothing, which was the same as they had been wearing—were wearing?—at the Maiden Pole.

"No, Lakenna," Branor said quietly. "What Destin had was the Eternal. And so do we."

Something inside one of the buildings noticed their presence. Lakenna knew it was evil. She did not know how she knew, only that she did. A door swung open, and the evil stepped into view. The muttering stopped, and everything turned deadly quiet.

The evil moved closer. The thing was massive and possessed overwhelming power. It had the body of a giant male human with wide shoulders, long, thick arms, and enormous legs. The huge head, however, resembled that of a bull. Two horns projected sideways with the pointed ends curving forward. Glowing red eyes pulsed in fury as the creature regarded the humans before it. Somehow Lakenna knew it was the Mighty One of the North. Her mind quailed in fear. She had been prepared to face a siyyim—but not a Mighty One! Her heart thudded inside her chest. What lunacy was this?

The North regarded them for what seemed ages. *How dare you presume to interfere? Leave, or be squashed like the worms you are!*

Lakenna's skull vibrated with the voice. Were she and Branor about to appear—dead—in the midst of those watching the *Wifan-er-Weal*? Her mind demanded that she turn and flee. But from her spirit surged an answer.

"We are warriors of the Eternal! He has called us to stand in the gap, and so we stand! You will not have the Land!"

The North laughed. The central square rang with it. *The Covenant weakens daily. Our power is upon the Land as it has not been in centuries. You are too late. Be gone.*

Something came together in Lakenna's mind. "Then why does the West seek inroads through Clan Arshessa? We beat the West back when Tellan renounced his partnership with the pagans. Now we come against you."

A shocked silence reigned—but only for a moment. A vortex of power built around the huge demon. The swirling mass gathered speed, and dark red lightning flashed within. The square crackled with energy, and the nauseating stink increased. The humming vortex rose higher and higher until it completely covered the creature like a shield.

Then, with a mind-numbing roar, the Mighty One attacked.

Harred leaped forward without hesitation, knowing it was imperative to dispatch this first man and the second as quickly as possible. Deflecting the heavy swing with a sharp clash of blades, Harred moved inside the man's guard and drove a knee into the groin, followed by a forearm to the throat.

Tay *oofed* and staggered backward but did not go down, face registering surprise at the unorthodox tactic. He tried to bring his heavy sword back up—but too late. Cat-quick, Harred surged straight in and drove half a cubit of sharp steel just below the big man's breastbone. Tay's face twisted, and he crumbled to the ground facedown as Harred withdrew his blade.

Elmar and a Dinari partner trotted out, grabbed the fallen man and his sword, and pulled him aside to clear the field.

Harred had showed his foot speed and quickness, but not

much else, and he was determined to dispatch the next big man without giving Maolmin any clues as to his swordsmanship.

Keeping his mouth open with seeming fascination, Harred watched Elmar and the other man drag Tay away. Harred had positioned his side to the remaining four, pretending to be unaware that the rite called for the next opponent to engage him immediately.

Seizing the bait, the second rushed ahead without announcing himself, sword held high in a killing stroke.

Harred saw the movement out of the corner of his eye and dove. Tucking into a ball as he hit the ground, he rolled into the man's feet, bowling him over. The warrior hit the ground with a heavy thud. Whipping upright, Harred lunged straight back, but the man scrambled up with desperate speed and managed to partially deflect the thrust. Even so, Harred's blade opened a long deep slice across the man's upper chest and left shoulder.

Both male and female voices screamed encouragement, pleading with the second warrior to kill this Arshessa and end it quickly. Harred was only vaguely aware of the clamor. He shut it out, alert only for Elmar's warning should someone slip in and try to betray the rite.

The wounded swordsman shook his head like an angry bull and came more slowly and deliberately this time. Though taller than the first, this large, muscled Dinari was not as heavy and moved lighter on his feet. But he too was a slasher, depending on arm strength to batter down his opponent's blade.

Blood spread a dark wet patch down the man's left side as Harred slid one way, then the other, dodging and deflecting the tremendous blows. Soon the wetness had spread to the top of the man's breeches. Harred kept lunging forward enticingly and then twirling sideways, leading his opponent around in circles as the man swung his heavy blade again and again in a vain attempt to split his moving target asunder.

Noting that the movements were slowing and the left hand's grip on the hilt seemed to be loose, Harred feinted, and for the first time, met the attack straight on. As their swords clashed hilt to hilt, Harred was able to thrust the other's blade down, then drive his point deep into the exposed belly.

A hush descended as the severely wounded man moaned in the dirt. Elmar and his Dinari partner came out and helped the warrior to the side where he could receive attention.

Two down, and Harred was barely winded.

The third opponent stepped forward. "I am Dandrict Reniloge." He drew his sword with a smooth easy motion and waited calmly. Cries erupted from the crowd again, angrier and more strident.

Harred took a moment to slow his breathing, hoping Dandrict would come to him. Not so. The man stood his ground with a relaxed stance, his face regarding Harred quizzically, as if examining a peddler's wares and deciding at what price to start the bargaining. Noting that this one's blade was smaller than the first two, Harred realized he and Dandrict carried the same type of sword. Commonly called a bastard sword, the hilt was long enough for a two-handed grip, but the blade was light enough to be wielded effectively with one hand.

The wind gusted, bringing another splattering of raindrops, but Harred welcomed it. Neither heat exhaustion nor sweat obscuring his vision was going to be a problem. Though his mouth was dry and he would have welcomed a drink of water, physically he was in better shape than he had dared hope to be at this point. With no cuts or bruises, he strode forward to engage Dandrict.

The preliminaries were over. The serious swordplay was about to begin.

After the two strong-armed bashers, the third one's swiftness was unsettling, and that almost ended it for Harred. Dandrict's sword was everywhere, putting a deep slice along Harred's rib cage and another on his left arm before he drove the man back a step and was able to pivot away, gasping as a lightning-quick thrust grazed his throat.

Then Dandrict was in his face again, the man's sword moving

swiftly and smoothly. But Harred had adjusted and retreated only a small step before the new onslaught. Then, he slowly drove the other swordsman back, showing Maolmin more of his true abilities than he wanted, but having no choice against such a highly skilled opponent.

Harred drove him one step backward, two steps, then a third. A frown appeared on Dandrict's face, and he disengaged and sprang sideways.

Harred followed and fought, heart blazing with an inner fire. When they broke from this exchange, blood flowed from Dandrict's sword arm. Soon, the Dinari was stumbling backward before Harred's ferocious assault, their swords swirling and clanging, cutting and thrusting. It ended with Dandrict on his knees, unable to continue, left hand grasping his right shoulder where Harred's blade had penetrated deeply.

Dandrict surrendered, and Harred spared his life. Elmar escorted him out of the arena.

Three down, but not without a price. More wounds marked Harred's body now—a second slice on the rib cage and a deep cut on the outside of his thigh where a partially deflected thrust had scored. The others were minor cuts.

Harred strode, bloodstained and fierce, toward the Sabinis guard, determined to dispatch the brash mercenary quickly before blood loss could become a factor.

As Harred closed, mind battle-focused, he noticed something that did not surprise him—raw fear lurking behind the guard's eyes. Though the guard drew his sword with a flourish, Harred *knew* the man was petrified. Here was a classic bully: brave when bolstered by numbers or in situation where any attack would be stopped quickly—as had been the case in Lachlann—but when alone against a worthy opponent, the deep-seated cowardice came out.

The mercenary stepped forward. "I am Mahone Tierney."

Harred stopped and tilted his head toward Breanna. "I'm leaving with the maiden, Mahone. The only question is whether you will be living or dead when I do. Why die like this when your employer decided he wasn't going to?"

Mahone swallowed, his eyes clearly agreeing. "Dandrict's the best I've ever seen," he whispered hoarsely. "I have no chance against you. In the Eternal's name, I beg mercy."

Something surged inside Harred. He engaged the guard and skillfully drove him to the middle of the field. Then, locked hilt to hilt and chest to chest, he hissed, "Next time I'm going to cut your face and you go down and stay down. Get back up, and I'll have to kill you!"

He shoved Mahone away and gave him a moment to prepare.

Confusion flashed across the mercenary's face, followed by relief. Then Harred was upon him. With a sharp blow, he knocked Mahone's sword aside. Then swinging his blade with perfect control, Harred opened a deep cut along the man's temple, a slash that bled spectacularly but did no real harm.

Mahone dropped convincingly to the ground and remained still.

Total silence reigned. No one stirred in the crowd though a steady rain was falling, with heavier bursts intermittently. Harred found Breanna's face as she stood by the Pole. Her hair was wet and plastered to her face, but she stood bravely, teeth chattering in the damp chill.

Realizing Mahone was done for, Elmar and the other man jogged out to carry the guard from the field.

Maolmin had begun rotating his neck and shoulders the moment Harred had started driving the third warrior backward. Eyes never leaving the swordplay, he had stretched his arms and legs. When Mahone had stepped forward, the High Lord had turned disdainfully away, drawn his sword, and gone though a lightning-fast series of drills.

At the hush, he pivoted and moved forward, sword point held low and to the side; both hands gripped the hilt loosely, almost casually. His gaze might have been on Harred's approach, but then again, it might not have been.

Harred stopped two sword lengths away. Black eyes slid over him and seemed to bore inside his very skull.

"I am Maolmin."

"I am Harred."

Utter stillness pervaded the High Lord's demeanor. Stillness and death. Maolmin wore it like a cloak. Raindrops splattered on his face and ran down his skin in small rivulets, but he took no notice. "You're good, Arshessa, but not good enough."

"You have no idea how good I am."

Something flickered inside those black orbs.

Pleased, Harred pressed on. "I know what you think my weaknesses are. I know how you plan to exploit them. Try it, and see what—"

Startled movement came within Maolmin's dead eyes. A reassessment and recalculation. "What is this?" he hissed in disbelief. Maolmin seemed to go inward for a moment. When his eyes refocused, he lifted his blade. "I must end this quickly."

He rushed forward, and it was like an avalanche roaring down a mountainside.

Stumbling backward from an attack of unbelievable speed and power, parrying wildly and struggling to keep his feet under him, Harred realized with growing desperation that he was totally outclassed.

Snarling behind the vortex shield, the North flung a huge fireball.

Branor raised a shield that was suddenly in his hands. The fireball beat heavily against it, then split into pieces and scattered on the square's cobblestone pavement. Another bolt and yet another smashed into the shields he and Lakenna held. The odd-shaped buildings loomed closer; the fetid air grew thicker. The background chatter increased, urging atrocities too depraved to contemplate.

Branor looked straight into the black depths of the *thing* before him. "You will *not* have the Land!" Pointing to the Mighty One, he roared, "I bind you, foul demon, by the power of the Eternal! Your power is bound!"

The North came at them, confidant in its awesome power, pressing with unholy force to kill and destroy.

Branor and Lakenna locked shields. Standing shoulder to shoulder, Branor fought as best he knew how. "I petition the Eternal," he gasped as the incredible pressure continued, "to strengthen the Covenant that has limited evil in the Land."

Lakenna prayed, "I ask the Eternal's forgiveness of our unfaithfulness and pledge to seek daily how to uphold the Covenant that we may be safe in the Land!"

Branor stood, but he and Lakenna were new to spiritual warfare, and here they were facing the unbridled strength of a Mighty One. The powers of darkness swirled within the vortex and threatened to overwhelm him. Branor's stomach heaved and twisted; bile rose, searing his throat, but he swallowed it back down. His whole being trembled.

Battered, he and Lakenna reeled backward under an unimaginable onslaught. His mind filled with vile, unthinkable images.

The pressure increased. Another fireball came hissing, lower than the others. Branor dipped his shield too late—and gasped when a piece from the shattered ball grazed his left leg. White-hot pain seared, bringing black spots to his vision. Swallowing a moan, he locked shields with Lakenna again right before three more fireballs slammed into them, one after another.

His leg throbbed, and he thought he might fall. How much longer could he endure this? He feared not long, and as the assault continued, despair threatened to engulf him.

Then Rhiannon joined the fight!

Her presence was a battle-ax that crumpled the North's forward surge and punched a gaping hole in the vortex.

"You are bound!" she shouted in righteous fury. "I am called to be Protectoress of the Covenant, and by the Eternal I bind you!" Her words were filled with power. Branor felt their strength, and so did the North. The huge demon shuddered and eyed the young woman warily.

"The Eternal is a redeeming God!" Lakenna flung at the North. "As he has redeemed me and all who call on his name, so will he redeem the Covenant. We claim its protection for us and all who fight for it!"

Astonished, Branor saw that Rhiannon held a flaming sword in her hands. He looked back at the North. Through the hole punched in the demon's shield, Branor noticed black reins running from the North and disappearing into the distance. The reins pulsed and writhed like a living thing—and Branor knew this was the Mighty One's connection to the siyyim inside Maolmin.

He shouted into the whirlwind at Rhiannon and pointed. She nodded her understanding. Holding the sword before her, she lunged through the hole, came to the black reins, and swung down with a sharp blow. The black reins parted cleanly.

The North bellowed in rage and frustration. Thunder boomed and tentacles of red lightning cracked across the leaden sky.

What about Maolmin? Branor wondered suddenly as he watched both ends of the reins wiggle on the ground. If the siyyim was bound, perhaps the man could be saved.

"I claim Maolmin Erian for the Eternal!"

The North sneered. It reached down and picked up the siyyim's severed end of the reins. "Your claim is empty. Maolmin has sworn his soul to me—of his own free will!"

Rhiannon pivoted and dealt a blow to the North himself. The Mighty One howled in pain and alarm. He dropped the rein, stepped back, and jerked the intact part of the vortex shield between himself and the red-haired spiritual warrior.

Pressing forward, her eyes blazing green fire, Rhiannon swung again. And again. Abruptly, the vortex disappeared.

The North shuddered as Rhiannon continued to rain strikes with the flaming sword. The demon winced in pain, roared, and lunged, a massive arm and balled fist coming down toward Rhiannon's head.

But she was equal to the challenge. She raised the sword, parried the blow, slid it smoothly aside, and then countered with a strike to the North's leg. Whimpering in agony and frustration, the North turned and swung again—but Rhiannon was upon him, her flaming sword cutting deeply again and again.

Finally, the huge demon turned and fled beyond the buildings and into the mist.

Abruptly, the pervading sense of evil all but vanished. They all felt the release. They fell to the ground in the spirit realm, spent and dazed.

Branor became aware of the Dinari Gathering again. His left leg throbbed painfully, and he could not put his full weight on it. The clang of swords rose over the shouts of the crowd. The spirit world faded, and he was back in Lachlann watching Harred fight for his life.

Lakenna and Rhiannon turned and looked at him with wide eyes. They both fell into his arms, crying. All of them shuddered with relief.

Harred's breath whistled in and out, ragged. He was a mass of blood and pain, his strength draining away by the moment. How he had survived this long against Maolmin, he did not know.

Somehow he parried another lightning-fast thrust, arm jarring from the impact, and stumbled back yet again, a fresh cut on his wrist. How could any man be this good? At this point attacking Maolmin was unthinkable. It was all Harred could do just to defend—if it could be called that.

The end had to be near. The crowd sensed it. Their screams for Harred's death intensified.

Moving with blinding speed, Maolmin was on him again, and this time Harred was driven to his knees.

It was over. He had lost! He tensed for the killing blow—

But it did not come.

Breath raw in his throat, he peered up. Maolmin stood frozen, face stilled in shock, sword point lowering slowly to the ground.

Wary, Harred came to his feet. Incredibly, a measure of strength flowed into his body and the pain dulled. *What was this?*

Maolmin shook himself and lifted his sword. "No matter," he hissed. His eyes were different, less intense. "I am still the better swordsman."

The two men circled, their swords ringing out as they clashed. Maolmin flowed in effortlessly as he probed, then slid away. He engaged again, with more force and speed. Harred found the strength to fend him off. A third time Maolmin attacked. Their swords clanged as blows and counterblows were exchanged. Then the High Lord backed away several steps, sword point held below his knees, and waited.

Harred stood, eyes wide, studying Maolmin with fierce concentration. Was this some trick? After being at death's door only moments before, had he now met Maolmin, one master swordsman to another, and not taken a step backward during three attacks? Something had changed, and it was as if the bout had started afresh.

Harred dared hope. He launched an attack, his sword a silver blur.

Maolmin met him with feral intensity. Steel rang on steel, then again, sharper. Left, right, at the knees, then the throat.

Lunge, attack, slide, pivot, and reengage.

The two fought at the very pinnacle of their deadly art. The brutal dance flowed up and down the crowd-lined arena, accompanied by shouts and pleading.

Overhand feint, side slash, parry, counter. Grunts as their blades arced and met.

Harred's shoulders burned. His arms were almost numb from the strain. His throat was raw from sucking the cool damp air. But he pushed fatigue aside. Breanna waited.

Finding reserves he never knew he had, Harred pressed harder, his sword alive.

Soon, like the third warrior before, Maolmin had to disengage

340

from Harred's relentless advance. The High Lord skipped away to gather himself, but he was moving backward again the moment Harred closed. Over and over Maolmin withdrew a few steps before returning with even greater determination. But he could not stop Harred's impetus.

Blood flowed from the High Lord through numerous wounds when Harred's sword finally bit deeply into Maolmin's side. Maolmin gasped and reeled away in stunned disbelief. The crowd shrieked. Then Maolmin lunged back in a desperate, almost suicidal effort to penetrate Harred's defenses.

Harred fended off the ferocious exchange, then pressed one of his own. He feinted low, avoided the parry, thrust high—

And drove his blade through Maolmin's heart.

An ear-shattering screech issued from Maolmin's open mouth, undulating eerily with the screams of the crowd until it faded into the distance. His sword slid from lifeless hands, and he crumpled onto the wet grass.

Harred's ragged breathing was loud in the stunned silence. Blood loss from his wounds added to the light-headedness of exhaustion. He wavered back and forth before steadying himself.

"*Nooooo!*" The inhuman cry rose above the quiet. Lomas leaped from the crowd behind Harred and raced toward him. The short rhyfelwr's face was twisted in rage, and he raised his dagger head high.

Harred turned around and stumbled, trying to lift his sword to meet this breech of the rite. But he was spent. It had all been for nothing.

Suddenly Elmar was there! Moving with a nimbleness surprising for his bulk, he tackled Lomas two strides from Harred. The two rolled on the grass, grabbing for the dagger.

Screaming in fury, Lomas threw Elmar off as if he weighed no more than a child. Lomas sprang to his feet and lunged for—

Tellan's dagger plunged hilt-deep into Lomas' chest.

The two stared into each other's eyes for a moment. Then Lomas's mouth opened, and the same otherworldly screech rose and then faded. He fell to the ground, dead, an arm's length from Maolmin's body.

Tellan bent down and wiped his dagger on Lomas's breeches. Straightening, he looked at the two dead men and nodded in grim satisfaction. He faced Harred but did not touch him lest he invalidate the rite. "A good day's work, warrior. Now, claim your reward."

Slowly, arms trembling, Harred managed to sheathe his sword after two missed tries. He walked with a loose-legged gait to Breanna.

She watched with shining eyes as he approached. Her black hair hung in straggling clumps from the cold drizzle. The flowing white dress clung wetly to her skin. Even so, she took Harred's breath away. When he stopped before her, they spent a long moment lost in each other's eyes.

Finally, Harred held out his right hand. "Breanna Caemhan," he managed, "before the Eternal and these witnesses, will you be my wife?"

Breanna's face glowed. "I will." Tears of joy ran down her cheeks. "With honor and pride do I take your name."

Her right hand came up to clasp his, and the *Wifan-er-Weal* was done.

Chapter Thirty-two

RHIANNON

O UTSIDE, WIND AND rain lashed the royal pavilion. Inside, the huge tent was packed with families of the noble maidens waiting for the Rite of Presentation. Fine carpets of alternating blue and yellow had been laid to floor the entire area. Braziers burned brightly with aromatic wood, and a dozen gold-plated lanterns, polished until they gleamed, hung from stands.

Royal attendants in high-collared blue coats had with brisk efficiency herded the young women to the middle. Rhiannon was last in line. She overheard snide remarks about the smell of sheep.

A wide area separated her and the other maidens from their families, and that was deliberate. For twelve centuries the Faber dynasty had remained apart from the six clans, a separation of power that had served the Land well. A woman marrying into the dynasty was required to publicly renounce clan and family ties in order to rule justly and wisely. The rite called for each maiden to be presented alone, and if marriage resulted she would come to the altar alone, family and clan left behind.

Lord Baird approached the royal party, who were waiting in a loose semicircle ten paces from the first maiden.

With Maolmin's death, the Dinari clan had no High Lord. Baird had been named acting High Lord at a hastily called meeting after the *Wifan-er-Weal*. His first official act was to include Rhiannon with those to be presented.

Rhiannon, Lakenna, and a limping Branor had just finished telling a flabbergasted Mererid about the encounter with the Mighty One of the North when Tellan had returned with the news. It had been a mad scramble to get her new gown unpacked and her hair brushed in time. And Rhiannon had found it very difficult to sit still. Even now her blood was still rushing from the thought of the incredible authority and boldness she'd had in the spirit world.

Queen Cullia stood half a step forward of her son and the handful of advisors. She dominated the pavilion with her presence. The creases in the queen's face could not disguise that she had been beautiful years ago. She wore a pale blue silk gown embroidered with pearls, and a coronet encrusted with diamonds rested on her gray-streaked hair. Her gaze was sharp and piercing as a hawk's as she watched Baird approach.

Prince Larien stood two steps to Cullia's right. He was a head taller than her. The cut of his coat emphasized his wide shoulders. Light brown hair was combed back and tucked behind his ears. A scar ran across a slightly crooked nose. Rhiannon thought it lent a rugged yet pleasing symmetry to his face.

Baird dipped one knee to the queen and kissed her offered hand. "Your Highness, Clan Dinari bids you and Prince Larien welcome." He grinned rakishly. "We commend your desire to save the expense of visiting the other clans by coming here first."

Laughter swept the pavilion. Lord Baird was in his element, not at all awed by the presence of royalty.

Cullia offered a cool smile as the laughter died down. "It has been much too long since the throne made an official visit to the highlands." She paused as a particularly strong gust cracked the fabric of the pavilion's roof. "Though I must say, the weather is as I remember." Another wave of amusement, mainly from royal advisors and attendants. "Well," she went on briskly, flicking a glance at the line of young women, "let us begin." She didn't add, *So we can be finished and on our way*, but Rhiannon and everyone else heard the tone.

Baird certainly did. His smiled never wavered, but his eyes flattened. Giving the queen a tilt of his head instead of the dipped knee protocol called for, he turned to Prince Larien. Cullia remained unruffled, but her nostrils flared and the creases around her mouth deepened, somehow conveying the trial of dealing with ruffians.

Larien and Baird bowed to each other and exchanged a few pleasantries. With posture erect and shoulders square, the prince projected the impression of studied calm.

Rhiannon tried to ignore a mild bout of queasiness. Understandable, but disconcerting. Her emotions had never been tugged in so many different directions in such a short time. Immediately after having her hopes dashed because Harred preferred Breanna over her, she had found herself trading blows with a major demonic foe in an ethereal realm. Now she was to be presented before the crown prince. Today the Eternal had opened the door, and she had stepped through it. But did that open door include marriage to the next Faber monarch? A young maiden's nervousness mixed with the courage of a victorious warrior, horror and pride that her father had killed a demon-possessed man before her. It left her feeling intoxicated and unstable, but exhilarated.

Trying to bring all that under control, she stroked her hand across the gown. It was emerald green, long, flowing, and very feminine. She loved the way the fabric swished around her strides. This was the first time in all her sixteen years she had worn silk. It was also the first time she remembered being glad she was a woman. The gown was beautiful but costly. Even with the extra coins from the one-time sale to Lord Gillaon, another piece of Mererid's family jewelry had gone to pay for it and the matching slippers.

Unlike Rhiannon's unadorned one, however, the gowns worn by the other young women displayed great wealth. Most had golden threads woven into the fabric, which shimmered in the lantern light. Several had small pearls embroidered into intricate patterns, some even extending down the sleeves. One notable dress, worn by a stunningly beautiful blonde whom Rhiannon had never seen before, had a bodice outlined with diamonds.

Until Rhiannon rushed up, the blonde had been last in line. Those slanted eyes had flashed with concern beholding Rhiannon's face and flowing red hair. Then the woman had taken in the plain gown and lack of jewelry. Smiling a dismissal, the stranger had turned toward the front, ignoring Rhiannon's greeting.

That insult still had Rhiannon's palms itching for her sword. Let this smug, soft-muscled beauty peer down her nose again, and she would behold Dinari steel! Then Rhiannon realized a scabbard would hinder the way her gown swished as she walked. Chewing the inside of her lip, she pondered that revelation for a long moment.

Larien and Baird finished their exchange and bowed to each other again. The prince nodded at the royal attendants. The background murmuring ceased as the first attendant offered his arm to an auburn-haired maiden of the Erian kinsmen and escorted her down a runner of red carpet to Baird, who formally introduced her to Cullia and then to Larien.

The Rite of Presentation, the first in almost two centuries, was under way.

The queen and prince exchanged formal greetings with the woman, and then she was led away. Another young lady was escorted to Baird, and the line moved up. The blonde slid forward with a sinuous grace that drew the eye of every man in the crowd.

Who was she? In the past, foreign nobility had, on occasion, sent daughters to be presented along with Land nobility. Those tilted eyes and high cheekbones certainly were not Dinari. And the cut and drape of her gown were different, somehow drawing attention to the curves underneath. One more reason for the men's attention.

Glancing at the surrounding crowd, Rhiannon found that she too had become the object of male scrutiny. One well-dressed young nobleman elbowed another and lifted his chin toward her. Their appraisal was much different from the insulting leer she'd received from the Sabinis guard in Lachlann. Surprised that she did not find this inspection displeasing, Rhiannon stood straighter even as her queasiness continued.

The line shuffled forward again. Cool beads of sweat popped out along Rhiannon's hairline as the nagging twist in her stomach built toward nausea. She chided herself at such a display of nervousness.

I have faced the Mighty One of the North this day. Maolmin is dead and the siyyim has left the Land. I walk in my prophecy. The Eternal is with me. This will be a simple introduction and greeting. Then I will be about my future as Protectoress of the Covenant.

She caught her father's and Mererid's eyes. They smiled encouragingly. That helped.

A young lady with curly brown hair and a stiff smile curtsied before Larien. The future king nodded pleasantly, then brought her hand to his lips. Rhiannon's knees began to tremble, and it became much harder to breathe.

Another maiden processed down the carpet. Baird took her from the attendant and introduced her. The line edged forward. Then again. And yet again.

Incredibly soon, only Rhiannon and the stranger remained. An attendant returned. The blonde took his arm and seemed to float down the carpet runner, her posture regal even as her hips swayed alluringly.

Baird beheld her approach with open-mouthed fascination. When the woman halted before him, Baird blinked and closed his mouth with a snap. He took her arm—then a frown wrinkled his brow, and Rhiannon realized that he did not know the woman either. His eyes darted among the crowd for a sponsor, needing an introduction himself before he could present this stunning beauty to the prince.

Lady Ouveau, the advisor immediately to the queen's left, made to speak, but Cullia made a slight gesture and Ouveau remained silent. The blonde waited calmly, profile turned artfully toward the prince. The diamonds outlining her full bosom sparkled. Larien's gaze kept traveling up and down her statuesque figure.

Nervous coughs came from the crowd as Cullia allowed Baird to dangle. Finally, she cut her eyes to Ouveau.

"Lord Baird," the advisor said, bringing her hand to her chest as she stepped forward, "I must beg your forgiveness. Lady Zoe is here at my invitation. With the unsettling events concerning High Lord Maolmin, there was no time to introduce her to you." She smiled. "May I have your permission to present our foreign guest to Queen Cullia and Prince Larien?"

Tilting his head in agreement, Baird stepped back.

"Your Highnesses, may I present Lady Zoe, granddaughter of Hansh Rajak, the emir of the island of Costos in the Southern Sea." Ouveau outlined the woman's impressive lineage.

Zoe held the prince's gaze a long moment before she spread her skirts wide and dipped a graceful curtsy. Larien looked stunned as he brought the woman's hand to his lips.

Someone nudged Rhiannon's elbow. Startled, she realized it was an attendant ready to escort her. Her heart thudded like a runaway horse as she took the offered arm and strode down the runner.

Rhiannon halted before Baird as Zoe was being escorted to where the other maidens were grouped around a table of refreshments. The prince's gaze still followed the blonde woman from Costos.

Lord Baird gave Rhiannon a quick wink as he took her arm from the attendant. "Your Highness, I have the pleasure to introduce Lady Rhiannon Rogoth, daughter to Lord Tellan and Lady Mererid."

Cullia nodded. "Greetings, Lady Rhiannon." Then, with an air of a task finished, she turned to Ouveau. "I am famished. Let us eat."

But Ouveau's focus remained on Rhiannon. From a distance, her plump figure and round face had seemed almost motherly. Close up, her gaze was hard and calculating.

Rhiannon's breath caught as she swallowed down a much

stronger surge of queasiness. Something was disturbingly familiar about Ouveau's eyes—

Baird gently tugged Rhiannon forward as he formally introduced her to the prince. Gathering herself, she dipped a curtsy to Larien, who slowly brought his focus back from Zoe. When Rhiannon straightened, he looked full at her—

And she *knew*.

Deep inside something surged, and she understood her prophecy with stunning clarity. All her former plans for how she would serve as Protectoress of the Covenant, galloping across the land like the Founders, crumbled at the realization that her destiny was indeed to marry into the Faber dynasty—and to be mother to the next heir. Her mind reeled as she struggled to maintain her composure.

From the look on Larien's face, he had felt the same impact. He blinked, then looked from her to Zoe, then back to her.

As if in a dream, she watched him bring her hand to his lips. His grip was firm, but not tight, the kiss warm and dry. And his eyes. She was getting lost in those eyes. They peered straight into hers with the same question that had just been answered within her spirit.

Then a half frown wrinkled his brow. "Where did you get these calluses?" he inquired, breaking the spell, his fingers exploring her palm.

"I—"

Cullia moved between them and deftly steered her son toward the refreshment table and the presented maidens. "Spend no more time with these girls than necessary. You must talk to the Costos woman. As you know, Ouveau and her husband recently visited that rich isle. They had a private dinner with the emir. That conversation contained ideas about trade that I find most intriguing." She hurried him away.

Rhiannon felt as if the sun had suddenly dawned and then just as suddenly gone behind a cloud. Alone, her mind still spinning, she grappled with the events of the past minutes. That quiet, still voice she'd heard before had not been the giddy hope of a starry-eyed youngster. The Eternal was indeed calling her to be the princess bride! And like Destin and Meagarea twelve centuries before, the moment she and Larien were formally introduced, they both knew it.

Larien *did,* didn't he?

She looked up. She and Zoe remained a few paces from the table where the others were pretending to eat as they preened before Larien. He nodded amicably to a young woman prattling away even as his eyes darted around until they rested on Rhiannon.

Her breath caught and a warm tingle shot through her. Then her heart stuttered when his gaze found Zoe. Those dark orbs held Larien for a long, intense moment. Finally, the prince swallowed and returned his focus back to a dumpy maiden offering him a tidbit from her plate.

Zoe and Lady Ouveau, who stood on the far side of the table sipping a cup of punch, shared knowing smiles.

Ouveau! With Larien's impact, Rhiannon had forgotten about the stomach-churning foulness she had felt while near the woman. And the movement inside the eyes that had been so eerily similar to Maolmin's.

Suddenly, Rhiannon wanted to pace. She needed to put all this into some semblance of order. Surely the senior advisor to the queen could not be harboring a siyyim? First a clan High Lord and now the throne—and the Faber dynasty itself?

No, not the Fabers. Rhiannon had not sensed evidence of the Mighty Ones' taint while close to Cullia, only disdain for all things Dinari. And most certainly there had been nothing demonic inside Larien. Only with Ouveau.

Pausing, Rhiannon wondered about her bout of queasiness while waiting in line. She had assumed it a simple case of nerves, but was it possible—?

She wanted to kick herself for being such a blind dolt. She shot a hard look at Zoe, then back to Ouveau. The senior advisor had taken Larien's arm and was leading him to Zoe while Cullia made final good-byes. Royal attendants appeared to escort the maidens back to their families.

Zoe's brilliant smile enveloped Larien. The woman's honey-colored hair shone; her gown and jewels glittered. Her stance was poised and regal, confident of her attraction.

A barb twisted in Rhiannon's heart when she saw Larien's mesmerized expression as he took the offered hand. The barb grew larger when she noted Ouveau's look of triumph, quickly masked. Zoe moved closer to Larien until her bosom just touched his arm. Her tilted, sloe eyes grew larger, more liquid.

Swallowing a lump in her throat, Rhiannon knew true despair. Why the *knowing* at the introduction? Had that happened just so she could watch him walk away with someone else—someone using demonic force to beguile the future king? What was she to do?

Then Rhiannon remembered Zoe's flash of concern when the woman had first seen her. And the young noblemen's scrutiny. And the Mighty One of the North edging back warily when she had declared herself Protectoress of the Covenant. And Harred's expression in the stable. And the way her skirts swished.

Rhiannon took a deep breath and for the second time that day answered the call to battle. She slid past the attendant coming for her and strode to where Larien was held in thrall.

"My prince," she said, halting at his side and holding out her hand, palm up. "You asked about my calluses?"

Larien blinked. "Pardon?" He tore his eyes from Zoe, who looked as if she could have bitten a nail in two. "Oh, yes." His voice became stronger. "Yes, I did."

Their gazes met again—and this time she knew they both felt the impact. Zoe's sudden intake of breath sounded like a hiss, and Rhiannon felt her hatred like a physical presence. Larien's eyes were becoming clearer by the second.

She continued to hold out her hand, praying desperately for him to take it, and almost sagged with relief when he did. She sensed every eye in the pavilion watching, every ear straining. Somehow she remembered to breathe.

He examined her palm, then scraped a fingernail lightly across the ridges and bumps. "This looks like a swordsman's hand."

"It is."

He regarded her with a perplexed expression. "You train with a sword?"

Inwardly cringing, she not did know whether to be mortified or proud. "Not a full-sized one—"

"Larien," Cullia inquired in a too-sweet voice, "have you hurt this girl?"

Maintaining his grip on Rhiannon's hand, Larien turned to answer his mother. He was outwardly unruffled, almost placid, but Rhiannon sensed he had an inner core that would not bend easily.

"I was examining Lady Rhiannon's hand." He put a slight but definite emphasis on *Lady*. "It seems the original Dinari blood runs strong in her veins. Lady Rhiannon practices regularly with a sword."

"Of course." Cullia's assessment of all things Dinari was plain.

Ouveau's and Zoe's gazes bore into Rhiannon, and she had the feeling both women wanted to plunge a dagger into her heart. She looked into Ouveau's eyes, then Zoe's—and understood what she saw.

The senior advisor's eyes shimmered dark red. Zoe's lips curled a bit before she regained control and smiled pleasantly.

Cullia flicked a hawk stare, piercing and full of power, to Rhiannon. "Please excuse us, m'lady. We will leave you to your sword drills." She nodded formally and reached for Larien's arm.

Rhiannon raised her chin. "I no longer do sword drills, my queen. I have found that scabbards and gowns interfere with each other."

Cullia turned slowly back, eyes glittering with a probing look of reassessment—but it was Zoe who spoke.

"How quaint," she said, her lilting accent soft and musical. "Still, I imagine your...skills...will be of great benefit shearing sheep when you return home."

Rhiannon locked eyes with the blonde. "Warrior skills are beneficial in all manner of endeavors. I have been trained to use every weapon at my disposal."

With a cold stare and bared teeth, Zoe acknowledged the challenge. "I see. Safe journey, Lady Rhiannon."

"Yes," Cullia agreed, turning to her son. A slight frown wrinkled her brow when she saw how he was looking at Rhiannon. "Larien, please. We have done our duty here. It is time for your seclusion." She took his arm.

As Larien moved away, his eyes caressed Rhiannon's face, silently communicating: *I will see you again.*

She returned an equally earnest reply: *I'll be waiting.*

Chapter Thirty-three

RHIANNON

"EVERYBODY'S TALKING ABOUT you and your calluses," Phelan announced as Lakenna escorted him into the Rogoth pavilion to dress for the banquet. He had a smudge on one cheek, and both knees were muddy. "I threw Chiam Fawr down and told him if he snickers one more time, I'll do to him what I did to that winged horror."

Rhiannon lowered the silver hand mirror and hairbrush. "Thank you for defending my honor, kind sir."

"You didn't kill a winged horror," Creag said petulantly as he took his cloak off the peg on a tent pole and swung it across his shoulders.

"I would have if I'd found the bow before Rahl did. With the bow Serous is making me, next time I'll kill two or three."

Branor smiled. "I pray that 'next time' will be quite awhile for all of us."

"I agree." Lakenna lifted a pitcher, poured water into a bowl perched on a battered travel chest, then wrung out a cloth and handed it to Phelan. She nodded toward the curtain separating Tellan and Mererid's part of the tent. "You'd better have your face scrubbed and be dressed for the banquet when your mother steps out."

The pavilion, which seemed tiny compared to the royal one, was divided into three sections by hanging curtains. A separate corner for Mererid and Tellan, and another for Rhiannon and Lakenna. Branor and the two boys made do with the crowded central area filled with their cots, two stools, the washstand, and two chests full of clothes.

Lakenna looked down at her own dress. For the banquet, she wore one of Mererid's gowns, a wine red that went well with her dark hair and eyes. At first, the tutor's Albane upbringing had made her hesitant about wearing a colored gown, but she had finally given in.

Phelan gave his face a quick wipe with the cloth, then sat on one edge of the largest chest and stripped off his dirty pants. Wiggling into a new pair, he looked at Rhiannon. "Serous says my bow is just about cured and ready. When we get back, you and Creag can take it out with me and see how far it shoots."

She paused in her brushing, fingers working the handle nervously as she regarded her brothers. "I..." She gave a quick smile. "I would like to go shooting with you two."

Creag said, "Don't worry about the calluses or what people are saying. They're just jealous because Larien spent more time with you and that Costos woman than with all the others put together. Calluses had nothing to do with it. You're the most beautiful one here."

Rhiannon was surprised to feel herself blushing. "Thank you, Creag. That's the nicest thing you've ever said to me."

He tugged at his cloak to cover his embarrassment. "It's the truth. You should have seen the men waiting to talk to Father afterwards." He grinned. "Mother's started a list."

"It's true, m'lady," Branor said. He was sitting on one of the stools in the common area. "You are radiant."

Rhiannon's blush deepened.

"What's this about a list?" Tellan pulled back the curtain. He held a sealed letter in his hand. When Creag explained, Tellan shook his head wryly. "That was a new experience—men elbowing each other to talk to me about my daughter."

"Best get used to it," Mererid said, stepping through. "This is just starting." She wore a gray wool with ivory lace outlining the bodice and cuffs. She took in Creag and nodded, then frowned at Phelan, who was still dressing.

Tellan handed the sealed letter to Creag. "This is for Lord Gillaon. It is the document formally breaking our trade agreement with him. Take it to Llyr and tell him to deliver it to Harred in the morning. I hear someone has provided a room at the Bridge Across for he and Breanna. I wish them well." He smiled at Creag. "We'll wait for you outside."

Creag took the letter and hurried out.

At the mention of Harred, Rhiannon examined herself and found no strong feelings. Admiration, to be sure. Both her father and Llyr said that the Arshessa was far and away the best swordsman they had ever seen, discounting the siyyim-enabled Maolmin. Once she, Lakenna, and Branor had cut off the siyyim from the North, Harred had faced the High Lord, man to man, and had—

Harred is a finely honed weapon, proven and available for the future.

She nodded at the revelation and tucked it away. She too wished the new couple well. Then she thought about Harred and Breanna in their room at the Bridge. And that made her think about Larien and seeing him at the banquet tonight. And Mererid's and Cora's talk with Vanora. And Larien and tonight.

Will he be true to what we both felt, or am I still dreaming a little girl's dream?

"I believe I heard Phelan mention a discussion with Chiam Fawr," Mererid arched an eyebrow at her husband. "Tell Rhiannon about your nice conversation with Lord Seuman Fawr regarding his oldest son, Peibyn."

Tellan's face soured. "Let's not spoil the evening."

Rhiannon laughed with everyone else, thankful for this warm, easy atmosphere now that Maolmin's dark cloud was gone. She gave her hair a last swipe with the brush, slid the requin in place, and rose to her feet.

Mererid inspected her from head to feet and nodded. "Rhiannon, while I assure you that nothing will happen with Peibyn," her eyes danced merrily, "I do look forward to the spectacle of Aigneis circling around the topic of courtship before she begins the real discussion."

Frowning, Tellan turned to Mererid, opened his mouth, and then thought better of it.

Girard pulled back the front flap and came in. Behind him came a royal attendant dressed in blue and yellow livery.

The attendant bowed to Branor. "Queen Cullia's greetings, Your Grace. She asks you to join her and Prince Larien at their table for the banquet."

Branor stood, rubbing his left leg. "I will be honored." He made to follow, then hesitated. He turned to Lakenna. "It would be a double honor for you to accompany me."

The tutor's face paled. "I couldn't possibly." Stunned, she shook her head. "The invitation was for you."

"Such invitations include a wife or companion." Branor looked at the royal attendant. "Correct?"

The attendant seemed as surprised as everyone else. "I think the queen assumed Your Grace would be unaccompanied..."

"Come now," Tellan said. "I've been to Faber Castle many times, and always with a female companion."

Lakenna recovered. "I cannot. My place is with Rhiannon."

"No, Lakenna! Please go," Rhiannon urged. "I will be fine." *Maybe.*

"Yes," Mererid and Tellan said together.

"I have no place with royalty. I must stay with Rhiannon." Lakenna's mouth firmed. "Nothing will call me away from that."

Branor nodded. "As with me, for the foreseeable future." He waited, but when Lakenna shook her head, he said, "I will return afterwards."

"Before you go," Rhiannon said, coming to a decision she had been wrestling with, "can I talk to you and Lakenna?"

They stepped behind the curtain into her and Lakenna's area. Quickly, Rhiannon told them her insight about Zoe.

"A lilitu," Branor said. "A lesser demon. Has to be."

Lakenna gasped. "We must pray."

The three of them joined hands and prayed a covering over Larien and a binding on Zoe. Rhiannon started to tell them about Lady Ouveau but decided to wait and see if they sensed the same about the senior advisor. Rhiannon also did not relate her and Larien's—*what*? Whatever it had been, it was too personal to share.

That done, they stepped back with the others, and Branor left with the attendant and Girard.

Mererid beckoned Rhiannon. "I have something for you to wear."

Hurrying through her and Tellan's curtain, she went to her small jewel box on the stand next to their pallet. She opened the lid and removed a gold and emerald necklace. Rhiannon gasped at its beauty. Mererid stepped behind Rhiannon, slipped it around her neck and set the clasp.

"There. My mother wore this for her wedding, and I wore it when I married your father." She smiled fondly. "Somehow it seems right for you tonight."

Tears came to Rhiannon's eyes.

Picking up a cloth, Mererid dabbed them away. "With your hair, red eyes will be a bit too much."

Rhiannon gave a half giggle. Then she clasped Mererid's hands inside hers. "Thank you," she said softly, her voice breaking.

"You are most welcome.".

Rhiannon squeezed harder. "Thank you for . . . everything."

Mererid's expression slowly changed. She searched her step-daughter's face. "Is there something else?"

Rhiannon enveloped Mererid in a full hug. "Only how much I love you. And how much I admire you. How difficult it must have been for you to step in after my mother." She felt Mererid shudder and heard her begin to weep. "I have no memory of my mother," Rhiannon continued, "only Father's stories. But you . . . you have always been and always will be Mother to me."

Mererid squeezed Rhiannon close. "Oh, daughter! Thank you. Thank you for this. You have given me the more precious gift."

She pulled away gently. Her face was wet with tears.

"Mererid! Rhiannon!" Tellan stuck his head through the curtain. "Lord and Lady Fawr have come to accompany us to the banquet. They're waiting outside." Then he seemed to notice the women's condition. "What's happened?"

Mererid laughed and wiped away her tears. "Two women talking, my lord husband." She turned and regarded Tellan. "Aigneis awaits us outside our tent?"

"They have requested the pleasure of *our* company at the banquet."

"Hmm." She kissed Tellan on the cheek. "Then we must go. Peibyn must have persuasive powers I am not aware of."

"I'd better go, too," Rhiannon said, feeling the nervousness return.

Mererid studied her for a long moment. "No, you stay here. I will *not* have Peibyn escorting you to the banquet. Much better matches are sniffing at the door. Your father, Phelan, and I will go out and greet the Fawrs. You will be 'finishing dressing' until your father comes back for you and Lakenna." She frowned toward the front flap of the pavilion. "I will stall until Creag returns. He's old enough to escort me, freeing your father for you." She straightened her dress and hurried away.

When Rhiannon stepped back to the main area she startled Lakenna, who was gazing into the hand mirror and arranging her hair. The tutor jumped and put the mirror down hastily. Red bloomed on her cheeks.

"I have never seen you lovelier," Rhiannon told her truthfully. "You would do well sitting beside Branor and Cullia." *And Larien.*

Lakenna made a derisive sound but seemed pleased at the compliment.

"You know, of course," Rhiannon continued, "that high-ranking Keepers like Branor can marry. In fact, I believe he is the only High Lord Keeper who is not already wed."

The tutor stiffened. "I am an Albane and will remain so." She looked down. "And he is noble born. That is where he is most useful to the Eternal."

Rhiannon let it be. Too many imponderables loomed this night. As they waited for Tellan's return, she gnawed her lower lip. Her prophecy. How was it to be walked out these next few moments? What if Larien didn't choose her? He would carry her heart away with him, but somehow—somehow—she would learn to live with it. But what if he chose Zoe? How could such *evil* be queen and mother of the heir? What impact would that have on the Covenant?

She stared at nothing for a long, intense moment. *I am called to be Protectoress of the Covenant.* She looked at her hands. In that spirit realm they had held a flaming sword. One like *Asunder.* With it, she had dealt the North a defeat straight from the legends of the Founding. She heard again the undulating wail issuing from Maolmin's mouth when Harred's blade stuck the fatal blow. And she remembered the ancient Dinari clan saying: *Pray. Sharpen your sword. Then pray some more.*

Decision made, she strode to her pallet and found her clan dagger. Taking two rawhide strings, she went back to Lakenna and began rolling up her own left sleeve.

"Here." She handed the leather throngs to Lakenna and placed the dagger on the underside of her arm. "Tie this for me."

The tutor's eyes widened and her mouth dropped in disbelief. "Whatever for?"

She met Lakenna gaze calmly. "You know what for. My lord father needed his this morning. I may need mine tonight." Though her voice was soft, it carried command. "Tie it."

Lakenna swallowed—and obeyed. With shaking hands, she tied the dagger and sheath to the arm and pulled down the sleeve.

They had just satisfied themselves that nothing showed when the front flap of the tent was pulled back and her father stepped in. He wore a faint smile. "Mererid and Aigneis. And here I was thinking all the combat was over once Harred and Breanna had gripped hands."

"No doubt Mother has Aigneis in full retreat."

"Aigneis is incapable of full retreat, but Mererid has her hemmed in nicely." Tellan folded his arms across his chest and regarded his daughter for a long moment, eyes full of love and approval. "As I have said before, here stands a woman, full grown and beautiful."

Her throat closed. Finally, she was able to say, "You know I love you, Father. But never have I told you how proud I am to be your daughter."

His eyes misted. Giving her a kiss on the cheek, he offered his arm. "Are you ready, Lady Rhiannon?"

Her heart thudding, knees shaking, she slipped her right arm through his and took a deep breath.

"I am ready."

The Rogoths and Fawrs joined the crowd heading toward the royal pavilions. All the Dinari kinsmen lords and their families had been invited to dine with their queen and prince. The storm was over now, and the night air carried a crisp chill. Torches were everywhere.

King's guards were in abundance around the largest tent, a not-so-subtle show of force. In addition to finishing the Rite of Presentation, Cullia wished to use the banquet this night to renew vows of fealty to the Faber dynasty and the Covenant. A wise move, given the throne's perceived weakness with all the rumors of King Balder's deterioration.

Rhiannon's feet took her through the wide opening of the high-pitched pavilion. The ladies wore gowns of every color. Their perfumes mingled with the aroma of fragrant woods burning in braziers, and the combination clogged her throat. With her stomach tied in a cold knot she almost gagged. Somehow she smiled and responded to greetings as she moved through the throng with her parents and Lakenna. Her eyes raced over the crowd to find Larien or Cullia, or even Ouveau, but the royal party had not yet made its entrance. Tables for the guests had been arranged in a loose semicircle focused toward the head table on a raised platform. Between them was the table for the maidens—

Her heart skipped a beat. Next to the royal table stood an ornately carved, waist-high pedestal. Atop it was a crystal vase, and in the vase rested a rose made of silver. It sparkled in the lantern light. The petals and leaves, even the thorns on the stem, were rendered in exquisite detail.

Lakenna had seen it, too. "Is that the same one Destin gave Meagarea at the first Presentation?"

"The same," Mererid replied. "It has been used ever since. At the beginning of the banquet, High Lord Baird will formally ask Larien if the Eternal has shown him a bride among those presented. If Larien answers in the affirmative, he will present that maiden with the silver rose. The maiden will signal her acceptance by returning the rose to Larien. And as with Destin and Meagarea, the marriage will take place immediately."

Rhiannon swallowed. *I want this over with, one way or the other!*

Still eyeing the silver rose, she grappled with the unbelievable suddenness of all this. This morning she was a young woman only weeks old in being acknowledged "Lady." Then before noon, she had held a flaming sword and battled face-to-face with a dread Mighty One. But what loomed now was even more mind-boggling: a possible betrothal and marriage, both within a turn of the glass. Princess and wife, with family and clan and her beloved highlands left behind. The capital city of Ancylar, Faber Castle, Lady Ouveau. And, of course, Cullia.

Rhiannon quailed. *No, Eternal, I cannot do this! You ask too much of me!*

Tellan elbowed through the press of people, leading her to the forward edge of the Dinari tables where he handed her over to a royal attendant. Other fathers were doing the same. The maidens were escorted to their table and left standing.

Running her eye over the others, Rhiannon realized she was

the only one wearing the same gown as at the Presentation.

"Ewe's milk," someone said.

Rhiannon turned to look. Standing beside her was the Erian maiden who had been first in line.

Rhiannon blinked. "What?"

"Nothing keeps skin softer than bathing in ewe's milk. Your skin's so creamy and perfect. You use it, don't you?"

Rhiannon wondered if the girl was an idiot or if this was some game.

"And your hair..." The girl sighed. "I would die for hair like that. My brother is demanding that Father approach Tellan for your hand. We will probably be seeing more of each other."

The girl smiled wistfully and wandered off. Then a cloyingly sweet perfume filled her nostrils.

"Lady...Rhiannon, isn't it?" Zoe approached in a rustle of rich silk. Jewels sparkled on her ears and encircled her neck, but those sloe eyes were dark and fathomless. She inspected Rhiannon from slippers upwards, then arched an eyebrow when she came to the face.

"Poor girl, you look as if you've eaten spoiled mutton. Or perhaps it's a reaction to some lotion you have rubbed on your calluses. No? Hmm. Well, all of this must be too lavish for one of your simple background."

Rhiannon's blood quickened. "I find my background most suitable. We are constantly dealing with predators. Recently, a winged horror thought it could take what was mine." She gave a cold smile. "I killed it." Zoe's mouth dropped open and her face lost some of its beauty. "So you see," Rhiannon continued, her voice deadly soft, "I stand ready for any challenge."

Zoe's haughty expression returned. Her musical accent thickened. "Larien will not forget my impact during the Presentation."

The dagger tied to Rhiannon's arm felt like lead. "You will not have him."

Zoe's voice became as hard as her glare. "If he chooses anyone tonight, sheepherder, it will be me. If not," a perfect eyebrow rose meaningfully, "then I will be around when the marriage bed becomes stale."

A wave of movement came from the far side of the pavilion. An escort of king's guards emerged from an opening curtain, the Faber banner high on a pole. Next came Queen Cullia, her hand resting on her son's arm.

Prince Larien took Rhiannon's breath away. He was the most handsome man in the pavilion. The most handsome man she had ever seen. Tall, lean, gracious. She had sensed an underlying gentleness at the Presentation when he held her hand, which had felt so warm and secure in his.

Will he be gentle tonight if I become his bride?

His scar gave him such a rugged look. She wondered what it would feel like when she ran her fingertips along it.

Attendants came and seated the maidens at their long table. Zoe was placed at one end, Rhiannon on the opposite end.

Larien helped his mother step onto the dais. Even from that distance, Rhiannon could see the richness of her gown, gold threads in the rarest blue black silk. Cullia had a fixed smile on her lined face as she nodded to the gathered nobles. Her hair was fastened in a tight bun under the diamond-encrusted coronet.

Then Lady Ouveau, head high and haughty, stepped up to the platform. A ruby necklace sparkled in the light. She was escorted by Branor, whose limp seemed more pronounced. Sweat beaded the Keeper's forehead, and Rhiannon could almost feel his nausea. She knew what he sensed.

Looking at those two powerful women, Rhiannon realized why this had to be so sudden, so quick, so public, so protected from interference. Trying to get past Cullia's prejudice and the evil inside Ouveau would be impossible otherwise.

But what about Larien? Was the *knowing* they had felt toward one another enough to overcome Zoe's bewitching impact? After the prayer of binding, could Zoe still affect Larien?

Everyone settled into their seats. Larien's eyes swept the

maiden table, searching. They came closer to where she sat. She waited, hands clammy. Cullia said something to him. He turned to her, listening, then replied. His eyes flicked back exactly where he had left off—and resumed.

They swept by Rhiannon, then whipped back! For a long moment, he looked straight at her. She returned it, hardly daring to breathe. Then he glanced at Zoe on the other end. Finally, he looked down and started drumming his fingers nervously on the table.

For the first time, Rhiannon had an inkling of *his* dilemma. At the very first of the Presentations, before he'd had the opportunity to meet the other clans' offerings, he had beheld Zoe—a cultured, exotic temptress, clearly born and bred for a crown. She would bring foreign contracts and wealth untold to the Faber throne, not to mention the envy of every man who met her.

As opposed to a poor Dinari! Worse, a girl from one of the smallest and poorest of the Dinari kinsmen groups! To be joined to such a one for the rest of his life? A callous-handed sheep-herder to be princess, queen, mother of the heir?

Lord Baird rose and approached the head table. The crowd hushed. Rhiannon's pulse quickened.

"Prince Larien Faber," Baird intoned, "before the Eternal and these witnesses, it is my solemn duty to ask if, after the Presentation of these maidens and your spending the afternoon in prayer and contemplation, the Eternal has made known to you your wife and our next queen."

Larien did not reply. He gazed at the tabletop, expression closed. The silence stretched. A puzzled buzz began. Rhiannon started to tremble.

Baird cut his eyes to Cullia, then back to Larien. "Prince Larien Faber, has the Eternal made known to you who is to be your wife and the next queen to rule by your side?"

Cullia became very still, then darted a quick look at Zoe. A pleased smile played at the corners of Ouveau's lips. Rhiannon saw Branor frown. He looked down the table at the prince. The puzzled buzz returned, stronger. Rhiannon's trembling increased.

Larien came slowly to his feet, and the buzz ceased abruptly. "Yes, Lord Baird," he said. "The Eternal has shown me my wife and the next queen of the Land."

Startled gasps came from the crowd. Loud, excited talk swept the pavilion. Zoe sat straighter.

Baird's mouth dropped open. "Th—then you..." He cleared his throat and lifted a hand toward the crystal vase. "Then you must offer the rose, Your Highness. You must proffer the rose to the one the Eternal has indicated."

Larien tilted his head in acknowledgment. He walked to the vase and removed the silver rose. Stepping off the platform, he strode formally toward the middle of the maiden table. If he veered right, his path would take him to Zoe. A left turn would take him to Rhiannon.

Zoe's eyes glowed in triumph as she waited, head held high.

Ouveau watched Larien's back with an intensity that was frightening. The ruby at her neck sparkled deep red.

Dry-mouthed, Rhiannon's hand crept toward her sleeve, wondering if she could find the strength to do what she must if Larien turned the wrong way.

The prince continued his slow march toward the table, the rose in his hand. The mouths of the girls sitting in the middle dropped wider with every step, and for a moment Rhiannon wondered if he was coming for one of them.

Larien stopped two paces in front of the table.

The crowd went completely silent. No one spoke or coughed or shuffled feet. Everyone's gaze rested on the prince and his historic decision.

He turned left.

The world spun. Rhiannon had to grip the edge of the table to remain upright. Trembling from head to toe, she watched him approach. Was this really happening?

Zoe's face paled. Disbelief and rage twisted her features into an ugly mask.

At the Rogoth table, realization hit Lakenna with the impact of a horse kick. Her mouth dropped open and her eyes bulged. *Of course. How better to fulfill it?* She shook her head. *I have been blind.*

She glanced at the royal table and saw Branor seem to put it together as well. He sat there with a look of stunned understanding, nodding over and over.

"Oh, my," Mererid breathed when Larien neared Rhiannon. "Oh, my dear, sweet girl." Tellan's face was unreadable as he watched the future king of the land come to marry his daughter.

Rhiannon's trembling ceased when Larien stopped before her. She stared up at the most beautiful, loving pair of eyes she had ever seen. Eyes to spend a lifetime with.

"Lady Rhiannon Rogoth," Larien said, "before these witnesses I ask you to be my wife and share with me the joys and burdens of ruling the Land and maintaining the Covenant." He held out the silver rose. "If the Eternal has moved on your heart as he has moved on mine, please return this rose to the vase, and there we will take our vows." He seemed so steady, calm.

Everything had been preparation of this moment. A *rightness* infused her from inside out. Rhiannon watched her hand reach out and take the rose. It was heavy, the stem warm from his touch.

Larien gave her a bow. He searched her face and managed to communicate: *Together, we can do this.* He walked back to the empty vase and turned around, waiting.

Every eye in the pavilion rested on her. The queen's hawk stare radiated a mother's disapproval strong enough to wilt a tree. Down the table Zoe had regained her composure and sat straight-backed, jaw muscles clinched. She and Ouveau exchanged looks, and the royal advisor's ruby pulsed an angry red.

Seeing that, Rhiannon realized with calm certainty that she was entering a contest being played for enormous stakes. Larien had found the strength to go against expectations, maneuverings, and centuries of precedent. Rhiannon understood that her first task as princess was to prove he had not made a mistake.

She came smoothly to her feet, chin high, shoulders square, red tresses gleaming in the lantern light. Holding the silver rose before her she glided toward the royal table, a picture of feminine grace perfected in all those afternoons with Mererid.

Larien and Branor met her at the pedestal. She put the rose back in the vase, amazed that her hand did not tremble. Larien reached up and removed her requin. Though his face was as composed as hers, for the first time she sensed his nervousness. Surprised, she ached to comfort him. Their eyes met, and she knew it was going to be fine. She faced Branor.

The High Lord Keeper gave her a quick smile, full of support and favor. "You're doing fine, my princess," he breathed, lips barely moving. Then he started the ceremony.

"The Rite demands that after the rose is given and returned, the statement of vows proceeds with all due dispatch, and is brief. Once the prince and princess return to Faber Castle, a celebration will be held with all the pomp and ceremony such an august event deserves."

Then Branor regarded her with gravity. "Rhiannon Rogoth, you are about to marry into the Faber dynasty. For twelve centuries the throne has remained separate from the six clans. Though it is understood that love for family and clan cannot be easily relinquished, it is necessary for you to set aside all such ties. Your allegiance will henceforth be to King Balder for as long as he shall live, and then to King Larien for as long as you two shall rule, then to your son, whom we pray will spring forth from your loins." He paused, then asked. "Are you willing to accept these historic conditions?"

"I am." Her voice was clear, firm.

Cullia's feet shifted. Her bright blue eyes seemed to be trying to wedge open Rhiannon's heart to determine what kind of person was marrying her son. Ouveau's glare was cold enough to make the night seem warm.

Branor faced Larien. "Larien Faber, heir to the throne, are you a follower of the Eternal?"

"I am." His voice was rich and steady.

"Are you joining to this woman unencumbered and of your free will?"

"I am."

Branor turned to Rhiannon. She felt his sense of urgency to get this done before Cullia or Ouveau or any possible calamity could stop it. He knew what was at stake.

"Rhiannon Rogoth, are you a follower of the Eternal?"

"I am."

"Are you joining to this man unencumbered and of your free will?"

"I am."

"Join hands."

Larien took both her hands in his, which were warm and comforting. He gave a quick squeeze. She returned it.

"I, Larien Faber," he said, repeating the vow after Branor, "take you, Rhiannon Rogoth, for my wife. I promise to forsake all others and love, protect, and provide for you as long as I have breath in my body. This I pledge of my own free will before the Eternal and before these witnesses."

Then it was her turn. "I, Rhiannon Rogoth, take you, Larien Faber, for my husband. I promise to forsake all others and to love, honor, and care for you as long as I have breath in my body. This I pledge of my own free will before the Eternal and before these witnesses."

It was done. Larien and Rhiannon. Prince and protectoress. Husband and wife.

EPILOGUE

ELMAR HELPED HARRED down the hallway. Thankfully, the room was on the Bridge's second floor and not the third. Two flights of stairs had near done him in.

"A bit more," Elmar grunted, almost carrying him now.

"I'm fine." His voice sounded far away even to himself.

Harred smelled the oil used to polish wood paneling. Or maybe it was Elmar's salve on the wounds all over his body. After arriving here after the *Wifan-er-Weal*, Elmar and Breanna had cleaned him and bandaged his wounds, and Elmar had forced a foul-tasting brew down his throat. He had slept dreamlessly on a pallet in the washroom until half a turn ago when Elmar had shaken him awake and applied fresh salve and new bandages. A lot of bandages. With them and the cloak Elmar had thrown over him, he had on more cloth than if he was fully clothed.

"Here we be." Elmar braced him against the wall with one hand and quickly opened the door with the other. He slung Harred's arm over his shoulder, then half-carried, half-dragged him inside and kicked the door shut.

The room was smaller than the one he and Lord Gillaon had stayed in for the wool sale. But it had the essentials: a wardrobe, a washbasin, and a bed. But where was Breanna? Belatedly he noted a dressing panel in the corner of the room. A lacy white robe was draped over it.

It seemed a long way to the bed, but they made it. Elmar removed the cloak and sat Harred on the bed. He grabbed him, put an arm under both legs, and levered him onto the mattress.

"I'm fine," the far-off voice said. Everything throbbed with pain.

Elmar stepped back and wiped sweat from his brow. "You sure you be up to this?"

"Of course." His voice didn't sound so distant all of a sudden. He took two deep breaths. The room became clearer.

Elmar lifted his chin toward the dressing panel. "We talked before I be going down to get you. She be understanding if you just sleep tonight and rest. Then in the morning..."

"I am fine." Harred focused on his brother-in-law. "I can do this."

"I know that. But tonight may not be..."

"Tonight."

Elmar shrugged. He made to go, then hesitated. He bent over and whispered, "Need any advice?"

Harred just stared.

"One thing your sister be really liking—"

Harred growled and pointed to the door.

Elmar grinned. "I be going now," he said loudly toward the dressing panel. And he did, shutting the door firmly behind him.

Harred sat up against the head of the bed, every muscle complaining, every wound throbbing. He waited, hardly breathing lest some sound cause his bride to delay or lose her nerve.

He thought briefly of Rhiannon. Elmar had told him of her marriage to Prince Larien. An astonishing turn of events—but then Harred remembered the fire in those startling green eyes and decided maybe not. She would become queen and raise the next king. He wished her only happiness. But now it was time to concentrate on the treasure he had found and claimed for his own.

Breanna stepped out from behind the panel. She wore a thin white nightgown. Her black hair was down, long and gleaming in the soft lantern light. She glided toward him with her natural grace. He struggled to sit up further, but she shook her head and quickened her steps. She stopped at the side of the bed and smiled at him, tilting her head in her endearing way.

He drunk her in, awed by the moment.

She placed one hand on his bandaged chest and gently traced his jaw line with her other. "Even after we spoke in the mountains and I said I would not refuse your suit, I thought I would never see you again."

He groped for something profound to say. "I could not live without you," was all that came. The words sprung from the depths of his being, and their truth filled the room.

Her eyes moistened. "I prayed every day for the Eternal's will to be done. I knew my father would deny your suit. I wanted you to win the *Wifan-er-Weal*, but I so feared you would not survive. I feared it so much that I almost wanted you to not appear at the Pole." Breanna searched his face. "You looked so alone standing there."

"No more alone than you when you grounded your staff. I knew then that we were one. That was all I needed." Harred took her hand. "You are all I will ever need."

Breanna climbed into the bed and melted into his arms. With her head resting on his shoulder, her feet came halfway below his knees. After a long luxurious moment, she rolled to her side, propped on an elbow, and gave him a look. "I have never bedded a rhyfelwr before."

"What!" he spurted, struggling to turn toward her. "Who *have* you bedded?"

She fought to maintain a solemn expression, but broke into giggles. "No one! Your wife comes to you virginal and pure." Her eyes danced merrily. "But Mother and I have talked in preparation for the Pole. We read some frank passages in Holy Writ. Within the bond of marriage, the physical love of a man and woman is celebrated as a beautiful gift from the Eternal." She snuggled back on his chest. "One gift Mother mentioned..."

Her soft lips found his neck and began nibbling upwards.

Heaven came down to earth.

Rhiannon awoke, momentarily disoriented. Everything was different. She lay on a much softer bed, under a thicker wool blanket. A body radiated warmth against her side.

It all came flooding back then. She was in the prince's—and princess's—pavilion.

She turned her head. Enough early morning light filtered through the top to see Larien's features. He slept belly down, face slack on the pillow, hair tousled.

Hardly believing this was happening—had happened—she reached over and played her fingers through his hair. At her feather touch, his breathing changed a bit, then resumed slow and steady.

His scar had felt just like she had thought it might. He had not minded her touching it. Or his lips. Or his chest. Or anywhere.

She had not minded his touch either. Not at all . . .

Rhiannon chuckled silently. *Yes, Father, your daughter is indeed a full-grown woman.* Married. Princess. Future queen.

She looked at Larien again and was overwhelmed at the love she felt for this virtual stranger. She had given her prophecy to the Eternal, and he had given it back in a manner and a purpose far beyond galloping through the land and slaying winged horrors. *I no longer do sword drills, my queen.* No indeed. Her future encompassed different battles fought with different weapons. And who would have thought part of it would be so . . . nice.

She heard faint murmuring of servants moving on the other side of the partition.

A new day was beginning. A new life. After a farewell time with her family, she would ride in the queen's carriage as the royal party journeyed back to Ancylar and Faber Castle. That should be an interesting time, days of travel one on one with Cullia.

Lakenna and Branor were coming as advisors to the new princess. Rhiannon knew she would need them.

And although Harred wasn't coming, she sensed that he and his swift sword would be available should she need them. *Harred is a finely honed weapon, proven and available for the future,* that inner voice had told her. She didn't understand it yet, but she felt strongly she and Harred were somehow joined in the task of upholding the Covenant.

She thought about Lady Ouveau. How far had the Mighty Ones penetrated Faber Castle? What positions of power and influence were controlled by demonic threads? How many clan nobility secretly served the old gods? When would Zoe show up again? Rhiannon had thought the battle might be over when the North had retreated into the mist. Now she knew it was just beginning.

There was much to do. But she put those worries away until later.

She took a long, luxurious stretch under the wool blanket and then leaned over and began kissing Larien's scar.

Wasn't her first task to prove he hadn't made a mistake?